O
OF
ANGELS

A Novel of Navy Nurses In World War Two

JOAN LA BLANC

Northampton House Press

ODYSSEY OF ANGELS. Copyright 2013 by Joan Hartzel La Blanc. All rights reserved, including the right to reproduce this book, or portions thereof, in any form.

This is a work of fiction. All of the characters, organizations, and events portrayed in this novel are either products of the author's imagination or are used fictitiously.

Cover image is adapted from a public domain U.S. Government poster produced during WWII. Original artist: John Falter. Ccver design and NHP logo by Naia Poyer.

First Northampton House Press edition, 2013. ISBN 978-1482622-52-2
10 9 8 7 6 5 4 3 2 1

ODYSSEY OF ANGELS

CHAPTER ONE
October, 1944

*G*olden light splashed across her face as Anna Donovan, Ensign, Nurse Corps, United States Navy Reserve, emerged from the first deep sleep since they'd left San Francisco. God only knew how long ago—too many blurry hours over too much ocean to make sense of with a mind still ticking to Eastern Standard Time. Even now she was awake only enough to be peeved that her seatmate had nudged her.

"What is it?" she said. "What's going on?"

Audrey Hoffmeister's bitten-down fingernail tapped the smudged glass of the small round window. "Look at that, kiddo. If that's not Australia up ahead, I'll eat my hat."

Anna blinked and peered beyond the engines to opalescent popcorn clouds drifting past the wing. Below, the sapphire taffeta sea was patched with surf-fringed turquoise. And on the horizon ahead, a green haze shimmered. "Could be," she said through the dank morning taste in her mouth. "Been flying long enough."

The intercom crackled and the garbled, metallic voice that had periodically addressed them since Oahu announced they were over the Coral Sea. "Where we gave the Japs the first dose of their own medicine back in May, '42. Lost *Lexington*, but stopped 'em from invading Port Moresby. A month later, we gave 'em a real licking at Midway."

Audrey said, "Ooh, I've got goose bumps. Like when we saw the *Arizona* the other day. Or whenever it was. How long's it been anyway?"

Anna shrugged. "No idea." By now the R5D transport reeked of sewage, garbage, exhaust fumes, cigarette smoke and old sweat. Her body felt battered and compressed, swollen ankles bulged over her shoes, and her khakis looked like a relief map of Death Valley. And people at home thought she'd be leading a glamorous life.

"And in half an hour, we'll be landing in Brisbane," the announcer went on. "Maybe if you're lucky you'll see MacArthur. Or his staff car."

Scowling, Audrey relaxed in the battered leather seat. "MacArthur! That yellow-belly. My fiancé said it was a crime the way he ran out on the Philippines. Saved his own hide and let his men pay the price."

From the seat behind them, Wilhelmina Stotter tapped her shoulder. "Anna, did you know the Japs torpedoed an Aussie hospital ship right off the coast here?"

Her voice was pitched a notch higher than the roar of the engines; still Anna wasn't sure she'd heard right. She half-turned to see the other nurse better. "What? The Japs torpedoed a hospital ship?"

Willi nodded, her dark gaze more earnest than usual. "Right after the Coral Sea Battle. Probably for revenge." She gestured toward the window. "Just out there somewhere."

With a jolt, Anna emerged from a stupor induced by 10,000 miles of entrapment in flying metal cylinders. And a night that had followed them all across the Pacific. "No. I never heard that. Did they sink it?"

"Well and truly. Tell you about it after we land."

Audrey leaned closer. "What'd she just say?"

"That the Japs torpedoed an Australian hospital ship near here."

Audrey's stone-gray eyes went wide. "Jesus. Never heard anything about that, did you?"

Still reeling, Anna shook her head. "Maybe it's a military secret. Bad for morale if we knew."

"I'll say! God. Didn't think even the Japs were that low." Her sigh was morose. "You're right. The Navy doesn't want us to know. So they tell us about the Geneva Convention and how safe we'll be." Another heavy sigh. "God. If this got around, who'd ask for hospital ship duty? One thing to be in harm's way on a warship, but on an AH—hell, we won't be anything but sitting ducks."

Wondering what other catastrophes had been censored from public scrutiny, Anna shifted her gaze to the sun-dazzled ultramarine below. So an Australian ship had died somewhere in these waters. God only knew where her husband's sub had gone down, or why. Not in any specific spot, just "somewhere in the Pacific." Now, flying above it, she recognized the futility of speculating where in this vast, sparkling graveyard he lay. It didn't matter, of course, in a cemetery that forever hid its dead from the living.

As she drifted into that old enigma again, she was only dimly aware when the wing flaps came up and her lurching stomach told her they were descending. A sliver of pristine beach, lace-edged with surf, slid under them, followed by another offshore island dappled with tropical greenery. Still dropping, they banked over a slender gray two-stacker steaming seaward on a wide bay. Upstream, this narrowed to a river the color of lime Jell-O where a taxiing seaplane trailed a wake like a chartreuse bridal veil. On one shore, shabby warehouses clustered around piers bristling with cranes and freighters, some trim in wartime gray, some camouflaged, most rust-streaked and hard-used in the desperate race to kick the Japs out of the South Pacific.

In the midst of such utilitarian ugliness, the sole white ship was almost incandescent in the tropical sunlight. Even before Anna noticed the green stripe and red crosses on hull, stack and deck, a pulse of recognition beat in her. Surely the fleeting glimpse on the Navy Nurse Corps recruiting poster hadn't produced this enormous sense of *déjà vu*. Of belonging. Of the certainty that this was where she was bound long before her final orders had been cut. That regardless of risks, she was damned well destined for this duty.

Audrey pointed. "Think that's ours?"

Anna nodded, imagining small boats packed with casualties tumbling toward them from bloody beachheads. Even if these boys couldn't see her name, this ship would be *Compassion* indeed, comfort, caring and healing, all delivered on clean sheets with good food and efficient medical personnel. Her eyes went moist.

"Yep," said Audrey with a knowing nod, "that's what she is. A big white sitting duck."

Anna's immediate instinct was to snap, "Do you have absolutely no faith in anything?" but, certain Audrey would only accuse her of being an unregenerate Pollyanna, swallowed the words.

Upstream, they circled over a city so large, so modern it could have been Boston, except for traffic flowing the wrong way. Then, dropping over red-tiled roofs and tank farms, they slammed onto a runway, bounced, and hit again. Tires squealed as they braked hard; the seat belt pinched her belly. Other planes flashed by. Men in foreign uniforms hunched over the wheels of scurrying service vehicles. And a red, white and blue flag with the Union

Jack and Southern Cross rippled above a terminal building.

Observing through the plane's tiny window, Anna wanted to celebrate, rise from her seat and shout to her weary fellow passengers, "Look out there, will you? My God, we're actually here, we're going to join our ship!" But long before she'd been transformed into to a naval officer at Newport, Rhode Island, she'd been imprinted with the desirability of decorum, of modest, unnoticeable behavior. Besides, after traveling to the ends of the earth with the people on this plane, she reckoned few would share her adolescent excitement. Audrey would undoubtedly tell her to act her age. Anna only hoped the Navy had seen fit to assign them different cabins.

* * *

As soon as they'd stepped off the jitney at the pier, Audrey surged ahead to catch up with a doctor who reminded her of Van Johnson. Overhead, between purple-bellied clouds, the noon sun blazed with equatorial intensity. The steamy air was heavy with the mingled odors of Diesel exhaust and oil, overheated metal, sewage, brackish water, creosoted pilings, and the spiciness of hemp lines. And that universal aroma of civilization—stale cigarette smoke.

Close at hand, nets swayed from cargo booms as crates and bales were hoisted aboard; winches whined and small gasoline engines sputtered. As the group Anna had joined in Hawaii filed up the gangway, Floyd Einhorn angled his Brownie at U.S. Navy Hospital Ship *Compassion* under the ship's flaring bow, then at the bridge, and the red and white Geneva pennant flapping from the forward mast.

"You sure can tell she used to be a cruise ship, can't you?" he said loudly to no one in particular. "Just look at her lines."

Audrey shot Willi Stotter an accusing glance. "Thought you said it's springtime out here. Feels more like summer to me."

Willi was an American, born and educated in Australia till her parents came home to Oregon at the outset of the war. "Best get used to it." Her accent was softer, more lilting, more intelligible than the jitney driver's. "It'll be even worse closer to the Equator."

Everyone groaned, but half-heartedly. At least they were here, on the far side of the world, where the seasons were upside down, the sun moved right to left across the sky, people drove on the wrong side of the road, and spoke with what sounded like an English accent, only harder to decipher. But Lord knew, they were resilient. Back in '42, when the Japs had bombed the northern city of Darwin, the government had proposed abandoning the top third of the country in case of invasion. Around the same time, not fifty miles from where this group was boarding a similar vessel, the hospital ship *Centaur* had been sunk just off the coast. In the airport, Willi had pointed out a poster depicting women in the water behind the sinking stern. The caption urged, *Avenge the Nurses!*

"At least, she wasn't carrying casualties," she'd added. "She was on her way back to New Guinea from Sydney. Middle of the night, but in full compliance with Geneva. No sense to it. No sense at all. Those girls never had a chance."

Not surprisingly, these stalwart Allies had rescued *Compassion* after she'd had a massive mechanical failure en route to Hollandia, New Guinea, with wounded from the Saipan campaign. Until the jitney driver had told them, Anna hadn't heard this heroic tale before. All their group had been told was that they were replacing medical personnel who'd been transferred off while the ship underwent a lengthy overhaul.

Next, Audrey asked Floyd if the ship was air-conditioned. Having known the dentist at the Philadelphia Naval Hospital, early on she'd complained to Anna he was a smart-mouthed Jew who thought he knew everything about everything. Still, she asked.

He lifted his cap and wiped his streaming forehead with a handkerchief. "See, she was built in '27, before they had the technology. And when they converted her in '42, the Navy was so desperate to get her on line, it must not've mattered."

"Jeez. We're all gonna melt."

The Van Johnson look-alike gave her a wink. "Don't worry, doll. It'll be cooler at sea."

Audrey simpered. Everyone else groaned. The gangway trembled as the group of nurses and doctors shuffled forward. Ahead of them the last of the enlisted men hoisted their sea bags and moved toward the deckhouse. At least officers didn't have to lug theirs aboard. Rank, after all, had its privileges. Anna thought this premise undemocratic but wasn't about to quibble with it now.

By the time she reached the OOD, raindrops large as half-dollars were pelting them from an isolated cloud. Trying to keep her orders dry, she unfolded them from her purse, and went through the prescribed boarding routine—salutes to the flag at the stern and the Officer of the Deck, then a brisk, "Ensign Anna Donovan reporting for duty as ordered, sir. Permission to come aboard."

The boy-faced jaygee slid a casual glance at her papers, gave a lazy salute and smiled with a mouthful of crooked teeth. "Permission granted, Ensign. Welcome aboard. Report to the wardroom, just forward through the hatch." He gestured toward an opening in the superstructure where the rest of the group had disappeared into the dimness.

All except Floyd and Willi. "Come on, Anna," he urged. "They're waiting lunch for us."

She stepped through the hatch into the metallic, faintly oily smell common to every Navy vessel she'd ever visited, including Dan's sub. Briefly emotional, she followed the other two forward, toward the aroma of fried onions and grilled meat that soon overpowered it. And started her mouth watering.

"Smells like we're having steak for our first meal."

Willi grinned back at her. "If we are, likely it's 'roo steak."

She was about to ask what 'roo was when they came into the wardroom, where a crowd of ship's officers waited to greet the newcomers. Oh well, she thought; if it was kangaroo, no sense turning up her nose at it now. Before they got home again, all of them would probably be eating lots of strange things. Including crow and humble pie.

Bring it on, she thought, following Willi and Floyd to one of the long tables where a grinning Filipino steward beckoned them to the last three empty seats.

CHAPTER TWO

Shortly after two on Christmas afternoon, Anna entered Cabin C-14 as *Compassion* steamed westbound on the Philippine Sea, somewhere between Guam and Leyte. Without so much as closing the door behind her, she stripped off the starch-stiff white uniform and tossed it on the bunk. Not only had she dribbled cranberry sauce on jacket, blouse, skirt and even the black necktie, they reeked of smoke from the blaze when the Catholic chaplain's birthday cake had gone up like the Hindenburg. An eye-opening finale to two hours of stupefying speeches and a gut-busting American feast.

Regarding the crimson stains, Anna could hear her mother's tight-lipped mandate, "Quick, rinse them under running water, or they'll never come out!" Instead, she brushed the taste of turkey from her teeth and splashed cold water on her face. She grabbed the jacket and removed shoulder boards, brass buttons and the one small service ribbon she was entitled to wear by virtue of having disobeyed no major regulations the whole four months she'd been in the Navy. Finally, she stuffed everything into the laundry bag for pickup the next morning.

The fleeting reminder of her mother drew her gaze to the pile of letters that had come aboard at Guam. Earlier, she'd had intentions of answering all five so she could enclose copies of the Official Souvenir Menu from the Officers' Mess. Now, stuffed with calories, sweating in the midday heat and still in her underwear, she settled for dashing off a few lines to her fiancé.

> *Jim, darling...well, as you can see from the enclosed, at noon chow today we had more "turkey & trimmings" than anybody could eat. But the most exciting part was when Father Luke's birthday cake burst into flames—because they'd used sparklers instead of candles! The skipper looked scared enough to order us to abandon ship. Luckily one of the stewards grabbed an extinguisher and saved the day. Afterward, there was plenty of cake left, but by then it was time for the "Special Holiday Movie", so we began leaving the wardroom... until Old Horseface remembered we hadn't sung the stupid birthday song. Once we'd done that, the stampede to the lounge began in earnest. Except for me. I saw Holiday Inn when it first came out, so here I am instead, telling you about my Christmas so I won't miss you so much. Last night I went to Fr. Luke's midnight mass and this morning the Protestant service, but it still doesn't feel like the real thing. Then again nothing feels the way I think it should lately. Maybe I'm finally getting detached. On the other hand, maybe I've just gone numb after 81 days on this tub.*

She intended to add to this before mail left the ship, which wouldn't be till they'd picked up more wounded from Leyte and ferried them down to the Army hospital at

Hollandia, New Guinea. Probably another ten days. So she slipped the flimsy onion skin sheet into an envelope, and folded a Souvenir Menu to fit inside. On the cover was an aerial view of the ship underway, but the picture was black and white, so you couldn't tell that the crosses on the stack and deck were red, and the stripe along the hull was green. On the second page was a list of every officer aboard; seventeen ship's company, two chaplains, fourteen surgeons, one dentist, twenty-nine nurses and two Red Cross workers. No mention of the eighty-seven Pharmacist's Mates who worked alongside them; they were, after all, enlisted.

The glorified Holiday Dinner menu filled page three. The back cover featured a group photo, taken when the ship's photographer had lined everyone up on the weather deck and snapped the shot from atop the pilothouse. Anna had smiled when he'd told them to, but had also lifted her hand in a Hi-Mom gesture that made her easy to spot, even in the far back. Old Horseface (Lieutenant Commander Norma Welch, the Head Nurse) had dressed her down for it, but Anna was used to reprimands. Not just for ignoring trivial orders or asking questions no one wanted to answer, but mainly for having failed to report her cabin-mate's pregnancy, thus preventing Patty's botched abortion and subsequent transfer off the ship. OH had warned that at this rate, Anna might stay in the Navy twenty years and never rise above Ensign.

As if she gave a damn; her future was with Jim anyway.

His letter at least begun, she glanced through the others, then addressed airmail envelopes and inserted the menus. This minor effort left her craving a nap. The cabin was sultry, but a fresh sea-smelling breeze drifted through the open porthole, while the pulse of the ship's engines, the monotonous whir of the ventilating blowers and the cheerful tick of her alarm clock were as relaxing as a lullaby. The only jarring note was the tinny jangle of Christmas music over the PA system; it had played since 0600, pausing only for the routine announcements that punctuated shipboard life at sea or in port, on ordinary and holy days alike.

She barely noticed them anymore, these orders to Station the Special Sea and Anchor Detail, or for Sweepers, Man your Brooms, or reminders that the Smoking Lamp is Lit, or the Gedunk was open till 1100 hours. When she'd first come aboard, she'd harkened closely to all this official chatter, even that which pertained only to all those nameless sailors who worked at jobs she could barely imagine in parts of the ship she'd never seen on any orientation tour. Soon, however, she'd grown used to this constant static, almost as quickly, and as effortlessly as she had the fact that it was Christmas again. And the war was still raging.

At Christmas, 1941, married only nineteen days, she'd had a rosy, heroic perception that the war wouldn't last long, certainly not this long. Then Dan's sub left Portsmouth, and she became another dutiful Navy wife, living at home, working at the base hospital, and, with every letter from him, growing ever more frightened, ever more isolated by fear she couldn't share with her parents. Submarine duty was hazardous even when everything worked well, but Dan's boat continued to be plagued by engineering snafus that had begun the day she was launched. Bad enough the old folks were already concerned that she'd married a Catholic, and an Irish one at that. At least she wasn't pregnant.

By Christmas, 1942, such problems had earned *Wolf Fish* time in a San Francisco shipyard, so Anna took a long train ride west and moved into a garage apartment with Dan. In March, when the sub sailed for the Pacific, she came home again, this time pregnant indeed. In June, an official telegram advised her that Dan was missing in action; in August her baby was stillborn. In October, worn thin by tragedy and her parents' incessant, hand-wringing concern, she'd taken a job on a Maine coastal island, where she'd spent Christmas, 1943. The next summer Dan was declared Killed in Action, so she joined the Nurse Corps.

And here she was, ten thousand miles from home with people she'd known less than three months, in a war zone on a ship that was basically a big white sitting duck, shielded from enemy hostilities by only her non-combatant status under the Geneva Convention. And Lord knew, in 1942, those rules hadn't kept the Australian hospital ship from being sunk only fifty miles off Queensland. And just the previous month, a Jap sub had launched a misguided torpedo at an Army hospital ship off the Philippines.

This tropical afternoon, however, those hostilities seemed as remote as civilian life, as distant as parents and friends and frigid New England. And Jim, who'd planned to spend the day with a cousin up in Camden, Maine. Or maybe it hadn't even turned Christmas yet on that side of the International Date Line; she still couldn't decipher global time differences.

Trying to connect with his reality, she gazed at the snapshot of a round-faced man, with round glasses and a kindly look, not exactly a smile, and pale hair blowing in a sea breeze off the pretty little harbor at East Point, Maine. As usual when he was on her mind, she fingered the engagement ring on a neck chain beside the dog tags that would identify her in the event she was unable to herself. But all she sensed was the great void between them, reaches of time empty of so much as the sound of his voice. Each day this vacuum was more noticeable, today most of all. Sometimes she filled it with purposeful activity, like writing cheerful letters home to keep everyone's spirits up. Or reviewing stacks of purple mimeographed sheets of emergency medical procedures every nurse was supposed to know by heart.

Now, however, she regarded the bunk, neatly and tautly made up even on a day guaranteed free of inspections. Tempting, that cave of sleep in which she might lose herself for an hour or so. Well, why not? She yawned, gave Jim's picture a last look, then slid her writing kit into a drawer, closed the hatch and headed for the bunk in anticipation of an hour or so of sweet oblivion.

Just as she stretched out, however, the boson's pipe shrilled over the PA system, a signal the next announcement was significant, not routine. The following, Now hear this! Now hear this! brought her to full alert. She tensed, waiting for the rest of it.

Sure enough, it concerned her, All duty medical personnel, report to Receiving and stand by for incoming casualties.

She groaned, stumbled from the bunk and groped her way into clean scrubs. Casualties? In the middle of an empty sea? Or were the Japs going after the fleet, even on Christmas? As if they'd ever honor a Christian holiday; December 7, 1941 had been a Sunday, but that hadn't stopped the bastards from blowing up all those ships before the crews even had a chance to worship the Lord.

Sighing, she combed her hair, swiped pale pink Tangee on her lips and left the cabin with an urgency that took over her senses whenever duty called. Heading toward the ladder, she met Wilhelmina Stotter and Audrey Hoffmeister in the passageway; the three were the most junior of the ensign nurses, therefore, resigned about having pulled duty on Christmas. But how bad could it be, they reasoned, with no patients on board and no watches to stand in the wards?

So how bad would this be, this unscheduled rendezvous with casualties? On the ladders down to F Deck, they speculated about what they'd find. The consensus was, wounded from a Kamikaze attack.

"Or maybe not," Anna said. "Remember that Hellcat that crashed into a carrier when it was landing? Only a few days after we left Brisbane, remember?"

"Oh yeah," said Audrey. "On the way to Peleliu. Before we had any idea what to expect."

"God, that was a shock," said Willi with a shake of her close-clipped auburn curls. "Three years in a city hospital, I thought I'd seen it all. But like they say in the movies, honey, you ain't seen nothing yet."

Receiving was a large amidships area with huge doors on either side of the hull; those on the starboard side were already open, a group of duty personnel clustered around the Medical Officer of the Day. Frank Sims was a redheaded Texan who, Audrey claimed, was the spit and image of Van Johnson except without the freckles. He was explaining that a boiler explosion deep in a destroyer's gut had scalded eight crewmen over most of their bodies.

"Now, there's no doc on a tin can," he added, "so they're high-lining them to us. From the sound of it, though, ain't much we can do." He gave a sardonic grin. "Except wish them Merry Christmas."

Anna caught Willi's gaze and rolled her eyes. Audrey giggled, which she did at virtually everything the man said.

Approaching from astern, the camouflaged destroyer appeared undamaged, at least outwardly. The late-day sea was so mirror calm that high lines were quickly shot in place to connect her to *Compassion*. Then, bobbing and swaying above the stream between the ships, eight litters were run across. After the injured men had been transferred to gurneys, the destroyer reeled in her lines and pulled away sharply, oily smoke roiling from one of her stacks.

Anna's usual duty in Receiving was to stand by as medical officers triaged incoming casualties, then, with information from conscious patients, or dog tags from those who weren't, she made up charts on which to record the doctors' orders plus her own visual observations. A few of these men were moaning, but none was capable of speech; all had been so cooked by live steam they were clearly beyond hope. Some appeared less severely burned, but lung damage wasn't as obvious as flesh peeling in shreds. The only treatment was palliative; intravenous fluids and enough morphine to take the edge off their agony, even if the dose proved more quickly lethal than tissue destruction.

Shuttering her mind to everything but the task, Anna did what she was charged with doing, then helped corpsmen transfer patients to the Burn Ward's immaculate white beds on the deck above. Even before they finished, both chaplains were on the scene. Father Luke wore a white stole around the neck of his khaki shirt and carried his portable communion set. Mark Whitmore came armed with only a Bible. He'd joined the ship at Guam just three days before, so all Anna knew was, he was a Methodist, spoke with what sounded like a hill-billy accent, and was married, to judge by the ring.

A fresh nursing shift relieved them at 1800. As they waited for the forward elevator, Willi said, "This has been the worst Christmas ever."

"But it beats hell out of the one my fiancé's having." As usual, Audrey sounded petulant. When Anna'd first met her, she'd called him Fred, but after that only, "my fiancé". He was an Air Corps ball turret gunner on a B-17 shot down over France a year before, a prisoner of war, PW, ever since. Compared to Anna's, Audrey's diamond was miniscule, which had moved her to ask, "Say, what line of work's your fiancé in? He must do okay if he can afford a rock like that."

"Oh, he's just a country doctor, but he's awfully busy with so many other docs in service." She didn't mention the polio-ruined leg. Early on she'd recognized Audrey as a woman she might work with but never regard as a friend in whom she could confide her most foolish secrets. Or much of anything else.

The elevator left them at C Deck. Heading forward to Nurses' Country, Willi said after she showered, she was going down to the wardroom for a snack. "Didn't think I'd ever eat after that monster dinner, but now I'm famished. Of course, it's been six hours."

Anna glanced at her watch; almost seven, or 1900 as the Navy reckoned time. In the press of the emergency, she'd lost track of time and bodily sensations, but now she was conscious of fatigue in every muscle and the gnaw of hunger in her belly.

"Once I didn't see how anybody could eat anything after working with casualties like those. Now, well....must be getting thick-skinned because I'm hungry too"

Audrey's reproving look did nothing to prettify her long, narrow face. "Not me. All I want to do tonight is write my fiancé about what happened today. So he knows my Christmas wasn't real merry either."

Stifling sarcasm, Anna said, "Well, good for you."

In her cabin, she peeled off the scrubs, stained now with the blood and plasma of the men she'd touched while getting information from their dog tags. Worn by all American service personnel, these small metal rectangles were engraved with name, rank, serial number, blood type and religion, basic statistics needed to identify anyone in any circumstances. According to corpsmen, they were particularly useful with battlefield corpses, even those which were only torsos.

This gratuitous information clashed with her previous assumption that men in battle died virtually intact except for neat little holes left by bullets bound for vital organs. Clean and quick and heroic, the way Hollywood portrayed it. Not at all like the burns and crush injuries she'd encountered in the casualties from the carrier. Or later at Peleliu and Leyte where machine gun and mortar fire, hand grenades and land mines destroyed human flesh in ways no training had prepared her soul for. Like seeing pictures of the devastation at Pearl Harbor, she thought, then flying over the ruined *Arizona* as the clipper from San Francisco came in for a landing. The realities of death and destruction far surpassed the graven images, the textbook descriptions, even eye-witness accounts from men barely able to speak of what they'd seen.

After a quick shower, she dressed in khaki shirt and slacks, and met Willi at the ladder down to the main deck. In the wardroom, a pall of cigarette smoke and the tang of brewing coffee now dominated the residue of the cake fire.

"I wonder if they have any marshmallows," Willi said as they headed for their usual table in the rear, where earlier they'd been the last to be served. Even on Christmas, rank had its privileges, and ensigns had the fewest. "I feel like a cup of cocoa. With a marshmallow on top."

"Oh, sounds good. Like something you drink after a walk in the snow." Even as Anna said the words, a pang of nostalgia coursed through her. Caught up in it, she pressed her lips together and pulled herself back to the moment by observing that across the wardroom, the MOD and a senior surgeon were huddled in what seemed an intense and possibly inimical discussion. At other tables, a few officers and nurses still in dress whites were socializing over coffee and turkey sandwiches. Some even seemed to be enjoying cake remains.

Almost immediately, a small brown Filipino steward in a white jacket appeared to ask what he could get them. "Coffee? Iced tea? Milk? Turkey sandwich? Nice piece of Padre's birthday cake?"

"Is the milk real or powdered?" Willi asked.

"Oh, sorry, nurse." His face crumpled like a child's

about to cry. "But nice and cold."

"Then make cocoa with it, okay? With a marshmallow on top."

"Me too," said Anna. "And a turkey sandwich. And a piece of cake, please. Unless it's poisonous."

The dark eyes widened in horror. "Oh no, nurse. Plenty good, except for icing. Butter and sugar, they burn real fast."

Willi watched him scurry back to the galley. "Wonder who had the bright idea to use sparklers instead of candles?"

Anna smiled. "How many were there?"

"I heard twenty-six."

"Oh, he's only my age then. Gee, I thought he was older. At least thirty. Maybe because he's so serious."

Willi shrugged. "All I've ever noticed is what a dreamboat he is. But don't tell Floyd Einhorn I said that." Willi blushed, confirming Anna's suspicion that Willi and the ship's dentist were sweet on each other. Or maybe just in a state of lust; there seemed to be a lot of that going around. In their case, they'd started as seatmates, first on the Clipper from San Francisco to Pearl Harbor, then on the shuddering R5D transport that had flown them the rest of the way to Brisbane. While she'd been stuck with Audrey all the way from Norfolk, Virginia.

"But why would he be jealous of a homosexual?" Anna said. "I mean, if scuttlebutt's right."

Willi rolled her dark-fringed green eyes. "You don't believe that, do you?"

Anna shrugged. "Oh, I don't know. It doesn't matter anyway. It's not like he's looking for romance."

The steward had just set down their food when the two chaplains came in, glanced around, then wandered toward them. As they took seats across the table, Anna felt the usual warm reaction to Luke's physical presence. Was it possible, she wondered, for a fairy to exert that sort of attraction? Of course, there was his resemblance to Dan; even in wrinkled and stained khakis, he reminded her of him—the same waving dark hair, crystal blue eyes, florid complexion and features her mother would call "a map of Ireland". She didn't know what nationality Salaunas was—maybe Italian—but the resemblance was stunning, even down to the same gift of the Blarney.

Beside him, Mark Whitmore seemed merely pallid and dull. And sad, so undeniably sad. Just as she'd probably appeared after her first experience with the terminally maimed.

As the steward hovered, Luke ordered two turkey sandwiches with cranberry sauce, cole slaw, iced tea and a big piece of cake. Mark asked only for coffee, then noticing the nurses' cocoa, changed his order.

"Not hungry, I bet," Anna said after the steward left.

The wide-set gray eyes met her gaze. He shook his head, glanced down at his hands and began turning his wedding ring.

"Your first experience with fresh casualties?"

He nodded. "See, till I joined this ship, I was stationed at shore side hospitals. The injuries there aren't so new. And men like the ones we just saw wouldn't have made it that far."

Anna brought the mug to her lips but the cocoa was too hot to sip. She wiped marshmallow froth from her upper lip with the napkin. "It took me a while to get used to it too. But at first . . . Luke, remember when you took me to see the casualties from that carrier?"

He nodded, shook a cigarette from the Luckies pack in his shirt pocket and flicked flame from a chrome lighter with the Navy officers' insignia on it. "See, she was new and green, so she was horrified. But she did a fine job. Kept smiling, even made a joke with one man who was fully conscious."

"Don't remind me." She felt a blush rising. "The others were burn cases. He'd been crushed from the waist down. He was in good spirits, but we couldn't save him." She blew on the cocoa and managed a small, steaming sip. "He was funny, though, said I was the first white woman he'd seen since he left San Diego. 'And some of them wasn't white, if you know what I mean.' All I could think of was, 'All cats are gray in the dark.' Then I worried I'd shocked you, Luke."

He exhaled blue-tinged smoke away from the table. "Well, you might have if you were Catholic. But I'm never surprised at things Protestants say."

Willi and Anna laughed, while Mark regarded them with a look that suggested the same horror Anna might have felt had anyone made a joke when she was still subsumed in the despair of dealing with patients for whom there was no help. Still, he cleared his throat and said, "I understand you're not just any Protestant though. Your father's an Episcopal priest, right?"

When she said, "Please don't hold that against me," she expected him to grimace. Instead, a grin lit his eyes and softened his face. Before he could answer, the steward appeared with his cocoa and Luke's meal-sized snack.

As Luke lifted the first sandwich to his mouth, Willi said, "Well now, padre. Bet you'll never forget this birthday, will you?"

He bit, chewed and swallowed, Adam's Apple bobbing. "If only for the fireworks."

"Did they do that last year?" Anna asked. "I mean, bring you an incendiary cake?"

"Wasn't aboard yet. Still in Baltimore, training for the chaplaincy at Johns Hopkins. No one knew it was my birthday. And no one who did know even remembered."

"Not even your parents?" Anna asked.

His gaze went distant; his face hardened. "No. They died when I was twelve. In a car wreck. And my brothers and sisters, they're not really flesh and blood family, so they never remember. I did have one card though. From a nursing sister who was there the day I was born."

"The day you were born," Anna said slowly. "In Baltimore? Is that where you're from?"

He nodded. "My father was a pediatrician and my mother was a baby nurse. They couldn't have children of their own, so they took in foundlings. I was the first."

She felt her mouth gape, her heart begin to race. Until she told herself it was sheer coincidence that he'd been born in Baltimore the same day as Lorraine Cropper's illegitimate son, immediately signed away for adoption. The rest of it, the resemblance not so much to Dan Donovan as to the Irish priest in Lorraine's photograph, might be pure wishful thinking. Or a need to rejoice in a happy possibility, however remote, on a holiday marred by tragedy on a passing destroyer.

Momentarily speechless, she let Willi direct the conversation to more prosaic matters. By then her sandwich was history and the cocoa was tepid, yet still warm enough to be comforting. At least to her mouth. Still, musing on the possibility that this priest could be Lorraine's son, she was jolted back to the moment only when Mark asked where she'd spent the previous Christmas.

She brightened. "Well, I was working on an island off the Maine coast, and I couldn't get home…"

"Home? Where's that?"

"Portsmouth, New Hampshire. Anyway, some friends on the island invited me to their dinner. I enjoyed it. It snowed, and one guy was on leave from the Air Corps. Everybody told funny family stories, and I called my parents…." She took a deep breath as private details filled out the coalescing memory, stirring up emotions she hadn't realized were still stewing within it.

"Oh?" His smile was polite, reserved. He hesitated a moment. "Hope you don't mind if I mention it, but I understand you're a war widow."

She was startled for no sensible reason: her marital status was far from a secret. Yet tonight the topic seemed inappropriate. Feeling prim, she nodded. "My husband was engineering officer on a sub. It just…it just never returned from a patrol." A shrug, as if she needed to convince him Dan's death was but another ordinary aspect of her life. Like having had dinner with the Croppers last year. Or being the daughter of a priest. Or having dishwater-blonde hair.

"Sorry," Mark said quietly. "That must be rough."

She nodded again and drained the rich chocolate sludge in the bottom of the mug. "But life goes on." Even to herself, she sounded like a damned Pollyanna. "Now, why don't you tell us what you did last year?"

While Mark sketched a domestic picture of a wife and two kids in Charleston, South Carolina, her mind flitted again to the rumor Luke was a homosexual. Even as she speculated, *Judge not that ye be not judged* echoed in her head as if spoken by her father from a nearby pulpit. Then she asked herself why Luke's sexuality mattered anyway, except as a distraction from the war and its effect on her life. Gossip like this and all the rest that circulated on this ship was generated, she suspected, in the common need for diversion on a vessel that endlessly circled the Pacific, steaming back and forth between invasions and fleet hospitals, and never reaching home port. Yet she'd requested it, her mother thought because she hoped to find Dan out here. But Anna had sniffed and said, "No, Mother. I just want to do something in the war. Something I'm trained for. Something important."

It was eight-thirty when they finished picking at crumbs;

the cocoa mugs had been refilled, the dirty dishes cleared, and they'd all managed to swallow some of the smoke-tasting cake. They'd talked about previous Christmases, and families, and home, almost everything except the moribund men living out their last few hours down on E Deck. Mark had begun stifling yawns and Luke had finished the cigarettes in his pack. Willi kept glancing at her watch as if she had something else to do. Still, Anna sensed that none of them was anxious to leave this circle of camaraderie and return to their solitary cabins, solitary memories, solitary emotions. Even when they ran out of conversation, pushed back chairs and headed toward the ladder, their reluctance resonated with her own.

Suddenly, she was filled with the need to embrace them one by one, experiencing their warm and living presence against her body for a moment before they parted. She didn't of course, would have been embarrassed to admit the impulse even to Willi. So they climbed the ladder to C Deck; she and Willi said goodnight to the chaplains and started forward to Nurses' Country.

"Now don't forget to pray for those men," Luke called. "Won't save them, but it might ease their suffering."

"My father says prayer is our Christian duty, even when it's only, Thy will be done," Anna rejoined.

When the men had resumed the climb to male officers' quarters on B Deck, Willi said "Don't know about you, Anna, but I'll be praying their suffering ends, stat. If they're going to expire, let it be quick."

"Amen to that." Even as she spoke, she wondered if the chaplains or her father would consider the thought a form of apostasy. As if wishing the suffering a speedy death dishonored the premise that life was sacred and a medical professional's duty was to preserve it as long as possible. No, she decided; *Thy will be done* overrode all personal intentions.

In her cabin, she gave her face a quick once-over with a washcloth, undressed, and climbed into the bunk. Now the breeze from the porthole carried the scent of rain, smelling just as it did at home in summer. Yellow lightning flashed on and off against distant clouds and thunder muttered behind it, just as they did at home too. The ship was pitching slightly, a gentle roller-coaster motion that recalled lines she'd learned somewhere, maybe in a hymn, or a grammar school poem: *Rocked in the cradle of the deep, I lay me down to sleep....*

Old words, an archaic, sentimental concept, yet they triggered a landslide of emotions, like rocks down a hillside of memory. In the passageway, the carols played on and on, the same twenty or thirty that had endlessly cycled throughout the day in cheerless juxtaposition to the losses that now surfaced in her; Dan, the baby, her troubled friend on the island, the first casualties from the carrier, today's scalded sailors, the wounded from Peleliu and Leyte, and thousands more she'd yet to meet.

"Jesus, Jesus," she whispered, using the prayer of last resort she saved for those moments when despair rendered her unable to say more. Or when there was no time for a specific petition, as had been the case in Receiving earlier, when *Jesus, Jesus* implied *Keep my hands from giving pain; help them to comfort and heal.*

Tears filled her eyes, diluted sorrow. At least for now. As for next Christmas, well, surely she'd be home by then and married to Jim, therefore no longer susceptible to it. But that was a year away; all she really needed now was to get through tonight.

* * *

Three days later, all the scalded men had expired, two in the wee hours before the next morning, the others at longer intervals. Luke and Mark shared the funeral service on the fantail. As the bodies were consigned to the deep, the bugled taps stirred what Anna considered useless emotions; regret and frustration and sorrow, even a deep, quiet strain of anger. Glancing over from the podium, Mark's gaze connected with hers in wordless commiseration, but Luke merely stared over everyone's heads at the sea, his face a grim mask.

At the mortality conference afterward, however, though she'd resolved to keep her mouth shut, she was compelled to ask, "Since these men didn't have a chance to begin with, why were they subjected to the stress of a high-line transfer? Couldn't corpsmen on the destroyer do everything we did for them?"

Commander Tomlin, the CMO, sighed. He was a compact man with a thick neck and a beefy face, the sagging lines of which gave him an aspect of profound weariness. As if he might have asked the same question of some higher authority and come away with an answer that had left him unsatisfied and peevish.

"That was their CO's decision, Miss Donovan. A tin can's a small, cramped ship with a small, cramped sick bay and no medical officer. Their skipper ordered the transfer so the crew would think heroic efforts were being made to save them. When in truth, nothing could have. Now, any other questions?"

"No, sir," she said. "Thank you." And realized that to this there was only one real answer; in war, people died. You couldn't save them all. She'd read BuMed statistics on the percentages of battle casualties who were saved, compared to the Civil War and World War One. Impressive, a cause for hope, for optimism. Still, there was the grim fact that some were beyond help from the first minute.

Maybe, in the long run, it was all a matter of *Thy will be done,* after all.

CHAPTER THREE

The afternoon Father Luke was attacked, Anna was working the afternoon shift on H-13, officially Neuro-Psych, unofficially the Nut Ward for battle fatigue casualties. Some had self-inflicted wounds; others were recovering from injuries, but were convinced they were still in combat. A third group was physically undamaged, but beset by symptoms ranging from violent outbursts of rage to fits of weeping. A few were manacled to their beds; one was in a straitjacket. Others appeared normal, at least physically. Their eyes, however, had a haunted, distant quality, as if instead of shipboard realities, they were watching a movie. Not some clean Hollywood version of war, but the real thing, the dirty truth that generated a soul deep pain even heavy-duty morphine couldn't touch.

H-13 was no nurse's favorite duty. Not only were the patients frequently stereotyped as cowards or moral pygmies, it was also the hottest, noisiest ward, far astern on the lowest habitable deck where oily fumes from the engine room tinged the air, and the churning of the screws was like a washing machine that never quit. At first Anna had griped like everyone else about such conditions. But before long, she'd realized working there gave her a chance to spend more time with the chaplains; both wrote up their chart notes at the nurses' station, usually with coffee, often with conversation. Besides, a double complement of corpsmen staffed the ward, handling scut duties and leaving her free to dole out meds, give sedative shots, dress wounds, chart vitals, and generally serve as mother hen.

The day was a Saturday toward the end of January; *Compassion* was eastbound to Guam with a capacity load of wounded from Luzon beachheads. Both chaplains were already on the ward when Anna came on at 1500. Engrossed in the previous shift's chart notes, she was only dimly aware of their presence, the dance music spinning on the chief's record player, and the noisy poker game on the port side. It was the steamiest part of the day, so most patients were dozing or reading books from the portable library the Red Cross girls wheeled around.

Just as Jo Stafford went into *I'll Walk Alone*, a muffled shout grabbed Anna's attention. A few beds from the station, she saw Luke struggling with a wheelchair patient. Before she could react, the chief corpsman bolted across the deck and forced the young soldier into a headlock. Another corpsman led Luke to the nearest empty bed, yelled at her to phone the MOD and bring a shot of chloral hydrate. As she made the call, she glimpsed a red stain spreading across Luke's shirt. Her hands began to shake as she prepped the hypo and rushed it to the chief.

By the time the drug had reduced the attacker to a limp lump, the corpsman had pulled up Luke's shirt; a fountain of blood spurted from a gash under the right rib cage. Anna grabbed a stack of gauze compresses, pressed one over the wound, forced a professional smile and willed composure into her voice.

"Okay now, padre, just lie still. You're going to be

fine."

Luke's face was dead white, but he managed a small grin. "Don't worry, Anna. Only a few cuts."

The compress was soon saturated, so she replaced it with a double layer. In the background, an excited hubbub from the other patients subsided only when the chief ordered them back to their beds. Then, bringing a basin, he stepped up and offered to relieve her. After he took over, she assessed Luke's other wounds -- a couple of superficial slashes on both forearms and a deeper cut across the chest.

Smiling again, she took his hand. "The MOD's on his way. Are you in pain?"

"Some. Not a lot, though." He winced as the chief pressed another pad over the major wound. Still, the red flow continued. Anna pictured the complex system of veins and arteries supplying the liver, and knew this wasn't a hemorrhage mere pressure was going to control.

Where was the damned MOD anyway?

She glanced up as footsteps approached in the passageway, but Mark Whitmore was the only one who hurried toward Luke's bed. "What happened?" he asked of no one in particular, then came closer, studying the other chaplain with a grave look. "You okay, padre?"

"Fine." The smile was half-grimace. "Nothing to worry about."

"Guy had a knife," the chief said. "Must've snuck it off the chow tray and sharpened it on something." He shook his head. "Never know what these nut jobs are gonna do."

"We were just talking," Luke said. "Like we do every day. Then he lunged. Never saw it coming. Finally got the knife away, but he got me first."

At eighteen, the soldier was the youngest on the ward, but had been in combat since October, first on Leyte, now Luzon, where he'd earned hero status by rescuing three buddies pinned down by a sniper. Afterward, however, he'd gone berserk and begun firing at everything that moved. Eventually overpowered, he became another of the involuntary passengers on H-13. Now he was locked away in a quiet room.

The chief nodded to Anna for more compresses. "Seen this happen a time or two before." His tone was matter-of-fact, as if this event were not extraordinary. "Doesn't look too serious, padre, but the docs might decide you need surgery anyway."

As he spoke, a surgeon and two corpsmen pushed a gurney off the stern elevator. The MOD repeated Anna's cursory examination, then ordered the sailors to take Luke up to surgery. She trailed behind in hopes of saying something spiritual, something reassuring. But the men moved too fast. All she could do was give Luke a thumbs-up as the elevator swallowed them.

Back at the station, Mark slid a cup of coffee across the counter. "Here. Fresh joe. If you're as shaky as I am, you could use a pick-me-up."

Relieved to get off her feet, she sipped the steaming black liquid. "Thanks. Now that it's over, I'm . . ." She held out her trembling hands. "I can't believe what happened. With no warning. Just, all of a sudden."

He nodded gravely. "Hope they're right the injuries are minor. What do you think?"

"I think he'll need major surgery. This is one of those wounds that could be fatal. The liver might be damaged."

He gawked at the gratuitous medical detail. "Sounds bad. Maybe they'll have to transfer him to the hospital when we get to Guam."

"I doubt it. We can do everything they can." Her gut constricted at the notion he might leave before she could pursue the possibility that he was Lorraine's son.

"Is that right?"

"Sure." She had no idea if it was gospel, but it seemed

likely given the experience of the surgeons, the state of the operating rooms and the modern equipment on board.

"You know, he has such a gift for helping these guys. Can't imagine why anyone would go after him. Except the kid wasn't in his right mind." He shook his head slowly, fingertips raking his sandy crew-cut. "It'll be a real mess when veterans like that come back to civilian life."

His tone was so morose, she had to say, "You sound pessimistic."

"Sorry. I try not to let it show, but…well, there it is." The disarming grin flashed as if to give the lie to his words.

Her immediate inclination was to ask if he wanted to talk, but decided they didn't know each other well enough to share confidences. "Well, some day when we have more time, maybe I could talk to you about something. A… uh, a personal dilemma."

His eyes widened above the coffee mug.

"It's not about me," she said. "So I need some advice. She swallowed more coffee. "Actually, it concerns Luke. It's…well, a sensitive matter. So I need to talk in confidence." Good Lord; she hoped he didn't infer it had to do with Luke's sexual preferences.

He studied her with a patently curious expression. "I see. Well, maybe when we put in to Guam, I could borrow a Jeep and show you around. There's a swell officers' beach there."

Some Puritan strain in her stiffened. Silly, she told herself; he wasn't suggesting a tryst, just a venue for a private conversation. And perhaps a guided tour of a tropical island where he'd been stationed. All she knew now was Apra Harbor and that sliver of the Navy base between the piers and the Officers' Club. Besides, they were both respectable people, committed to loved ones at home. Then she remembered, "But I don't have a bathing suit."

He blinked with obvious surprise. "Oh, I didn't mean swimming. Just thought you'd like to see the beach."

She felt an abashed blush. "Well, okay then."

He drained the cup, got to his feet, checked the time. "Good. We'll plan on it. Now, been half an hour since they took him upstairs. Think I'll see what I can find out."

Watching him head toward the elevator, she observed the confident walk, the squared shoulders, the erect posture; hardly the same sad man she'd talked to Christmas night. Well good, he was getting his emotional sea legs at last. Then, as he waited, he turned and saw her staring at him. They both looked away quickly, but it took her a few seconds to redirect her concern to Luke.

That night she wrote to Jim about the incident, adding medical details about Luke's lacerated liver and the surgery that had repaired it, with a good prognosis. She also mentioned the possible connection to Lorraine, but decided not to tell him she and Chaplain Whitmore were going to discuss it. That news could well make Jim worry because she was spending personal time with a gentle, kindly man she saw daily and shared both medical and spiritual concerns with. She knew too well his conviction that she'd find another love out here amongst what he envisioned as multitudes of able-bodied and irresistibly handsome naval officers.

"Someone younger and stronger," he'd said before she left, "And whole, so he can take you dancing and sailing and mountain climbing. Someone who doesn't have to strap his leg into a damned brace every morning so he can hobble around on a cane the rest of the day." He hadn't verbalized the rest of it: that he couldn't have intercourse even in the standard missionary position; but she knew that was part of it. Thanks to his first wife, his heart was convinced no woman would love him as she might an undamaged man. In his mind it was only a matter of time before he got the dreaded Dear John letter.

Well, Anna thought, she couldn't undo what that other woman had done to him. But she could shield him from pointless speculation about her own fidelity. Even if it meant censoring portions of truth from letters as she wrote them.

CHAPTER FOUR

*A*fter they docked at Apra Harbor, Anna was tied up transferring disembarking patients to buses and ambulances. Then she worked on records for another hour before Mark reminded her of the Jeep ride. "It's the Exec's. I only have it 'til four. So whenever you're free. . ."

She ran to her cabin for purse and cap and followed him down the gangway. The pier was bustling with gray supply trucks provisioning them for the next deployment, front-end loaders, mechanical mules, cranes and a few Jeeps. He led her to one marked with two stars; the back seat was stacked with stenciled cardboard cartons.

She slid on dark glasses against the mid-day glare and hoisted herself into the front. Backing around to leave, Mark jerked his head toward the boxes. "Before we hit the beach, I've got to make a delivery. Stuff for the local church. The Exec's pet project."

"Oh? Secret stuff?"

He chuckled. "Not at all. Just food. Powdered eggs and milk. Canned vegetables. Rice. Dried beans. Spam. Lots of

Spam. Candy bars and soap. See, the Japs occupied Guam right after Pearl Harbor. Civilians damned near starved the whole time. We only retook it last summer." He turned a grin toward her. "Commander Beall believes we have a moral obligation to share our excesses with the needy."

"Oh, I agree. And do you deliver it just so you can use the Jeep?"

"Not just for that. You know what Jesus said: 'If you love me, feed my lambs'. Besides, there's always more than they need in the officers' mess."

Once they'd left the base's clustered Quonset huts, shabby little houses lined the pock-marked road. The air was steamy, vegetation lush, overgrown. Fetid odors wafted from piles of refuse. Between stands of palms, she caught glimpses of steep hills, rocky cliffs, dazzling surf breaking on reefs.

As he drove, Mark described the campaign to retake this island a month after the bloody fight for Saipan. "Natives there believed the Jap propaganda that our troops'd torture them and eat their kids. So a hell of a lot of them jumped off cliffs into the ocean." He sighed. "Makes me wonder what lies our government's told us about our enemies."

The remark moved her to tell him about Jean Cropper's brief, doomed affair with Wilhelm Himmelreich, a survivor of a German U-boat sunk off the coast of Hope Island, Maine. "Such a needless tragedy." She sighed. "Sometimes I can't see any order to the world. I want to make sense of these events. But everywhere I look I feel more bewildered."

His nod was solemn. "Thank God Luke's going to be okay. I know nobody's exempt from harm, but on a ship as safe as ours…" He shook his head.

The church where he stopped had a California-mission look, but with stucco peeling like a bad case of sunburn and painted surfaces faded to raw wood. As they approached, clusters of scrawny rag-clad kids ran alongside calling, "Padre, padre!" Parking in an unpaved, trash-strewn alley, Mark left the Jeep running and disappeared into a tin-roofed cinder block building behind the church. Besides exhaust, Anna was almost overpowered by the stench of garbage and sewage. And engulfed in a world foreign to any she'd ever known, surrounded by gap-toothed, brown-skinned little people chattering in an unknown tongue, hands outstretched in supplication. All she knew was they wanted something. And she had nothing to give except a white woman's nervous smile.

Relief swept her when Mark returned with a hunch-backed priest and three sturdy young men babbling Pidgin English. Within minutes, they'd unloaded the Jeep, called a torrent of thanks and lugged every carton into the ramshackle building. Then Mark stooped to the kids' level and, with a soft-eyed expression, handed out candy bars until there were none left.

Business-like again, he reversed onto the street with a whine of gears. "Thought the colored folks at home had things bad 'til I came here." He shifted and headed downhill toward the coast, shimmering in the distance. "Now, tell me what's bothering you about Luke. Besides his health."

Heart hammering, she condensed Lorraine's story. Then, breathless about revealing her suspicion, gave him the punch line: "Now I think the baby she signed away in 1918—in Baltimore, mind you—I think it might be Luke."

Skirting a pothole wide enough to be a bomb crater, he nodded so casually she wondered if he was surprised. Then again, most clergy, including her father, were skilled at hiding reactions to shocking news. "Sounds plausible. You mention it to him yet?"

"Suppose he doesn't want to know."

"Then let him decide." Letting go the gearshift, he

patted her hand as she clutched the seat for balance. "You'll have plenty of chances to talk on the way back to Luzon. Want me to be there?"

She studied this. "Thanks. But better if you don't. He might think we're in cahoots."

He smiled, brushed her hand again. "Well either way, you have to tell him."

The beach was a strip of sugar-white sand fringed with palms and bracketed by rocky headlands. Offshore, breakers rippled over an unseen reef. A few men in black Navy-issue trunks and women in bathing suits--off-duty nurses, Mark said, waving at them--were soaking up the tropical January sun. The scene was a jewel-toned travel poster, except for a rope dividing the beach into sections for officers and enlisted. And, at its far edge, a tangled mountain of rusting metal.

He nodded toward it. "Leftovers from the fighting. In three weeks, we lost almost two thousand men. Those wrecks came from the reef where the LCIs got hung up."

She pictured landing craft impaled on coral, their passengers pinned down and helpless in the defending barrage. And wondered how long it had taken the blood to wash from this now-pristine beach.

Leaving shoes and socks in the Jeep, they rolled up their trousers and stepped around recumbent sunbathers toward the water. And talked about other beaches they'd known. Her favorite was Kittery, Maine, his, Myrtle Beach, South Carolina. "Seems a million miles away," he said, his gaze on incoming ripples swirling sand around their toes. "Another lifetime."

"Is that where your kids were in that picture you showed us Christmas night?"

"No, that was Coronado. Right before I left for Pearl. A year ago."

"Haven't you had any pictures since?"

He shook his head without meeting her gaze.

"Why not?" The closeness of their bare feet suggested an intimacy that emboldened her to prod for an answer he might otherwise be reluctant to give.

He turned, shoulders hunched, mouth tight. "It's personal. Not something I want to talk about."

"Oh," she said. "One of those things. Guess I'll have to figure it out for myself."

"Look, Anna. It's no big mystery. See, my wife didn't want me to join the Navy, and that's one of the ways she punishes me."

"Oh. I see. Forgive me for saying it, but that seems, well, sort of mean, don't you think?" She turned to gauge his reaction, but his gaze was focused on pink whipped cream clouds festooning the horizon.

"Well, maybe." His hands were clenched at his sides. "You may be right. She loved being a minister's wife, but not a chaplain's. I didn't see the difference, except we weren't living near her family anymore. Or maybe I'm missing something."

Anna shrugged. "Possibly she's afraid. You know, that something will happen to you out here. I felt it when I was married to Dan. Not terror, just a sense he wouldn't come back. Of course, he was on a sub that had problems from the start."

His gaze clung to her face. "But when he didn't, you dealt with it. I doubt Lynette could."

Her smile was automatic, like the comment: "Everyone's different. I'm sure once you're home again, she'll be fine."

He nodded, face bleak in the harsh sunlight. Neither of them spoke for a minute. Then they began sketching life stories, innocuous little vignettes that disclosed neither secret longings nor buried sorrows. Even when she confided she'd lost a baby, she willed emotion from her voice. All the while the surf foamed and hissed; gulls swooped for picnickers' crumbs; cigarette smoke mingled with whiffs of suntan oil and Noxzema, and the northerly breeze carried the familiar stench of rot from the heaped metal up the beach.

She was about to suggest they sit awhile, when he glanced at his watch. "Good Lord, quarter to four. Got to get back before this bucket of bolts turns into a pumpkin."

At the ship, she barely had time to thank him for the ride before he spun the Jeep around and roared off in a cloud of gravel. After she watched him bounce along the pier, she climbed to the quarterdeck, grabbed letters from her mail slot, and headed to Nurses' Country. Two were from Jim, postmarked a week apart. Impatient for his advice about Luke, she skimmed past reports of Hope Island's state of health to the heart of his letter: that her path had crossed that of someone who might be Lorraine's son was beyond coincidence. It was divinely ordained and she had to take it as far as she could.

The tears of relief took her by surprise. Wiping her cheeks, she decided to visit Luke in the quiet room on E Deck. Not to tell him, not yet, just to reassure herself he needed to know.

Now three days post-op, Luke's skin was slightly jaundiced, and he appeared shrunken, physically diminished as many patients did after surgery. His chart, however, recorded excellent progress. The head of the bed was elevated so he could read mail and smoke, and his smile told her he was happy to see her. She stayed only until a corpsman brought his chow tray, just long enough to tell him about the Jeep ride with Mark. Not quite long enough, however, to become convinced she had the right to forever change his life with her news.

CHAPTER FIVE

*T*wo days later, *Compassion* steamed out of Apra Harbor at first light. A hundred miles west, the weather thickened into a hard-blowing storm, so the ship slowed to avoid overtaking what Floyd Einhorn declared a typhoon. During the five-day run back to Luzon, Anna planned to give Luke a wheelchair ride to the weather deck, an open area cluttered with exhaust vents, horizontal lockers and lifeboats rowed along the rails of the highest accessible deck on the ship. Corpsmen and nurses often wheeled convalescents up here to take the sun. Now, with no other patients aboard, it seemed the perfect spot to deliver her heart-stopping news.

It was Sunday afternoon before they ran out of clouds, wind and rain. By then, other nurses had been giving him so much attention, she sensed an unofficial competition to see who could spend the most time with him. So, before anyone else grabbed him after noon chow, she stepped behind his chair and suggested a trip to the top deck. "Be a nice change of scene, and the sun's lovely after the storm."

He grinned up. "They tell me I'm white as a dead fish."

"Not quite, but the fresh air will put roses in your cheeks."

From the far end of the table, Mark sent her a knowing smile. Pushing Luke into the forward elevator, she rang for the top deck. There, midday sunlight was blinding on white-painted surfaces and bleached wood decking, so she wheeled him to a small patch of shade in the lee of the pilothouse, then sat facing him on a storage locker. The sky was enamel blue, streaked by high-altitude remnants of the storm, the sea an ultramarine chop frothed with whitecaps. A cool, salt-tasting wind swept the open deck, but the sunlight was hot on her skin.

She slipped on sunglasses and asked how he was feeling now. "I mean, really feeling."

He lit a smoke. "Still so damned weak. Taking a lot longer to come back than I thought."

"Has anyone explained liver function?"

"My father did, once upon a time. He was so sure I was going to be a doctor he answered every medical question before I had a chance to ask. That's why they named me Luke, of course."

She took a deep breath. "About your surname. What nationality is Salaunas? Italian?"

His face sobered, eyes deep in shadow. "No, Lithuanian. Second generation."

"You said your parents took in foundlings?"

He nodded, inhaled on the smoke. "Turned our house into a veritable orphanage. After they died, the Sisters of Charity took it over. That's when I started thinking about becoming a priest. If they'd lived, I probably never would have."

She tried not to look too interested. "Oh? And do you know anything about your…uh, your natural parents?"

"Not a thing. Actually, I didn't know I wasn't born to the Salaunases 'til they died."

She glanced away from his intense gaze toward the brownish fumes from the stack. Occasional downdrafts wafted warm oily exhaust, while the ventilator funnels poured out the usual smells of cigarettes and perking coffee, as if at any time of night or day, someone on duty within the ship's innards was smoking and drinking coffee.

"Well. That must've been a shock. Did it...uh, did it start you wondering about them? Your biological parents?"

His face went wistful. "All us kids wondered about our parents. We all dreamed one day they'd come and take us home. Then we'd be happy."

"Weren't you happy in the orphanage?"

"Happy as you can be in an institution. We knew things'd be much better with our real parents." A short, tense laugh. "Of course, now I realize we were there because they didn't want us. We were bastards. The shameful secret they couldn't let the world see."

Her heart softened with pity for the smashed illusions, the lost innocence of his childhood. "Well, maybe you were wanted, but they had no way to care for you."

His eyes narrowed, only the bright blue visible in the shadow of his heavy brows. "Then how come they didn't look for me?"

"Maybe . . . maybe they didn't know where to start."

His laugh was a short, cynical cough. "That's no excuse, Anna. All us kids were born in the same hospital. And my parents never sealed the records. In case somebody wanted to find us."

She aimed her gaze skyward and prayed, Lord, help me know what to say. A formation of four-engine planes appeared between shredded clouds, too high to hear or determine whether they were friends or foes. She crossed herself mentally before she said, "You know, Luke, I've met a few unwed mothers in my nursing career. Most were too ashamed to look for their kids. Or they'd married, and didn't want their families to know."

"Yeah, I've told myself that too. But the reasons don't matter."

"Maybe not. But . . . wouldn't you like to know who you came from?"

He stared off across the endless blue surging around the ship. "Once, yeah, it seemed important. But not anymore. I know I'm God's child regardless of who they were. Or what sins are on their conscience."

"Gosh, Luke. Don't you want to know anything?"

He regarded her so intensely her defenses felt penetrated. "Anna, all these questions of yours . . . are they purely academic?"

"Well . . . actually, no," she stuttered, mouth going dry, heart hammering. "Actually, I think . . . I mean . . . I may know your mother." She paused to gauge his reaction, could detect none on his face, though his fingers were tightly clenched. "See, last year, a friend in Maine told me she had a baby. A boy. On Christmas Day, 1918. In Baltimore. In a hospital run by the Sisters of Charity. Later she showed me a picture of his father, and . . . well, you look just like him."

A frown gathered his brows. "No. No, that's ridiculous. Impossible. Can't be."

"Well, I only know what she told me. And if you want, I'll tell you the rest of it." She waited, her own hands tense in her lap. Luke closed his eyes, slumped in the chair. Wind blew open the bathrobe, exposing skinny white legs, the calves dark with hair. With sunlight harsh on it, his face registered more pain than when he'd been stabbed.

It seemed a long while before he spoke, and then his voice was faint. "But does she want to find me?"

"Well, she prays for you every day. What do you think?"

"Don't know, Anna." He closed his eyes so tightly the

skin crinkled around them. "Does she have other children?"

"No. But she and her husband are raising his orphaned nephew."

"Her husband... my father?"

"No. He knows about you, though. So if I tell them I've found you, it won't be a rude shock."

He stared through her for what felt a long time. "Oh God, Anna. I don't know…"

"Then think about it a while longer." Fighting off disappointment, she got to her feet. "Right now it must be awfully confusing."

Without further discussion, she wheeled him back to his cabin. After she helped him into bed, she considered knocking on Mark's door just down the passageway. But why? To alert him to Luke's dilemma? And receive his assurance that her intrusion would work out well? Or to connect on a personal level? Ah, that was it. Connecting with Mark suddenly seemed excessively important. Even desirable.

Stung by remorse, she nonetheless detoured to pass his door. It was open just enough that she could see him at the desk. Before he caught a glimpse of her, she ducked down the nearest ladder and hurried forward to Nurses' Country. She'd intended to write to Jim about Luke, but confided in her journal instead.

* * *

Back on station, the ship picked up what scuttlebutt declared the last casualties from the Philippines. Now early February, they were to transport them to Hollandia, then head north to a new campaign involving Marines. As usual, both medical staff and ship's company were betting on which island was next. So many were now in Allied hands, the only logical choices were Iwo Jima and Okinawa. To make the wagers more interesting, the betting pool was widened to include time and date of the first landings.

At chow one evening, OH told them that sailors bet on everything, from duration of a campaign to the number of casualties they'd pick up. "Once I even heard some betting where the next seagull would shit. Then they divided the weather deck into squares with chalk. Like Bingo."

Audrey said, "I thought betting was against regulations."

OH rolled her eyes. "Honey, if we ever enforced every reg, there'd be a mutiny. On this ship, it's all about morale. And not just the patients'."

By now Anna saw Luke only when the schedule allowed her to eat at regular hours. He was so distant, however, she assumed she'd been too quick to share her theory of his parentage. She mentioned her disappointment to Mark the next time he was on H-13.

Seated across the desk with his usual coffee, he toyed with the sugar canister. "Actually, I think he's scared to find out. I told him, anytime you have a chance to learn the truth, seize it. Even if it hurts. Only way you'll ever make peace with it. Of course, now he knows you have this information…" He brought the mug to his lips. "…it's going to eat at him 'til he hears the rest of it."

"I hope so," she said. "Lorraine's a wonderful woman. And his father was an Irish priest. Catholic, of course."

Mark's eyes widened. "Really? Now that might knock him for a loop. I mean, knowing he's the result of a priest's sin. But then again, maybe he'll want to find him." He drained the coffee in one gulp and got to his feet. "God only knows, Anna. I sure as hell don't. I don't know the answers to anything these days."

Without excusing himself, he hurried from the ward. She stared after him, wondering what had pushed him to leave so peremptorily. This shift in moods tempted her to get into his mind, the way one might pry open a clock that kept erratic time. With Luke, her imagination drew a line at personal speculation, as if his celibate status placed him beyond her right to curiosity. With Mark, the only deterrent was the glaring truth that his mental state was still none of her business, however intriguing she found it.

* * *

Compassion stood off Leyte for most of that week. Saturday evening, up to capacity, she weighed anchor for Hollandia. By now Luke was on his feet again. Leaning on a cane, he was celebrating morning mass, hearing confessions, even officiating at funerals. Still, Anna sensed he was ducking her. As if she intended to back him up to a bulkhead and demand he hear all about Lorraine Cropper. Like a mother forcing a kid to swallow castor oil. Finally, with a *the hell with it* sense, she decided the Lord wanted her to tend to her own business.

From Hollandia, they steamed north for four days, then put into Guam again. Apra Harbor was so crowded they had to anchor out, loading stores and refueling from lighters alongside. Besides a couple of cruisers, a transport and some LCDs were also being replenished. Even tied up, this armada looked so mighty, it was easy to believe the coming campaign would be over quickly, with few casualties.

At chow that noon, Anna voiced her optimism.

"Don't kid yourself," said OH from down the table. "I've heard that scuttlebutt about every landing since Guadalcanal. And so far, they were all worse than we expected."

"And the closer we get to their homeland, the harder they're going to fight," said Floyd, who had recently turned into a fount of all wisdom and all knowledge, whether anyone sought it or not.

At the other end of the table, Mark's face was troubled. "But wouldn't we do the same thing in their shoes?"

No one answered. Beside him, Luke stared into his soup.

Just then the boson's pipe squealed, heralding the commencement of liberty. Everyone bolted their food and hurried from the wardroom. On his way out, Mark asked if she wanted another Jeep ride. "Luke's coming too, but we can squeeze you in. Dinner at the O club afterward. My treat."

Eager to leave the ship's confined spaces for any reason, she said, "Good. It'll give me a chance to talk more to Luke."

But even in the packed launch, the priest's dark mood was an ever-present cloud. And in the Jeep he chatted with Mark in the front seat and ignored Anna, who was sharing the back with food cartons destined for a church halfway up a steep hillside. The road was a shambles but the brilliant view of Agana and the sea was worth the jolting ride.

The moment they pulled up, Guamanian nuns in tattered habits flocked from a patchwork school like gulls going after crumbs on a beach. Mark jumped from the Jeep to help carry in the cartons, while Anna sat regarding the back of Luke's neck in a discomfiting silence. It was only when he lit a cigarette and began smoking in short, quick puffs that she realized he was as nervous as she was.

Ridiculous, she thought, then said, "Luke, am I imagining it, or are you angry with me because I said I might know your mother?"

He went on staring at shadows on the pocked plaster wall directly ahead. "Listen, Anna, I know you meant well, but…well, I wish you never had. It's changed everything for me."

"Everything? What do you mean by everything?"

He tapped a smudge of ash over the side of the Jeep. "Oh, my sense of my past. My identity. Even the way I feel about myself."

"Sorry," she murmured, feeling unfairly accused. "I only told you because I thought you deserved to know. Sure, I knew it might upset you, but I had to take the chance. The rest of it's up to you. I mean, you don't have to follow up on it. And I'm not going to tell Lorraine anything either. So it's all up to you."

He didn't answer, but continued the fast, nervous consumption of one cigarette after another until Mark returned, climbed in and started the engine.

For the rest of the afternoon, even during dinner, Luke's sullen mood weighed on her, distracting her from Mark's travelogue. But afterward, on the launch returning to the ship, Luke leaned over and murmured, "Listen, Anna, I've been thinking about what I said earlier. And I apologize. You were right to tell me about your friend. It's just that…well, I don't know what to do now."

Astonished at the abrupt change of heart, she said, "Looking at my pictures might be a start. Maybe when we get back to the ship…"

His nod was tight.

She glanced over at Mark just as he gave her a surreptitious thumbs-up.

In her cabin, she grabbed the envelope with personal photos, then walked aft on C Deck down the long passageway that housed a veritable shipboard village; post office, barber shop, library, Gedunk, ship's service, miniature chapel and various offices. In the chaplains' office Luke was at the far desk under the porthole, Mark closer to the hatch.

Dropping into the chair between them, she dumped the pictures on her lap. Somewhere nearby, a radio blasted out Tommy Dorsey's *Boogie Woogie*. It was dark now; the open porthole exhaled humid air redolent of dank water and exhaust fumes from launches alongside.

After she'd sorted the pictures, she passed Luke all those of Lorraine with Cleve, with Johann, with Jean and Alex, even one with Jim. Meanwhile, she explained how Lorraine had come from Louisiana to Hope Island in the 'twenties as Cleve Cropper's mail-order bride, and how she was connected through him to his niece Jean, who'd died in childbirth the past summer.

Luke absorbed this information, nodding, and asking occasional questions, such as why Lorraine had had her baby in Baltimore, and if she had other children. And inevitably, "And who is my, I mean, her son; who's his father?"

Her gaze slid to Mark's; his held a warning.

"Hmm…she didn't say much about him. Just that he lived in her hometown. He was a…a respected member of the community. And they were deeply in love."

He frowned down at the pictures. "Then why didn't they marry?" She heard the flare of anger. "Or was he already married?"

"She didn't say."

"Are they still in touch?"

"Uh, I don't think so. But I believe she knows where he is."

His sigh was morose. "God, I don't know what to do. If I thought it'd make her happy, well, maybe I'd contact her. But it sounds like she has a good life. I might just throw a monkey-wrench into it."

"Well sure, that's one possibility." Mark reached for the pictures and shuffled through them. "On the other hand, it could give both of you something you've never had."

"What does your heart tell you?" Anna asked.

Luke's face turned wistful. "This is all too good to be true."

She glanced again at Mark. Even immersed in Luke's dilemma, she was strangely tempted to stare into his eyes, be drawn into his thoughts, admit him to hers. Her heart rate accelerated until she took a deep breath and forced her attention back to the moment.

"Well, the only way to find out is to get in touch with her." She reached for a pencil from the cluttered desk, then printed Lorraine's name and address on the envelope. "Here, this is where you can write to her." Gathering up the pictures, she stuffed them back inside and dropped it onto his desk. "Keep these as long as you like. And if you want more information, you know where to find me. Now, I'm going to write my fiancé and tell him how things stand."

Instead, back in her cabin, she yielded to the pull of fatigue generated in the long day and the wine she'd had with dinner. She intended to sleep, but when she closed her eyes, Mark Whitmore kept glowing in her mind, a distant candle the wind of reality hadn't yet blown out. Nor would it, she realized, as long as she let it light up her imagination.

Harmless, she assured herself. Just a diversion, an entertainment, a distraction. As innocent as reading a novel or watching a movie. Nothing could possibly come of it.

CHAPTER SIX

*A*s *Compassion* steamed closer to Iwo Jima, flashes brightened the night sky; the ensuing thuds vibrated through the ship. The night before the scheduled landing, medical personnel lined the rails to watch the man-made thunder and lightning display, now in its third day after months of aerial bombing.

Anna was shocked at the general jubilation, as if no one had been through this before and couldn't picture the transports wallowing behind the warships, their holds full of young Marines who, tomorrow before daylight, would breakfast on steak and eggs, then, laden with weapons, ammo, radios, field rations and entrenching shovels, haul themselves hand over hand down cargo nets into landing craft rocking on the sea below. Approaching a beach supposedly secured by Allied shelling, they'd be cocky with the same *espirit de corps* of Marines in the O Club. Then the boats would grind onto the sand, men would splash overboard, rifles above their heads as they waded toward shore. And the unseen enemy whose inescapably heavy fire would pin them down in the surf. Or on the sand, if they made it that far. Wave after wave would go ashore, all innocence and energy, until they stumbled over fallen comrades on the beach. After a while, medics would move in to treat the wounded and evacuate them in the same Higgins boats and LCIs that had brought them from the transports. Later, another team would remove dog tags from the dead, both those bodies still intact and those blown apart, these metal rectangles the only remnants of their identity.

Dear Lord, she prayed; *let this not be as bad as I think it'll be.*

She didn't realize Mark was beside her until he cleared his throat and spoke her name. Surprising she hadn't noticed, given her recent sensitivity to his presence.

"You thinking about the kids on the troopships?" he asked. "The ones who won't be alive this time tomorrow?"

"No. I was thinking about the half-dead ones we'll get in Receiving."

He shook his head. "God. I really wanted this duty. You know? Being close to the action. But now I'm considering asking for transfer. Somewhere the tragedy wouldn't seem so immediate. So inevitable. Maybe a hospital on one of the secured islands."

"That makes sense. The worst casualties would've died before they got there, so you wouldn't have to see them."

He scratched his head and scowled across the restless water. "Sounds cowardly when you put it that way."

"Sorry. Didn't mean it like that."

"I know you didn't." He inhaled the cigarette-tinged night air. "Well, maybe it'll be easier after I get used to it."

"No, it won't. It's easier before you know what to expect."

"God." He watched the flashing horizon, then twisted his wrist so a deck light shone on his watch. "Well, time to start the weekly prayer meeting. Think tonight I'll invite folks to ask the Lord to bless our work. I just hope nobody says, 'Jesus, help us beat the crap out of those Jap sons-of-bitches.'"

She laughed. "What'll you do if somebody does?"

"I guess, just say Amen." He cleared his throat. "You planning to come?"

Burdened with heavier thoughts than usual, she'd intended to pour her heart into her journal, but Mark's plaintive tone made her say she'd be there.

"Good. Maybe you could volunteer to pray too."

"And say what?"

His face was in shadow, but she felt he smiled. "You've got a better sense of that than I do."

Back in her cabin, she paged through her dog-eared Book of Common Prayer for a collect. None seemed appropriate, but in the back was one she'd cut and pasted from *Forward Day by Day* before she left home. She took it along in case the Spirit moved her to read it at the prayer meeting. Something she could write her father about later, something to connect them in that same Spirit.

In the crew's mess, she joined Willi at the officers' table. Three sailors with guitars accompanied the hymns, just the first verses of those everyone knew, *Rock of Ages* and *Jesus, Savior, Pilot Me* and *Faith of our Fathers*. A few men rose when Mark asked for prayers. And sure enough, one said what he'd been afraid of, except this bluejacket said "shit" instead of "crap", and "bastards" instead of "sons of bitches", then apologized profusely.

When no one else volunteered, Anna rose, cleared her throat and spoke her paraphrase of the original words: "O God, our country has called us away from our homes and work, to serve your people in danger. We believe you are with us. We do not ask to escape duty, hardship or danger. We ask for strength to keep pure, courage to face the unknown, and patience to bear what is dull and hard. Bless and protect the homes we have left behind. Keep our people from worrying about us, and return us to them, if it be thy will. Amen."

Willi clasped her hand as she sat again. From the lectern, Mark sent her a tender look. Then, in his deep Southern-tinged voice, he said, "Our Father and our God, You know we hate what we have to do out here. We hate that tomorrow we'll have to take on casualties from this new invasion. We hate what's happening to these young men, and we hate seeing the damage to their young bodies. But we know if you were here, this is what you'd be doing, even if you hated it too. So walk with us, Lord, and make us strong, and kind, and gentle, and patient, and tireless to do your will. But please, make it end soon. In the name of the Father, Son and Holy Ghost, Amen."

Anna made the sign of the cross, then joined in The Lord's Prayer and *Onward, Christian Soldiers*. Everyone sang loudly, righteousness in their voices. While they were still singing, she left by the after hatch, went up to Nurses' Country, then lay in her bunk, not just listening to the continuing whump of big guns, but feeling the reverberation in her body as flashes lit the overhead

After Taps came over the squawk box, she tried to clear her mind for sleep. But there were all those images of Marines packed into the transports waiting for the last dawn some would ever see. Who among them would spend this night sleeping?

She didn't either, distracting herself instead with recollections of the service, the hymns and Mark's sermon. And before long, the man himself. Nothing specific about him, just the quivery excitement she was beginning to feel in his presence. Not a new feeling: she'd first noticed it four years before, when she'd met Dan on the Orthopedic Ward at the Portsmouth Naval Hospital. And more recently in the Hope Island clinic when she worked with Jim.

No, she thought; not the same feeling at all. Those other times, it had turned serious. This never would. Of this she was certain.

She was equally certain, however, that at some point in whatever time remained until the war's end, it would take shape and morph into something else entirely. What she could not presently say. Nor was she ready to face yet the small but intensifying conflict between her conscience and her heart. Like a storm she could see approaching, but was powerless to flee despite the harm it might do her.

CHAPTER SEVEN

One morning two weeks later, Anna forced down a bowl of oatmeal with the other junior nurses in the wardroom. It was gummy, gray, lukewarm. But no one griped. They never stopped complaining about powdered eggs, but they swallowed this swill without a word. And all because of a damned rumor. If a crate of real eggs had come aboard at Saipan and the CO had shared them only with a chosen few, so what?

But Nell Owens thought a boycott would give the Supply Officer the message: "After all, we work as hard as anyone on this ship. Our morale's important too."

What everyone really needed was respite from the casualties hemorrhaging out of Iwo Jima. The first time they'd ferried six hundred to the hospital on Guam, liberty had been cancelled without explanation. The next time, they'd been diverted to Saipan, where they'd tied up only long enough to offload patients and take on provisions. Now, steaming back to Iwo's white hellhole, they were scheduled for an underway fuel replenishment. A routine maneuver, but excitement was so high you'd have thought they'd be getting eggs, not oil.

She was still playing with the porridge when the squawk box announced the oiler was coming alongside. Leaving the cold dregs, she fell in with others heading topside. The sea was flat, sunlight pale as lemon juice, sky a dull blue. On the weather deck, medical personnel lined the rails of what they laughingly called the Sun Deck, because OH had once told nurses they could sunbathe there. But only in shirts and slacks so they didn't inflame sailors with lust.

By the time she found Floyd and Willi, the oiler had fired lines to support heavier lines and hoses that would transfer fuel to *Compassion*'s bunkers. As usual, Floyd was teaching, even if no one was listening. "Really tricky maintaining separation between ships running side by side like this. Because hydrodynamic tension can suck them together at the rate of twenty feet a minute." When no one commented, he trained his binoculars on the camouflaged ship trailing them far astern. "And that tin can back there can't come any closer 'cause having a warship escort makes us subject to attack."

Anna regarded the sapphire stream separating them from the oiler. "I thought this part of the Pacific was safe."

"Remember the *Centaur*, Anna?" Willi said. "They thought they were safe so close to the coast. Listen, a sub could be tracking us right now."

Floyd pointed to the oiler. "Only need one torpedo to take out that tanker; the rest could be for us."

This gloomy news was interrupted by cheers as three lumpy canvas sacks came bobbing across the first high line. Movies and mail; this ephemera connected them to home and boosted morale as effectively as liberty. When Anna had first come aboard, she'd been shocked that medical professionals on a non-combatant ship might have morale problems. That was before Peleliu, Leyte, Luzon and Iwo.

She hadn't seen Mark on deck, but as she studied the

oiler's gray pipes and booms, she heard his voice nearby. On this deployment, she'd been assigned solely to Receiving; both chaplains circulated there too, but the only time she saw them socially was at chow, when there was a mob present. For reasons she chose not to analyze, she was more relaxed with Mark in a mob.

When the operation had been underway for twenty minutes, the distant destroyer suddenly picked up speed and veered off course. Heavy smoke billowed and her siren whoop-whooped across the hazy sea. Floyd had just muttered, "Uh oh, could be trouble," when the oiler's PA system ordered her crew to abort the UNREP and go to battle stations. Sailors on deck scrambled to retrieve hoses, booms and lines. Alarm bells clanged, the haze from her stack changed to a black boil, and the bow wave rose as she altered course away from *Compassion*. At the same time, nearby speakers erupted into an urgent, "Now hear this: All hands into life vests. Proceed to boat stations and stand by to abandon ship. This is not a drill."

Not a drill? Her gut clenched. Before she could join the rush to the storage lockers, Mark stepped over with a vest for her. She was tying it when Floyd lowered the glasses and pointed toward the destroyer. "For Chrissake. There's a damned Jap on her tail."

Squinting, Anna made out an airborne speck, like a distant mosquito. She expected it to drop a bomb or torpedo, but instead it plowed right into the slender ship. Orange flame flared; a heartbeat later, the blast slammed them like a hurricane gust. Everyone on deck gasped.

"Shit, there's another!" someone yelled.

Flying low, the single-engine plane came out of nowhere. Even before it was in range, the oiler's deck guns began firing; they sounded puny, like corn popping. But abruptly, the aircraft angled off, wheeled around and changed heading. Anna held her breath as it skimmed the waves toward them. Toward *Compassion*? No, that couldn't be. The pilot was confused, or blind to their markings. Or didn't know the Geneva rules.

Yet on he came, bearing for some low, vulnerable spot on the hull. The snarling engine drowned out everything else, even the squawk box and the shouts of those on deck. She wanted to look away, but couldn't wrest her gaze from the whirling propeller, the canopy behind it. Was she hallucinating, or could she make out the pilot's helmeted head, scarf and goggles, even a sadistic grin? Easy pickings for a coward, now they truly were a big white sitting duck waiting to be slammed in the belly, forbidden to take evasive action or shoot at it with anything larger than a sidearm. At least there were no patients aboard, thanks be to God.

At the last second, Mark yanked her to him. Burying her face against his life vest, she smelled faint mildew. Jim's face flashed by, like someone's on a passing train. Then the scream of the plane's engine filled her head as she waited to die. Instead, with a great rush of wind, the Zero pulled up and roared overhead. Still holding her breath, she watched it soar over the stack, but the prop caught the red and white Geneva pennant and chewed it up, along with the tip of the forward mast.

Willi yelled, "Son of a bitch Kamikaze!" Suicide bombers were nothing new; in October they'd damaged or sunk seven carriers off the Philippines. But this was the first they'd seen, so close Anna got a whiff of gasoline-tinged exhaust and a glimpse of paint peeling from the red sun on the fuselage.

She exhaled, backed out of Mark's arms. "Is he... is he coming back?"

His eyes widened as he watched the receding plane, now circling and descending to wave-top altitude again. "Looks like he's going for the oiler."

By now the other ship was stern-to, kicking up a green wake as she put distance between them. Still, Anna clearly saw the Kamikaze smash into her close to the waterline. First came the flash, then the concussion. The crowd groaned; Willi huddled closer to Floyd. The PA system broke in: lifeboat drill was cancelled; all hands were ordered to duty stations, boat crews, to stand by to pick up survivors.

Creaking and straining, *Compassion* leaned into a tight turn to port. Beyond the stricken oiler, smoke poured from the crippled destroyer, now lying on her side, stacks immersed, screws still clawing the air. Closer, the oiler too was spouting flames amidships, where heavy Bunker C bubbled from her gashed side. Men were plunging overboard, surfacing through the thick oil with faces coated, whites of their eyes bright against the black slime.

By the time *Compassion* had slowed, boat crews had lowered launches and begun plowing toward clustered survivors. Mesmerized, Anna watched the rescue operation as she might a movie. Until Mark tapped her arm. "Come on, Anna. Let's get down to Receiving. God knows how bad it's gonna be."

She nodded, barely able to look away from the flames, the smoke, the broken ships, the struggling men in the sea. Until he grabbed her hand and pulled her toward the nearest companionway.

* * *

For the next seven hours, they were flooded with casualties and survivors from both ships. The destroyer had gone under quickly; those who'd gotten off were either burned or injured by shrapnel from the exploding magazine. Surprisingly, most had been able to swim to the rescue boats. Some of the oiler's tanks had been breached, but her cargo of heavy oil wasn't burning, nor was the black layer on the water. Small fires still smoldered on the ship, where a skeleton crew remained aboard for damage control. Most of her survivors were in good shape, though a few had been torn up in the Kamikaze's impact. These were picked up first, the rest retrieved as fast as possible. The main problem was the black oil that coated their skin, like makeup on minstrels. Corpsmen swabbed it from their faces and cut saturated uniforms from their bodies. And all the while, Anna worked on charts.

More insidious were the effects of contaminated seawater. Most who'd been blown off the ship had inhaled or swallowed it as they'd surfaced through the oil-covered water. She was reaching for one man's dog tags, when she realized his eyes, dark as the oil on his skin, were focused on her name badge.

"Donovan," he muttered hoarsely. "Not Rosemary Donovan from Brooklyn, New York, U.S. of A., are you?"

She was about to say her husband had had a sister named Rosemary, when he turned his head and vomited a cascade of oil-specked seawater onto the corpsman beside him. "Oh shit," he groaned. "Must've swallowed half the damned ocean. Up me nose, in me eyes, likely up me arse too."

She leaned over with the stethoscope, heard rattling in his chest. Noticed the elevated pulse, the struggle to breathe, oil residue in folds of skin. Smiling the specious professional smile, she tucked the sheet around him and hung the chart on the gurney. "How about I come see you when I get off duty? Then we can talk about Rosemary Donovan. Okay, Chief?"

"Don't forget me, doll," he said, and retched again.

After everyone in the water had been picked up and processed, medical personnel secured Receiving and trooped up to the wardroom. Stewards met them with fresh coffee and stacks of sandwiches.

Sitting at last, Anna felt fatigue stiffening every muscle. Yet she was strangely ravenous, almost too busy eating to notice when Mark sat beside her. He ate silently, like everyone else; in spite of the day's excitement, the main conversation at the table was requests for condiments.

She ate fast, didn't wait for dessert before she got to her feet. "Excuse me. Going to look in on a patient I saw earlier. He may have been a friend of my husband's. I want to find out while he's still able to talk."

Mark said, "I'll come too. And say a prayer. Then I have something to tell you."

She shrugged. "If you want." From the next table, Luke's gaze followed them from the wardroom.

On F-10, the duty nurse said Chief Bryson had been moved to a quiet room. Comatose, he was in an oxygen tent, skin and lips cyanotic, breathing raspy and labored. A corpsman beside the bed glanced up from a comic book and shook his head. Anna went over and picked up the man's limp, cool hand. The wedding ring stirred up images of a wife and kids. If he'd known Dan, it was too late to find out now.

Still, she had to try. "Chief Bryson. It's Anna Donovan. Remember me?"

No response, not even a change in the labored respiration.

"Might as well get out of here," she murmured to Mark. "Nothing we can do."

"Wait. I want to pray."

Knowing it would be, "Lord, into thy hands I commend his spirit," she backed away and made the sign of the cross. Then with a last sad glance at the patient, followed Mark between rows of men who, this time the day before, had been safe and whole on their safe, whole ships. Turning on her cheerful smile, she gave a thumbs-up to those whose gazes trailed them from the ward.

While they waited for the elevator, Mark withdrew a folded envelope from his shirt pocket. "Let's go topside, shall we? Want you to read something."

"Okay. Maybe some air would help." She glanced at the bulkhead clock. Nearly 1900. "Be nice to watch the stars come out too."

"Might remind us God's still in his heaven, even if all isn't right with His world."

Low above the eastern horizon, a waxing moon floated like a piece of orange peel in the deep purple sky. Its glow silhouetted the crippled tanker wallowing ahead of them. Floyd had said the skeleton crew had stabilized her, shorn up the damaged hull, stopped the flood of seawater and gotten her underway at half speed.

"Now there's a miracle," Mark said as they came out on the open weather deck. "Scuttlebutt is, we'll escort her back to Saipan and offload the new casualties before we head to Iwo. So we'll be a couple days behind schedule."

She waited for him to bring up the letter, or whatever it was. Deep in her core, fatigue had swollen to a monster that made her drag her feet and long for sleep. But around the edges, nerve endings sizzled, as if another force, unexpected as a Kamikaze, was about to slam her.

He leaned forearms on the railing. "Anyway, this was in the mail we picked up this morning." He patted his pocket. "From my wife. First in two months."

She'd barely scanned her own mail earlier. "Oh, you must be relieved."

"No. Not really." He cleared his throat. "See, she...uh, she wants a divorce."

"Oh? Is that a shock?"

"Guess it should be. But after everything else that's happened today..."

She groped for a response. "Uh... does she say why?"

"Yep. She's fallen for somebody else. Another minister. Older. A Widower. Pastor of her parents' church. Claims they're both lonely and turned to each other for comfort." He held out the letter. "Here, read for yourself."

"Thanks. I'll take your word. Sorry. That must hurt."

A long, rueful sigh. "Yeah. If I could feel anything right now, it'd probably be hurt."

"I'm so numb I haven't even opened Jim's letter yet."

"Not expecting a Dear John too, are you?"

Another time the suggestion might have sent her into a tailspin. "No. But nothing's ever certain, is it?"

He tucked the letter back in his pocket and clasped her hand on the railing. The feel of it was sure and warm and firm. "You know," he said after a while, "I feel like I've watched everything today in a newsreel. As if it didn't happen to me. Know what I mean?"

She nodded. "It's strange. After five months, I thought I was used to the war. But today it was right here. I mean, we could be dead now too."

He shook his head, a slow, eloquent gesture conveying emotions too complex, too raw to speak. Beyond the rail, the waves caught golden slivers of moonlight. The air was brisk and salty, but overhung with the smell of oil, and inexplicably, cordite.

"You know," he said, "maybe that Jap did hit us. And we are dead. And on our way to hell."

She shivered as if the wind were Arctic, not equatorial. Then, while the sea hissed along the hull and the moon ascended, they leaned on the rail in a companionable, comfortable silence. In the bowels of the ship, the engines maintained their steady rhythm, unnoticeable as her own pulse. From the deck below, snatches of conversation drifted between another man, another woman. Quiet, earnest words, murmured intimately as if full of dark personal secrets. Still, her mind kept flashing to the unbelievable sequence of events that, within minutes had taken them from the war's safe outskirts to its very vortex.

Images flashed, vivid on the screen of unbidden memory: the first flaring explosion on the destroyer, and in what seemed a heartbeat, the second plane hurtling toward them. Like a newsreel exploding from the screen, unstoppable as time itself. That frozen moment when it screamed at them, head on. The moment she'd faced her own death.

The shivering escalated to shaking as she watched again and again, heard the snarling engine, the muted shouts of others on deck and smelled the exhaust as the plane lifted above them. Her teeth began to chatter as a chill unrelated to the ambient temperature set into her flesh. She hugged her arms around herself, but composure continued to elude her.

Mark regarded her a moment, then pulled her to him, pressing her to his chest as he'd done as death zoomed in that morning. "It's okay, Anna," he murmured into her hair. "It's okay. The plane's gone. He didn't hit us. Remember? He hit the oiler, but didn't sink her. See? She's underway just ahead. She's all right. We're all right too. It's over, Anna. It's over."

Still trembling, she huddled against him. "Every time I close my eyes, I see it. Coming at us. As if it'll never be over."

He patted her head, reminding her of her father's way of comforting her as a child. "Sure, it will," he said. "You've just been through too much today. All those casualties. And that man who knew your husband. It's too much."

She tried, but couldn't speak.

"Know what you need?"

She pulled back with a startled sense the mood was about to change. It usually did when a man asked that particular question. "No. What do I need?"

"Brandy. Or whiskey. Don't have brandy, but I do have some bourbon. For medicinal purposes, of course. Come on. It'll fix you right up."

"Oh, I don't know…"

"It'll do you good. I promise."

Sensing a crossroads moment, she said, "Well, maybe just a little."

Then, for the second time that day, she let him lead her to the companionway and down the ladder. In B deck's dim passageway, they passed a dozen closed doors before he unlocked his. "Come on in," he whispered. "It's okay."

Inside, the only illumination was the porthole, a pale eye filled with moonlight. Mark closed the door, switched on an overhead light, tossed keys to the desk, and his hat to a hook on the door. "Sorry I can't offer a snifter. Only glass I have's in the head. Have a seat while I fetch it." He pulled out the desk chair. "Won't be a minute."

By now the trembling had eased, so she perched on the chair and took deep calming breaths while he went for the bottle.

"Here," Liquid gurgled. "Just enough to warm you."

She held the glass with unsteady hands before she sipped. Liquid fire burned her tongue and trickled down her throat, reminding her of a night when she'd drunk brandy with Jim, then seduced him. "Gosh, Mark. What is that?"

"Fine Kentucky bourbon. 101 proof. So sip slowly."

She took another small taste. Her taste buds had gone numb, so this one seemed smoother. "Aren't you having any?"

He shrugged, leaned against the desk and picked up the bottle. "Guess I should. So I'll sleep better." He tilted it up, swallowed a couple times, set it down. His eyes watered. "Not used to hard liquor. But tonight it's just what the doctor ordered. Feel better now?"

"Uh-huh." She drank until the glass was empty. The

whiskey burned all the way down.

"More?"

"Oh. Just a drop. To help me sleep too." She shuddered, knowing what she'd see behind her closed eyelids. Or maybe she'd imagine instead the panic on *Centaur* when she blew up without warning in darkness like this. Or the final scene on *Wolf Fish* as she died. Oh God. Now she truly was connected to all the lost ones.

Mark poured more, swigged some for himself, cleared his throat a couple times. "Maybe...don't know how you'd feel about it, but maybe it'd be better if you...well, if you stayed here tonight." He gestured toward the lower bunk. "Not much room, but we could curl up together. Then you wouldn't be alone with the nightmares."

She swished the potent liquid around in her mouth and pondered his suggestion. Another crossroad, another choice of paths, with only a gauzy notion that one could lead to trouble.

"Don't get me wrong, Anna. I'm not talking about anything improper. Just holding each other. You know." He shrugged. "I mean with our clothes on."

She studied laugh lines around his eyes, frown tracks between his brows, parentheses bracketing his mouth. Alcohol had soothed raw nerves, but she had the sense of impending danger, this time not from an enemy plane or sub. Yet his eyes were so innocent she found trust easy. She got to her feet, drained the second drink. "Well, maybe for a little while."

He smiled, came to her, arms encircling, fingers in her hair. His beard scraped her cheek as she inhaled the stale, end-of-a-long-day masculine smell, and waited for him to release her. When he didn't, she pushed him away. "I thought we were just going to sleep."

He laughed tensely. "Whatever you want, Anna." Excusing himself, he went into the head.

She debated taking off her uniform, decided not to. If comfort was what they sought, why undress? She did, however, remove her shoes. But almost changed her mind when he came back in skivvies. "I thought we were keeping our clothes on."

He glanced down, as if surprised he was in his underwear. "Sorry. Guess I forgot. I'll get dressed again."

"Never mind. It'll be okay."

"Well, if you're sure…anyway, let me get in the bunk first so you can escape anytime you want." He grinned, then turned off the light, climbed in and moved toward to the bulkhead.

Feeling stiff and awkward, she stretched out hesitantly, turning on her side away from him. Then, with eyes pressed closed, she focused on the subterranean vibrations of the ship, that familiar constant of shipboard life. Not like visions of the Kamikazes, or the bewildered faces of the day's patients. Or the fact that she was in bed with a man who wasn't Jim.

At first she lay tensely, nerve endings tingling. But when Mark offered no further conversation, no kissing, no romantic gestures, she began to relax. For a while, he stroked her hair, but soon his hold loosened; his muscles relaxed. And when he began to snore, his solid flesh-and-blood presence was more calming than the bourbon.

The day retreated. She drifted into a restless doze peppered with images that often jolted her awake. When they did, she lay quietly fingering her engagement ring until they faded.

* * *

When she awoke again, it was to a change in his breathing rhythms, an acceleration of his heart rate as they cuddled, still spoon fashion. Even half-asleep, she realized he'd gone beyond the need for simple platonic comfort.

She pulled away, but his arms tightened, holding her to him, pressing his erection against her buttocks. "Oh Mark, no," she said loudly.

His breath quickened against her neck. "Please, Anna."

She wrenched out of his grasp and swung her legs to the deck. "I thought you just wanted to hold me."

"Look, we don't have to have intercourse. Just…touch me. You know. Please?"

She groped for her shoes in the dimness. "That's disgusting." She sounded stern, as she did with patients immobilized by casts who often begged her to relieve their sexual torment.

"But it wouldn't be infidelity."

She felt her way to the desk chair and put on the shoes. "We'll talk about what it'd be another time."

Without further conversation, she left the cabin with energy generated in self-righteous shock. As she hurried down the passageway, a jaygee coming from the bridge said good morning. She nodded but didn't meet his eyes.

In C14. she stood under the shower longer than they were supposed to, pretending she was in a summer rain on the rectory lawn. Then, forcing her mind to the day ahead, wrapped up in a damp towel, flopped on the bunk and watched shreds of pink dawn brighten the porthole.

At 0530, she put on a clean uniform, made up her face and went down to the wardroom. She'd planned to go to mass, but shame stopped her. What the hell had she been thinking, lying with Mark, yet reacting like a prude when he behaved as any normal man would have? Even Jim wouldn't have been content to just sleep.

When Luke came into the wardroom, she gave a sliver of thought to confessing, but instantly vetoed the idea. What would a celibate priest know about the passion bred of propinquity, or of the need for respite from the terror of loneliness?

He took the chair beside her. "You're up early this morning."

She shrugged. "Bad night for sleeping."

"Maybe you could use a bit of good news, then."

She gave him a dull-eyed glance. "What's that?"

"I want to contact your friend." His voice dropped a notch. "The woman you told me about."

His meaning took a moment to register. "Oh, that is good news. But why now? I mean, what changed your mind?"

"Yesterday. When I thought the world was going to end, my worst regret was that I didn't know her." His shoulders moved casually as he sipped from the steaming mug. "So maybe it's time you told her about me."

She fought off the urge to hug him. "Oh, I will. Soon as I get off duty, I'll write her everything. She's going to be so happy."

When the steward brought coffee refills and cheese Danish, his kindly expression combined with Luke's news began to undermine her tight control. Before she felt them, tears slid down her cheeks into the coffee. Sniffling, she was aware of Luke's concern and the glances of others entering the wardroom. But no one made a move toward her, nor asked what was wrong. Not surprising, given what they'd all experienced the previous day.

By the time Mark came in, she was dry-eyed again. When he sat down, she excused herself and left the table. Of all the horror the past twenty-four hours, what had happened with him was the most scalding. She'd had nothing to do with the Kamikaze, or the death of Chief Bryson. But she'd been fully responsible for what had happened with Mark.

Even more horrifying was the possibility that she'd wanted it to happen.

* * *

On the way to the wardroom that evening, she dropped a letter to Jim in the post office. The mess was more crowded than usual, but it was a quiet group, few of the usual jokes going around. Without speaking, Anna took a seat near Audrey and waited for her plate: Spaghetti and meatballs and canned mixed vegetables covered with orange dressing that came in gallon cans. She shuddered, and bit into a dry roll to calm her roiling stomach. When the queasiness passed, she managed a few bites before Mark came in. Her table was full, so he went to another. Lines around his eyes seemed deeper, aging him. She'd noticed the same effect in her own mirror that morning.

After he came in, she nibbled a bit more and pushed the plate away. When the Filipino steward reached for it, she said, "Sorry. Not very hungry today."

"Yes, ma'am. Lot of nurses, doctors too, they not hungry today. I bring you nice chocolate pudding. You eat, remind you of your mother. You feel better then."

Across the table, Willi said, "Like all it takes is chocolate pudding."

But spooning it into her mouth, saving the whipped cream for last, was indeed peculiarly comforting; until she got up to leave, and Mark rose too. She hurried out, but he caught up in the passageway. "Wait up, Anna. We need to talk."

She shivered. "Nothing to talk about."

The caged bulb at the foot of the ladder glowed on his gathering frown. "Maybe you don't need to, but I sure as hell do. If I promise not to touch you, will you come out on deck?"

"Oh, I guess." Walking quickly, she led the way outside. A few others were at the rail, including several huddled couples. She found a spot away from the glare of deck lights. "Now. What do you have to say?"

"My God, what do you think?"

Feeling like an affronted spinster, she shrugged tightly.

"First off...well, I'm sorry as I can be about...uh, what happened. I swear I didn't have that in mind."

"It's okay. I've been married. I know about...uh, how men are. Anyway, nothing happened."

"Still, I hope you can forgive me."

"There's nothing to forgive either. Now forget it."

She felt his gaze, intense even through the dimness. Down the railing, a nurse's shrill laugh erupted like the opening notes of a Harry James trumpet solo. "Well, thank you for that," he said. "I'd hate to think it'd stand between us. I value your friendship too much to risk it for such a stupid reason."

She forced a smile and stepped away. "Don't worry about it, okay?"

"Oh, by the way, Luke tells me he wants you to contact his mother. That's good news, isn't it?"

"I've decided to ask Jim to tell her in person. Be easier than in a letter."

"Good idea. You can give her details later."

"Uh-huh." She waited, but he said nothing more, so she told him she was dead on her feet and excused herself. As she walked away, she felt him watching, but couldn't imagine what was on his mind. Nothing seemed to matter except getting into the bunk, closing her eyes. And praying for respite from the various nightmares of the past two days.

CHAPTER EIGHT

The last Higgins boat had just churned away from the embarkation ladder when the rumbling vibration of the anchor chains erupted like some monumental digestive process in the ship's belly. As crewmen secured the doors in Receiving, Anna took a last look at the distant white hump of Mt. Suribachi, then returned to the ashen-faced Marine in the line of incoming casualties. According to his dog tags, he was nineteen, but could've passed for forty. He'd come aboard with the last of the ambulatory ones; the more seriously wounded were now being flown out from the island's patched-up airstrip. Officially the campaign was over, but hold-out Jap snipers in caves were still picking off occupying troops with deadly precision.

"Hear that, Private Sorensen?" She stripped bloody gauze from his mangled left hand. "We're getting underway. After the doctor sees you, we'll put you to bed on the ward. Bet it's been a while since you slept on clean sheets. Or drank iced tea."

He nodded, eyes downcast.

"When did you land on Iwo?"

"Uh...not sure. Last month, I think."

"So you were there for most of the campaign."

"Yes, ma'am. 'Til the grenade got me. Good I ain't a lefty or my writing days'd be over."

She glanced at the bloody tangle of tendons, bones and skin as the squawk box crackled static. The usual double "Now hear this," was followed by the announcement that they were steaming toward Guam; after that, they'd head for Pearl Harbor. "We'll be taking some convalescents for further care. Then having some routine maintenance in a shipyard." The announcer paused, then added. "Which will give everyone a chance for liberty."

"Oh. Pearl," the patient sighed. "What I wouldn't give to be back there."

"Have you been there before?"

"No, ma'am. See, when we left Dago we went straight to Iwo. But everything I ever heard about Pearl, gosh, sounds like heaven. Say, think I'll be one of them convalescents going with you?"

She smiled. "Could be. Especially if you'll need long-term care."

To distract him from these hopes of heaven, she told him what she knew about the lesser paradise of Guam. His eyes glazed over, so she realized her travelogue was no match for his recent morphine shot. Patting his shoulder, she moved on to the next boy, and the one after that. And kept at it until she'd charted them all. Some were on gurneys, but the ambulatory injured were likely to be patched up and returned to duty in time for the invasion of Okinawa. Then, that of Japan's south island. And God knew where after that. It didn't matter; the small islands were only previews of hell. Going into the Japanese home islands would be the real thing.

* * *

On Monday, 9 April, *Compassion* stood out from Apra, every bed occupied by Iwo convalescents. That night at chow, after non-stop talk about Honolulu bars where the liquor was cheap and the entertainment exotic, OH announced that nurses would bunk in quarters at the hospital, and Special Services would run buses to town, in case they wanted shop. And to the beach, so they could sunbathe. "Because I know my girls don't give a rat's ass about partying in bars," she concluded.

Everyone laughed and began to chatter about what they'd buy in Honolulu. With nowhere to spend it except for small items at Ship's Store, their wallets were fat with back pay.

On the fourth day out, Anna was in her cabin when the CO came on the horn. The news was always dramatic when he addressed them. This time his voice was so somber she had an instant presentiment of tragedy.

"My fellow shipmates," he began. "Today I have the sad duty of telling you our commander-in-chief, President Franklin Roosevelt, died yesterday in Warm Springs, Georgia." He cleared his throat. "Vice-President Truman has taken the oath of office and assumed the duties of president. And as I speak, the chaplains are planning a memorial service so all hands can pay their respects to our leader's memory."

Up and down the passageway, hatches burst open and women called to each other in tear-thickened voices. "Oh this is terrible," said one. "Just terrible. What'll become of the country now?"

"Don't be silly, ladies," said OH with her usual authority. "Roosevelt's only been a figurehead lately. Haven't you noticed how sick he looks in all the newsreels?"

Craving spiritual reassurance, Anna headed for the chaplains' office. Only Mark was there, face furrowed as he pored over some official manual. Since they'd left Iwo, she'd seen him only briefly; at chow, meetings, and almost daily on her ward. But he no longer lingered for coffee and conversation, as if steering clear of any close contact that might turn intimate.

She paused in the hatchway until he looked up. Unsmiling, he waved her to the chair by the desk. "Terrible news, isn't it?"

She nodded and sat, carefully smoothing her skirt over her knees. "That's why I'm here. I need you or Luke to tell me not to be dismayed. Tell me America will survive without FDR."

The dark eyes studied her, but backlit by the porthole, his expression was unreadable. "I'm sure you know that as well as we do, Anna."

"Okay. But I want to hear it from someone with greater faith than mine."

He laughed wryly. "That'd be Luke, then. Not me."

"I'm sure your faith's every bit the equal of his."

"But can you trust the faith of someone with clay feet?"

"I trust my father's faith, and I'm sure he's as human as you are." She waited but he didn't answer. "Besides, I've missed you. I was hoping you'd take me for another Jeep ride last weekend."

He pushed his seat farther from the desk, as if to maximize the distance between them. "Sorry. Luke came along and we had so much stuff, there wasn't room for anybody else." His gaze dropped to the volume on his desk. "Been working on the memorial service, but I guess he's still with patients, trying to keep up morale." He ran his finger around the khaki shirt collar. "Those kids are more devastated then the rest of us."

"They're young," she said, "but hardly kids after what they've been through."

Sorrow softened his face. "Yeah, that's the hell of it."

For a moment they regarded each other across piled papers on the gray steel desk in that gray-painted compartment with the gray ocean flowing by and the gray deck vibrating underfoot. There was, she thought, a profound reassurance in the constancy of such shipboard sights, smells, and sounds, even the monotonous predictability of routines. If the Navy was a microcosm of the American government, Roosevelt's death would delay the progress of the war by only a heartbeat.

She wanted to touch Mark's hand, but he'd folded his arms behind his head, and leaned the chair back so he was beyond reach. Possibly to underscore the fact that they were off-limits to each other? She got to her feet. "Well, I won't keep you. Just wanted to see you at closer range than I have lately."

He glanced up but didn't stand. "On Anna. I wish…"

"What?"

"Oh, just that we could talk more. But I'm so damned busy lately . . ."

"Well, maybe at Pearl, you could show me around. You were at the hospital there, weren't you?"

"Yeah. I'd love to, but I've made plans with another chaplain. Knew him when I was stationed there last year. He and his family live in quarters, so we're going to catch up. Otherwise…" A shrug completed the thought.

Disappointed, she compressed her lips and stepped toward the hatchway. "Well, let me know when the memorial service is, okay?"

"It'll be in the plan of the day."

She thanked him formally and left the office. As she headed forward, Luke got off the elevator, a green stole around his shoulders, prayer book in hand. His face brightened when he saw her, but she'd gone beyond needing his counsel. She said only, "I'm looking forward to the memorial service. It'll comfort everyone," and kept going.

At chow, no one talked of anything but FDR's death. Anna might have too, had she not been alone with Mark again. And realized how sensible he was, maintaining distance between them. For all their religious backgrounds and noble intentions, they were two ships steaming side by side, sucked together so imperceptibly they could come to grief before either could change course. Thank God he wasn't going to let that happen.

* * *

The morning of 20 April, the ship entered Pearl Harbor with sailors in dress whites standing at attention along the rails to honor *Arizona* and *Utah's* battered hulks. The solemn moment evaporated, however, when *Compassion* tied up at an auxiliary pier, where the promise of liberty hung in the air like an exotic perfume. By the time the patients were debarked into ambulances and busses, it had become a fever in the blood of everyone who was going ashore. And in duty personnel who had to stay aboard, a flood tide of envy.

Finally turned loose at noon, Anna, Audrey, Willi and Nell followed a crowd toward Nurses' quarters. Mark walked part of the way with them, so jaunty he seemed years younger. Later, surveying her image in the head mirror, Anna noticed her own cheeks were pink and her eyes had lost the dull glaze of the past weeks. She hadn't realized she'd begun to look middle-aged until she surveyed this improvement.

While they were changing into khakis, Willi announced she'd decided to go sightseeing with Floyd, and wouldn't bunk with them after all.

Watching her leave, Audrey murmured, "Hmm. Must be shacking up."

Anna said she had no idea, which was not wholly true. Then she squared her cap, swiped on fresh lipstick, and joined Audrey in a fast walk toward the Honolulu bus.

* * *

Sunday evening, there was a luau at the O Club for *Compassion*'s medical staff. Some old hands declared it odd for attendance to be mandatory. All Anna knew was, liberty ended at midnight and partying was a swell way to wrap it up. She'd had enough freedom for a while anyway, had spent half her back pay on sundresses, sarongs and a two-piece bathing suit, the rest on a hair cut in a civilian beauty parlor, and exotic feasts in Chinese and Polynesian restaurants. Only sunbathing at Waikiki was free.

That afternoon, the beach was so travel-poster perfect, she and Audrey stayed too long and were late to the party, which put them at least one drink behind the others. Only Floyd and Willi arrived after they did.

Audrey nudged her. "What'd I tell you? See how guilty they look?"

"No more than a lot of other couples. Like Nick and Nell. And Ed and Polly."

Audrey sniffed. "She must be a Jew too, don't you think?" She stared as the suspect pair approached the bar where they were sipping their first Mai Tais.

Anna lifted her glass as if in salute, said "I have no idea," and swallowed a copious mouthful. Then, drink in hand; she followed the party past undulating hula girls and a ukulele band to a lanai outside. Beyond a border of palms and spiky plants with fuchsia blossoms, low sunlight intensified the aquamarine and cobalt striations of the harbor. Even their fellow officers had been transformed; men in garish print shirts and shorts, nurses in sundresses with flowers in their hair, leis around every neck and tans on every bright-eyed face.

Stationing herself where she could survey the crowd, Anna sipped the sweet rum-laced concoction, too delectable to drink slowly, but so instantly warming, she knew if she didn't pace herself, she might slip over the edge of sobriety, then make some nasty remark to Audrey which, though relevant and perhaps even funny, she'd regret later. So between sips, she nibbled on puu-puus from a leaf-lined tray. And wondered where Mark might be.

While she was looking, Luke caught her eye. Still in dress whites, he sat at an inside table with the Red Cross girls and the baby-faced surgeon who was sweet on Jill, the one with Orphan Annie hair. Ignoring them, Anna refocused on the crowd. When she finally glimpsed Mark walking across the lawn, her heart thudded, as if she still had a tenth-grade crush on a senior track star. Now, just like that exalted personality, he gazed right past her, then joined some surgeons who were inspecting a pig on a spit as if it were an anatomical display. Behind them, Tiki torches wavered in the last rays of the sun, fat and red above the water. She was about to walk over when Luke beckoned her to his table.

Dragging her feet, she joined him just in time to get in on a scintillating discussion of mail. The others were concerned that there'd been none at Guam, and if any had come aboard here, liberty had gone before it had been sorted.

Ironic, she thought; mail hadn't mattered until now, now that they were about to sail again. In the space of three days, they'd become civilians again, with no taste for shipboard routines. Like all the men on all the other ships of all the other fleets, they'd return from liberty only reluctantly. But return they would, of course, for as long as they had to.

After the hula girls retreated to wolf whistles and cat calls, a pot-bellied Hawaiian began chanting native songs no one could dance to, so those at the table drank more Mai Tais, tried to figure out what was in the puu-puus, and described their respective liberties. She tried not to stare at Mark, but her gaze kept wandering. Finally he noticed, ambled over and squeezed in between her and Willi.

Luke greeted him with the glare of a reproving chaperone. "So tell us, Rev. Whitmore," he said with faint sarcasm, "has your weekend been as decadent as everyone else's?"

Anna was shocked, but Mark only drawled, "Well, not really decadent, but it sure was different."

"Why?" she asked in mild alarm. "What did you do you can't do on the ship?"

He grinned. "Nothing much. Except sleep in a big soft bed as late as I wanted, and eat Southern fried chicken, and reminisce with Dick. Then he tested his sermon on me."

Jill yawned. "That's not decadent. It's a busman's holiday."

"Sounds exciting," said Gladys, the other Red Cross worker. She was a forty-something spinster who prided herself on eschewing makeup. And men. Except for Luke. Audrey's theory was that both were homosexual, therefore perversely attracted to each other. Anna had found her theoretical description of their activities too disgusting for comment.

"Life at sea's exciting enough," Mark replied. "I needed peace and quiet."

At dusk, white-jacketed chefs carved the pig into greasy, aromatic chunks, and grass-skirted girls dished out unidentifiable foods with unpronounceable names, either served on or wrapped in shiny leaves. Inside, the band kept plunking away and a pearlescent evening coalesced, while the breeze wafted the dankness of harbor water overlaid with a heavy tropical sweetness. In this paradisiacal setting where it had begun, the war had shrunk from a volcanic morass that chewed up young men and spat them into the ship's wards, to the flat dimensions of newsreel footage. Anna's previous life too seemed as insubstantial as a recurrent dream, parents and friends and Jim characters in a drama set in a rugged land where even in April, spring was still a chilly promise.

At ten, the CMO announced the final drink call and a last dance before the busses returned them to quarters. "Muster on the pier in uniform at 2330. Be there. Or be AWOL."

The collective groan was barely audible over the lead-in to *Now is the Hour*. Anna's eyes misted; the music recalled Dan and Jim and their hours for farewells. She leaned toward Mark and asked if Methodists were allowed to dance.

He grinned, pushed back the chair. "Only when the bishop's not around."

She followed him outside, past club staff removing the pig carcass, to a far corner where he paused, gathered her in a loose hold and danced them away from the wavering torchlight. The air was cool, damp, aromatic of stale food, cigarette smoke, low tide, and a floral fragrance, heavy as a Woolworth's perfume. Before long other couples packed the floor around them, swaying and cuddling together like lovers for eternity.

In the midst of such overt sensuality, Anna began to feel awkward, lead-footed, and judgmental, a true woman of Puritan stock. Impatient with herself, she leaned her head into the curve of Mark's neck, closed her eyes and pretended he was Dan. But his skin smelled of Lifebuoy and Mennen Skin Bracer, and his breath was un-tinged by the cigarettes Dan had chain-smoked. Still, he felt familiar. Well, of course; hadn't they spent a night together in this same embrace, only horizontal?

For a while he hummed with the music, then began mouthing words about sailing across the sea.

She sighed. "At least we'll be on the same ship."

"Yeah, right now. But someday we won't be."

She pulled back to search his eyes. "Why did you say that?"

He shrugged. "Oh, just wondering how much time we have left."

"What, 'til the war's over?"

"Something like that." He drew her to him again. And resumed dancing and humming. Then his footsteps slowed and he sighed her name. Again, and yet again.

"What?" she asked.

"Do you know how lucky you are this isn't Friday night? Lucky we have to go back to the ship, I mean."

She was about to ask what he meant when he pressed his hips against hers so she could feel his desire.

"Oh that." Her laugh was stuttery, nervous. Behind him, Luke approached, as usual, serious of mien and manner.

He tapped Mark's shoulder. "Mind if I cut in?"

Before he could answer, she said, "Sorry, padre. I'm already spoken for."

He glowered, gave a curt nod and retreated.

"God bless that man," Mark said. "Your guardian angel."

" I don't need a guardian angel."

"Well, he thinks I do. Actually, the way you look tonight, you could use one."

Her nursing school friend Margie would've come back with a witticism indicating she was flattered but not interested. Anna, on the other hand, could only blush and wonder what he was saying. Then, under the influence of his warm proximity and more drinks than she could count, she let her body interpret.

They danced until the music ran out. Afterward, hands still linked, they joined the reluctant parade to the gray busses outside where bored sailors waited to drive them to the pier. At the curb, Mark brushed a kiss on her cheek and peeled off toward his friend's quarters. And Anna poured herself into the bus and stared out the window at lights of the base reflecting in the harbor. So much for liberty, so much for music and dancing, she thought. Now was the hour for *Compassion*'s inevitable return to the war.

At the pier, the ship's spot lit white bulk contrasted with the dirty gray of two oilers, three refrigerated cargo vessels, a salvage ship and a seagoing tug, all being loaded even at midnight. As personnel mustered at the foot of the gangway, someone wondered if they'd be sailing with the auxiliaries, since they weren't combatants either. No one, not even Floyd had an opinion.

The formation was ragged at best. Someone said mustering on the pier wasn't usual procedure; something was going on. Finally, when all hands except two Firemen Apprentices had been accounted for, everyone dragged their bags up the gangway, saluted the OOD, and headed for their cabins

On board, the prevailing smell was of fresh paint, but beneath it, Anna noticed none of the chlorine that usually laced the air after patient areas had been disinfected. Odd, she mused, too tired to speculate further.

At precisely midnight, the deck began to vibrate as the engines accelerated. The whistle blasted, lines were hauled in, and a tug nudged them toward the channel. She had just stumbled into her cabin when the squawk box announced a meeting in the lounge at 0800 the next morning. Down the passageway, Audrey muttered, "Oh shit!"

The tinny official voice added, "Meanwhile, all spaces

below the main deck are off limits except to personnel with specific orders. Now, carry on."

Now what? She wondered. But even escalating curiosity was no match for the combined effects of alcohol and fatigue. Besides, mail had been distributed. She began to dig into her pile, but suddenly, it was all she could do to strip off her uniform before she collapsed on the bunk.

CHAPTER NINE

During the night, Anna awoke to the creaking of the ship as she pitched in heavy seas. At first she couldn't remember having returned, but when nausea rose in her throat, the luau came roaring back. She barely made it to the head to vomit up the undigested contents of her stomach. Her skull ached, eyes burned and even brushing her teeth didn't banish the acid in her mouth. Hurrying back to the bunk, she huddled under the covers and let the ship's motion rock her toward a queasy sleep.

She was almost under when Audrey tapped on the hatch, pushed her way in, then dropped onto the empty bunk. "God," she groaned. "I've been puking my guts out. You too?"

"Must be something we ate."

"Or drank. Anyway, what do you think about the lower decks being off limits?"

"No idea."

"Well, let me tell you what Polly thinks."

"I'm too sick to care."

Audrey rose on one elbow. "Listen, Anna. This could be serious. See, Polly thinks we're carrying something forbidden by Geneva. Like tanks or ammo, or new weapons for the Okinawa campaign."

"Oh, that can't be true. If it's forbidden, we wouldn't carry it, would we?"

"If things got bad enough, maybe we would. She said at Iwo we lost more men than the Japs, and Okinawa's bigger and closer to Japan. So, maybe top brass threw that swell party so we'd be too sick to worry about it."

"That's crazy. We're Americans. We don't break international laws."

Her laugh was bitter. "Sure. And we always tell the truth about everything." Sighing, she got to her feet and headed for the hatch. "Mark my words. This could be trouble."

It was a ragged group that assembled again after a breakfast no one ate. Some had brought coffee from the wardroom where the docs were dispensing anti-emetics, to be taken sublingually for the fastest results. Still, speculation rustled in the air like a flight of invisible birds, until the CO came in and told them to sit.

After a long sip of coffee, he cleared his throat and said he knew they were curious about the restriction to the upper decks. "The fact of the matter is," he added, voice a notch higher than usual, "we've been pressed into service to transport a marine battalion to Guam. As you know, this is forbidden by the Geneva convention, so our passengers have to remain below decks, out of sight in case a sub's trailing, or a plane spots us."

Before he could say more, Mark jumped to his feet. "Excuse me, sir. May I ask why we've been put in harm's way like this?"

"That's only in theory, chaplain. In this part of the Pacific, the risks are negligible, and we maintained utmost secrecy boarding them, so the chance of attack's virtually nil."

"On December 6, 1941, the chance of attack on Pearl Harbor was virtually nil too."

A suave, handsome man with immaculately combed silver hair, the CO began to twist his Naval Academy ring. "I understand your concern, chaplain. And if this weren't vital, believe you me, we wouldn't do it. But desperate times demand desperate measures. Now, if I may continue…"

"First, sir, I'd like to go on record as strongly protesting. Our mission on this ship is healing, not transporting combat troops. Particularly when it's forbidden."

Captain Martin's smile was stiff, his face slowly flushing. "I couldn't agree more. But it wasn't my decision. So I repeat: this is war. You saw the suicide planes last month. They're only going to get worse as we close in on Japan. And if we invade, none of the rules will matter a good damn."

"Well, now, sir," Mark went on in his laconic drawl, "that means the odds are even higher that the next Kamikaze won't just fly over." He took his seat again. Two rows behind, Anna could see only the back of his head, but knew his mouth would be tight, hands clenched into fists.

The rest of the day, under the soporific influence of the anti-emetic, she was too stupefied to worry about the contraband passengers. She also had three weeks' mail for distraction. Including one from Lorraine, exuberant about the news of Luke. She skipped through those from Margie, Alex Cropper and her mother before she read Jim's. Three, oddly subdued. Why? Because he was still dealing with a Maine winter? Or had he lost faith in their happy ending? Had time eroded his trust, or had she been unconsciously communicating her off-color interest in Mark? That settled it, she thought; she'd just have to try harder to reassure him of her love and fidelity. Whatever happened with Mark,

Jim would be her North Star for as long as the universe endured.

* * *

By evening chow, she'd slept so much and eaten so little, hunger dominated her thoughts. At least until she came down the ladder and saw Mark waiting outside the wardroom.

Audrey elbowed her. "Surprised he's not in the brig, the way he mouthed off to the old man this morning."

"Oh, he was just standing up for his beliefs."

"Well, we all have beliefs, but we know when to keep them to ourselves."

Anna let the others precede her into the wardroom before she said, "Well, chaplain. What do you have to say for yourself after your speech this morning?"

His grin was thin. "Sit with me, and I'll give you the straight skinny. Unless you're afraid being seen with a troublemaker will give you a bad name." He took her elbow and steered her into the wardroom. "Luke already thinks we're too friendly."

They headed toward an empty table as the ship rolled so steeply they had to lean uphill to reach it. Stumbling into chairs, they unfolded napkins on their laps.

"That's silly," she said. "There's plenty of friendly couples." She gestured at other pairings: Nell and Nick, Polly and Ed, Willi and Floyd, among others she wasn't sure about. "Why's he worried about us?"

"Because I'm clergy and you're a preacher's daughter, so he holds us to a higher standard. You're on a pedestal, like The Blessed Mother. You shouldn't even be tempted."

"Oh, that's just silly."

"Yeah, but he says now we chaplains have to maintain the highest personal standards, or morale could suffer. The

Navy's set a bad example, so we have to try harder."

She studied the serious set of his features until the steward arrived to ask how they wanted their prime rib cooked. When he'd scurried away, Mark said, "Gosh, prime rib on a Monday evening? Must be a bribe, like the party last night. To make us forget we're defying Geneva."

"Wonder if the Marines are eating this well too."

He nodded. "Went down a while ago to confer with their officer in charge. Got to keep 'em happy, you know, or they'll start raiding nurses' country for nookie."

She gasped. "When did you start talking like a swabbie?"

"Sorry, Anna. Don't know what's happening to me lately. Talking dirty. Mouthing off to the CO." He sent her a sidelong glance. "Lusting for you."

Lusting for her? Shocked but not surprised, she watched the steward set down a plate with a slab of pink meat, a landslide of fries, and a mound of cole slaw like Suribachi.

"Actually, that's why I stayed with my friends at Pearl. Actually, I did want to show you around. But I was afraid it might give you a bad name." He shrugged, stared wide-eyed at his own arriving plate, then doused the fries with enough catsup to suggest an arterial bleed.

"Don't worry about that." Uncomfortable with the issue, she anointed her beef with horseradish and began taking small, tentative bites. It tasted life-giving, as it might to a starving person.

Mark put away half the food on his plate before he paused to swig iced tea. "Anyway, Anna, I agree with Luke. I need to …well, start behaving like a man of God. In thought, word and deed."

She went on eating but what was left of her appetite receded like a spent wave. She pushed the plate away and regarded him, observing that he no longer wore his wedding ring. "Well, okay. I don't want to be a thorn in your flesh."

"It's not just my flesh," he said with a nervous laugh. "Even before Luke said anything, I was concerned about what's going on between us. I mean besides the lust."

"Oh? What else is going on?"

"Mm...don't know what to call it, but I'm always finding excuses to be with you." He shook his head. "At Pearl, I stayed busy with my friends. But last night, there it was again. Maybe you could call it a thorn in the flesh."

She let her breath out slowly, unnerved that the admission intrigued her. "Oh. I didn't know. I mean, that there was more to it than...you know."

"I reckon that's what the good padre's most worried about, not the... you know."

She glanced around at stewards bracing themselves against the ship's careening, at familiar faces clustered at the long tables, at the layered clouds beyond the portholes. She wished she could say something wise and clever, but was stymied by the usual Yankee reticence. She settled for, "Oh, you're just lonely, Mark. And hurt. After that Dear John from your wife."

He shook his head and finished the beef, blotting up juices with a roll. "Anna, it's not just loneliness that attracts me to you."

Her cheeks grew hot, but before she could answer, Luke entered the wardroom, shoulders slumped, eyes dark-shadowed. He lurched toward them and dropped heavily into a chair across the table. When a steward brought his platter, she passed rolls, asked if he'd heard from Lorraine.

He nodded, knifing the meat into pieces before he took the first bite. "Said the news was an answer to every prayer since I was born."

"Good. Are you going to write back?"

He broke a roll in half, stuffed it into his mouth, chewed furiously, then washed it down with iced tea. "Of course.

She wants to know every last detail of my life."

"How do you feel, hearing from her?" Mark asked.

Luke shrugged and continued eating the way everyone else was; as if ending a long fast. "Good as I can on a day like this. When I figured out the Navy follows the rules only when it's convenient. God, if we thought the Japs were doing what we're doing…"

Mark said, "But we don't expect them to play by the rules."

"So, does that make it right for us to flout them?" He shook his head. "Meanwhile, we have to do our duty just as if everything was by the book. For me, it's confessions and Mass for the Marines every morning. And whatever other spiritual help they need, whenever they need it. Business as usual, no matter what."

Mark nodded. "I'm holding prayer meetings and Sunday services. And taking over the Red Cross ladies' duties. And refereeing boxing matches."

"Boxing matches?" Anna asked. "You?"

"Part of the plan to keep them busy. Keep their minds off the war. And nurses."

"Well, anyway," Luke said, swiping another roll through a gravy lake, "all we can do is minister where we're needed and stay true to our principles. No matter what the Navy does."

Smarting with his sanctimonious tone, she had to say, "That goes without saying, Luke."

"Then keep praying, Anna. That we all have the strength to resist temptation."

Mark shifted in the chair so his knee touched hers under the tablecloth. "Who are you worried about, padre? Our illegal passengers? Or us up here?"

Luke pushed his plate away, got to his feet, hands braced on the table as the ship went into a long slow roll, so steep only green water showed beyond the starboard portholes. "What do you think, reverend?" His blue gaze bored into Mark's dark one.

"I think your concern is unnecessary."

Luke straightened up, eyed the bulkhead clock. "Hope you're right. Now, if you'll excuse me, I have work to do."

Anna watched him stagger toward the passageway as the ship rolled back to port. Then, mumbling something about writing letters, she got to her feet. Mark said her name, then quietly, "You know I can't protest the Navy's violation of the rules and disregard them in my personal life, don't you?"

She kept her voice steady. "Of course."

"I want your respect too."

"You already have that."

His gaze swung to the porthole, to the slow rise and fall of the horizon, then back to hers. "In spite of what happened before?"

She nodded, and with as much dignity as she could muster made her way past other tables, clutching chair backs and stanchions as the deck tilted. The next roll was so steep, a collective moan rose from other diners. China crashed to the deck all over the wardroom. As they went on leaning, she closed her eyes and whispered, "Jesus, Jesus," until the ship hesitated, then slowly pulled herself upright again.

At the ladder, Anna grabbed the railing, had her foot on the first rung when Mark laid his hand on her forearm. Stepping down, she let him lead her behind a stanchion. The kiss was so sudden she had no time to react.

He released her slowly. "Sorry. Couldn't let you go without doing that. To seal the deal."

"What deal?"

"The one about honoring our principles. No matter what."

Breathing fast, she closed her eyes. Some perversity in

her nature urged her to ask for a kiss of the head-to-toe sort she'd remember long after the desire it triggered had subsided. But she knew it would only tempt her to follow him to his cabin and break every rule they could before they returned to the safety of their moral convictions. To seal this deal with a completely smashed commandment, not just lust in the heart.

Before she could pursue the notion, the babble of approaching voices made her break away and clamber up the ladder as if fleeing a tidal wave, then hurry forward on C Deck. Even when she was inside C-14, her heart kept banging and the touch of Mark's mouth still pulsed on her own. She stood a moment clenching fingernails into her palms and breathing deeply, until the control she prized seeped back, like ice water dousing the fire in her body.

Then she lay on the bunk and read all Jim's letters again as the ship wallowed westward in seas dark and rough as the hide of a dragon.

CHAPTER TEN

*L*ate on the afternoon of 30 April, Anna, Polly and Willi were in Nell and Audrey's cabin practicing manicures on each other. Forbidden anything more colorful than natural polish, they'd been experimenting with a wild red and a pink that was beyond shocking. Their intention was to wipe these off with polish remover before chow time. Until Nell proposed they keep wearing it and see if anyone noticed. Or took any punitive action.

"After all, nobody's going to die if a few nurses wear red polish," she added.

Her implication was clear. For the past week at sea, Anna had been conscious of escalating tension in herself and her fellow nurses. Oh, brass had kept them busy enough with the usual lectures and conferences, even some newly-released movies. But the possibility of repercussions from violating Geneva had swollen to an inescapable cloud, like a huge, angry typhoon that dogged the ship despite every course change.

At least now the long, sluggish voyage was over. As *Compassion* slowed to enter Apra Harbor, word went over the horn to station the special sea and anchor detail and the Guamanian cliffs and hills came into view from the porthole. The languid air was sweet and fresh, but from below decks, blowers wafted the smells of massed humanity: sweat, cigarette smoke, hair oil and excrement, the animal emanations of concupiscent young men crowded into small, steamy spaces for eight sultry days and nights.

Beyond the breakwater, the ship stopped just out of the channel. Anchor chains rumbled, engines reversed to imbed the flukes, and mechanical sounds faded to the faint purr that never totally diminished even at anchor.

Polly glanced out. "Well, we made it back okay. Now all we need's a transport. Obviously we can't debark those guys at a pier, or everybody'll know what we've been doing."

Anna hadn't seen the chaplains all day; she assumed they were holding last services, hearing final confessions, giving communion. Maybe even praying with the troops. She had no idea of their routines, hadn't talked with either man for a week. By this time, however, all pretense of secrecy had fallen away. Twice, Marine officers had dined in the wardroom; some even roamed freely around interior spaces in the superstructure.

Meanwhile, the evaporators were faltering; showering had been restricted the whole cruise. The laundry too was feeling the pinch; the last time nurses had had clean whites was before Hawaii. And there had been no ice for days.

Now, with the ship at anchor, sounds from below were clearly audible. Metallic thumps, hatches slamming, the muted odd expletive. Purposeful, energetic activity.

"Guys must be rounding up their gear," Nell said. "Kind of sad when you consider what they're facing. God, if only we could give them all a goodbye kiss."

"They'd rather get laid," said Audrey in her usual dry tone.

Willi said, "Isn't a kiss before dying better than nothing?"

Without hearing more, Anna began to imagine a marathon of osculation. The idea blossomed like a summer weed. "Why couldn't we? Kiss them goodbye, I mean."

Nell only shrugged. Anna had always considered her the most daring of the junior nurses: besides the powdered eggs rebellion, she'd also led a brief, ineffectual boycott of creamed chipped beef. Not recently, though. Maybe Nick, or one of the other brass, had warned her to tone herself down. The Navy could break the rules right and left, but God help any upstart nurse who tried to change anything, even something innocuous, like breakfast.

But kissing the boys goodbye, Anna thought; why not?

When they went to chow that evening, *Compassion* was still alone in the anchorage. Scuttlebutt was, after dark an APA would steam alongside to transfer their passengers to Okinawa. Before any senior nurses joined them at the table, Anna began laying out her plan, so far still in the vague stages. The trick was to get into the routine so rapidly the Master at Arms would be caught off guard, thus enabling them to dispense as many kisses as possible before they were herded back to Nurses' Country. Or the brig.

As they plotted, OH came into the wardroom. Sober-faced, she strode to the lectern and stood waiting until everyone grew quiet. "Ladies and gentlemen," she began in a grave voice, "I know y'all have had enough bad news lately, but this really hits close to home." She paused. Tension crackled in the air like static electricity in the desert. "Yesterday, a Kamikaze hit *Comfort* off Okinawa. Twenty-eight dead, forty-eight wounded, including some nurses."

"Dear God," Nell breathed. Throughout the wardroom,

other faces mirrored her wide-eyed horror.

"See, she and *Relief* were taking on casualties, and a tin can was making smoke. But the sonofabitch got through anyway. Hit her fairly high, so she didn't sink. But it must've been a hell of a mess. At least it's convinced brass the rest of us'll need escorts from now on."

She paused. No one stirred. Willi's face was dead white.

"Anyway, we'll have a memorial service after we leave Guam. Meanwhile, we'll have to cover *Comfort*'s deployment as well as our own. Because she'll be out of action indefinitely. Now, carry on, ladies."

When she finished, stewards began silently passing out a meal that looked and smelled like low tide. One identified it as tuna curry on toast. People were still regarding it with disgust as OH made her way between the tables, stopping to ask if anyone knew someone on *Comfort*. No one did: her medical personnel were Army.

After OH had taken a seat at her usual table, Willi began pushing slime-green peas around with her fork. "Kind of makes you wonder if what we just did, you know, transporting Marines, was that why they went after *Comfort*?"

"But how would they know?" Nell asked. "Those guys were never on deck."

Polly said, "Maybe they didn't know it was us. Maybe to them all white ships look alike. Or maybe we weren't the first to do it."

Dutiful as chastened school girls, they eventually finished what was before them. But as they dug into red Jello with pineapple chunks, Willi slammed down her spoon and sat bolt upright. "Well, it makes me so mad I could spit nails. Nobody's safe out here. We could bloody well have been hit too."

Nell said, "And we could yet. Okinawa's still not secured."

"At least now we'll have a warship escort," Polly put in.

"Huh! Fat lot of good some rusty old tin can'll do us," said Audrey. "The one with the oiler that time never got off a shot before the Jap hit him."

"Ed says they're supposed to lay a smoke screen," Polly came back.

"Didn't keep *Comfort* safe," said Nell.

Muttering, they sucked up the Jello and more coffee than usual. Cold tea was available, but without ice it soon warmed to the temperature, someone said, of spit. At least the sunset was brilliant—huge mauve clouds with flaming edges filled the sky for a few glorious minutes before they turned ashen. Like a marvelous idea that had lost its punch, Anna thought, sensing that no one was inclined now to pursue the kissing plan.

She waited until OH and most of the men had left the wardroom before she turned to her friends at the table. "Well, girls, what do you think? Shall we kiss the boys goodbye?"

"Damned right." Willi held up her scarlet-tipped fingers. "We got away with this, didn't we? And now they know what happened to *Comfort*, I bet other girls'll sign on too. Let's ask around."

In the next half hour, the five original conspirators surreptitiously recruited sixteen more volunteers, including Jill, the Red Cross girl, though Gladys declined with a firm, "Hell, no!" Then, intent on cleaning up, Anna went to her cabin, and scrubbed at spots on her least dirty uniform. Showering was forbidden, but she sponge-bathed, then sprayed Shalimar with the perfume atomizer from home, washed her hair in the basin and fluffed it with her fingertips. As she finished, Audrey came in, in uniform, cap pinned on her fuzzy new perm. Her hot pink nails glowed but she needed a lipstick.

Anna handed her a Tangee that still had some life left,

then grabbed a new Yardley she'd bought in Honolulu—a fire-engine red that'd leave brilliant prints on the departing passengers. For no reason that made sense, it seemed important not merely to kiss them, but to leave them conspicuously marked.

Squinting into the mirror, Audrey swiped color on her thin lips. "Don't know what my fiancé'd say about this, but what he doesn't know won't hurt him. How about your guy? You gonna tell him?"

"Sure," she said glibly, as if she told Jim every detail of her life. "After all, it's an official protest. By Navy nurses, not their fiancés."

The galley was closed, stewards off duty when they assembled in the wardroom after eleven. Furtively, as if involved in high treason, Anna divided them into groups to work both the forward and after gangways. Then, as if she wasn't already nervous enough, Audrey had to say, "Hope you didn't tell the chaplains about this. They'll report us for sure."

Nell snickered. Polly squinted out the nearest porthole. "Okay, the transport's coming alongside. Now. We all know what to do, don't we?"

The plan seemed simple. As Marines emerged from below, each nurse would walk with one of them until he mustered off, then plant her painted lips on his cheek. If he turned suddenly, he'd get it on the mouth instead. Then they'd start on the next group. With fifty men apiece to kiss, no one could slow the line by chatting or getting into a clinch.

"Remember, girls" Willi added. "These blokes'll try anything. So be quick and don't make them think you want more."

Nell said, "Maybe we should carry rubbers, just in case."

"Nonsense!" Anna said firmly, faking more confidence

than she felt. "We're Navy nurses, for God's sake. We know how to keep men in their places. Besides, every sailor on both ships'll be watching. They won't let anything happen. Now. Freshen your lipstick and get ready for action."

When ramps to the transport were secured, the mutineers lined up in the shadow of the deckhouse. She hadn't seen Mark all day, but now she spotted him at the forward gangway with a Marine captain, a gunnery sergeant, and the Officer of the Deck. Toward the stern, Luke towered over a similar group at the after gangway.

Audrey pointed. "Look, Anna. Your pet padres are handing out Bibles. What'll they think about what we're doing?"

"Damned if I know." She glared until the first troops spilled up the companionways, in fatigues and helmets, rifles over their shoulders, bulging packs on their backs. Floyd had said they carried everything they'd need for the first few days in combat…if seventy pounds of survival gear didn't drown them in the surf going in.

From their respective positions near the companionways, Polly and Anna signaled their groups forward. Trying to appear calm, Anna led hers toward the debarking passengers.

The first was a blue-eyed, pink-cheeked kid who looked too young even to shave. She smiled and fell into step beside him. " Hi, Private. What's your name?"

His eyes widened. "Uh, Gus, ma'am. Short for Augustus, after my dad."

"Where you from?"

"Nowhere you ever heard of. 'Less you're from Wisconsin too."

It was a short hike to the gangway. "No, but here's a little something to remind you of home." She leaned up, kissed his smooth cheek and quickly backed away. The sergeant checked off his name; Mark said "God Bless you, son," and pressed a small black testament into his hand.

"Thanks, padre. And thank you, nurse." Gus touched the red lip print on his cheek and hurried across the gap to the other ship. Anna blew him another kiss, then headed back to the next Marine in line. By now those spilling up the ladders were panting in anticipation. Unfortunately, the Officer of the Deck's initial surprise had worn off too; before more nurses could proceed, the Master-at-Arms hustled toward them, police whistle blasting.

"You nurses, all of you, return to quarters. On the double."

In their earlier briefing, she'd told the others to ignore such commands. Her own courage, however, was ebbing fast. Until she caught Mark's grin and thumbs-up.

Next, the Exec came on the horn with the same order. Pretending they hadn't heard, they approached the stalled line of Marines. Meanwhile, corpsmen at upper deck rails were cheering and hooting, while sailors had gathered at every vantage point on the massive gray transport. In spite of official imprecations to cease and desist, the line began to move again. Eventually those in command seemed to give up, but Anna was sure the reprieve was only temporary.

After this brief delay, the night became a blur of young faces, some with mouths turned to hers, others just cheeks. A few blushed and refused, while many went for a full embrace, the feel of breasts against their chest, the smell of a woman's neck, or a torrid kiss involving teeth and tongue. One after the other, nine hundred thirty-three men poured up into the sultry night to savor a moment between the minor hell of shipboard captivity and the greater, still unknown hell of Okinawa. For the minute they walked the deck together, they were the American ideal; clean-cut, hard-bodied Marines, and angels of mercy as pristine as the girls back home. Anna felt as if all of them were celebrating the last of these boys' innocence, the end of their youth. For some, it would be one of their final memories.

Yet while it was happening, her mind was fixed on the pure joy of this fleeting personal contact, not the next deployment or the likelihood they'd meet some of these boys again as incoming casualties, but on this moment when all of them were still upright, still strong, still whole and full of life.

Then they were gone. The last man to file off halted briefly on the gangway and called back, "Hey, blondie! Meet me in Fargo after the war, okay?"

Anna waggled both arms and shouted, "Sure," before he disappeared in the human line being herded into the transport's steel belly.

On *Compassion*, a certain hollowness echoed in the stale air wafting from the empty spaces below as deck crews secured the gangways and retrieved lines, while a flock of nurses like white gulls stepped up to the rail to watch the two-stacker drift across slack water. Then her screws began to churn and her deep-throated whistle reverberated across the harbor. Everyone waved until her stern passed, wake splashing *Compassion*'s hull as she made for the breakwater. Except for a red mast light, she sailed blacked out, but Anna could hear her engines for a long while as she stood out to sea.

Suddenly stung by these boys' dismal prospects, she bit her lip to stifle tears. Until Mark approached with a smile that lit his eyes. And her heart. "Hey, Anna. That was a swell thing y'all did for those guys. Whose idea was it?"

"Uh...actually everybody's. Guess we'll catch hell, but after we heard *Comfort* was attacked, we stopped worrying about it."

"That took guts."

She shrugged, glanced at her watch, amazed it was almost two. She started past him, but he caught her arm. In the harsh deck lights, his face was lined, dark with beard, and he smelled of old sweat. Yet she wanted him. Just like that, without preamble or poetry, she wanted him.

She stammered, "Uh… going to turn in now?"

He nodded, gaze intense. "Been a long night."

Before she could ask to go with him, Old Horseface shrilled down from the deck above, "Donovan, if you're not up here in three minutes, you'll be in so much trouble you'll think you're in a Jap prison camp."

Instead, she gave him a mirthless smile. "Now the fun begins."

In the wardroom, the culprit nurses stood docile as cattle as the Chief Medical Officer dressed them down. As for punishment, he was quite clear. "First, ladies, you've forfeited your next liberty. Second, tomorrow starting at 0600, you'll help corpsmen clean the entire ship 'til every ward's ready for patients again. I don't care if it takes all day, and Sunday too. Reveille's in three hours, so hit the sack, stat."

She stifled a groan and joined her chastened sisters plodding up the ladder. The Head Nurse's scowl was menacing, but as Anna passed, OH gave her a surreptitious wink, as if she recognized Anna as one of the ringleaders. She hoped so. Because it had been one hell of a fine evening. And no one in authority had even noticed the illicit nail polish.

* * *

Mark was alone at a wardroom table the next evening when the reprimanded nurses filed in after everyone else had eaten. By then, they'd finished the monumental job of cleaning the ship, but their hands were raw from scrubbing bulkheads, decks and befouled heads, and most were coughing from chlorine fumes in the steamy heat below decks. The corpsmen they'd worked with had been kindly and considerate, urging them to rest, bringing cold Cokes from the gedunk and sandwiches at noon. But when Anna's period started and she told OH, the Head Nurse had only brought her a Kotex and told her to keep working.

Only at 1700 had they been allowed to retire to their cabins. Showering was once again permitted and the laundry was back in action, so fresh uniforms were finally available. Clean from the skin out, Anna inhaled the cool breeze coming in the portholes and joined the other nurses at two tables. As they waited to be served, Mark came over, the usual grin splitting his face.

"That was fine work y'all did last night, ladies. I know y'all caught hell for it, but just thought you should know I approve…on behalf of the entire Methodist church."

"Does that mean God approves too?" Audrey asked. "Or would we have to ask Father Luke about that?"

"Wouldn't hurt to get his opinion." He was standing behind Anna, hands on the back of her chair. Unseen by the others, he massaged her shoulders with his index fingers. "Now. Anyone wants to talk more, I'll be in the office, oh, another hour or so. Have a nice meal."

As he walked away, she felt the covert scrutiny of those at the table. Oh, what fine gossip that would make—the engaged preacher's daughter and the married minister! If those two pious souls couldn't resist temptation, what hope was there for anyone else?

Silly, she told herself; no one had seen him touching her. Or recognized her longing for him the night before. Sure, they'd danced at the luau, but he and Luke were a usual part of their wardroom clique. Why should she be discomfited and uneasy? Unless, of course, her conscience was trying to get a message through the static of passion.

After the meal she waited until everyone else had left before she went up to the chaplains' office. Approaching, she worried that Luke might be there, but according to Mark, he'd gone ashore for the evening. "Think he has a boyfriend here," he added.

She sank into the chair by his desk. "Oh Mark, that's terrible. You don't know what you're talking about."

He shrugged. "Ask anyone. It's common knowledge. Really, Anna. How many secrets do you think there are on this tub?"

She closed her eyes and shook her head,

"Anyway, I hoped you'd stop by tonight. Want to ask you something. Don't know how you'd feel about it, but see, I've got this idea…."

She held up her hands. "Listen, if it involves kissing Marines, don't even think about it."

He laughed. "Not at all, it's just that, well, next time we get to Pearl, how'd you like me to show you around? Like you wanted last time. See, I was only stationed there four months, so there's a lot of Oahu I haven't seen either. And I can use my friend's car anytime. How's that sound?"

She stifled a yawn. "Ask me tomorrow when I can think straight."

"Sure. But in the meantime, picture the most beautiful beach in the world. Prettier even than Waikiki. And only an hour from Honolulu." He cleared his throat. "Maybe we could spend the night there."

Spend the night? Shock cut through the fatigue. She rolled her eyes.

"Separate rooms, of course."

"Of course." She got to her feet, yawned, didn't even try to cover her mouth. "But who knows if we'll get back to Pearl again?"

He rose too, so close she could smell his aftershave, feel his warmth. "Sure we will. Hospital here's real crowded, so we may have to take the next casualties there. Maybe pick up another load of gyrenes too."

"Oh, surely not after what happened to *Comfort*."

His laugh was bitter. "Listen, Anna, we're all expendable. See, last year at Pearl, six LSTs blew up in one of the lochs. They were nested together, taking on fuel, so they went up like…like Luke's birthday cake. After that, the Navy decided to separate them. But some top brass said no, that was the fastest way to load. It was a calculated risk they had to take, even if it meant more loss of life."

"But we're the people who keep the boys alive and send them back to duty. We're not expendable, are we?"

"Oh, Anna," he drawled. "You're sweet, but you're awful naïve."

Even as he slipped his arm around her, she retreated into an eat-drink-and-be-merry sense of these days on this ship, of her work, and most of all, this flirtation, or whatever the hell it was. For all she knew, next time they stood off Okinawa, *Compassion* could be blown to smithereens by a Kamikaze. Or torpedoed anywhere on the ocean. If there were no rules governing risk, surely those concerning something as minor as fornication were suspended too.

She edged closer, slid her arms around his neck, nuzzled his cheek. His lips came down; his hips pressed hers, reaffirming desire. Would he pursue it to its natural end if they went away together? She had no idea, but if given the chance she intended to. By golly, yes, she would. The hell with the pretense of virtue.

Admitting her own wicked intentions gave her a comforting sense of detachment from the war and everyone at home, especially the faith of her parents. And most of all from the shifting and ephemeral rules that no one obeyed anymore. Perhaps because they sensed, as she was beginning to, that the fate of the world was not in their hands. All of them, righteous Allies and evil Axis combatants alike, were nothing but ants, following orders they didn't understand from authorities who lied and manipulated them into doing their little jobs, scurrying around madly for a Cause they didn't understand, then numbing their souls with feeble, fleeting pleasures: eating and drinking and copulating until they were satiated. And incapable of further feeling, reasoning, or resisting.

There now, she thought as she went forward to Nurses' Country, quiet and hushed as night enclosed the ship. Her apostasy was complete. God help her.

CHAPTER ELEVEN

Although scuttlebutt was that the next deployment would be to Okinawa, instead the ship cruised adjacent waters rendezvousing with ships damaged in ever-more-savage Kamikaze attacks. One listing, charred flat-top transferred a hundred-eighty patients from her sick bay, most horribly burned, including one of their surgeons. A few miles away, a destroyer had picked up seventy-three men adrift in the sea after their light cruiser had gone done down. None had had more than minimal medical attention. Once they were aboard, *Compassion*'s surgeons worked 'round the clock, the burn wards filled, and chaplains conducted six funerals.

Last to come alongside was a damaged battleship with over a hundred casualties from her crew, plus an equal number she'd picked up from smaller ships that had been sunk. By 10 May *Compassion* was filled to capacity without having come near the beachheads.

When they'd completed these transfers, the ship came about slowly, engines laboring as speed increased. Anna was busy charting new arrivals in Receiving, but even in the noise and confusion, she heard the squawk box announce they were bound for Pearl again. Before anyone could react, the CO took over. She braced for another dose of momentous news, invariably tragic. This, however, was the antithesis of tragic: Germany had surrendered two days before.

After a brief, stunned silence, cheering rumbled up from below, reverberating in steel overheads, bulkheads and decks until the ship was alive with it. Relief weakened her knees and sent a vision, like a newsreel played too fast, of transports packed with troops from the European Theater steaming toward them to beef up the mighty force that would soon invade Japan. And, Lord willing, end the conflict once and for all.

Later, at chow, Audrey was bubbling with confidence her fiancé would soon be released from the PW camp. And Floyd said, "Well, now it's only a matter of time until the Japs call it quits too. See, B-29s are fire-bombing the hell out of their cities, and the battlewagons are bombarding Kyushu. So I'll lay odds we won't have to invade."

Everyone at the table heaved a collective sigh. No one concurred with all his opinions, but they did this one because it gave credence to their own wishful thinking. Then a new round of betting began in earnest.

As they neared Pearl, however, scuttlebutt began to undermine the mood of ebullient optimism. Anna's crumbled like a sand castle at high tide when she heard they'd be ferrying more Marines back to Guam. Too logical: six weeks into it, the fight to take Okinawa still raged, chewing up Marines and soldiers alike. And in spite of Floyd's assurances that the Allies wouldn't invade Japan, he admitted having heard that military high commands were stockpiling able-bodied men for cannon fodder on the beaches of the home islands.

Damn it to hell, she thought as she went to chow the last night out. Ignoring her female associates, she made straight for a table where Mark sat with some doctors. The only empty seat was at the far end, but when the others left, he moved to the chair beside her.

"Don't look so gloomy, Anna," he said with his bright minister's smile." We're steaming for Pearl. And an overnight liberty."

"I know." She pushed leftover beef stew into a compact pile on the plate so he'd be less likely to realize how much she'd wasted of an above-average meal. Or comment that she'd lost weight. "But it's only one night. And then we'll have more Marines aboard. I guess you're right. We are expendable."

His smile faded. "I hear that transports from Europe drop off five-thousand troops at a time in Hawaii, and go back for more. They're piling up faster than anybody can move them."

The steward glided up, asked if she'd finished, then whisked the plate away with a cluck of his tongue. "But I'll have pie, please," she called after him.

Mark studied her. "Hey, let's forget the damned war. And think about what we talked about before. Okay?"

She drew a deep breath. "Oh, I guess."

"Good. Then soon as phone lines come aboard, I'll call Dick about the car. If he gives me the green light, we can take off whenever liberty goes."

A reluctant joy poked at her, like shafts of sunlight pushing through clouds. "But suppose he doesn't?"

"We'll take a taxi." He shrugged, grinning. "Cost an arm and a leg, but hell, it's only money."

Under the tablecloth, their fingertips touched briefly with a promise that quickened her heart rate. "What'll you tell him about the car?"

He shrugged. "Oh, just that I'm showing some nurses

around Oahu. Not a complete lie. He's not half as judgmental as Luke, but I still don't want to give him the straight skinny."

"Oh, Luke! What'll we tell him?"

"Nothing. He'll be with a bunch of priests in Honolulu anyway."

"Good. I'd hate for him to write Lorraine. She'd tell Jim, for sure."

He rubbed the back of her hand. "Look, let's not talk about Jim, okay? And I won't mention my wife either. It'll just be you and me at Kailua."

"Okay." Smiling, she turned her hand over so his fingers pressed against her palm.

Their eyes held; he swallowed hard before he pushed his chair back and got to his feet. "Then we're all set. Now, I'm going below to see if anyone wants me to pray." He leaned down. "Hell of a thing, isn't it? Going from lust to prayer without a second thought? Hope the Lord understands."

"My father always says, if the Lord doesn't understand us, no one does."

She watched him hurry from the wardroom, then went up to her cabin in hopes of catching a nap before she went on duty at 1100. But anticipation of the weekend tingled in her like twenty cups of coffee. It wasn't dampened even by prospect of the night on a ward full of recent amputees. At least Willi would be sharing the duty. If anyone could, she'd keep Anna's mind from wandering to the coming assignation with Mark. If indeed that was what it turned out to be. After all, he'd promised separate rooms. Whether she wanted them or not.

* * *

On F-10, the amputees were so recently post-op the shift

was double-staffed. When Anna came on, corpsmen were still giving pain shots and sleeping pills. She hadn't worked this ward before, so she studied charts while Willi went from bed to bed assessing each man for signs of trouble- pallor, labored breathing, blood seepage, agitation, odors of suppuration or incontinence, or a dozen lesser indications of trouble.

Watching, Anna noticed one corpsman had been occupied with a single patient since she'd come on duty. When she went over to investigate, he jerked his head toward the man in the bed. "Special request, Miss Donovan. Swabbie here wants to talk to blondie."

She turned on the professional smile as she approached. The patient had the smooth face of a boy, but had lost both legs above the knee, the left arm at the shoulder. Dressings on the stumps had been changed an hour before, but were already damp with seeping plasma. "Hi. I'm Nurse Donovan. You wanted to see me?"

He made a mock salute with his remaining hand. "Yeah. Need another shot, but the medic here says not for three hours. And I hurt awful bad."

"Where?"

He grimaced at his bandages. "Where'd you think? Everywhere but my good arm."

"Okay. I'll see what I can do."

"Please, nurse."

She nodded and closed the curtain around his bed. Checking his chart at the desk, she saw her signature on the entry from Receiving, and her own handwriting recording his vital statistics. Obviously she'd seen him when he'd first come aboard. Yet she had no recollection except for a fleeting image of a pale sailor in shredded dungarees, tourniquets on both legs, pressure bandage on the stump of one arm. He'd been only one of a score of maimed men she'd met that day, processed and passed on to other hands.

She prepped another hypo of morphine, pulled up a chair beside the bed. "Well, sailor. I see your name's William Harrison. Do they call you Will? Or Bill?"

"Billy," he muttered through clenched teeth.

"Okay, Billy, I'll give you another shot in a few minutes. But first, why don't you tell me where you're from?"

He rolled his eyes. "Bet you never heard of it—Ogallala, Nebraska?"

"Actually, I think I might've passed through there on a train a couple years ago."

"Yeah. The Union Pacific." An almost-smile. "My folks have a farm twenty miles south. When I get back, my girl and I are going to get married and move in with them so's I can help the old man." The smile went dark; he squeezed his eyes closed. "Least that was the plan 'til this happened. Now, what good'll I be on a farm? What good'll I be anywhere?"

She winced, asked what ship he'd been on.

"*Ferguson*, a DE. Jap got us off Okinawa. I was coming up the ladder from the engine room when he hit. Don't know how I got out, but I ended up in the water. Thought I was lucky; most of my shipmates, they never had a chance." Tears jumped to his eyes. "Didn't know how chewed up I was 'til the cruiser pulled us out. Bad enough I lost all my gear, all my pictures, even one of my girl. And now my legs and arm. Should've gone down with the ship too."

She took hold of his thick-fingered hand, which was picking nervously at the sheet. "But your parents, and your girl, they must be awfully glad you didn't. See, my husband went down with his ship. So I know how it feels when that happens to somebody you love."

He studied her as if debating her veracity. "But now I'm

going to be a burden. Now I can't help anybody. Instead, they'll have to take care of me."

"Listen, the Navy's not going to send you home like this, you know. First they'll fit you for an artificial arm and legs, then train you to use them. You won't be as good as new, but you'll sure be better than you are tonight."

He shook his head silently, dislodging tears that trickled down the sides of his face into his blond crew cut. "No, I won't. Don't even want to go home now. Don't want them to see me like this. It'll kill Mom. And my girl— I know how that'll go. She'll tell me nothing's changed. But before long, there'll be somebody else." He sighed from the depths of the darkness in his soul. "Japs couldn't kill me, but that sure will."

Willing back emotion, Anna stroked his hand. "Look, Billy, we have two fine chaplains on this ship. Talking to them might make you feel better. And they'd be glad to see you any time. Even right now. Shall I call one?"

He grimaced. "Don't bother, nurse. They've already been around. Give you a Bible and tell you to keep praying. But it's all bilge water. They can't help. Nobody can help."

She moved her fingers to his wrist and checked his pulse: rapid but strong. "I know everything looks awful right now. Later, when the pain stops, life will seem a lot better. I promise."

"No, it won't, nurse. It never will again."

Out of words, she sat holding his hand for another five minutes on the off-chance the first shot might still kick in. Beyond the curtain, other patients were snoring faintly; from the deck above came a muted crash; bedside curtains swayed as the ship rolled, and underfoot the engines maintained their constant low-level thrum.

Relieved when his eyes finally closed, she stood to leave.

He was instantly awake. "Hey, nurse, you promised me

another shot, remember? But stay till it knocks me out, okay?"

With both his thighs swathed in gauze, the only readily-accessible muscle was the upper right arm. He twitched as the needle bit in. "Sorry," she whispered, swabbing the site with alcohol. He gritted his teeth, so she sat with him again until he began to untense, eyes closing, mouth sagging. When he was deeply under, she retreated on tiptoe.

At the station, Willi was slugging down coffee and working on charts. Anna recorded the second shot, noting, "Pt. very depressed; possible suicide risk." Then, helping herself to coffee, she wallowed in relief that Billy Harrison would be leaving in the morning, that a whole series of nurses would be dealing with him all the way back to Ogallala, Nebraska. Sure, she'd do her job for this shift, but then she would not think of him again, nor any of the other chopped-up boys whose bulky dressings covered irreversible trauma. That she hadn't instantly remembered seeing him when the flesh hadn't yet been sutured over the severed ends of bones, muscles, tendons and blood vessels indicated her growing detachment. Inevitable and necessary, yet somehow saddening.

She wasn't alone: she'd observed such a casual attitude in other medical personnel as well. In fact, they'd done so many amputations recently, one surgeon had joked, "Sharks'll really be feasting in our wake tonight." The vision of appendages dumped overboard with the garbage swam in her head for days afterward. Sure, on this ship they were removed from war's screeching engines, screams and concussions, from the stench of burning metal and flesh, from the terror of those on sinking ships. But these images burned in her brain so brightly she might as well have witnessed them first-hand.

Then she pictured Billy and all the anonymous sailors in engine rooms, fire rooms, boiler rooms and other dark below-deck spaces where moving machinery required constant attention. When she'd joined the ship, the acclimation tours hadn't included the berthing areas where boys fresh from boot camp slept cheek-by-jowl in cramped stacks, or the heads where they defecated without privacy in troughs of running water. Once she'd observed some sailors washing their dungarees by tying them to ropes and dragging them overboard. Another time, she'd noticed work crews grinning up from scaffolds rigged over the side so they could chip paint. The only enlisted men she knew by name were the Pharmacist's Mates they worked with and the wardroom stewards. But the others –especially the colored cooks—were invisible and anonymous, screened from nurses not just by commissions but gender and race as well.

Consequently, she rarely thought of them or the small, monotonous jobs that kept the ship functioning. Until that night, when she easily imagined all the faceless others on all the ships all over the Pacific. Not combat troops, true, but just as surely in harm's way. Just as vulnerable. Just as expendable.

Then, as she often did in the face of war's overriding truths, she felt shrunken, useless and increasingly numb.

* * *

The next morning she was helping with breakfast trays when *Compassion* steamed past *Arizona*. Few of these patients could handle utensils, so she fed those who couldn't, then assisted with toothbrushes, sponge baths and bedpans. Billy refused her aid, nor did he acknowledge their talk the night before. Ironic; she'd forgotten him earlier, now it was his turn.

Even after the next shift came on, she and Willi helped ready the patients for transfer, so it was almost nine when they came up to the wardroom. Outside the portholes were the gray warehouses of the auxiliary pier. The gangway was down, but Mark was nowhere to be seen.

They ate quickly; the powdered scrambled eggs were grittier than usual, bacon just this side of rancid, toast cold, coffee bitter. When the other nurse asked about her plans for liberty, Anna said only, "Mark's borrowing a friend's car to show me around the island."

Willi's brows inclined just slightly. For Audrey, Anna would have manufactured a more elaborate evasion of the truth. With Willi there was no need, nor did she ask more. Just as well: by now, Anna was quivering inside, as if a lightning bolt was about to wipe out her plans. Like the hand of God intervening to keep her pure.

Sure, she thought; as if the Lord had stopped watching the war to make sure none of its players deviated from the straight and narrow.

Mark came charging into the wardroom as she was about to go to her cabin. He was freshly shaved, flushed, trim in neatly-pressed khakis. He pulled her aside as two ship's officers rushed past, then eyed the brown splotches where a patient had splashed coffee on her uniform.

"Dick's bringing the car to the pier at ten." His voice was higher than usual. "I'll take him home, then come back and wait for you in the wardroom. Okay?"

She nodded and smiled a confident, serene smile, as if she'd gone off with men for nefarious purposes a hundred times before.

He blinked a couple times and touched her cheek with trembling fingers. "You're going to love this beach where we're going. Real quiet and pretty. Since liberty starts so late, thought we could stay tonight, and see the rest of the island tomorrow."

"Oh, you've been there before?"

"Last year, with Dick and his family." The electric grin

lit up. "Swell place for a honeymoon."

"You have to be married to have a honeymoon," she said primly.

He drew a deep breath; the intimate, confidential smile didn't fade. "No, you don't. Just in love." Blowing a kiss, he hurried out to the deck as the squawk box announced liberty.

Echoes of his words followed her to the post office. Without scanning, she took her mail to the cabin and tucked it under the pillow. She was tempted to see if Jim had written more glowing reports about a nurse he'd just hired, but didn't want to clutter her mind with speculation about his doings. Or anyone else's. In fact, while she showered she resolved to ponder nothing baffling. Including Mark's confusingly casual mention of love.

CHAPTER TWELVE

She'd seen Waikiki and Diamond Head and Honolulu on the previous liberty, but as Mark steered the '41 Dodge along a waterfront highway, he told her those tourist traps were hardly the best Oahu had to offer. "Just look at that Anna," he added, with sweeping gestures toward steep emerald hills on one side; and on the other, a lapis lazuli sea edged with turquoise. Even the sunlight was extraordinary, so clear and golden it seemed liquid.

She'd noticed the Eden quality of the island before; today it seemed even more intense. Of course this Eden would last no longer than the original, but that it blossomed on the very edge of the war's black vortex gave it an allure that heightened sensation even more than the fact that she was traveling with a man she had no moral or religious right to.

Since they'd left the ship, of course, they'd been only two proper naval officers, saluting the Marine sentry at the gate, maintaining a respectful space between them in the front seat and saying nothing they might censor in the presence of others. If Mark was seething internally too, he gave no indication except perhaps to talk more than usual, explaining every sign, every landmark, every geographical curiosity as if to make sure she really did see Oahu. She'd nodded and smiled and made small chirps of interest, but her mind was brimming with more personal questions. For one, where would they stay? Would he register as a married couple? And most important, were his intentions as impure as hers?

The air blowing in the windows was merely warm, but her palms were moist, while sweat plastered her shirt to her back and unfurled the curls in her hair. She'd expected to feel glamorous and desirable; instead she might have been working on H-13 in mid-afternoon of the hottest day of any tropical summer.

Mark drove for almost an hour before he turned onto a lesser highway toward the nondescript buildings of a small town. He slowed. "Well, here we are, Anna. Kailua. Ever heard of it?"

She shook her head, mouth too dry to speak.

"Beach is the best anywhere. And wait 'til you see where we're going to stay. Why, you can sit on the porch -- they call it a lanai -- and look right out at the ocean. So pretty you want to stare at it all day." He shot her a grin. "Except I'd rather look at you."

Her staid Puritan self could only simper and wish she'd taken repartee lessons from Margie. "Sounds beautiful."

"There's the lane." He pointed to an opening in dense roadside vegetation, braked hard and swung onto a shell track between walls of greenery abloom with large, gaudy blossoms. The only plants she recognized were palms of several varieties. After bouncing along a rutted surface for a few hundred feet, he braked in front of a rambling white two-story house with columns like a Southern plantation.

Two cars stood in the drive. A neat sign in the yard read "ALOHA HOUSE GUESTS".

Parking under a low palm, he sauntered toward the front door while she sat trying to appear pure and innocent. And married. Then, aware of her empty ring finger, she fished the engagement ring from under her shirt, unclasped the chain and slid it on, When she turned the diamond out of sight, it could have been a wedding ring. In case anyone noticed. Or cared.

For the next few minutes, Mark talked to a large woman in a flowered muu-muu who kept shaking her head and pointing back toward town. As he bounded down the steps and into the car again, Anna realized he'd been turned away.

Even so, his tone was confident. "They're full up. But the lady told me about another place the next lane over. Said it's just as nice." He backed around, expression cheerful, though sweat darkened the underarms of his khaki shirt.

"I'm sure it'll be fine," Anna said as if she believed it.

At first glance though, the smaller, boxier house with weathered vertical siding didn't look nearly as fine. Except for a weedy patch of grass in front, thick growth surrounded it like a jungle. Two stories, with porches on each at one end and across the front.

"Keep your fingers crossed," he said, exiting. This time he didn't quite bound to the door. She looked away, inhaling a warm, humid breeze fragrant of flowers and damp earth, and faintly, of seawater on hot sand. Again, she twisted the ring and touched the diamond and tried not to think of Jim. And wondered if Mark had to force thoughts of his wife from his mind today too.

He was gone almost ten minutes, but when he returned, the grin was reassuring. "Come on." He grabbed their bags from the back seat. "They only had one room, but it has twin beds. Hope that's okay. At least the landlord didn't blink when I registered as mister and missus. Guess if they asked for marriage certificates, they'd never rent the first room."

She drew a quick, sharp breath as he started down the path toward the house. At the rear, they climbed outside steps to the upper porch, where he pointed toward a sliver of pale aqua sea framed by palm fronds. Dutifully, she said it was beautiful, and followed him inside to a door just beyond an old-fashioned bathroom. A utilitarian setting for any drama: narrow beds spread with faded floral fabric, white-painted metal headboards and on a wicker table between them, pink artificial flowers stuck in a green glass vase. Above the beds, high-set jalousie windows overlooked more jungle growth and the white-tiled roof of a nearby building. Walls and ceiling were white planking, with a slow-turning ceiling fan. The floor was sea green, worn bare in spots, with a grass rug between the beds. Sand gritted underfoot and the air smelled of mildew.

"Well, what do you think?"

She turned on one of her ersatz smiles. "Mmm...It's fine."

"Not exactly the bridal suite." Mark set the bags on folding chairs, the only other furnishings in the room.

"That's okay. We're not exactly a bridal couple."

"Sorry. Other place is much nicer. Didn't think it'd be full up this early."

She didn't answer, hoped her face didn't reflect a hunch the Lord was trying to tell her something she preferred not to hear.

He took off his hat, raked fingers through his brush-cut hair, then set it back on. "Gosh, all of a sudden, I'm starved. What about you?"

Food was the last thing on her mind but she said, "I wouldn't mind some lunch. Why?"

"Noticed a Gedunk on the way in, so how about I pick up a couple hamburgers while you get ready for the beach? Won't be but a few minutes."

She told him that was a splendid idea. Relief flooded when he left. Until she noticed a hand-lettered sign thumbtacked to the back of the door: "No ALCOHOL, no FOOD, no SMOKING, no LOUD NOISE on premises." Since it didn't forbid fornication, she assumed illicit sex was the room's principal use.

Trying not to imagine further, she withdrew her bathing suit from the overnight case and undressed. There was no closet, so she hung the uniform skirt and shirt over the chair back, then quickly pulled on the two-piece sky-blue suit she'd bought in Honolulu on their last liberty. She'd lost so much weight since that the top hung loose on her breasts; she draped a towel around her shoulders so Mark wouldn't notice. That done, she peered through the window trying to see the ocean, but the branches were too thick. From below, the smell of garbage wafted up, and the outside shower was splashing, girlish voices giggling.

After a few minutes, she sat on the edge of one bed and tried to remember why she was here. Because Jim had a new nurse he thought a lot of? Hardly; in her heart she knew that no one, not Delilah herself, would be a threat to her. Jim wasn't a man who gave in to passion without commitment. This article of faith was imprinted on her heart.

No, this was purely about her attraction to Mark, one that had recently escalated into an irrational craving. How often had she remembered their night together with regret she hadn't taken it further? But no, she hadn't wanted to be that shipboard cliché, the sex-starved nurse furtively indulging her passion in an officer's stateroom. Like her hapless cabin-mate, Patty, the one who'd slept around. And had had an abortion, then an emergency hysterectomy, then a transfer off the ship. God forbid she should be another Patty.

When he'd been gone twenty minutes, she used the bathroom, then came back and paced the small room, wondering if he'd been in an accident, or arrested by the Shore Patrol for falsifying his marital status in a hotel register. Or maybe he'd met someone he knew, like the head of the Chaplains' Corp. Or worse yet, Luke. All the reasons she hadn't previously considered came tumbling out of the dusty corners of her mind until she was ready to start hiking toward the highway to flag down a Honolulu-bound bus.

Then a car door slammed; footsteps took the outside steps two at a time and someone whistled tunelessly. Maybe not Mark after all; she'd never heard him whistle before, though whistling was forbidden on the ship because it might be taken for the boson's pipe.

Bursting into the room, he handed her a grease-spotted paper bag and tossed his hat to a bed. "Sorry I was gone so long. Saturday afternoon. Everybody has food on their minds."

He began to unbutton his shirt while she held the warm bag and inhaled the aroma of fried onions. Feeling suddenly devilish, she said, "Guess they all want to EF."

"EF?" He stared a minute, the grin spreading until his eyes crinkled. "Sometimes I forget you were married to a Navy man. Well, now you know about me, don't you?"

"Uh-huh. But you're a minister. Honoring your vows."

He averted his gaze. "Don't count on it, Anna. After all, I couldn't get separate rooms."

She pointed to the list of proscribed activities on the door. "Look at that."

Wagging his head, he glanced at it. "Guess we'll have to have our picnic on the beach then. Give me a minute to get ready, okay?"

When he took his overnight bag to the bathroom, she concluded he didn't expect to take her to bed right away, if at all. A peculiar disappointment suddenly smudged her mood, so perceptibly she could've sworn the sun had gone behind a cloud.

Whistling tunelessly again, he came back to the room in black, skin-tight navy-issue trunks, towel over his shoulders. Trying not to notice the rest of him, she focused on his face; even so, peripherally observed sandy hair on chest and legs, and other physical geography she hadn't before, even the night they'd slept on his bunk. Her body warmed, heart thudded, breath quickened.

Then, racking her mind for something memorable to say, settled for, "Do you know the way?"

"The way? Where?"

"To the beach."

"Oh that. Sure. Just out the lane." Moving quickly, he dug into his suitcase, brought forth a tight white roll. "Even comshawed a blanket so we'd have something to lie on."

"You've thought of everything."

He nodded and swung open the door. Two dripping young women wrapped in towels scurried into the room across the hall.

Anna pushed their door closed again. "Wait a minute, Mark."

"Why?"

She set the food bag on a chair, took the towel and blanket from him and tossed them on one bed. "Let's hold off on the beach a few minutes, okay?"

"Fine with me." His voice sounded strangled and his gaze dropped to her chest. She thought of crossing her arms so he couldn't see how bony she was. Instead, she took his shoulders and pulled him to her. The skin of their bellies met, moist and warm, then their lips and teeth; his mouth tasted like Black Jack gum. Overhead the fan squeaked with every revolution. Across the hall, the young women were laughing in their room, and a plane snarled across the sky.

For a moment the need was hers alone; then it ignited in him, caught and flared like fire spreading between the LSTs he'd told her about. So urgent, so overwhelming they barely had time to shed their bathing suits on the way to the bed. It groaned under their weight; the springs commenced to protest and the headboard banged the wall. In some still rational part of her brain, Anna wondered if they were violating the NO LOUD NOISES rule. But when her own voice added to the clamor, she was beyond caring.

Afterward they lay in a sweaty embrace, regaining their breath, their consciousness of each other, of the surroundings. And finally, of the protection neither of them had thought to use.

"Dear God," he breathed against her hair. "Can't believe I didn't think about it. And it's not like I didn't bring any." He squeezed her to him, then rose swiftly, plucked the towel from his piled things and handed it over. "Jesus, what can we do now?"

She calculated briefly. "I don't think there's anything to worry about. This ought to be a safe time. And as soon as we get to the beach, I'll go in the ocean; that'll make it even safer."

He rolled his eyes. "Good you're a nurse. I'm ignorant about that sort of thing."

Jim and his gross of rationed condoms flew through her mind like a bird looking to build a nest. "Don't worry. I'll teach you everything I know."

He groaned and pulled on his trunks. "Better late than never, I reckon."

* * *

Once she'd had the therapeutic surf plunge, they wolfed down burgers and soda from bottles, then lay side by side on the woolen blanket with U.S. NAVY on it. The beach was wide and white and far less crowded than Waikiki, the ocean the color of lime sherbet, a few clouds drifting by like colorful smoke puffs. Offshore, two tiny islands were miniature emerald pyramids. The surf was soft foam except farther out, where dark-skinned boys balanced boards on incoming swells. Offshore, a white two-masted schooner rode the wind under full sail. And on the horizon an outbound flat-top was a dim gray shape.

She pointed. "Guess we can't get away from the war even here."

Mark raised his head to peer at it, but continued to lie on his belly, one hand possessively on her bare midriff. "Looks like she's headed Stateside."

"Lucky for her."

"Maybe she's that carrier we rendezvoused with last week. Going back to a shipyard."

"Can't tell if she's listing, but the repair ship could have taken care of that."

He leaned over to kiss her, then stared into her eyes at close range. "Wish I could forget the war as easy as I forgot the damned prophylactic. Every swabbie on the ship knows better. God. Talk about careless!"

"Maybe if I hadn't seduced you out of the blue like that...."

"That's no excuse. I'm old enough to know better. I could kick myself."

"Don't worry, Mark. My husband was Catholic; I'm familiar with the rhythm method."

"But you had a baby, didn't you?"

"Only because we wanted one."

"But you don't now."

"Not under these circumstances. Of course not."

He studied his fingernails. "What'd you do if it happened?"

She swung her gaze to the fading carrier again. "Not what my cabin-mate did."

"Ironic. The last Protestant chaplain was involved in that mess, wasn't he?"

"Uh-huh. Just think; if he hadn't been, you and I might never have met."

"Hope there's never a day you wish we hadn't."

She stroked his cheek with possessiveness born of recent intimacy. "There won't be," she said, faking the confidence she was so good at offering patients.

He kissed her again, sweeter, longer. "Listen, Anna, just for the record, if something did happen, I'd marry you, you know."

She reared back in surprise. "Marry me? But how could you? Aren't you still married?"

His mouth twisted into a bitter expression. "Maybe not. I never hear from my wife, so I have no idea. In fact, if it wasn't for my parents, I wouldn't even get news of my kids."

She patted his shoulder and massaged the tight tendons of his neck. "Well, it's nice of you to say that. About marriage. But you needn't worry. Really."

He grinned. "Maybe it's wishful thinking, not worry."

She didn't ask him to elaborate, was afraid of hearing a love declaration she wouldn't know how to respond to, even if she believed it. Wasn't love what men always proclaimed to women they wanted to sleep with? A minister especially would have to convince himself love was involved in order to justify adultery. On the other hand, she had no illusions about what she felt for him. If it was love, it wasn't the sort the Bible promoted, except in the context of "Be fruitful and multiply".

The sun had retreated behind the verdant nearby

mountains when they went back to the room. This time the loving was more deliberate, less reckless. Still, it left her breathless with pleasure. And hungrier than she'd been in weeks. Mark remembered a restaurant on the highway, so after they dragged themselves from the bed, they walked into town and found the American Café right where he'd said it'd be. Not surprisingly, the low white building was painted in horizontal red stripes with random blue stars. The sign out front advertised "Home Cooking Just Like Mom's".

A long line snaked across the parking lot toward the entrance. Lots of sailors in whites, exotic-looking girls, and couples in civvies, clinging to each other with undisguised intimacy. Half an hour later, they'd progressed only as far as the Tiki bar; it didn't serve alcohol, so Mark brought cokes to sip as they advanced toward the smells of hot grease and cigarette smoke, and the thump of a neon-flashing juke box. They'd almost reached the hostess when an older couple sailed by with two soldiers in their wake, one in a wheelchair, the other on crutches, an empty trouser leg pinned up.

"That's the thing to do these days," Mark muttered as he watched them being led to a booth. "Pick up cripples from a service hospital, take them home for the weekend, take them to church, take them out to eat, take them to visit your friends. Then take them back."

"Why do you sound so bitter?"

His gaze went distant. "Oh, I guess because my wife did it in San Diego. She loved doing good works. But she loved being seen doing them even more."

She felt herself retract, didn't remind him they'd agreed to keep others out of their assignation. Impossible, she realized now, the others were with them, mentioned or not. And she realized that though she was probably at a safe point in her cycle, she'd worry about an accidental pregnancy until she got her period.

Oh God, the Lord really was trying to tell her something. And now it was suddenly much easier to figure out what it was.

CHAPTER THIRTEEN

*M*ark dropped her at the ship before dark the next evening. While he took his friend's car back, Anna plodded up the gangway with the fatigue born of two sleepless nights in a row. Friday on the amputee ward had been a non-stop grind, the past night a round of loving and talking, with only a few dozes to keep them going. Obviously, despite his previous noble mention of separate rooms, their mutual goal had been sexual satiety. More lies, she thought; humans were more skilled at lying to themselves than she'd ever realized.

She made it to her cabin without seeing anyone she preferred not to, like Audrey, Luke or OH. After a shower, she flopped on the bunk with the previous day's letters from Lorraine, Margie, Alex and her mother. All seemed stale, as if she'd read them before. Or paraphrases of the same litany. Even Alex's doings were trivial, his anticipation of being transferred to the Pacific half-hearted. Compared to the brilliant new memory filling her mind, all other news was irrelevant.

She saved Jim's until last, held her breath as she

skimmed his account of the new nurse's capabilities. If he wasn't smitten with her, he gave that impression. Suddenly she slipped into the beyond-caring mode again. What did it matter if he slept with her, or she slept with Mark? If she conceived, had to take a medical discharge and go home in ignominy, so what? The war, the killing, the horror would grind on without her. *Compassion* would continue to ferry casualties to hospitals and return for more. Her duties would be absorbed by the other nurses, as Patty's had been. One way or another, the war would end. And her destiny would unfold despite her best intentions.

Then she read Jim's last paragraph:

> *I'm delighted that Ellen's working for me, but she can't take your place, even as my nurse. You brought so much more to our work than anyone before or since. Even before we loved each other, there was a special element to our days in the clinic; I guess it was the promise that we could be more to each other. And now, from 10,000 miles away, your letters continue to strengthen that promise. Obviously, I can live without you, but after the war, I hope I never have to, even for one night.*

She re-read it, tears of relief gathering behind her eyes, while in her soul, guilt began to fester like a case of gangrene. Jim's fidelity really hadn't been the issue, after all, rather the mindless mandates of a wanton streak that ran through her like a river, broad and quiet until it narrowed into wild rapids in a part of her soul she'd rarely allowed herself to visit. The first time was the night she and Dan got engaged; she hadn't yielded before because it was common knowledge that a man might enjoy, but not marry, a "bad girl", especially if he was Catholic and she Protestant.

With Jim, their engagement hadn't yet become formal when she'd seduced him. And now Mark, who'd had every intention to walk the straight and narrow path that clergyman were sworn to follow. And might have, had she not tempted him beyond endurance.

She wanted to find some excuse, some explanation, but there was nothing that could whiten that stain in her. No, it wasn't a sin mortal enough to keep her out of heaven, but now that she'd recognized it, she could hardly call herself a good Christian, could she? Though she would, of course, would maintain that pretense as long as possible. Which, if she turned up pregnant, might only be a couple of months.

* * *

The next morning, she slept through departure, and woke only when dawn paled the sky to feel the engines pushing the ship westward again. Later, on the way to the wardroom, she checked the duty roster. No patients were aboard, so it would be another training cruise, not just to keep them current with medical breakthroughs, but to occupy the minds and use medical personnel's excess energy. Since the kissing mutiny, busy-work and nit-picking inspections loomed even higher on brass's priority list. Being a great believer that the devil found work for idle hands, her mother would have been in full accord with this philosophy.

What had happened to her then? Anna wondered. Recently, she'd been working harder than ever in her life, yet the devil had still found work for her hands. And the rest of her body.

The morning's session was to acquaint nurses and corpsmen with new techniques for managing burn cases. So far, nothing was posted about off-limits spaces, so she wondered if they were carrying Marines after all. Then at chow, Floyd announced scuttlebutt had been wrong.

"Guess they learned their lesson. Or maybe they don't need them now we're getting all those troops from the ETO. All we picked up were some corpsmen strikers we'll train on the way out. And a field hospital with supplies for a year."

Willi had just said that *Centaur's* cargo had been something similar, when the steward set down Anna's coffee. Out of nowhere, another memory intruded; two years before, almost from the moment she'd conceived, several smells had turned her stomach: coffee, bacon and cigarette smoke. Traces of all three now hung in the air, but nothing triggered that tell-tale queasiness, though maybe the day after was a bit soon.

"Thank God," she breathed, adding quickly, "I mean, that we're not carrying more combat troops, that is."

That night, a movie she'd never heard of was showing in the lounge. Another cornball musical, with no recognizable stars, but she joined the usual gang to watch. The feature was preceded by Movietone News of Nazi death camps recently liberated by Allied troops in their sweep across Germany. Images of corpses piled like firewood slowed her breathing, while footage of the living skeletons staring at the camera brought bile to her throat.

"My God," Nell whispered. "Makes you think twice about having kids, doesn't it? Who wants to bring a child into a world where civilized people can do this to other civilized people?"

No one answered. Mercifully, the black and white horror show unfolded for only a few more minutes. Then the audience was treated to a Technicolor fantasy about a showgirl singing and dancing her way into the heart of a hard-boiled producer.

"I wonder," Willi asked as they made for their cabins afterward. "Is there really such a thing as happily-ever-after?"

Without thinking, Anna said, "No. There's only today. Don't count on anything beyond that."

"Weekend not what you hoped?"

"No, it was swell. But it's over. Fun's temporary; the war goes on forever."

Nell said, "Too bad there's no Marines on board. At least we could look forward to more kissing. Now that was a hell of a lot of fun."

Polly groaned, "The day after though, that was pure hell."

"Must be like getting knocked up," Audrey said. "Fun while you're doing it, but hell afterward."

"Depends on the circumstances," Willi said.

Wincing, Anna prayed Please, God. Please not in these circumstances. But even as she did, she heard her mother's favorite homily, "The Lord helps those who help themselves." And Anna hadn't. Hadn't given a thought to anything beyond gratifying her own need. For closeness. Intimacy. Respite from the war. And the fleeting delusion of love.

But when she was alone in the cabin, guilt began to fade, like photos of concentration camps, and recollections of young amputees, and knowledge she'd been unfaithful to Jim. And she was left again with the ashen sense that these things mattered indeed, but not enough to shake her from the cold numbness that had set in during eight months on this ship. These days, the only time she really felt alive was in Mark's presence. And when she wasn't, even guilt seemed preferable to apathy. Guilt at least was something you could feel. Something that let you know you were still a living, breathing part of the world.

* * *

Trapped in the next day's training session, Anna's attention kept wandering from the topic—the new air mattresses to be installed in the burn ward. Once they might have seemed as miraculous as penicillin and sulfa drugs. But in her consciousness she kept hearing lines from an old poem about the inability of even the most noble intentions to change human nature. Though they rarely saw the end results of the healing initiated in *Compassion*'s wards, medical personnel were constantly impressed with statistics, with the high percentage of casualties that would be restored sufficiently to return to combat. So far she hadn't heard how many of these, however, were likely to need them again. As for the rest, those damaged too severely to be of further use to the military, like Billy Harrison, no one asked if they wanted to be kept alive; they just were. Then forever after lived with absent limbs or deformed faces, lost eyes or shattered nerves, any of which would preclude a normal life.

So all the noble intentions and excellent work of all the medical professions all over the world could not eradicate these inescapable souvenirs of war. Or was being alive, in any condition, preferable to the alternative?

That evening, Luke joined Anna's clique at chow. After everyone else left to stare at another starlet-studded B movie, she asked if he'd heard any more from Lorraine.

His smile was unusually warm. "Yeah. Two letters at Pearl. Told me all about her life. And the island. And everybody there. I love reading them. Can't wait to meet her and find out about my father. For some reason, she won't tell me 'til we meet in person."

"Is it important to know about him?"

He gave her a strange look. "Funny, all those years I didn't care, now I want to know everything about my background." His gaze went pensive, distant. "I always knew, at least since I found out the Salaunases weren't my natural parents, I knew my childhood wasn't normal. Guess I'm trying to get it back."

"It reminds me of a verse in the Old Testament. *I shall restore the years that the locust hath eaten.* Do you know it?"

"Ah, yes. The second chapter of Joel." He nodded emphatically. "Exactly how I feel. Thanks to you, Anna."

"And our chance meeting out here on the other side of the world."

"But it was your choice to take it further. You could've just as easily backed off, and I'd never known."

"Well, I thought about it, but then I realized it was part of the Lord's plan."

He signaled the steward to refill his coffee, then doctored it with sugar and canned milk. Just like Lorraine, even to tasting and swirling in more sugar. He sipped, and lit a Lucky Strike. Her brand too. "My feelings exactly. Part of the Lord's plan." He inhaled deeply. "Now. How are you doing these days?"

"Oh, all right I guess. The heat's taken my appetite. But otherwise, I feel ...oh, like I'm in a dream where nothing's real. And nothing matters except work."

He studied her so intently she began to squirm. "Nothing? Not even your fiancé?"

She tensed. The line he'd crossed was as indistinct as longitude and latitude demarcations in the ocean. "Well, of course he's important. I'm talking about other things. Like what the Nazis did to the Jews. And what becomes of our casualties after they leave the ship. Questions like that. I mean, it isn't that I don't care. I just don't feel things like I did when I first came aboard."

He nodded. "You're more detached now. Should make your job easier."

"Yeah, I guess so." She didn't add that such numbness reminded her of the bleak year after she'd lost Dan and the baby, when detachment had been an obsession.

He massaged his jaw with graceful, slender fingers. "You know, I hear that from a lot of medical people lately. One surgeon said he felt like a sponge that's soaked up all the horror it can absorb."

"Don't you feel it yourself?"

"Oh, I'm sick of the war, sure. But, well, maybe I'm tougher than most people. Because of the way I grew up. Besides, I have the Church for strength. In fact, last weekend I was on a retreat with some priests from Honolulu."

She raised her eyebrows as if this were news. "And this sustains you?"

He nodded, drained the coffee in one long gulp and stubbed out the cigarette in a brass ashtray fashioned from a shell casing by some gung-ho machinist's mate. "Reminds me my life's in our Lord's hands. And my job's to share his gospel with people who don't know it. Or have stopped believing."

"Well, I still believe we're doing the Lord's work. I just don't feel it the way I used to."

His gaze darkened to indigo. "Maybe you're seeing too much of Whitmore."

Her heart clutched, but she quickly came back with, "Oh Luke, he's as spiritual as you are."

"Really? Then where was he last weekend? On a retreat too?"

Swallowing shock, she willed her sympathetic nervous system not to blush. "I don't know anything about that."

"Good. I'd hate to think you did, Anna."

"And I'd hate to think you're as judgmental as you sound. It reminds me of another scripture: *Let him who is without sin cast the first stone.* So I'm not going to judge you for some of the rumors I've heard."

His mouth gaped, as if he'd actually been slapped.

Without waiting for a reply, she excused herself and walked purposefully from the wardroom.

But as she stomped up the ladder to C Deck, her cold anger began to soften like ice cream in the sun. Pity was the puddle it left. One day Luke would learn the circumstances of his conception. And perhaps bring that judgmental strain to bear on his own parents. She dreaded that Lorraine might suffer it; bad enough the guilt she'd already borne. But even worse, Anna was saddened she could no longer count him a friend, except in the context of whatever beliefs coincided with her own. Certainly he could never be her confessor. Because he seemed to have her on a pedestal.

And that was the last place she belonged. Or wanted to be.

* * *

The day before they reached Okinawa, her period started. Relief sweetened her outlook on the rest of her life. Breathing a prayer of gratitude, she went down to breakfast in hopes Mark would be in the wardroom. He wasn't, though a steward reported seeing him earlier. So, ignoring Audrey's wave, she went up to his office, seated herself primly beside his desk and waited until he finished a phone call.

He hung up; both said "Hi," in unison, then regarded each other across stacked papers and an open Concordance. Considering how close they'd been at Kailua, she found it odd they hadn't spoken personally since. Maybe he'd had a sweet letter from his wife. Or had become immobilized by terminal guilt.

He reached for her hand, smiled hesitantly. "Glad to see you, honey." His voice was tighter than usual. "Missed you this week."

"Oh? Well, you've probably been as busy as I have." A

deep breath. "Anyway, just thought you'd like to know, nothing happened in Kailua. I mean, nothing we didn't want to. You know."

His expression sobered. "Funny. I almost hoped it had."

"Oh Mark, how could you?"

"I know. Doesn't make a lick of sense. But even if we didn't end up together, I'd be happy to know you had my child."

Stunned but touched, she sat mute. Until the old Yankee sensibility flooded her. "Well, that's easy to say now, but the reality—well, it's just shoddy. Back Street. No man of God should have a secret like that on his conscience."

"It's not shoddy, Anna. You know I'm in love with you."

She extricated her hand and fluttered her fingers in dismissal. "I don't want to talk about it anymore. It was a nice weekend, but nothing happened. By the way, I think Luke knows we were together. At least he suspects."

His sigh was a lamentation. "So I heard. Evidently somebody saw you getting out of the car Sunday night. He wouldn't say who. But this ship's like a small town: everybody knows everybody else's business." Another sigh. "I told him there was some mistake, but he didn't believe me. Sorry, Anna. I'd hoped maybe we could go to Kailua again. But now….. Oh well, we can always have a night in my stateroom now and then."

"No, we can't," she said in the frostiest tone she could muster. "I can't do that again. In your cabin or anywhere else."

His face clouded. "I thought you enjoyed …uh, being together."

"Sure. But I don't enjoy the way I feel now. And if I'd turned up pregnant…" She shuddered. "It was adultery, Mark. You say you love me, but I don't love you. I love Jim. I don't know how I could've done that."

Shaking his head, he gazed toward the porthole and compressed his lips.

"I thought it wouldn't matter. But it does. I wish we'd never gone."

When he looked back, he seemed to be controlling tears. He reached for her hand again. "I don't know what to say, Anna. I thought we cared for each other."

She glanced toward the busy passageway outside, the Main Street of the community activities that comprised the ship: they were far from alone. She withdrew her hand and got to her feet. "I think I only did it because I thought Jim was falling for his new nurse. Now I'm sure he's not. But I was unfaithful anyway. And I can't undo it."

Mark said only, "Oh, Anna." As she moved toward the open hatchway, Luke appeared. He stopped short, mouth agape, then gave a curt nod and brushed past to his desk. Groping for an innocuous exit line, she said to Mark, "We'll talk about that patient another time then, okay?"

She left, sensing silence hanging like a dark curtain between the two men. A few months before, they'd shared both their vocations and her friendship. This three-way relationship had not become a love triangle, but that she'd come between them bothered her more than the reasons why. Or even the inevitability that one day she would.

CHAPTER FOURTEEN

*P*ossibly because she'd been involved in the Kissing Mutiny, or was still persona non gratis for failing to report Patty's pregnancy, or was suspected of compromising a chaplain, Anna's duty on the deployment from Okinawa to Pearl was consistently nights on H-13. Now, however, with so many battle fatigue cases aboard, it was just one of three such wards where the quiet rooms were filled with NCOs and junior officers. Rumor had it there was even a bird colonel berthed somewhere in Officers' Country. Fortunately, her patients were passive ones, those who stared into space, wept silently into their pillows or huddled on their bunks.

The only time she interacted socially with these men was during the hourly bed checks each night. Regs forbade locking any berthing space for fear patients would be trapped in an emergency, so it was essential to keep constant track of them. Presumably for her safety, a corpsman accompanied her as she made rounds, shining a flashlight into each quiet room to make sure the occupants were still alive and well. More often than not, they were awake most of the night, requesting coffee, a smoke or a sleeping pill. More rarely, they wanted to talk.

The first night out, one who did was a young Marine captain, clean-cut and handsome as a recruiting poster. But his mind was empty of memories: of his previous life, he remembered only that he was from Richmond, VA, and a Naval Academy graduate. Without his permanent service record, only bits and pieces of his history were available. Another man from his unit, however, knew the captain had fought in the Guadalcanal, Saipan, Peleliu and Iwo Jima campaigns. Scars on his belly suggested recent surgeries, but he could tell them nothing of the where, when or why of them. All Anna knew was, medics had found him sitting on an Okinawa beach, without a weapon, helmet in hand, passively observing landing site activity. With no idea of how he got there, or what his part was in the invasion.

At the midnight bed check, Roger Armistead was sleeping. An hour later, however, he was wide awake and alert enough to ask her to talk with him. Before she did, she finished rounds, sent the corpsman back to the ward and returned to his room. Leaving the hatch open, she pulled up a chair and turned on a medium-warm smile to indicate interest but not enthusiasm.

"Okay, Captain. What would you like to talk about?"

The returning smile warned her of excessive interest, though all he said was, "Oh nothing special, nurse. See, I've forgotten everything I know, and this time of night, it drives me crazy. Maybe if you talked about your life, it'd help me remember mine. At least give me something to think about." The accent was soft, similar to Mark's but more cultured: Southern Gentleman born and bred.

Sounded reasonable, innocuous. "Okay. What would you like to know?"

"Your life story."

She laughed. "I'm afraid that'd take more time than I can spare."

"Well then. Just the highlights, okay?"

"Okay. Highlights. First, I'm from Portsmouth, New Hampshire. Ever been there?"

He shook his head. "Can't recall. Your folks still live there?"

She nodded. "My father's an Episcopal priest."

"Oh?" his face brightened. "I'm Episcopalian too. From the ground up. Even went to an Episcopal prep school. St. Peter's in Richmond. Ever heard of it?"

Confused that he could remember this alma mater, she said she hadn't.

"Not many people have. It's really small. Anyway, where'd you train to be a nurse?"

"Boston. Massachusetts General Hospital."

"Join the Navy right afterward?"

"No. Worked at the Portsmouth Naval Hospital a couple of years."

"Then did you join up?"

She decided to omit the Dan segment of her life. "No. I worked in a clinic in Maine awhile. But I wanted to do something important in the war. So here I am." Aware she'd said enough, she glanced at her watch. "Sorry, captain. Have to get back to my other patients."

His eyes took on a new intensity. "Just one more question, please. Not that it's any of my business, but I bet you have a sweetheart somewhere, don't you?"

She pulled out the ring on its chain from under her uniform. "A doctor in Maine."

His face registered nothing, but his mouth formed an O. "Well, that figures. A pretty girl like you. Should've known."

She ignored the comment. "And what about you? Do you have a girl back home?"

"Hope not. Hate to think somebody's waiting for me, and I don't even know her name."

She got to her feet briskly. "Well, I'm sure you're going to remember everything pretty soon. Now. I have to get back to work. I'll look in again in an hour."

"Can we talk more then?"

"Sorry. I'm 'way behind on charts. Maybe tomorrow night."

"Promise?"

"If I can. Goodnight now."

Back at the station, she pulled his chart, read the diagnosis of hysterical amnesia, and noticed Mark's notation that he'd visited him that afternoon. "Pt can't remember how he knows, but he's a skillful chess player."

Off duty at 0700, she headed to the wardroom and joined Mark at a table with Ed Bryson, the Supply Officer. She waited until they'd finished discussing the weather, then asked what Mark could tell her about the Marine on H-13. "I see you played chess with him yesterday."

"Yep. Swell way to get patients to talk. Why? What do you want to know?"

"Well, last night at a bed check, he told me he went to an Episcopal private school. Did you know that?"

"No. But I'm not surprised. Probably one of those places where they have chess teams, not football squads."

She gazed at his face, noting a smear of egg yolk at the corner of his mouth. And was momentarily discomfited by the remembrance of his chin grazing hers. "Is he one of your special cases?"

"Yeah. Got a hunch I can help him remember. In fact, I gave him a copybook so he can write down any recovered memories. You going to talk to him again?"

"He wants me to."

"Good. Maybe that'll help prime the pump."

"The only thing is, I can't get personal, so I'm not sure what to talk about."

He drained the coffee and blotted his mouth with the napkin, which took care of the egg yolk, but not recollections of his skin on hers. "Then tell him about that island in Maine, and what happened with the U-boat. Bet you've got plenty of yarns like that. You'll know where to draw the line."

"I hope so. Thanks."

Excusing herself, she headed toward the table where her female colleagues were evaluating the real eggs on the menu. The consensus was, they should have gone to a hatchery instead of the galley. When her own plate arrived, the hard-fried specimens the steward slid under her nose were so smothered in rancid bacon grease she couldn't tell if they were fresh or not.

* * *

As soon as she came on duty that night, Anna scrutinized Armistead's chart for Mark's notes: "Pt. not interested in chess today, only my life story. Wants me to take him topside for fresh air. Showed him how to open the port by his bunk, but he really wants a turn around deck."

It was 0200 before she found time for the Marine. By then she'd rehearsed a hyperbolized version of the U-boat sinking, which she recited like a dramatic reading. When he appeared only moderately interested, she kept adding details about the Navy's involvement and the fugitive they'd hidden in the hotel. She didn't mention Jean's subsequent pregnancy, because she had a creepy feeling that behind his concentrated but genteel gaze, the captain was mentally undressing her.

The third night, Mark's notes recorded that he'd taken Armistead to the main deck in a wheelchair. "Asked him if it reminded him of any other ship he'd been on, but he said no, and seemed apologetic, as if he'd disappointed me."

Later, when she asked Armistead if he wanted to talk, he said he was awful damned tired from his outing with the chaplain. "Next time, he's promised I can walk with him. Depends on the weather, he says. But come see me tomorrow night, nurse. And tell me more stories. I love the sound of your voice. It's so sweet, I can hear it the whole time I'm falling asleep."

"Or maybe all that exercise will jog your memory, and you'll be able to tell me a story."

His smile was wan. "I'll do my best, ma'am. Cause I want to make you happy. I sure do want to make you happy."

Red lights flashed in her mind as she walked back to the station. An innocent remark? Or an indication he was fantasizing? Even without a professional answer, she was nagged by an insistent hunch that the man was an unexploded bomb, the contents of his memory ready to blow up at some provocation neither she nor Mark could foresee.

But when he was sleeping at subsequent bed checks, she told herself Luke's stabbing had conditioned her to expect the worst. Ridiculous, she thought; these patients were nothing like that one. These were docile, Roger Armistead mannerly and well bred, his personal remarks likely the result of isolation from his own reality. Loneliness and lust were a powerful combination, but she couldn't see them leading to an attack with an improvised weapon. Nonetheless, she alerted the corpsmen to check his chow trays and make sure he withheld nothing that could be sharpened into one.

She considered sharing these vague suspicions with

Mark, but their paths didn't cross the next day. That night on the ward again, she read he'd given Armistead "as complete a tour of the ship as I could, including a look into the wardroom. Spirits seemed better, and he was grateful for my efforts. Still no recall, however."

At midnight, the patient was sitting up in bed, covers folded neatly over his lap, like a well-bred invalid receiving visitors. On the bedside table was an orderly stack of magazines, a *Leatherneck* on top. She took the usual chair, smiled the usual neutral smile. "I hear Chaplain Whitmore gave you a tour of the ship today. Didn't all that fresh air make you sleepy?"

He shook his head, scratched the pale stubble of a fresh crew cut. "Had a nap after chow, so I'd be wide awake when you came around."

"Well, good. Then I'll tell you about the Kamikaze that buzzed us a couple months ago."

"If you don't mind, ma'am, I'd rather hear more about you. And your boyfriend. I mean, this doctor you're engaged to. Is he your first love?"

She inhaled away a premonitory tightening in her chest. "No. I married my first love, but he was killed in action two years ago."

"Oh?" He stared a while. "Two years? And you're already engaged to a new man?"

She let the smile fade. "That's none of your business, Captain. Now, unless you want to talk about something else, I'm going back to the ward."

"Only trying to be friendly." His eyes darkened. "Anyway, have you always worn your hair that short?"

"Navy regs."

His gaze raked her like an inescapably bright light. "Bet you're a real looker with it long." She was about to cut off further conversation when he added, "Listen, miss. Do you have a picture of yourself I could have? One I can look at when I can't sleep?"

She rose quickly. "Sorry, none of myself. Just with friends."

"Bet he has one, though. Your boyfriend, I mean."

"Of course."

"Nude? "

She stifled a gasp. "Okay, that's enough. I'm getting you another sleeping pill right now."

"And when he can't sleep, I bet you crawl in bed with him. Lucky guy. Bet that'd work better for me too. Better than any sleeping pill ever invented."

She virtually goose-stepped to the hatchway. "I'll send the corpsman in with the pill."

At the station, she ordered the corpsman to make sure the patient swallowed it with no tricks. "And from now on, don't let me go into his room alone."

"Make a pass at you, did he?" Bobby McWherter was one of the new boys fresh from Pharmacist's Mate's "A" school, so eager to learn the ropes he was often underfoot like a friendly puppy. But the first day they'd worked together, she'd detected a Boston accent, a streak of intelligence and a natural talent for medicine.

"Oh, you know how it is." she said lightly.

"Don't worry, ma'am. He won't get another chance long as I'm on duty."

Had she seen Mark in the morning, she'd have reported the incident. As it was, she charted neither her impromptu visits nor the patient's verbal pass. She'd done nothing improper, but neither had she shaken loose any fragments of memory. Not only had her contacts with the captain been psychologically and medically unproductive, she'd been naïve thinking they might be. And saw no need to record this lapse of judgment on an official document.

The next night, she dealt with Armistead brusquely, briefly, coolly. Still, at each bed check, he implored her to stay and talk. "Just for a minute, if I promise to stay in line." His remorse touched her heart but didn't shake her resolve.

Mark's record of his visit earlier that day said only, "Pt. more quiet than previously—not interested in chess or talk or prayer. Seems to have regressed."

At chow on the fifth night, they learned arrival at Pearl would be delayed by a gale along their course. Seas were high, speed reduced. On Armistead's chart, Mark had written only, "Saw pt. for half an hour, claimed he wanted to sleep." And so he appeared on the first bed check when she shone the light into his room. Relieved she didn't have to interact with him, she prayed he'd sleep until morning.

At 0100, however, his bunk looked empty. She came deeper into the room with the flashlight. Sure enough: Not only was he not in it, the covers were tidily pulled up, as if he never had been. She sent Bobby to check the head, but he wasn't there either, nor in any other quiet room. Dread tightened in her, until Bobby suggested the patient might have gone forward to bum coffee on H-11. "Want me to find out?"

Anna said she'd do it. In the hushed quiet, even her rubber-soled steps echoed off the bulkheads. The charge nurse on that ward, an older jaygee who hadn't participated in the kissing mutiny, said she hadn't seen the patient, but asked if Anna had called the Chief Master at Arms to report him missing.

"No, I wanted to be sure he really was. We're still looking."

"Do it now, Donovan," she snapped so sharply, Anna automatically saluted.

The CMAA's response was terse: He'd send a search team, stat; meantime she and the corpsmen were to leave no space unexplored. Before they arrived however, she dispatched Bobby up to Officers' Country to rouse Mark.

"Don't tell him what's happened. Just say he's needed here."

His eyes widened; he saluted and took off at a run.

By the time the chaplain got there, the CMAA's people were slamming lockers so loudly every man in the ward was awake. The sight of Mark, even unshaven and in rumpled khakis, was oil on the troubled waters of her nerves. The effect, however, lasted only until she told him about the missing patient.

He blanched. "God, Anna. Where could he be?"

"Well, he's nowhere on H Deck. Don't know where else they've looked."

"Bridge been notified?"

"Why the bridge?"

"Because it could be a man overboard."

"Oh no. I didn't think of that."

He nodded, glancing around as if seeking clues others had missed. "Likely the CMAA's alerted them already. You know the drill, don't you?"

"I think so. Don't they blow the whistle a lot and put boats over and steam in circles? But they can't do that at night, can they? And in seas like this, God, they could run him down."

He stood regarding her with a look that mirrored her own chaotic mix of fear and frustration. "Glad I don't have to decide what to do."

"Overboard, though. You really think he'd have done something like that?"

"Hard to tell. This afternoon, he said he appreciated my help, but we weren't getting anywhere. Said you didn't want to talk to him either, because he'd gotten out of line."

"Oh, not seriously. He just asked too many personal questions."

He glanced toward the CMAA's scurrying team. "Think I'll look around his room. In case he left a note."

When he came back, the *Leatherneck* was folded under his arm. "No note, but I did find that copybook I gave him. I'll take it back to my cabin and see what he wrote."

By 0700, there was still no sign of Captain Armistead. Bobby McWherter reported that the entire ship had been searched twice, with particular attention to lifeboats, a prime refuge of goldbrickers since the age of galley slaves.

After they handed over the ward to the next shift, the CMAA came to escort her and the duty corpsmen to the Exec's office. "He's holding an inquiry to determine what happened."

"I know the way, Chief."

"Just a formality, ma'am."

But when they left the elevator at C, she concluded his real aim was to keep her and Bobby from talking to the unofficially curious. To judge by the glances along the way, their number was legion.

Commander Scott was a remote figure; his cool aloofness stemmed, it was rumored, from having lost two sons in combat. If he had, there was nothing in his Spartan office to hint at such family ties, at least no framed photographs.

Beginning with Anna, he interviewed each separately. She answered as fully as possible (What time did you last see the patient? Was he awake? What was his mood?) but volunteered nothing. She was relieved he didn't ask if they'd had any personal contact, though Bobby McWherter might innocently reveal that they had.

The commander's last question wrapped up all the others. "Miss Donovan, do you have any reason to suspect Captain Armistead might have deliberately gone overboard?"

She weighed her answer a moment. "Well, he was troubled by the memory loss. But he didn't seem suicidal. Of course, I'm no expert."

"But you've stood NP duty often enough to have some idea."

"I've had patients who seemed hopeless, yes, but this man was nothing like them."

He cautioned her not to discuss the matter with anyone and dismissed her. By then, it was nearly 0800. Mark didn't answer her knock at his cabin, nor was he in his office, so she went to chow. Every nurse at the table pounced, wanting the "real dope" about the incident. With a locking gesture over her lips, she said she couldn't discuss it. Nonetheless, each expected her to confirm some rumor or other. So while she ate, she kept shrugging and apologizing, and glancing around for Mark. She was almost finished before he came in and proceeded to an empty table.

Despite an urgency that tempted her to sprint, she ambled over. When she described the Exec's questions, he said, "Yeah, talked to me too. He's talking to everybody who ever charted anything about the man."

"What did you tell them?"

"Not much. Just explained my notes. When he asked if I thought the patient might have deliberately gone overboard, I said there was no reason to think so."

"So did I. But what about the notebook? Anything in it that might help?"

His nod was slow and serious. "Sorry to say, I think he knew what he was doing."

Her mouth gaped; she covered it with one hand. "You mean…?"

"Yeah. He didn't just go for a stroll and lose his footing. But that's what I told the Exec. I never mentioned the notebook, and he didn't either."

"Why didn't you?"

"None of their damned business."

She studied his face as anger tightened his jaw. "I don't

understand."

"Look, Anna, if they told his family, that's all they'd remember, no matter how fine a record he had. Anyway, he wrote some other stuff I don't want anyone else to read. So it's just between us. You'll understand after you read it. I mean, if you want to."

"Why wouldn't I?"

He stared, as if debating his answer. "It's disturbing. And I don't want to keep it around."

She waited as he disposed of a mass of watery scrambled eggs and a grease-oozing sausage. Compared to his previous demeanor, he seemed sure of himself, determined in a cause, like the day he'd protested the Marines on board. Admiring him in spite of herself, she felt the warm edges of desire crowd her mental processes. She hated that, that even preoccupied with a life or death matter, she wanted him.

God, could she be another Patty after all?

Oblivious to the shift in her mood, he swiped the last toast crust across his plate and regarded her as if he'd forgotten she was there. "Sorry. Guess I'm not with you. Trying to figure out what to write his parents."

She winced. "Well, at least you know what not to tell them."

CHAPTER FIFTEEN

They docked at Pearl the next morning about ten. Liberty wouldn't start until 1200, so, yawning in the glittering sunlight, Anna leaned on C Deck railing and watched the slow parade of wheelchairs and crutches down the gangway. Last, the NP patients shuffled ashore in robes and slippers. Their listless gait reminded her of a line of shackled prisoners.

She didn't hear Mark approach until he appeared beside her.

"Well, there they go," she sighed. "All but our Marine."

"One besides him too. Died on H-11 last night. Saved every sleeping pill he ever got, and took them all at once. But nobody's supposed to know that."

"Of course not. It'd undermine morale if people knew some men would rather die than go on fighting."

He shook his head in a slow, sad way. "Another ugly little story to make us doubt our cause."

"God," she said. "No matter how much we do...."

"What?"

"Nothing changes, does it?"

"Not that I can tell."

As the last patients filed aboard the gray buses on the pier, a distant siren rose and fell once, signaling noon. Simultaneously, speakers all over the ship announced liberty. Mark wound his watch and reset it.

"Want to go ashore? Have lunch at the club and read the notebook?"

The night's adrenaline drain had left her with serious fatigue, but his suggestion revived her like a whiff of pure oxygen. "If you think I should."

"Here, then. Put it in your purse." He handed it over, still wrapped in the *Leatherneck*. "I'll deep-six it into the wake when we're underway again."

Stuffing it into the bag, she followed him down the gangway. On the pier a line of sailors and nurses extended back from the base bus stop. She hadn't seen Luke all morning, but the back of her neck prickled, as if he was spying from a porthole on B Deck. Or maybe one of his minions was peering down from Nurses' Country. She hated seeing him in the same dark light as she did the mean-spirited Down Easters who'd maligned Jean as she lay dying. Who, unable to forgive her alliance with the German sailor, had neglected her even in the hospital. Instead, she wanted to love Luke for being Lorraine's son, but it was hard to charitably bear his judgments of Mark, however deserved. Maybe one day, life would slap it out of him.

At the Navy Exchange, she stocked up on Pond's Cold Cream, Drene shampoo, Lux soap, Mum deodorant, Ipana, Kotex and a new red lipstick. She was waiting for Mark outside when an arriving bus disgorged more nurses, including Willi with Floyd in tow. They asked her to join them for lunch in the cafeteria, but before she could invent a credible excuse, Mark showed up and they hustled aboard.

"Think they're spying for Luke?" she asked as a sudden ugly notion gripped her.

"Not them. But plenty of others know we're running around together."

"When he told me you'd been away with a woman, I said, 'Let him who is without sin cast the first stone'."

"But he is without that particular sin. Too bad sodomy's not one of the Big Ten."

She twisted her face into an expression of disgust. "Oh Mark, that's terrible."

He shrugged. "Maybe. But true."

"Gosh, I hope Lorraine never finds out."

"Why? Isn't it enough she's found her son? Does he have to be perfect too?"

She pondered the question until the bus sighed to a stop at the manicured O Club entrance. Inside the air-cooled dimness, they followed the blare of the juke box to a rear bar with a view of the harbor and Ford Island. The contrast between the sun-filled windows and the interior was momentarily blinding, but she could tell the place was crowded. Mark suggested she wait on the lanai while he went for drinks.

Outside, a water-smelling breeze sifted through a manicured border of neon-bright tropical plants. She found a table away from the crowd, and sat where she could watch the door before she surreptitiously withdrew the notebook. It was the kind you could buy at Woolworth's, with a black and white marbled cover and blue-lined pages. Exactly like one she was using as a journal. And an earlier one in which she'd practiced cursive writing in third grade.

Mark came out trailed by a waiter with drinks and hamburgers on a tray. When he'd set them down, Anna inhaled the aroma of grilled meat and fried onion. "Oh. Just like Kailua."

His grin was wicked. "Except we can eat these while they're hot."

She averted her gaze primly, told him she couldn't wait to read the book, and lifted the sandwich to her mouth. At first, the taste was of rare beef, tomato, relish, onion. Then something sweet made her lift the top.

"Oh No. Pineapple? Whoever heard of pineapple on a hamburger?"

He laughed. "It's standard here. Didn't you notice at Kailua?"

She studied his face to see if he was kidding. "You mean…?"

He grinned. "You were too besotted to notice."

"No. Just preoccupied by…you know. The thing we forgot."

"I forgot." He mopped her chin with his napkin. The grin faded. "Damn. Now all I can think of is how it was that day."

"Well, all I can think about is this notebook."

He picked up his burger. "Hope it doesn't shock you."

"After eight months with sailors and Marines and doctors, nothing's going to shock me."

After removing the pineapple, she put away the burger in a few fast mouthfuls, wiped her fingers and opened the book. Beyond the shredded spine where Mark had ripped out old pages, the writing was small and precise, hardly the rambling, haphazard penmanship of someone desperately seeking clues to his identity.

Beginning on 4 June, Roger Armistead described fragments of his forgotten years on Guadalcanal; the hospital ship to Auckland and there, a series of surgeries that left him *finally able to shit without the damned bag.* Then, as he was about to be shipped back to the States for discharge, he convinced a medical board he was fit for duty and was sent to Saipan. But after that, the campaigns ran together in his mind, a blur of bloody surf and ruined beaches, bodies, body parts, sniper fire, explosions. Confusion and chaos. He'd also been on Peleliu, and Iwo, which he remembered for the big white mountain. But after the landing on Okinawa, his memory shut down, leaving him to wonder, *What did I do I can't remember?* And conclude, *Must be pretty bad. When people won't tell you anything, it's usually pretty bad.*

In the next entry two days later, he began to ramble, a series of disconnected suspicions that Anna had turned against him, because "The Padre" had told her what he'd done on Okinawa. This act had to be egregious. He'd convinced himself it had probably involved abandoning his men and leaving them helpless under fire. Short of going over to the enemy, abandoning your men was the worst sin in any Marine's book. Previously, however, he'd been sure Anna liked him in a special way, *maybe even enough to get in bed with me one of these nights. Boy, wouldn't I love that!*

The next paragraph was filled with graphic descriptions of what he'd do if she let him.

Stunned by the neatly-penned obscenities, she looked at Mark. "No wonder you didn't want the Exec to see this. He might think I led the guy on."

He gave her a wry grin. "Yeah. A girl who'd kiss fifty Marines in one night might do anything."

She grimaced and read on. Two days later, he'd written the final entry:

Well, that's never going to happen. Because just now she cut me off, like she can't stand to look at me. Like I'm a yellow-belly who betrayed my men, and the Corps and my country. Oh God, if only I could've slept with her just once, I wouldn't hurt like it does. If she hadn't been so nice in the first place, it wouldn't seem so bad now. As it is, I don't want to go on. Wish all this shit was over. But it never will be. That's it. The way I am now, they'll never send me back to combat, just give me a Section 8 discharge. No woman will ever want me now, except whores.

The rest of the page was filled with doodles, indecipherable scratchings and symbols, hieroglyphics of a despair that standard language couldn't express.

But then he began writing again.

Well, maybe I'd better take care of it myself. Do what cowards always do...take the easy way out. They always said it was a sin and you'll end up in Hell, but that's got to be better than the hell I'm in now. I only hope Jesus understands. I hope Jesus forgives me. And the folks back home never find out.

Tears filled her eyes; she made the sign of the cross over her heart. The Marine's final words had been written after her last visit, just before he'd left the bed and ducked up the companionway to the main deck, then made his way aft.

She closed the book and wiped fingertips across her cheek. "Oh, this is so sad. That poor man. If only...."

"What? If only you could've saved him?"

She nodded, took a long swig of the rum and coke, watery now with melting ice.

"Surely you're not thinking if you'd gone to bed with him he wouldn't have done that, are you?"

She drank more, fast. "It's crossed my mind."

Mark rolled his eyes. "Don't be silly. Every deployment we make, some patients lose the will to live. You can't get in bed with all of them."

She leaned back in the chair, glass in hand. "Don't you be silly, Mark. I was just wondering about Roger

Armistead." She drained it, thrust it toward him. "Could I have another, please? I feel like getting drunk."

After he'd gone inside, she reread the journal. And tried to recapture expectations of her conversations with the Marine. Mainly, she'd hoped they'd stimulate flashes of recall, followed by a flood of recollections, restoring his identity and enabling him to resume his life. But apparently nothing had convinced him he'd followed the path of honor, through Guadalcanal, Saipan, Peleliu, and Iwo, all the way to Okinawa.

God, how much honor, how much heroism did he demand of himself? And at what cost?

Mark came back with fresh drinks, slid hers across the table. "Okay, then, let's get drunk." He shrugged. "Not much else to do when something like this happens on your watch."

She took a copious swallow. Evidently unstirred, the rum on top was eye-opening. "Poor guy. He was damaged so much worse than we realized."

"Actually," Mark said, "those things he wrote about you, they weren't so abnormal. Plenty of guys fantasize about nurses. I've heard a few confessions."

Shaking her head, she stared out toward a yard oiler creeping along in the channel. A haphazard little tug pushing a barge that refueled ships in the harbor. Another of the small, unnoticeable pieces of the war. Like the equivalent human detritus, the victims of battle fatigue.

Mark withdrew his hand, shifted his gaze from her. "You know, I think I understand what he must've gone through. It's bad enough for us. Dealing with casualties over and over and over, and not knowing when it'll ever end. Not even knowing where the hell we are, half the time. Or where the fighting is." He shook his head, drank down an inch.

She nodded. "Even on that big plot board in the

pilothouse, you can't tell what's happening. We're just out here somewhere, doing what they tell us to. Without knowing where we fit into the big picture. And the casualties, well, we see them for a few days, and then they're gone, and we never know what becomes of them."

"That's it. We're stuck in the middle of a story without a beginning or end. Reading the same pages over and over. And never getting anywhere. Cut off from our families and our friends, with nothing but each other to hang on to. And that poor bastard didn't even have that. Just this big question about what he did on Oki. No wonder he lusted for you. You must've been his last hope."

His last hope. More unwelcome tears. Then quickly, more rum and coke.

"Don't feel bad, Anna. Even if you'd let him have his way with you, it wouldn't have changed anything. That guy needed more than a roll in the hay."

"I know." She sighed and finished the drink. "Too bad Luke didn't talk to him. He has all the answers. At least the big one; it's all a matter of faith. I mean, the true faith. His faith."

Mark's expression went sour. "For him, church dogma's a suit of armor."

Regarding her empty glass, she wondered what would happen if she had a third drink. Sure, it might wipe out speculations about the dead Marine, but probably also render her unable to climb the gangway. When she pictured herself being carried aboard, limp in the arms of one of the CMAA's men, she pushed the glass away and got to her feet. To her relief the room did not begin to whirl, and she could still walk.

"That's it," she said. "Let's go. I'm drunk enough."

Mark laughed, following as she picked her way back inside, then out the main door into dazzling late afternoon sunlight. They had to wait five minutes, but when the base bus arrived, the first off was OH, followed by her second in charge, Young Horseface, then Gladys, and the Exec, and finally, respectfully deferring to those who outranked him, Luke brought up the rear. They headed inside, probably for a few hands of bridge. Everyone saluted in passing, so fast, so automatic she didn't notice whether his look on her was jaundiced or not.

"Speak of the devil," she whispered when she'd collapsed into the bus.

"Good they didn't get there earlier when you were reading the notebook. Might've started them wondering if we were doing more than enjoying each other's company. Bad enough we do that."

When they arrived at the auxiliary pier, Mark herded her toward *Compassion*'s gangway behind two staggering sailors. She hoped that in contrast she'd seem only sad to anyone who might be spying. Surely they'd understand; after all, the Marine had gone missing during her shift. Surely any nurse would react with such regret and sorrow.

She marched directly up to her cabin, kicked off her shoes and dropped on the bunk as the narrow space began to whirl. She'd intended to read the notebook again, but when she closed her eyes, a fretful sleep soon bore her to a less complicated region of her soul.

CHAPTER SIXTEEN

At chow that evening, with every nurse at the table gabbing about shore-side minutiae, Anna had no chance to hear Mark's plan for the notebook. Then, as soon as dessert was served, the Exec took over the lectern and rapped for attention. Her skin began to crawl in anticipation of some troubling new announcement, perhaps about another shipload of Marines below decks. Or the public deportment of one junior nurse and an infidel chaplain.

Instead he talked about Armistead's disappearance. "Now, I know there's been speculation," he said in his papery, old man's voice. "But from interviews with staff and Chaplain Whitmore, I've concluded he wasn't able to sleep, and took a turn around the deck. But it was rough that night, and he hadn't been aboard long enough to get his sea legs. So he lost his balance. Or slipped on the wet deck and went over the rail. Ironic, considering the hazards he'd faced in combat." He shook his head, face more ashen and lined than usual.

"Of course, we can't lock our NP patients in. But from now on, we can't let them go topside. In this case, the chaplain was being charitable when he gave him a tour of the ship. But if he hadn't, the man might not have known his way around. And tonight he'd be in the base hospital instead of…" He gestured broadly, "…out there in a watery grave."

Someone sniffled at a nearby table. Anna clutched her fingers in her lap.

Before the tides of pathos rose higher, Commander Scott turned the meeting over to the Chief Medical Officer. Anna tensed further and glanced down the table at Mark with a *Now what?* look. His face betrayed nothing except rapt attention.

"Ladies and gentlemen," Dr. Tomlin began, "when we get back to Guam, we're going to offer anyone who's interested a chance to transfer to the hospital there for a while. See, our next deployment's Ulithi, an atoll about 350 miles southwest of there. Maybe you never heard of it, but it has a deep-water lagoon large enough for the entire fleet to anchor." He withdrew a pack of Camels from his shirt pocket and carefully lit one. "Now. With the Okinawa campaign winding down, we'll stand by as fleet hospital there for the next six weeks. And we won't have enough patients to keep all of you busy, hence the offer of TAD. So think it over. Guam's good duty, with four-section liberty. You can sign up any time before we arrive."

Audrey hurried over after they were dismissed. "How about it, Anna? Want to try working ashore for a while?"

"Don't know. Have to think about it."

"Think about it?" Willi chimed in. "You mean, find out where Mark's going?"

"Don't be silly," she said, as if that wasn't her exact intention. Before Audrey could comment, she hurried out to the deck as they got underway. The whistle blasted, pier lights receded and a tug nudged the ship toward the channel. The routine rarely varied, yet she felt the usual surge of exhilaration. And made up her mind that no matter what Mark did, she wanted to experience every situation shipboard duty afforded. Including the Ulithi deployment.

When they'd cleared the harbor mouth, she took the magazine with the notebook still inside to his cabin. The compartment was dark, but she could make out his form on the bunk. "Anytime you're ready, we can…you know…deep six this stuff."

He got to his feet, switched on the desk lamp. This close, he smelled stale, in need of a shower. Like the morning at Kailua. "Later. After taps. Meanwhile, why don't you lie here with me? Like we did that first night, only without what happened later."

The idea had such appeal she knew it would undo her in only a few heartbeats. "Thanks, but I'll be better off in my own bunk." She thrust the magazine at him. "Here. I'll meet you in the wardroom after taps."

As she pulled the hatch closed, he sighed, "Oh, Anna."

With purposeful steps, as if on official business, she walked to the ladder down to C deck and forward to her cabin. But even there, she was still with him, racked with wanting so intense no spiritual homily could touch it. Finally she found Jim's most recent letter and focused on memories of lovemaking with him. The problem was, they'd become as faded and monochromatic as his picture taped to the bulkhead, whereas those of Mark were still technicolor brilliant, still pulsing in her body.

Then she remembered what he'd said that afternoon, about having only each other to hang on to. "Poor bastard," he'd said of Armistead. "He didn't even have that." They at least had each other, she and Mark and Audrey and Willi and Floyd and all those who worked on this ship; islands of refuge in the relentless monotony of duty. Her refuge with

Mark was often spiritual but just as often sexual; with the others it was the continuity of duties, shared attitudes about people like OH, and common recollections of these months together. Armistead hadn't had those either.

The year before, when Jean Cropper had died, she and Jim had tried to ascertain at what point they might have intervened in her fate and changed the ending. But however they re-wove the facts, in the end they had to acknowledge that some situations have the pall of doom about them from the outset. Some are irreversible even with the best intentions.

And that, she concluded now, had been the irony of Captain Armistead. That for as often as he'd eluded death on the battlefield; it had found him anyway in the safety of a hospital ship's belly, surrounded by people who were trying to help. But hadn't realized for him, there was no earthly help.

* * *

At eleven, she combed her hair, swiped on fresh lipstick and met Mark in the wardroom. Proceeding aft, they descended ladders to H Deck. The ward had been cleaned and disinfected, was hushed and dark except for emergency bulbs in their tiny cages. First they went to the quiet room that had been Armistead's, sat on the bed and read his entries again. For her, they were no less painful than they'd been at first reading. Then, retracing the route Mark had used when he'd given the tour, they climbed ladders to the fantail and emerged into the night.

At the stern, a light glowed above the Stars and Stripes whipping in the breeze. The deck was littered with coiled lines, chains, canisters and unrecognizable pieces of equipment, the light so dim someone who didn't know the area might trip, especially on a stormy night. This sea was slick, the swells shallow; still, someone unfamiliar with the ship's routine lurches and shifts might be unbalanced.

From the flagstaff amidships, the wake five decks below was a maelstrom behind the flared stern. Salt tang prickled Anna's nostrils, though the air flowing over the vessel also brought the pungency of cigarette smoke and stale coffee, and the omnipresent oily, metallic fumes of overheated machinery. Easy on such a night to picture other dramas played out here when this had been the P&O liner *SS Maui*; couples clinging, kissing, stirring up passion, then racing to their staterooms to indulge it. The contrast with what had happened to Roger Armistead was chilling.

"Want to say anything before we drop it?" Mark asked.

She could have used a thousand words, but said instead, "Well, only... I'm sorry we couldn't help him."

"Same here," he muttered hoarsely. "Lord knows, I regret that."

Without further ceremony, he tucked the magazine around the notebook, leaned over the rail and let it go. They stared down for the fragment of a second it tumbled into the boiling prop wash and was sucked out of sight.

Anna said, "I feel like singing *Eternal Father*."

As they mouthed the words, she thought first of Commander Stark at Jean's funeral, then of the memorial service she'd planned but never held for Dan. His memory had receded, yet this night they were connected by the same ocean, and the death of another man whose physical remains would be assimilated by the same primitive elements. She wished she could speak her heart to Mark, but sensed he was subsumed in his own mysteries, too personal and private to share.

After a few minutes, he looked up from the sea, turned from the rail and held out his arms. "Now. Can I hold you awhile? Or is that too much to ask?"

She shook her head and came into his familiar embrace.

At first, his lips were on her cheek. Until she turned so they connected. For a moment longer, she was strong and self-assured, but then fatigue and the experience they'd shared combined to make her kiss an invitation to more primitive sharing.

He slipped one arm around her as they proceeded toward the bright portholes, the spot-lit red crosses, the activity of those who conned the ship. They were well forward when she remembered to ask if he'd decided to sign on for TAD at the Guam hospital.

"No. I already know Guam. On the other hand, Ulithi sounds like an exotic tropical island I might never see otherwise."

"Oh, good. I was hoping you'd go."

He squeezed her hand as they climbed the last two ladders to B Deck.

By then it was nearly midnight. The ship had a buttoned-up feeling, the long passageway to his cabin quiet, other men tucked into their bunks, sleeping or engaged in some sort of sexual activity, reading, writing letters, or whatever else they did in the privacy of their staterooms.

She could not have said what they were about, but she knew full well what Mark had on his mind. As did she. After all they had only each other for comfort. Especially tonight.

CHAPTER SEVENTEEN

On Sunday, 17 June, *Compassion* anchored in Apra Harbor only long enough to disembark those leaving for the fleet hospital—sixteen nurses, both Red Cross girls, five surgeons and thirty-some corpsmen. And Luke, of course. Of the junior nurses, only Willi and Anna remained aboard; even OH had chosen the luxuries of life ashore. In her place, they got Young Horseface.

Lieutenant Commander Ethel Durrand was a hatchet-faced spinster with all of OH's worst qualities plus some of her own. OH had a certain Savannah charm; her mint-julep accent softened even harsh orders. YH, on the other hand, hailed from Detroit and took pride in a blunt, no-nonsense manner. With no other ensigns to notice, Willi and Anna figured she'd be on their case at every provocation.

Waving as the packed launch churned away from the ship, Anna was nibbled by a hunch that this six-week hiatus could well eventuate into a permanent separation. From personal experience, she knew human intentions counted for little in this gigantic scattered conflict. Floyd had just illustrated that premise with an account of *Missisinewa*, a fleet oiler sunk by a Jap suicide sub in Ulithi's supposedly-secure lagoon.

Willi watched the captain's gig approach the landing platform before she turned with a faint frown. "Gee, Anna. Maybe this was a bad idea after all. I mean, staying aboard when we're the lowest nurses on the totem pole."

"Well, then, we'll let them catch us doing something awful, so they'll throw us in the brig and we won't have to work."

Her dark eyes twinkled. "Awful? Like what? Sleeping with the dentist? Or the chaplain?"

Anna laughed in spite of herself. Below, the arriving officers stepped up the embarkation ladder in order of rank; the CO first, then the Exec, finally the CMO, all three stiffly resplendent in Dress Whites.

"Look at those stuffed shirts," she murmured. "Do you think any of them are sleeping with anyone?"

"Floyd says Commander Scott and YH do."

Dubious, Anna said, "I bet not. She looks like a woman who's never had any."

Willi giggled. "Reckon anyone ever thinks that about us?"

The question was discomfiting, perhaps because it resonated with those Anna dared not ask herself. When she didn't answer, Willi changed the subject, as if it had been academic anyway.

* * *

That evening, the wardroom had a quiet, cozy ambiance. With half the medical staff absent, the rest clustered in self-conscious new camaraderie, mingling even with those they'd previously ignored. Like shipwreck survivors in a nearly-empty lifeboat.

When he came in, Floyd made straight for Willi, Anna and Mark. He was disheveled, as if he'd been blown in by a Force 10 gale. Patting down the corkscrew growth of an old crew cut, he took a chair across from Mark. "Say. Any of you know anything about this place we're going?"

Willi slid platters of ham sandwiches and potato salad toward him. When the steward brought iced tea, Floyd asked if the cook could make him a grilled cheese instead. Until then Anna had no inkling he kept Kosher.

"Only that it's a fleet staging area," Mark said. "Why? What do you know?"

Anna cringed in anticipation of one of Floyd's encyclopedic avalanches.

"Well, it's an atoll like Kwajalein, with this huge natural harbor. Used to be Jap territory, but they pulled out last year and we took over. Actually, it's a string of little marshy islands, but the Seabees have turned it into a tropical paradise. With a hospital and a theater and a desalinization facility and a sewage treatment plant, and a big chapel. And oh yes, a fleet recreation area. The men'll love that. A place they can drink their beer ration. Big deal, two cans a week."

"I meant, what're they going to do with us?" Mark asked.

Floyd fluttered his long bony fingers. "I'll be working on the teeth of every man on every ship out there. Guess you'll just have to keep on saving souls, padre."

"God, Einhorn," Mark laughed. "Sometimes you tempt me to blaspheme."

After chow, they wandered into the lounge to watch another of the worst movies Hollywood had ever made. No one, not even Floyd, had ever heard of it. The prevailing theory was that the brightest and best films went to the carriers, cruisers and battlewagons, leaving Service Force auxiliaries with these dogs. Their only redeeming feature was that they were easy to parody, easy to poke fun at. And doubly easy to forget.

In the darkness of this one, she let Mark hold her hand. When it ended, he leaned toward her and asked if he'd see her later.

Annoyed by his assumption she was ready to hop into bed again, she snapped, "Told you I'm going to write letters."

"To Jim?"

"Probably. That might be something you should try. Writing to your wife, I mean."

He winced, then shook his head and sighed, "Oh, Anna," as he walked away.

* * *

In the morning, medical staff met with the CMO to learn details of the Ulithi mission.

"Even with Okinawa close to being secured, there's still plenty of Kamikaze action between here and there," he explained, "so the repair ships are working overtime. Some of the damaged ships still have wounded aboard. Last month it was a carrier with a hundred sixty-seven casualties, including one of their medical officers. We'll take the worst cases for long-term care, and there's a hundred-bed hospital on the island for backup. I expect it'll be light duty, and we'll all have time ashore. Can't compare with Pearl or Guam, but it's still R and R."

He'd just dismissed them when a radioman hurried in, message in hand. Sensing a new crisis, Anna watched him read. The frown was a tip-off that he'd call them back. They settled into their still-warm chairs again.

"Well," he said with a grave air. "Maybe it won't be R and R after all. This is from an AE en route from Pearl. Half her crew's down with dysentery, so she needs medical assistance. ETA at Ulithi is 1600 today." He glanced at his watch. "By then, I want a team ready to assess the situation. Meanwhile, who can give us the skinny about dysentery, as opposed to common diarrhea?"

The first hand raised was Bobby McWherter's. "Sir, I don't know anything about dysentery, but what's an AE?"

Everyone smiled, even the CMO. "Ammunition ship. Bound from Pearl fully loaded. In Navy lingo, Flying Baker. The red signal flag. Not a ship we want sailing around with half her crew out of action. Now, let's get back to dysentery."

Floyd's hand shot up. "It's not a dental condition, but there was an outbreak at the hospital where I interned." His preamble led him into a dissertation on the most common form, caused by the *Shigella* bacillus from contaminated food. In crowded living conditions, it could rapidly escalate into an epidemic. His description of symptoms, high fever, abdominal pain, bloody diarrhea, weight loss and dehydration, was so colorfully graphic even some doctors groaned.

"And how is it treated, Doctor Einhorn?"

Anna suspected he was patronizing the dentist, but Floyd handled every question with aplomb, including, "How do you recommend controlling it on the AE?"

"Well, first you determine the source of contamination. Like the water supply, or food handlers. Meanwhile, you treat victims with replacement fluids and electrolytes, usually per ora, but IV in severe cases, with an antibiotic. With supportive therapy, it resolves in about a week. Main thing's to keep it from spreading."

Commander Tomlin stroked his jaw and got out his cigarettes. After he lit up, he was quiet a moment. Anna held her breath, waiting for the next test. But he said only, "With your experience, Floyd, we need you on that team. That is, if we can pry you out of your dental chair."

"Happy to help, Commander. But would you want somebody who'd been handling stool samples working in your mouth?"

The other man actually laughed for the first time in Anna's memory. "Good point, doctor. Well, at least we can consult with you."

When he dismissed them, Bobby McWherter was waiting in the passageway. He greeted Anna brightly, like a special friend. Or someone with a shared secret.

"Hi, Miss Donovan. Just wanted you to know, I got the orders I put in for. To a cruiser, one of the big ones. Chief Pettingill in the pharmacy, he served on her once. Says she's the best damned ship in the fleet. In the old days, she took President Roosevelt on cruises. Then she helped blast the Japs out of those islands off Alaska. And a couple months ago, she took a bomb from a suicide plane. Went right through her, top to bottom, but she made it back to California on her own. I'll be joining her when we get back to Guam."

"Oh my. That sounds exciting. But I didn't know you wanted to leave us."

"Oh, don't get me wrong. I love this duty. But a capital ship, that's something else. I reckon the way things are going, the war'll be over pretty soon and I might not get a chance to go in harm's way, like they say." His eyes sparkled. "But something else I wanted to tell you. About that Marine that went missing?" He edged closer, lowered his voice. "I never told the brass about you and him. I mean, how he got fresh with you. And always wanted to talk to you. I seen you didn't chart it, so I reckoned it wasn't none of their business. Especially since they decided it was an accident."

"Thanks, Bobby. I felt that way too."

"Anyway, ma'am, maybe we'll work together again before I leave. Except it don't sound like we'll be getting any nut jobs here."

Later, she reported this conversation to Mark as they observed their half-speed entrance into the vast sheltered sea enclosed by Ulithi atoll. If she hadn't known it was a major Navy outpost, she'd have seen only a pretty blue lagoon surrounded by a necklace of islands so tiny they were barely visible above the jade-green shallows. An incongruously exotic setting for the somber gray and camouflaged vessels swinging at anchor in the cobalt deeps beyond. Widely spaced for safety, this armada comprised a carrier, battleship, two cruisers and a number of destroyers, LSTs, oilers, repair ships, reefers and other auxiliaries. Serving as water taxis between them and shore, Higgins boats and LCIs spewed wakes like chalk lines on blue taffeta.

As usual, Floyd identified them all by category. Including the toxic ammo ship, anchored far enough from the others to be conspicuous.

As he talked, Anna scanned the tropical shoreline with binoculars, observing clusters of Quonset huts, a tank farm, palm-thatched huts along the water, trucks and Jeeps on roads between. And soaring up from a runway extending into the water, a two-engine R4D transport roared above them. Higher and louder than the Kamikaze, it still ignited a flare of memory.

Floyd waved one arm toward the scene. "Seabees built all that just since we occupied it last fall. Got rid of the mosquitoes but couldn't improve the climate."

As if on cue, some fluffy pastel clouds slowly congealed into a large dark umbrella. When the heavens opened up, the rest of the world disappeared behind a silver curtain. The air turned cool and sweet. Anna had been about to say the weather wasn't that bad, when the deluge stopped as if someone had turned off a faucet. The sun emerged, hotter than ever as steam misted up from the water.

At chow time, the wardroom wasn't much cooler, but huge fans stirred up an artificial breeze. As they ate, she began to feel displaced, with no clear sense of her new duties. If this was R and R, it seemed reasonable to expect a peaceful hiatus between eight months on line and the biggest invasion of all. She wanted to enjoy the placid present, but an old calm-before-the-storm sense warned her to stay on guard for the next suicidal patient, the next potential catastrophe, the next lapse in her own sanity. As if there was nothing to count on but uncertainty.

She was about to retire to her cabin and commit this formless anxiety to her journal, when YH banged a spoon on her iced tea glass and said she wanted to meet with the nurses, stat. Willi shot Anna a look that said, See, told you she'd start throwing her weight around.

In the lounge, however, YH stood silhouetted against the sun-filled portholes while everyone took seats. Then, smiling, she said. "Now ladies, this isn't an order, but with the heat like it is here, I think we can all dispense with the white hose. And the garter belts and girdles."

Anna glanced sidelong at Willi's skeptical expression.

"Unless you'd rather keep them on. But the less we have to wear, the better. Of course, this means keeping your legs shaved and your skirt over your knees. And if some visiting brass holds an inspection, well, we'll have to be in full uniform. But for now, we need to be comfortable. Any questions?"

Pleasantly stunned, Anna wondered why she'd given permission to flout the uniform code even slightly. What next, red fingernails?

On the way out, Willi had a possible explanation: "Floyd saw her coming out of the Exec's cabin this morning. So you know damned well what they did last night."

"Hope it lasts," she said, remembering Mark's comment

that the Marine had needed more than a roll in the hay. All of them did. But when that was all they had, a roll in the hay was better than nothing, wasn't it?

* * *

A few nights later, she took Bobby along on bed check in the burn ward. She'd met the officers in quiet rooms on a previous shift, but still scalded by recollections of Armistead, wanted to avoid further incidents. These men, however, were so heavily sedated they barely knew she was a woman. Nor were any alert enough to talk except when necessary. And even if they'd wanted to go overboard, none could have managed without assistance.

Drinking coffee between bed checks, she asked Bobby to tell her about his postwar plans. It was the sort of conversation officers weren't supposed to have with enlisted men, but she didn't know one, except maybe the Horseface girls, who hadn't.

"Guess I'll keep working in medicine," he came back. "Not a doctor; my family don't have the money to send me to college. But if I start making my ratings, I'll go for twenty."

"How does your girl feel about that?"

His grin was disarmingly dimpled. "She wants what I do. Ever show you her picture?"

Anna said not, whereupon he produced a dog-eared, tinted shot of a red-lipped, rosy-cheeked, green-eyed girl with flowing auburn curls.

"Very pretty," she said. "And I bet she's Irish too."

He smiled at it, tucked it back in his dungaree shirt pocket. "You're Irish, yourself, aren't you? I mean, with a name like Donovan?"

"No, that was my husband's surname. My maiden name was Moss."

His gaze focused more intently on hers. "Oh, you were married?"

She nodded, and gave the standard synopsis of the Dan years. "It's been two years since he was lost. Now I'm engaged to a doctor in Maine."

"Yeah, I heard that." A sudden blush flooded his freckled face. "I mean…well… maybe you don't know, but the men, the other corpsmen, I mean, they talk about the nurses. Not gossiping, I mean, just interested." The blush deepened to maroon. "Especially the lookers like yourself." He leaned forward to pour more coffee.

"Thanks. That means a lot coming from someone with a sweetheart as pretty as yours."

"Don't mention it." He belted the steaming coffee, glanced at his watch and excused himself to hustle down the ward toward another corpsman filing lab chits. She was relieved he'd left; his next question might have been, "If you're engaged, why do you run around with Chaplain Whitmore?" Since corpsmen were apparently discussing her, that issue could have surfaced. The Kissing Mutiny too could have augmented the image of her as loose, perhaps available. Maybe even Bobby questioned her behavior with Captain Armistead.

Another of her mother's favorite admonitions was, "One must avoid evil and the appearance of evil." Perhaps she'd avoided neither. And here she was, late at night, in a tete-a-tete with a corpsman who, in spite of his guileless persona, might well report her friendliness.

Hell, she thought; there were no answers to life's riddles these days.

Then she asked herself, When had there been?

CHAPTER EIGHTEEN

Late on the afternoon of 26 July, *Compassion* steamed past the breakwater at Apra Harbor and glided toward the Navy piers past a score of smaller vessels at anchor. When they'd tied up, Anna looked for the TAD people to welcome them. Instead there were only the usual line handlers, base officers and ambulance drivers waiting.

At the rail beside her, Mark said, "Huh, that's strange. Thought sure Luke'd be here to find out how many commandments we broke at Ulithi."

Her lips tightened and she said nothing.

"Oh, well. He'll probably start giving us hell soon enough."

"Anyway," she said vacuously, "it'll be nice to see everyone again."

"You going ashore when they announce liberty?"

"Yep. I wrote so many letters at Ulithi, I'm out of stationery. What about you?"

He nodded. "Thought I'd look in on some friends at the hospital. See if they've heard anything about him lately."

"Who, Luke? Why? What do you think he's been doing?"

He shrugged. "You never know. Just thought if he decides to accuse us of anything, it'd be good to have something to throw back at him."

"Oh, Mark, that's so pointless. All it'll do is stir up bad blood."

Sighing, he watched a gray Jeep bouncing along the pier.

"So let it alone, okay?"

"For now. But if he gives us any static, I'm going to dig up everything I can on the guy. Don't want him making trouble."

"Listen, if we get in trouble, it'll be our own doing."

He shook his head, but said only, "Oh Anna."

* * *

The next morning after breakfast, the returning personnel filed up the gangway without fanfare. All except Luke. Later, when Audrey glanced into her cabin, Anna asked about him.

"Not sure where he is. He got special leave to work with civilian priests, so we hardly ever saw him. Anyway, how was Ulithi?" Her tone was so off-hand, Anna assumed she wasn't interested in chapter and verse.

"Pretty. But hotter than hell. How was it here?"

She shrugged. "When you're working, one hospital's the same as any other. Except nobody got seasick. Kind of missed it. And the patients were mostly convalescents. Well, anyway, I gotta unpack. Catch up later, okay"

Chow at noon was a welcome-back feast the likes of which they hadn't seen in months. With supply ships in and out of the lagoon, they'd eaten well at Ulithi, but this was beyond compare; lamb chops with mint jelly, twice-baked potatoes, tomato aspic and Parker House rolls fresh from the galley oven. Afterward, OH gave a speech about how she'd never had such swell chow, even before the war. "I doubt they eat this good even on the big new AHs. One of them put in here last week. Patient capacity eight hundred. And totally air-conditioned. The times, they really are a-changing. Meantime, Kamikazes are still terrorizing the fleet and the Japs are all but licked, and don't have the sense to know it, so we've got plenty of work ahead."

Then YH droned on for twenty minutes about how everyone at Ulithi performed like champs in spite of intense heat and the constant menace of Jap air attacks. She made it sound so hazardous, Anna could hardly believe she was talking about them.

Next Commander Tomlin described their mission, with heavy emphasis on the dysentery epidemic. He also recited impressive overall totals; casualties treated, returned to duty or transported back to Guam for further care, even the number of dental patients.

In spite of endless cups of coffee, heads began to nod. Mark kept glancing at the clock; he'd invited Anna along again when he distributed donations around the island. It was after three, however, by the time the brass had finished their monotonous reports. The only item that held her attention was the skipper's promise of a picnic the next afternoon.

Later, as she and Mark started down the gangway, Bobby McWherter and another sailor caught up with them. In starched whites, sea bags over their shoulders, they headed toward a jitney on the pier.

"Are you joining your new ship now?" she called after them.

Bobby turned and saluted. "Right, Miss Donovan. She tied up an hour ago."

"Well, we're going to miss you. Come back and see us

sometime."

"Sure thing. And I'll send you a postcard from Tacloban. That's where we're headed tomorrow."

"Tacloban? Where's that?"

"Leyte. Scuttlebutt is we won't be there long, though. Sailing with a task force for the next invasion. Anyway, nice working with you, Miss Donovan. You too, chaplain."

Snapping a last crisp salute, he and the Yeoman Second boarded the gray jitney with a stenciled cardboard sign in the windshield: USS INDIANAPOLIS CA-35.

"Good luck, Bobby." she called as they ducked into the little bus. It made a flatulent sound as it pulled away. "Gosh," she said to Mark, "I almost told him God Bless You. But I didn't know how he'd take it."

"You should have anyway. No sailor in his right mind's going to object when his favorite nurse blesses him."

"I'll do it later then, in my prayers."

* * *

From her cabin the next morning, she watched an outbound warship glide past—long and low, sailors manning the rails. Hoping to catch her name, Anna hurried out to the deck and read the letters on the stern. Sure enough; Bobby's cruiser. She waved, but by then the ship was well into the anchorage, moving smartly seaward, signal flags fluttering, a purposeful haze wafting from her stack. Anna watched until she'd cleared the breakwater and disappeared in the blue enormousness of the Philippine Sea. Then she went back to her cabin, put away laundry and dashed off a quick note to Jim.

The picnic that afternoon took place at the same officers' beach she'd once visited with Mark. Now they were openly part of a paired-off group, Willi and Floyd, Nell and Nick, Polly and Ed. Around them other couples reclined on Navy-issue blankets on the sand and drank icy beer from paper cups. In the shade of a pavilion, wardroom cooks were dishing out a proper American picnic; hot dogs, burgers, baked beans, potato salad. Close to the water, some junior officers had set up a volleyball net, while a few bathers dared the surf.

Anna still hadn't seen Luke, though Mark reported he'd come into their office earlier. "And was reasonably friendly," he said. "As was I."

"Well, good," she said in a preachy tone. "One expects no less from chaplains, even of differing denominations."

She caught her first glimpse of Luke when they went up for food. He was at a table with his usual cronies, OH, YH, Gladys and the Exec. Mellowed by the recent R and R, she went over and said, "Good to see you again! Missed you while we were gone." A fabrication: all she'd really missed was the niggling awareness of his constant scrutiny.

Smiling more widely than usual, he got to his feet and enveloped her in a loose, abashed hug. "Wish I'd had time to miss anybody, but I was so busy I hardly ever saw people from the ship."

"That's what Audrey said. Something about you working with local priests. I hope you'll tell me all about it."

"Sure." He leaned closer. "Meanwhile, I want to talk to you about something else."

"Oh?" Ah, there it was, the familiar anxiety again. "What's that?"

"Something you need to know. Tell you later. Maybe after chow. If you can get away from your friends for a while." He nodded toward Mark in the chow line, "Maybe we could walk down the beach a ways."

"Well, okay. If we're not here eating, we'll be out there." She gestured across the sand. "Come by when you're ready."

"I'll find you." A certain grim quality to his voice sent waves of dread through her. Gritting her teeth, she joined the others, got a tray of food and took a seat beside Mark on a picnic bench. As she dug in, she noticed someone had carved the image and the caption *Kilroy was here* into the planked table top.

"Floyd," she asked automatically, "who's this Kilroy that turns up everywhere? I even saw him when we cleaned the ship after the kissing mutiny. Somebody drew him on a bulkhead with lipstick."

Floyd's eyes took on an expectant gleam. "Glad you asked, Anna. The original Kilroy was an inspector in a shipyard. See, if he painted that on the bulkheads, it meant they'd used the proper number of rivets. Then sailors started spreading it around. Now, hell, he's like a gremlin. Except they're on planes."

He seemed about to add more, but before he could, she thanked him and resumed eating.

While everyone was still working on the food, Floyd got to his feet and announced he was about to recite a poem written by some unknown sailor on Ulithi. Willi groaned and said it was too long. But he went ahead anyway, charging through all four verses from memory. A smattering of applause and half-hearted laughter followed.

Evidently encouraged, he went on: "Now I'll tell you about the wreck there." He sipped his beer, wiped foam froth on his forearm and began recounting the *Mississinewa* story. "Brand new ship, but after a Jap mini-sub torpedoed her, she burned like hell and went down in a couple hours. Even now you can see oil leaking from her." He shook his head, his expression mournful. "Oh, the sheer wastefulness of war!"

Before he could begin a new story, Willi chimed in. "But in some ways, it was a real holiday. Why, we even saw a USO Show. Dorothy Lamour was supposed to be with them."

Audrey gasped. "Was she really?"

Willi tittered. "No. No Andrews Sisters either, or Dick Haymes or Tommy Dorsey or Bob Hope. But the singers did some fine impersonations, and the band sounded just like TD's. While they were performing, the usual Zero flew over. He came over every night at the same time and bombed hell out of some palm trees, but once we got the all-clear, the show went on. Next day the singers came aboard and serenaded our patients. Then they all got in their airplane and flew off to another island."

This reminded Audrey and Nell that at the Guam hospital they'd endured a rigorous inspection by touring BuMed brass. Anna was only half listening when Mark whispered, "What was the padre telling you a while ago? He sure looked serious."

"Don't know. Wants to walk with me after chow."

He shook his head, with that familiar heavy sigh. "Bet a dollar it'll be more of the old morality line." His gaze wandered across the pavilion to Luke's table. The bitterness in his eyes made her look away. "Just remember, Anna. That guy has no room to throw stones at anyone."

"Is that your text for tomorrow's sermon? Let him who is without sin, etcetera?"

His eyes softened and his fingers brushed her forearm.

It was after three before Luke wandered toward the blankets where the four couples sprawled in a stupor induced by the heat and overindulgence in beer and food. Down the beach, somebody's portable record player wafted reasonably recent Hit Parade favorites. The air was soft; a wispy sea breeze rustled palm fronds. Another day in paradise, Anna thought, noticing a carrier on the horizon and the usual line of B-29s taking off with firebombs enough to cook half of Tokyo.

The men were toweling off when Luke strolled up to the

blanket. He nodded at the others, then held out a hand. "Ready for a walk, Anna? "

She let him pull her to her feet, fluttering fingers at Mark as they set off through lapping shallows along a rim of hard-packed sand.

At first Luke talked only of his work on the island. "Mostly we rebuilt churches, a few schools, and some social halls. Also, I got to say Mass. In English, but they translated it into Chamorro too. Anyway, it felt good being constructive and useful. Not that I'm not useful on the ship, mind you, but it was different working with my hands."

"Noble work," she said. "I'm impressed. But is that what you wanted to tell me in the middle of a picnic?"

He frowned, extracting a cigarette from a mashed Luckies pack in his shirt pocket. He backed up to the breeze to light it. "No. This is something else. Actually, I didn't intend to mention it, but seeing you and Whitmore just now well, do you know how it looks, Anna? You and him, I mean?"

She stopped walking, dug her toes into the sand. "No. How do we look?"

"Like you don't care who knows you're having an immoral affair."

"Oh, for God's sake, Luke. That's absurd."

He exhaled fragrant smoke. "Before Ulithi, at least you were discreet. Now, you don't seem to give a damn. Either of you."

She inhaled sharply and buttoned the shirt over her bathing suit so he wouldn't accuse her of trying to vamp him too. "Luke, what business is it of yours what we do?'

"Well, if you were anyone else, I wouldn't care. But you're special. You know. Because you put me in touch with my mother. So it makes me sick to see you behaving like a... well, to put it bluntly, like that nurse that got in trouble last year. Like a common street tramp."

The slap she aimed at him was light, but her palm felt bee-stung afterward. He gaped, his eyes watered and his hand flew to his cheek. "Hey, I'm only the messenger."

"Yeah, but that was a message you didn't need to deliver. Just your judgmental opinion."

He shrugged. "Sorry if that's how you see it. But there's something else you need to hear. And it's not just my opinion."

They resumed walking, stiffly apart. Anxiety was full-blown now, tightening her hands into fists at her side. "What's that?"

He went on smoking, staring grimly at the war wreckage down the beach. "If you really care for Whitmore," he said then. "you're going to be hurt. Because he's not what he seems."

"Oh? What does that mean?"

"Well, mainly that you're not the first nurse he's played fast and loose with."

Her heart seemed to stop, but she managed to go on walking. Her voice sounded small and thin. "How could you possibly know that?"

He smoked the cigarette down to a nub, threw it to the beach and kicked sand over it. "You know the hospital Exec, the guy he borrows the Jeep from? They were at Pearl together last year. Seems he had a girlfriend there, a nurse, and another at the hospital here before he joined us. He told me one night when we were having a drink at the club. Then he asked if Whitmore had a girlfriend on our ship too. Now, that's not something he'd have said without reason, is it?"

No longer capable of walking, she sank to the sand. It was warm and powdery on the skin of her legs and starkly white against the Ulithi tan. "What reason, though? Why would he want you to know?"

Luke squatted beside her and lit another cigarette. "Not

sure, but I sensed something, maybe a little malice. Or envy. Maybe because Whitmore's getting away with something he isn't. Maybe he even wanted to stir up trouble."

"Well, if he did, he couldn't have found anyone better to tell."

He looked over with patent disbelief. "Is that what you think I'm doing, Anna? Stirring up trouble?"

Her answering look was equally dubious. "Aren't you?"

"Not at all. You're the only one I've told, the only one I intend to tell. And that's only for your own good. So you don't take him seriously. Don't do anything stupid, like breaking if off with the doctor in Maine because some smooth-talking two-timer's turned your head. Apparently your fiancé worries about that anyway. Or so Lorraine says."

She slumped, seeking cracks in his logic. Or a hint of *schadenfreude*.

He sighed out a cloud of smoke. "I'm truly sorry, Anna. And I don't blame you for being hurt and angry. But I can't in good conscience let you get your heart broken, can I?"

"No, of course not." Her mouth tasted bitter, like quinine. She almost said, "Too late now," but realized it wasn't. Instead she said, "I wouldn't have anyway. See, I still love Jim."

He stared toward a line of incoming breakers collapsing in foam as they rolled toward the beach. "You do?" he asked. "Explain that to me. Because I don't understand how you can do what you're doing with Whitmore if you love Jim."

She pondered a lengthier explanation, but drained by shock, said only, "I don't know. Unless it's the war. And the work we do. Oh, I know you claim you don't, but the rest of us need respite and comfort. And what feels like love. After all, look at the other couples on the ship. Some are serious, but for most of us, well, it's something else. Maybe a Protestant weakness. Which I don't expect you to understand. You find your love elsewhere."

His jaw turned rigid; Dan's had done that when inexpressible anger seethed in him. In his case, when he realized his boat's engineering problems were only a flyspeck on some obscure BuShips report. She wondered what had fueled this man's anger. Perhaps a suspicion that Mark had told her of his aberrant love preference?

"But you two aren't even discreet about it," he said.

By now her energy was so depleted, she could barely conceive of walking back, rejoining Mark, and behaving as if she knew nothing of his...what? Romances? Dalliances? Casual sexual encounters? At least she wouldn't see him that evening: he'd be busy fine-tuning his next day's sermon for the base chapel. God. Maybe his previous girlfriend would even be in the congregation, gazing at him with wistful longing. Then she flashed back to the first liberty in Pearl, which he'd told her he'd spent with friends. Had he rendezvoused with another former lover too? Suddenly, even the Kailua memory was sullied by a suspicion that he hadn't been there with the other chaplain's family at all, but with her, or some other nurse as naively complaisant as Anna was now.

No, her heart was not broken, but her trust was disintegrating like a building under bombardment, chunks of it falling away and exposing her to an ugly, devastated world.

She clambered to her feet, told Luke she was going back. She felt they'd been gone a long while, was surprised they hadn't come very far, so returning, she had little time to rearrange her face and compose her agitated thoughts.

As they approached, Mark jumped up and stood, hands on hips as he squinted at them in sunlight dazzling off the ocean. When they were within hearing range, she said to

Luke, "Let's talk again soon; I want to know more about your work here."

With a stiff smile and a quasi-salute, he took off at a lope toward the pavilion.

She turned back to Mark. "Well, I don't know what you want to do now, but I'm going back to the ship."

"Oh? Why's that? Tired?"

"Yep. Too much beer, too much sun."

"Well, then, I'll go too." His tone was normal, neutral. "Still need to polish tomorrow's sermon."

On the bus to the pier, he held her limp hand and asked what Luke had talked about. She said, "Nothing much. Mostly what he did with the local priests. Like you thought."

"Huh. Bet he didn't tell you everything he did with them."

She took the deepest possible breath and stared at the passing blur of vegetation, Quonset huts, warehouses, pier-side buildings, gray ships and eventually, the familiar white one. She didn't meet his eyes; she was certain hers would betray the disillusion and disappointment that burned in the rest of her body. Tonight, drained of energy and optimism and hope, she'd let him think she was merely tired. Tomorrow would be soon enough to hit him with what she was really feeling.

CHAPTER NINETEEN

Aware that Mark expected her to hear his sermon, at breakfast Anna excused herself on the basis of a mild hangover.

He regarded her with concern. "Everything all right otherwise?"

"Oh, sure. I want to write some letters before we sail. Besides, I heard your sermons at Ulithi. Nothing could top them."

She was relieved he didn't ask her to cite texts, reprise messages or describe a favorite. "Well, see you later then. We can talk more, maybe even have a nap. Preacher's prerogative, you know, the Sunday afternoon nap."

Recollections of her parents' habit came back from life on the far side of the world: her mother's post-prandial plea they were both tired, her father from doing the service, she from producing a monumental dinner. Surely they'd just napped, at least in Anna's time. Now, connecting them to Mark seemed a sacrilege, and visualizing in the same breath, an obscenity.

She shrugged, headed toward the ladder, said, "We'll

see," and left him alone at the table. From across the wardroom, she felt Luke's concentrated scrutiny like a flashlight beam. Two men of God, she thought, each more self-righteous and judgmental than her father had ever been. Of course she hadn't known him at her age, when he'd been an Army chaplain in France during World War One. Once in a while, her mother alluded to a French nurse he'd known over there. Some rancor always colored her remarks about Claudine, some tinge of ancient jealousy which Anna had never taken seriously. Until now.

Mark wasn't at noon chow, but shortly before *Compassion*'s scheduled departure, he hurried up the gangway. With a deep Ulithi tan contrasting with his dress whites, he was so handsome, her heart did an adolescent flip. As if last night's sleep had totally flushed his manifold sins and wickedness from her memory.

He saluted the OOD, then waved up. "Stay there. Be right up."

Breathing slowly for composure, she stared down at line handlers on the pier and deck hands securing the gangway. Then Mark was beside her, the usual grin deepening the grooves beside his mouth. She was almost overcome by the urge to kiss his lips, then kick him in some sensitive part of his body.

He glanced around, nuzzled her cheek. "Missed you at church earlier. And you missed a hell of a spread at the O Club afterward."

She took another deep breath. "What was your text for the sermon?"

"Let not your heart be troubled," he said. "John 14. You probably know it."

She switched her gaze toward the hazy mountains beyond the warehouses. "Last year, my father preached on a line from *This is my Father's World*: 'that though the wrong seems oft so strong/God is the ruler yet.'"

"That's not a Biblical text."

Annoyance soured her voice. "No, but it could be a paraphrase."

"Well, anyway, sorry you weren't there."

"Was I conspicuous by my absence?"

His face tightened. "To me, at least."

As she gazed into the distance, she felt his scrutiny so intensely she began to suspect he intuited her dark mood. Maybe he was even worried about her talk with Luke. Good, she thought; let the bastard stew a while.

After the PA system ran through the usual commands to the crew, the deck began to vibrate; lines snaked through the widening gap of slime-green water where chunks of garbage whirled in the eddies. Winches squealed; a downdraft from the stack brought warm exhaust. Although blowing the whistle was standard departure procedure, this time Anna jumped when it blasted overhead. The ship drifted outward; a tug alongside swerved them slowly about. The engines stepped up their pace and the breeze freshened. Behind their wake, the green Guamanian hills receded. Ahead, a bruise-blue veil hung over the Philippine Sea.

Mark pointed. "Say, looks like we're heading into a storm. Good time for a nap." He paused, studying her with faint curiosity. "What do you think, Anna?"

She glared. "You inviting me to your cabin?"

His shrug seemed too casual. "Can't think of a better way to spend a rainy afternoon."

"Oh, all right. After I change into khakis."

"Don't be too long."

By the time she'd hung up the dress whites, the sun had gone dim as they plowed north into a cloud mass filled with chartreuse light. For a while the sea was strangely slick, an ominous dark green that stirred images of prehistoric swamps. As Anna climbed the ladder from C to B Deck, she felt the ship shudder and hesitate, as if seized by a giant hand, then plunge like a roller coaster. In the passageway on B, she grabbed the rail along the bulkhead and felt her way up the sloping deck past the Ops Officer's headlong dash toward the bridge.

By the time she reached Mark's door, the angle had leveled off, the ship convulsing with the effort to right herself. Gradually, she began to rise as steeply as she'd previously descended. Off balance and without knocking, Anna hurtled into his cabin. It was dark, but in a lightning flare, she saw him sitting on the bunk. Loud as hail, rain drummed on the overhead and a strange roar obliterated a squawk box message. What was it, all hands into life vests? To lifeboat stations? Prepare to abandon ship? This is not a drill?

Losing her balance on the shifting deck, she collapsed beside him. "My God, Mark. What's happening?"

He pulled her close. "Feels like a squall full of rogue waves."

She huddled, certain only of his warm proximity, a refuge from the cannonading of thunder so intense it might have been the boilers exploding. Non-stop lightning split the sky as the ship continued her wild see-sawing, slamming and thudding, stanchions and bulkheads groaning. A death agony, or merely a passing spasm?

Mark smoothed Anna's hair back from her face. "Let not your heart be troubled," he murmured. "Remember, the disciples in the storm were as terrified as we are. Even with Jesus right there in the boat."

Despite her terror, she had to say, "But you're not Jesus."

"Obviously. Or I'd be calming the waters, not lusting for you."

"God, Mark. Is nothing sacred?"

He laughed, kissed her and began unbuttoning her shirt.

Her rational self was all for stopping him, but her weak, trembling persona welcomed any distraction from the certainty that they were goners.

Afterward, however, tears gave her away. Previously, this physical intimacy had bulwarked her with the strength of his body, the force of his spirit. Now she felt only the loneliness of having indulged passion without regard to the ugly new truths about him. After the first lovemaking with Jim, she'd wept with relief and release. This was pure remorse.

Mark dried her cheeks with his handkerchief. But when his fingers drifted to her breasts and the C-section scar on her belly, she snatched his hand away. "No. Don't do that."

"Why not, sweetie? Storm's not over yet."

"Maybe not," said her tear-stained voice. "But we are."

His hand stopped moving. "What? What's that mean?"

"Luke told me yesterday. About your... your other women."

"My other women? What the hell are you talking about?"

"Your previous girlfriends. At Pearl. Here too. I mean, Guam."

"That's absurd." His voice was unnaturally tight. "Where'd he get that ridiculous story?"

"He says the Exec at the hospital told him."

He snorted with disgust. "And you believe that crap?"

"Don't know. I want to hear your side of it."

When he sat up, grabbed the sheet from the foot of the bunk and arranged it carefully over their bodies, she realized he was buying time to devise a placating line. Folding it back neatly, he lay down again, necessarily close in the narrow bunk but without the previous skin contact, the connection on several levels.

Then he sighed, staring at the springs of the upper bunk. "Look, sweetie, I'm not going to lie. Before I left San

Diego, my wife and I'd been having problems. So at Pearl, when I met this nurse well, let's just say I was weak and she was willing."

Something in Anna's chest contracted to a hard knot. "She's the one you went to Kailua with, though. Not the chaplain's family."

He closed his eyes, his mouth a thin, taut line.

"And that first weekend at Pearl, you were with her, weren't you?"

The query was a shot in the dark, but when he stiffened, she knew it had hit the target.

"But that night when we danced together, you wanted me. How could you?" Even as she spit out the question, she realized it was the same one Luke had posited: How could you love Jim and do that with Mark?

Another long silence, backgrounded by slashing rain, the creaking, straining ship.

"Now. What about Guam. Who was it there? Another nurse?"

He shook his head against the pillow. "No, a WAVE. Worked in the chapel office."

"An officer?"

"What does it matter? She was nothing like you."

"Oh, I'm special, am I?"

"You know that. Always have been." He groaned. "I love you, I'd marry you right now, if I could."

Suspecting he'd used the same words with other women, equally trusting, equally needy of hearing them, she clamped her lips closed.

"Listen, Anna. Suppose I gave you a ring. Would that convince you my intentions are honorable?"

"Last week it might have. But not today."

"Oh God." He turned toward the bulkhead, one arm over his face. She sat up, reached her underwear on the deck, slacks, shirt and finally shoes.

"Don't leave yet. Please. We need to talk."

"Nothing more to say."

As she covered her nakedness, she no longer felt beautiful, as she had in past lovemaking. Now her body was just one of many he'd enjoyed. If that possibility had crossed her mind before, hunger for him had shoved it into a dark corner. Naive as a high school freshman, she'd been quick to suspect Jim of sexual attraction to his new nurse, but not this man to whom every woman on the ship, including butchy Gladys, seemed drawn, perhaps by hopes of indescribable raptures in his bed. Obviously, too much temptation even for a man of God. At least this clay-footed man of God.

He was still huddled under the sheet when she was ready to leave. The rain continued, but the sky was lighter, the sea now more gunmetal than obsidian. With her hand on the door latch, she wanted to fire off a parting salvo that might haunt him as Rhett Butler's exit line would forever echo through Scarlet O'Hara's dreams. All she could devise, however, was a feeble, "The least you could do is say you're sorry."

But before he could say anything, she slammed out. Hurrying forward, she passed Luke's door. Fighting off the impulse to confront him, she resumed her flight forward to the ladder, then down to Nurses' Country, to C-14 and a pile of letters she needed to read again. And again and again, as many times as it took to convince herself Jim loved her so much that Mark Whitmore was nothing more than a transient amusement, a distraction, a palliative to the discomforts of life on this ship. She also wanted to be able to regard him as a skilled seducer, a corrupter of innocence, and trouble disguised as love. But blinded by need to whatever he was or was not, she could no longer pretend she hadn't been equally complicit in their affair. Even today, in full awareness of his past transgressions, she'd let him do nothing she hadn't wanted him to do.

"Damn him," she said loudly as she banged the hatch closed. "Damn him to hell, the son of a bitch!"

CHAPTER TWENTY

For the next five days, she spoke only when necessary to both chaplains, sitting with neither at chow nor at staff briefings. If Willi noticed the breach, she didn't mention it. Just as well; she'd probably have given short shrift to any man who proclaimed love in the same breath he admitted infidelity. That Anna hadn't recognized Mark's proclivities might make the other nurse suspect she was either blind, stupid or sex-starved. Anna was afraid she was all three, but wanted Willi to think better of her.

On Friday, 3 August, she and Willi were at the rail when *Compassion* anchored in Buckner Bay, Okinawa. Sailors on landing craft below had just begun offloading pallets of medical supplies when the CO came on the horn. They barely glanced up, but personnel on deck tensed for whatever momentous announcement invariably followed the solemn, "This is the Captain speaking."

"Bet the Japs have surrendered," Willi said.

Anna thought it unlikely; only the day before they'd picked up casualties from a sunken destroyer. She crossed her fingers and under her breath, said the Jesus, Jesus prayer. The omnibus prayer, the one that covered all worldly fears.

"Ladies and gentlemen," began the strained voice. "Today I'm grieved to report the loss of the heavy cruiser *Indianapolis*, CA-35. Sunday night between Guam and Leyte, she was torpedoed and sunk, with heavy loss of life. There are some survivors, but I have no other information. Meantime, let's observe a moment of silent prayer for our two crewmen who transferred to her on Guam: Pharmacist's Mate Striker Robert McWherter and Yeoman Second James Creesey." The intercom went silent except for some background static. Then the CO cleared his throat. "That is all. Carry on."

"Lord," Willi breathed. "I saw that ship on her way out Saturday morning. And that corpsman, wasn't he one of the new ones came aboard at Pearl last time?'

Aware her lips and chin were trembling, Anna swallowed hard. "I was on the gangway Friday afternoon when he and the yeoman were leaving. He couldn't wait to get on a warship. God. He was only nineteen."

"Past tense, Anna?"

She stared blankly, then said, "Okay. He is nineteen," with only a pretense of optimism.

Numbed by the news, they stood a while longer as the unloading progressed. As always, shipboard routines continued uninterrupted, even when tragedy came close enough to touch. With this one burning in her bloodstream, she thought of Mark. She hadn't seen him all day, nor cared to. Until now.

"Think I'll go look for the chaplain," she said.

And Willi said, "Yeah, I might find Floyd too."

Only Luke was in the chaplains' office, his face grave. Feeling boneless, she dropped into the chair beside his desk. "Where's Mark?"

"Ashore, looking at the new base chapel. Why?"

"We saw Bobby McWherter last week when he was leaving for the cruiser." She shook her head, groped for more words. "I feel so bad about what's happened, I don't know what to do. Maybe Mark's feeling that way too."

He scowled. "I heard you threw him over."

Disbelief held her inert. "But he's still a friend. That's not over, and I need to talk to him."

"Can't you talk to me, Anna? I knew Bobby too. He came to Mass almost every day. Anyway, we shouldn't feel bad: they could still be alive, you know."

She studied that dark face, still handsome though it no longer remotely reminded her of Dan's. "They said heavy loss of life. Sounds like there aren't many survivors. And new men on a ship might not know their way around well enough to get off in an emergency."

He leaned back in the chair. "Well, sure, it's a terrible tragedy, and I'm sad too. But at least the lost ones are out of the war. Beyond mortal suffering. At home with our Lord."

The words seemed only a smug schoolboy's rote answer to a catechism question. "Does that mean we shouldn't grieve for them?"

His eyes narrowed, darkening as they often did to indigo. "Grief is a human sentiment that denies spiritual truth that heaven's the ultimate goal of all souls. We should rejoice for those who have attained it."

Repressing shock, she got to her feet. "Well, Luke, I'm glad you've figured it out. Don't grieve; they're with the Lord. Is that what they told you when your parents died?"

His jaw dropped, eyes widened. A dark flush suffused his face and the pencil he'd been tapping snapped in his fingers. "That's unkind, Anna. And none of your business."

She was about to ask, "But why are Mark and I your business?" when it came to her that such logic was not going to ameliorate this intensifying contretemps. If she and he hadn't been connected through Lorraine, would her relationship with Mark have mattered to him, except as it reinforced some inherent Catholic suspicion that Protestants lacked moral fiber?

"Sorry, Luke," she said stiffly. "When you see Mark, please tell him I'm looking for him."

He nodded curtly, but didn't rise. "Of course."

Smarting from this exchange, she went back to the railing where Floyd and Nell had joined Willi. The unloading continued, the banter of sailors below a mundane backdrop to their stunned silence. Anna wanted to ask Floyd why Indy's sinking touched her so much, but knew he'd likely spout some convoluted explanation based on her association with Bobby McWherter. That wouldn't help; she needed more than psychology or Luke's glib spiritual whitewash. She needed Mark, damn it.

As the last loaded landing craft left, a launch came alongside with the Exec and some medical officers poised to step onto the boarding platform. Mark brought up the rear. God help me, she thought as he climbed the embarkation ladder: he was the only one who could possibly share her pain. She despised the weakness that fed this truth, but resisting it was futile. Although she no longer trusted his fidelity, she did understand his carnal weakness. Incongruously, there was also a strength in him that drew her, as adventurous men are drawn to Himalayan peaks on which they know there's a good chance they'll meet death.

High time, she thought, that she stopped deluding herself that she and he were not cursed with the same flaws.

* * *

Chow that night was tuna sandwiches with canned tomato soup; she barely touched either. Underway again,

Compassion was scheduled to rendezvous with a cruiser that had taken a Kamikaze. The Okinawa campaign had ended six weeks before, but these persistent, desperate suicide planes were still battering convoys gathering for the Japan invasion. Floyd had told them more men had been lost in these attacks than in the invasion itself. He didn't know the extent of this ship's damages, just that she was still afloat, making half speed and packed with casualties.

"But obviously," he added, "she got off a distress signal. I wonder if Indy did. Heavy loss of life, they said. I wonder how heavy?"

"Complement of a CA's about twelve hundred." said Nick. "But even if she didn't radio, Tacloban had her ETA. When she didn't arrive, they'd have known where to start looking."

"Remember the *Hood?*" Floyd didn't wait for an answer. "British battle cruiser. German dreadnought *Bismarck* sank her in May, '42, Went down so fast, there were only three survivors from a crew of fourteen hundred." He shook his head, his close-set eyes darker than usual. "Times like that, nobody's got a chance."

After this dialogue, all of them had comments. Even without answers, the speculation continued. And each new theory painted a possibility more horrific than the last.

Engrossed in them, Anna was sipping the now-cold soup long after everyone else had finished. Then Mark came in. His gaze swept the wardroom before he spotted her group. He'd never asked permission before, but now he wanted to know if he could join them.

Floyd nodded. "Maybe you can tell us more about Indy."

He took the chair beside Anna. "All I know is what I heard ashore this morning." He shook his head morosely. "She was torpedoed. And there aren't many survivors."

"Bobby said she was a tough ship," Anna put in.

"Couple months ago, a Jap bomb went through her hull. But she still made it back to California for repairs. Hard to believe she'd go down so fast the crew couldn't get off."

"And on the way back, she set a new speed record between Frisco and Pearl," Nick said. "Fast ship can usually outrun a sub. Unless she was in economy mode."

Mark helped himself to the sandwich platter. As the others went on talking he murmured to her, "Salaunas said you wanted to see me."

She willed herself to ignore his masculine late-day smell. "Yes. I thought you might be feeling as bad as I am about Bobby."

He gazed past the sandwich into the landscape of his thoughts. "Well, I feel like hell, all right. But not just about him."

"Oh?" She stirred the soup into a small red whirlpool. When a ship went to the bottom, she wondered, did suction leave a vortex where it had been?

"Know what I mean?"

She flashed back from the image. "I think so."

"So when he said you wanted to see me, I thought… I mean, I hoped…"

"What? All was forgiven?"

"Something like that."

"That's funny. Luke said he thought we were over. You and I, I mean. As if we couldn't go back to being friends."

"He has no idea what human love is. Probably never experienced it in his own life."

"Maybe. Anyway, he said he's sad about the lost men. But not grieving. He's rejoicing they're with the Lord."

He frowned and bit into the sandwich. She pushed away the soup bowl and the plate with crusts, then focused on the notions others were positing. Whenever gaps appeared in their certainty, they filled them with theories. Perhaps it was the nature of medical people to be uncomfortable with unknowns and variables, to crave definition and order. And the illusion of certainty.

After the steward cleared her place, he brought a slab of vanilla-chocolate-strawberry ice cream, melting on a plate hot from the dishwasher. Spooning it up, her gaze wandered to Mark's suntanned hands and forearms. The white band where his wedding ring had been was no longer noticeable. Were the internal traces of his marriage similarly obliterated? And what did it matter anyway?

She sat a while longer before she excused herself. "Talk to you later," she told him on the way out, then went up to write to Jim. He hadn't known Bobby, but she could freely describe her emotions relative to his possible loss. Sharing the stuff of her soul with Jim had been the Mount Everest of her year on Hope Island. Even at ten thousand miles, she could still share it. At least the part about *Indianapolis*.

CHAPTER TWENTY-ONE

After *Compassion* debarked survivors from a sunken destroyer at Buckner Bay, their wounded, plus those from the damaged cruiser brought the patient census up to half, and put medical personnel to work again. Not as intensively as on other deployments, but enough to remind them war still raged nearby. Even after news of the new superbomb dropped on Hiroshima, all Anna could imagine was a continuation of the same routines they'd followed since October.

One evening at chow, the issue moved her to ask OH how she'd stood four years of this duty. "It's so predictable. No matter how many casualties we pick up, there's always more out there. Sometimes I feel like Sisyphus pushing the stone up the hill."

Commander Welch's lined face softened, but the no-nonsense façade didn't slip. "Well, maybe if I'd known it'd go on so long, I'd have felt like you do. But see, at first we thought it'd be over in no time. A year, tops." She shrugged. "Then it got bad and we didn't have time to think. Wounded piled up so fast they loaded 'em on anything that floated just to get 'em to safety. Sometimes they got medical attention; sometimes they just lay out in the weather until we arrived."

She shook her head; gray strands in her black hair caught the light. "Back then, whenever things got so busy I didn't have time to pee, I'd remember the nurses they captured in the Philippines. Mostly Army, a few Navy. Even starving, they set up dispensaries for other prisoners, and made do with whatever Red Cross supplies got through. When they were rescued a few months ago, they were so emaciated they hardly had any boobs. At first we didn't know what'd happened to 'em. All we knew was, no matter how hard we had to work, we still had three squares a day, and clean bunks. I mean, when we had time to sleep." Her gaze wandered across the crowded wardroom. "Sometimes it helps to remember people who have it worse. Which is almost everybody, when you get down to it. Especially the poor devils on Indy."

No one applauded, but Anna was tempted to.

* * *

They'd just tied up at Apra Harbor the afternoon of 9 August when the squawk box announced one of the new hospital ships had arrived with *Indianapolis* survivors the day before. "We don't have the official count," the CO went on, "but there's about three hundred."

As usual, Anna and her group were outboard on C Deck, squinting in the incandescent sunlight at patients being littered into ambulances on the pier. "Three hundred?" Floyd said. "Out of twelve hundred that sailed out of here the other week?"

"Can't be right," Mark said. "Must mean three hundred wounded." He paused, squared his hat. "Listen, Floyd, let's haul ass over to the hospital. The Exec's a friend of mine;

he'll give us the straight skinny."

Floyd unfolded himself from the railing. "Think I can pass as the new Hebrew chaplain?"

She expected Mark to grin at this absurdity, but he said only, "Let's go, then."

They headed for the ladder, hustled down the gangway, then quickly disappeared behind a warehouse.

The rest of the afternoon was torporous with heat, humidity and anxiety. Anna tried writing letters, but Indy questions shoved such good intentions from her mind. Picking up her prayer book, she paged to the section for The Burial of the Dead. As comforting as the archaic words could be, today none restored her "sure and certain hope of the Resurrection," or the trust that "the sea shall give up her dead."

While she was reading, word came over the horn that another atomic bomb had been dropped, this one on Nagasaki. The name meant as little as Hiroshima had earlier. Later in the lounge before evening chow, she wondered aloud why Tokyo or Yokohama hadn't been first.

Ed said, "Because we've already fire-bombed the hell out of them and there's no targets left."

"They used to call Nagasaki the San Francisco of the Orient," said Nell. "It was the setting for that opera about the Japanese girl who falls in love with an American Navy Officer."

"Oh, Madame Butterfly," Willi said. "Since Pearl Harbor, they're not allowed to perform it in the States. Maybe because the Navy man's a real jerk."

No one commented, as if they'd never known a cad like Lieutenant Pinkerton.

When a steward announced supper, Anna rose with the others, then stopped short at the sight of Mark and Floyd in the passageway. Mark's face was bleak, but Floyd's was that of an Old Testament character who has just witnessed the wrath of Jehovah first-hand.

"What is it?" she stammered. "What'd you find out?"

Floyd said, "Too much. See, when they said three hundred survived, well, that was it. Half of them are in the hospital here. You can imagine the shape they're in."

One of the surgeons asked, "Three hundred total? That's all?"

"Uh-huh. The rest are gone. Nine hundred. Including the two sailors who transferred from us."

A stunned silence filled the big space. "How in hell could that be?" Ed said.

Standing with shoulders hunched, Mark said, "Because nobody looked for them. Don't ask me why. All I know is, they were in the water four days and nights. With the sharks."

Before anyone could react, he nodded at her, jerked his head toward the passageway and mouthed, "Come on."

Leaving the group in the lounge still reeling, she followed him out on deck.

"Floyd and I are going to the club," he said. "Never knew what people meant when they said they needed a drink. Now I do." He extended his hands in one of *those I give up* gestures. "Want to come?"

Of course she did, if only to be in his company. They headed for the gangway, Floyd and Willi in their wake. On the pier, Mark walked so fast she had to scurry to keep up, skirting puddles, potholes, coiled lines, chains, barrels, crates, front end loaders and dozing mechanical mules. Another hospital ship was moored at a pier ahead; her stern stack and low silhouette marked her as a new one, the name across her transom, *Tranquility*. Unsullied by rust that streaked *Compassion*'s hull, her white paint gleamed in the sunlight. She even smelled fresh, as if her moving parts weren't overheated, overworked and oozing grease from every fitting.

"That's the ship brought them yesterday," Floyd said as they approached. "One of six just coming on line. Built down the river from Philly. Started out as tankers, but when it looked like we were gonna invade Japan, they converted them to AHs instead."

Willi smiled up at two nurses regarding them from the main deck rail. "I'd love a tour sometime. Think they'd show us around?"

"Maybe they could tell us more than we found out at the hospital," Mark said. "Only let us talk to five men. The CO made it okay, but he wasn't one of them."

Thursday night Happy Hour, the club was buzzing with Navy men, Marines, nurses, WAVEs, a few Brits, even some Aussies and Kiwis, all tossing back drinks at a dime a pop. Mark led them to a table far from the bar, the blasting juke box, a miasma of cigarette smoke and bursts of raucous laughter. She and Willi ordered rum and cokes; Mark asked for bourbon, neat. Floyd wanted only ginger ale.

"Look, y'all," Mark said when the waiter had departed. "let's don't talk about Indy any more. Okay? Let's just drink and forget."

"That's where us Jews have it all over you Goyim," Floyd said. "We've lived with shit like this so long, it feels natural. We don't need alcohol to make it easier."

"Shit like what?" Willi said.

"FUBAR. You know. Like SNAFU, only worse."

"Situation Normal All Fouled Up," Anna explained in case anyone didn't know.

"Not fouled up, Anna. Fucked up. FUBAR means Fucked Up Beyond All Recognition."

Across the room, Nell and Nick came in with Polly and Ed and wandered toward the table. When they'd taken seats, Mark advised them of his moratorium on Indy talk.

"Nothing to say anyway," Nick said. "Somebody screwed up. Or got careless." His shrug was casual. "Happens all the time. You don't hear about it, though, 'til lots of people die."

The drinks came; the new foursome ordered. And someone fired up the juke box with a recent Perry Como record, *Hubba, Hubba, Hubba*. The words were garbled, but throbbed with American bravado, American muscle. American revenge for Pearl Harbor.

Mark swigged; the rest of them sipped.

"Anyway," Floyd said, holding up his ginger ale, "one day soon the war'll be over and we'll go back to our lives as if none of this ever happened."

"Damned straight," said Ed. "And the first thing I'm going to do is buy me a shiny red Pontiac."

"Not me," Nick said. "I want a Lincoln Zephyr. I'll take Ford products over General Motors cars any day."

Anna shifted her gaze to Willi. Even with the drink to her lips, her face was pained. Leaning toward Floyd, she asked, "When did Indy go down?"

"Sunday, about midnight. She was due at Tacloban the next day. But it was late Wednesday before a PBY spotted them. And then only by chance. Worst of it is, most of the crew survived the sinking. But after all that time in the Philippine Sea…" He shook his head, his long face more lugubrious than usual.

Mark shot him a sharp glance. "That's enough, Floyd. Let's talk about what you're going to do after the war."

Floyd blinked, drew a deep breath. "Same thing I'm doing out here. Practice dentistry. Only in Philadelphia, PA, USA. Thought you knew."

"How would I know? It's probably the only thing you never told us."

Everyone laughed except Willi. "I think Mark meant, what kind of car are you going to buy?"

"A Packard." His voice was rough. "It'll make me look successful even if I'm not."

More laughter, too loud, too long. The others' drinks came. Except for Mark, the men talked of automobiles, comparing preferences, arguing their relative merits with a fervor Anna couldn't understand. Even Nell took sides, voting for a convertible, preferably a Plymouth, preferably yellow.

When Willi volunteered nothing, Polly asked if she'd be going home to Oregon when they finally got back.

"No. Philadelphia. See, I'm going to help Floyd in his practice.. And ride around in his Packard."

Anna gaped. As the others went on talking, she whispered, "Are you two engaged?"

"Unofficially. But this isn't the time to mention it."

Anna grabbed her hand. "But it's such good news."

Willi's smile was watery. As if word of another ship torpedoed in the middle of the night had rekindled her grief about a friend lost on *Centaur*. Had she bargained on so many painful connections? Had any of them bargained on the hard truths they'd learned out here?

"What about you, Anna?" Polly said. "Will you be married as soon as you get home?"

She shrugged, reluctant to discuss wedding plans with Mark beside her. "That'll depend when Jim can get away from his practice."

Mark reached for his drink and drained it in one gulp. His face was a perfect blank, but when his gaze flickered to hers, sorrow dulled his eyes. He looked away quickly, held up his glass until a waiter came over. Everyone ordered another round.

Sipping the second drink, Anna listened as the conversation returned to the material blessings of post-war life. An odd counterpoint to the repressed images of Indy's crewmen dying in the water the week before. Nine hundred, they'd said. About as many Marines as she and the other nurses had kissed. Nine hundred more grieving families. Nine hundred more empty chairs at Christmas dinners. Her own personal losses were only two drops in the ever-moving stream that bore so many mothers' sons away.

She drank until the rum and coke was gone, asked for a third. The last time she'd overindulged had been at Pearl, after the Marine had gone overboard. Her drink of choice, she reckoned, for the hard times. When no matter how much she learned, facts failed to illuminate the situation. And the answer to each question led only to others even more complex. Like trying to work your way through a labyrinth with no logical center.

FUBAR indeed.

* * *

Sunday afternoon, as *Compassion* idled northward toward an unannounced destination, the squawk box announced the memorial service for the two lost sailors. Anna hadn't seen Mark since they'd stumbled aboard Thursday night; a steward said he'd requested chow brought to his office until after the service. Her first inclination was to track him down and find out why. Except she already knew.

Everyone but duty personnel was packed into the crews' mess, officers and enlisted crammed in without segregation, except for Negro cooks and boiler tenders who were relegated to the back of the big space. She'd expected Mark to be in charge, but when Luke joined him at the lectern she concluded the tragedy had nullified, or at least minimized their private, personal differences.

There was no formal liturgy; each chaplain read scriptures and said appropriate prayers. For his homily,

Luke's theme was essentially what he'd told her; death was a spiritual homecoming, cause for rejoicing, not weeping. In contrast, Mark spoke from the helplessness she'd observed Thursday evening.

In conclusion, they sang *Eternal Father,* just the first verse, the one everyone knew. Joining in, Anna sensed that whenever she sang it, in whatever circumstances for the rest of her life, this would be a defining moment. As usual, it stirred her to tears. Not enough to spill over, however, just enough to clog her nose and thicken her voice. She couldn't remember the last time she'd allowed them to flow freely.

After the benediction, Mark disappeared in the crowd. Determined to find him, she looked in his office, then his cabin. The door was ajar; he was seated on the edge of the bunk, arms on his knees, a red-bound volume in his hands.

She said, "Hi. I looked for you after the service. Wanted to tell you, your sermon was perfect. My dad'll be thrilled you used his text."

No light came on in his eyes. "Couldn't think of a better one. Because my heart wasn't in it. I only preached it for the men."

"Your heart wasn't in it? Why not?"

The shrug was dispirited, vague. "Guess I've had to preach too many like that. You know. Be of good cheer; the Lord is with you even unto the gates of hell. Lately they're nothing but words."

"Oh, Mark. You're not losing your faith, are you?"

He shrugged. "Would you blame me?"

She inhaled, prayed for words. But who was she to give them? Just her father's faithless daughter. "I hate to hear that. Let's talk about it, shall we?"

"Maybe later. Right now I need a nap."

"Well, then, I'll let you rest. But how about after chow tonight?"

"Yeah, maybe."

Reluctant to leave, she blew him a kiss and pulled the hatch closed.

* * *

Mark didn't appear in the wardroom until most of the others had left. His face was puffy with sleep when he took the chair beside her. "Feel better now?" she asked.

"Some. At least I slept. Been having trouble with that lately."

The steward arrived with the usual Sunday night supper, canned mushroom soup and a grilled cheese sandwich, garnished with a dill pickle. Mark bit into it before he tasted anything else. "War really must be winding down if we're getting pickles this good."

She smiled, tempted to touch him, rub his hand, caress his face; freshly shaved with a touch of dried lather under the ear. "And real eggs," she added.

"When did we have real eggs?"

"This morning. Didn't you eat?"

"No. Just had coffee." He took a bite of the sandwich and rolled his eyes. "Cheese is better too. Not the usual Velveeta."

"Anyway, maybe after you eat, we could go out on the fantail. Ought to be cooler there. Then we can talk about what you said this afternoon."

He stared a moment, then looked away. "Why do you care, Anna?"

A dozen answers, none relevant, raced through her mind. "I don't know."

He slurped up more soup, chewed the sandwich, signaled a steward for iced tea, then resumed eating, but slowly, not the way he usually did, as if he had more to do than time to do it. Finally, he shoved the dishes aside and waved off the proffered block of melting ice cream.

"Well, I don't know what there is to say, Anna, but sure, let's talk."

They walked aft along the main deck, keeping pace with the ocean running alongside, which produced the illusion they were standing still. At the rails, other couples were inhaling fresh sea air and holding each other with a tenderness that suggested safeguarding rather than seduction.

On the fantail, he greeted a boatswain's mate Anna didn't recognize. Of course, his flock comprised every Protestant on the ship, not just medical personnel. She waited at a discreet distance while they talked. When the sailor left, she stood beside Mark, elbows on the rail, close but not touching. The big flag whipped in the breeze; the wake boiled out from under the stern, leaving an ephemeral foam trail back to the horizon.

She said "I haven't been out here since the night we …you know, after we lost the Marine."

"Ironic. Because I feel just as helpless as I did then. Maybe even more so."

"I know. Why is that? He was just one man. Bobby, I mean. I didn't know the yeoman or any of the others, but it still feels worse." She inhaled deeply of the damp, salty air. Quivering above the horizon, the sun was a fat orange flaming between crimson cloud stripes. "Look at that. It's so beautiful. But what did it look like to those men in the water with all the sharks?"

He groaned. "That haunts me. All that time, and none of us knew. And we were even out there that night. At least on the same sea."

"I try not to think about it. But then my mind starts up again. And I keep wondering, did Bobby even get off before they went down?"

"I talked to a corpsman who stood watch with him

earlier that night. Said he didn't see him afterward. But he was bright. Might've learned his way around before it happened, so I bet he did."

"Oh, God, I hope so. I hate to think of him trapped in some dark flooded compartment with the ship breaking up, and no way out." She swallowed hard as an old image of Dan intruded. "He was so excited and hopeful about going to a cruiser."

"Yeah." He compressed his lips. "Young men never worry about danger. When I think of how many have died like that... have to wonder why I even bother."

"Bother? With what?"

"Oh, this job. You know. Trying to give them courage and strength and faith. And what for? So they can stay alive a couple days longer?" He shook his head slowly. Sunset burnished the lines of cheekbones, nose and chin, and accentuated the creases beside his mouth. By now she'd collected a hundred mental portraits of him, but sensed the combination of vulnerability and strength in this one would stay with her into senility.

Laying her hand on his forearm, she was conscious of the warmth of his skin under her fingertips. "Tell me," she said then. "Is this a new feeling? Or just worse right now?"

The breath shuddered into him. "Not new, but definitely worse. And not just because of what happened to Indy. Ever since we talked about...well, my carnal weakness....I've been looking at my life without the rose-colored glasses. Wondering what kind of man I am under the ministerial robes. An alabaster sepulcher. A fake. And now this, this..."

"What? Apostasy?"

"Apostasy. Yeah. That's a nice way to put it." A half-hearted grin flashed on and off, fast, like a neon sign. "Whatever you call it, it makes me wonder if I can stay in the ministry."

The finality of his summary made her gasp.

"Oh, don't worry, Anna. I'm not going to quit; I'll do this as long as I have to. And the other night at the club, if anyone had asked about my post-war plans, I'd have said I'll go back to Carolina and find a church that needs me. But how can I when I'm starting to doubt the Lord even knows we're here? Or cares." He shook his head with visible sorrow. "Then there's my personal behavior. How can I preach morality when I'm not leading a moral life?"

She edged closer, aching with his pain. And wondered if her father in World War One, doing essentially what they were doing, had ever doubted. He'd already been ordained when he'd volunteered for the Army, leaving behind his wife, pregnant with Anna. But his doubts wouldn't include personal recriminations, would they? Then again, she'd never expected to have this sordid stain on her own conscience either.

Finally it came to her to say, "I hate to think anything I did contributed to that. But I wanted you, Mark. I tempted you. Don't deny it. I'm not blameless either. As for the other, you may doubt your own faith, but you're still helping others believe. And you certainly give me comfort."

He turned quickly. "How can I?"

"Well, I guess because you were with me the last time we saw Bobby. When the Marine went overboard. And the Kamikaze buzzed us. And oh, other times when I was troubled."

He hunched his shoulders and squinted at his clasped hands.

"Sometimes you're a man of God, and sometimes you're a man of the flesh. But no matter which, I never feel lost when I'm with you. Or hopeless."

He drew a deep breath, then reached out to her, hesitantly, as if he didn't trust her words.

In his familiar warmth, she felt the echo of her own heartbeats, her own respiration, her own sorrow. "And I don't want to feel that way tonight," she said.

He brought her closer. "Even though I'm a Doubting Thomas? And a letch?"

"Maybe tomorrow it'll matter again. But tonight I don't give a damn."

His smile was tentative. Behind him, the last tattered remnants of sunset flared, then turned to ashes, like a fire dying. Or a life force flickering out. A fleeting image of Indy's crew watching each sunset darken their hopeless, watery world made her shudder.

She pressed her face against his neck. "Let's go to your cabin," she murmured, in case he hadn't inferred the rest of the suggestion.

CHAPTER TWENTY-TWO

The war officially ended on 14 August but *Compassion's* personnel didn't get the news until the next evening at chow. After the CO announced it, dead silence throbbed in the wardroom for the span of a heartbeat. Then it yielded to a jubilant cacophony; whoops, cheers, yelps, screams, applause, even foot stomping. They were hundreds of miles from another ship, but someone on the bridge began blowing the whistle, short blasts like the Man Overboard, but more than Anna could count. Nick said later it was forty-five, one for each month the war had lasted

When a strong male voice began singing *The Star Spangled Banner,* everyone stood at attention, hands over their hearts, tears welling. All except hers; recently a lifelong tendency to easy tears, one she'd always regarded as childish and embarrassing, had been transformed to stoicism, she presumed by repeated exposure to the pain of others. And while she was grateful for the hardening of her heart, she was also mildly troubled that even the joy of victory left her dry-eyed.

She'd just sung "gave proof through the night that our flag was still there," when Mark came up behind her, spun her around and kissed her full on the mouth. Others soon picked up on the idea and a spate of osculation seized even oddballs like OH and the CO, and YH and CDR Driscoll. Maybe even Luke, though Anna couldn't see him in the crowd. It might have been New Year's Eve in Times Square.

Eventually everyone sat down again and began chattering about post-war plans. When someone mentioned champagne, three surgeons and two ship's officers volunteered what they had in their lockers. The seven bottles they fetched seemed inadequate for such a crowd, so Mark and Luke were requested to perform incantations that somehow effected a loaves-and-fishes miracle. Or so it seemed. Perhaps because the bubbly was served in the tiny paper cups normally used to dispense pills, everyone had enough for toasts. First, to the best damned country in the world, the best damned ship in the fleet, the president, the Marines and everyone's mothers. On and on, until they ran out of ideas and champagne. By then it was almost eight and the stewards were trying to clear the tables to set up for breakfast, so the Exec suggested moving the party to the lounge.

Behind the bar was an upright piano left from the glory days of the SS *Maui*. After someone removed the dust cover, Floyd squatted on the low bench and dashed off a few arpeggios. The notes were tinny and out of tune, but good enough to get everyone singing again: *God Bless America,* then *California, here I come!* and *Remember Pearl Harbor.*

Halfway through *She's a Grand Old Flag,* Mark stopped singing and gave Anna a smile she knew well. "Come on," he murmured. "Let's celebrate somewhere quieter."

"Quieter? Like your cabin?"

He nodded; in his eyes she read the familiar yearning that inevitably drew them together.

Still, she said, "Well, I don't know. I'm awfully damned tired from all that champagne and everything."

He yawned. "Me too. So we could just sleep."

She shrugged and said, "Let's just see what happens," though she knew full well what would. Because the war had ended and the countdown had begun to the final voyage home. Moments like this that had previously stretched into infinity now were numbered, fleeting, precious. One did not waste them with feeble excuses like fatigue.

CHAPTER TWENTY-THREE

As *Compassion* stood out of Apra Harbor on 17 September, the Exec announced they were bound for an undisclosed port on one of the Japanese home islands. The next day, as they steamed northeast at a speed rarely tolerated by the frugal engineers, they learned the destination was Nagasaki on the southernmost island of Kyushu.

"A minesweeper has cleared the entrance, and a task force has secured the harbor," the Exec reported. "Presently they're evacuating Allied prisoners of war, PWs, from camps near the city. Two new AHs, *Haven* and *Sanctuary*, will transport those needing medical attention. Others will be accommodated on the escort carrier *Chenago*, the cruiser *Wichita* and other task force ships. We'll provide backup in case they find other camps in the area. We're hoping for a quick turnaround, with no liberty and no sightseeing. Not just because the city was devastated by an atom bomb, but until a month ago, these people were the enemy."

"No liberty?" echoed Audrey. "Hell. We may never get

another chance to see Japan."

Willi gave a disgruntled snort. "I don't care if I never set foot in that bloody country. And that bastard in the Kamikaze's the only Jap I ever want to see."

As usual, staff had assembled in the lounge to await chow, which, judging by luscious smells emanating from the galley, would be one of those special meals that invariably spoiled them for ordinary fare. Floyd suggested this one was probably intended to boost morale about deploying again instead of going home.

Despite scuttlebutt about an immediate return to the west coast, first the ship had made a wide sweep south and west of Guam picking up convalescing Australian and New Zealand casualties. Then, filled beyond capacity, they dropped off the Kiwis in Auckland, and made a speed run to Brisbane with the others. There, despite a rumor they might go into a shipyard for a few days, medical personnel were granted only eight hours liberty and told they'd be sailing the next morning. So they streamed into a city that wasn't exactly San Francisco, but it was large and modern and western-feeling, with electric trains, trams and busses, parks and churches, theaters and hotels, and lots of English-speaking white people fighting to treat their Yank allies to drinks and dinner, then more drinks. Lots more drinks.

When *Compassion* steamed down the Brisbane River the next morning, everyone was so hung over that no one griped about going to Japan before they headed for California. By noon chow, however, they'd recovered enough to be in complaint mode again.

Seated across the table, Anna watched the play of emotions across Mark's face, from apathy to curiosity and eventually interest. She wasn't surprised then, when he finally said, "Listen, y'all. Just think of it as a rare chance to visit the enemy's homeland. So we can see what their civilians went through. No matter which side they're on, civilians are innocent victims of any war."

Anna asked, "Was that what you said in your sermon on Love thine enemies?"

His gaze switched to hers with mild annoyance. "Don't remember. But I'm not preaching now. Because some folks on this ship will never pity them. Let alone forgive."

"Do you blame them?" Willi asked.

Late as usual, Luke slipped into a chair beside him and sipped his tomato juice. Next Mark asked, "Who said they were disappointed there's no liberty in Nagasaki?"

Audrey raised her hand. "I promised my mother one of those paper fans with a lacquered frame."

When the steward set down a basket piled with golden biscuits, he helped himself to two, then passed them to Luke. "Don't know where you'd buy something like that. Not likely there'll be any souvenir shops on the Nagasaki waterfront."

Willi said, "Only souvenir I'd want would be rubble from the atom bomb ruins."

Floyd gave her a sharp look. "That'd be like taking a bone from a Nazi death camp."

The ensuing silence was broken by the soft tread of the stewards as they set down platters of fried chicken, and bowls of mashed potatoes, gravy, corn pudding and cole slaw.

Mark sighed. "Will y'all just look at this? My favorite meal in the entire world." He raised his gaze toward the overhead. "Thank you, Lord."

So he still believed enough to be thankful, Anna thought.

As they dug in, conversation switched to food. It generally did whenever it was better or worse than usual. Before he picked up his fork, Luke bowed his head and crossed himself. "Too bad we can't go ashore. I'd sure like to see that Cathedral. Nagasaki's been the center of a

Catholic community since Jesuits came in the 1850s. Be interesting to know if Christians showed more mercy to prisoners than the average Jap."

"Germany's a Christian country, but that didn't do the Jews much good," Floyd said, gesturing with a half-eaten drumstick. His tone was usually one of wry humor; today it was strangely acidic.

Mark chomped into a chicken breast, rolled his eyes, then wiped his lips. "If we get a chance, we owe it to ourselves to see what our bombers did. All we know now is what they've done to us. And the mangled troops we've treated. There'd be a certain poetic justice seeing the devastation of their homeland."

"Maybe." Luke reached for his iced tea. "So long as we didn't gloat. You know, play the conquering hero. Or behave like rich tourists."

Down the table, OH said, "Pardon my French, padre, but that's bull shit. We don't owe those bastards a god-damn thing. Remember, they started it. They deserved every bomb they got."

Anna sensed Mark's discomfiture when he asked, "Whatever happened to Judge not that ye be not judged?"

"Fine for you, padre," OH snapped back. "You haven't seen the things I've seen. You weren't at Pearl during the attack. Or Guadalcanal for that bloody invasion."

He went on eating, gaze lowered to his plate. A small nod told Anna he suspected OH was right. Told her too he didn't want to pursue the conversation lest it turn to his personal disregard of other scriptural precepts. Like the seventh commandment.

Finishing quickly, he excused himself and left the table without speaking. Later she considered looking for him, but realized she had no balm for his soul. All she could offer were a few moments of physical pleasure to distract him from the ache of his own apostasy.

* * *

Compassion reached Nagasaki late afternoon on 25 September, the day after a task force had sailed with ninety-two hundred ex-PWs. The last hundred miles, the ship was accompanied by a destroyer which picked up a harbor pilot to navigate a channel so tortuous they had to proceed at half speed. A cold mist obscured surrounding hills and mingled with acrid smoke in a stench that suggested both raw sewage and incineration. Though noticeable offshore, as they proceeded upstream it became so overpowering that those on the open decks retreated inboard to watch their progress from the lounge.

"God, what is that?" asked one of the surgeons.

"Well, six weeks ago, forty-thousand human beings were blasted to smithereens here," Floyd said. "What do you think? Plus the Japanese burn charcoal for everything. Even run their cars with it. And whatever shit they don't fertilize their gardens with, they dump in the harbor."

On either side of the channel, flimsy matchstick houses clung to terraced hills. The waterfront was lined with large, low buildings and skeletons of others. Dark shapes of sunken ships rose randomly from the harbor; an up-thrust prow, a deckhouse with a disintegrating stack, and a stern, its barnacled prop half submerged. The scene was a monochrome watercolor, all shades of gray soft-edged by fog. And silent, the only sounds from people on board, no movement except for the destroyer preceding them. *Compassion* followed her toward another tin can at anchor, and then, close abeam, veered to starboard. As they idled toward a wharf, two serious-faced kids squatting on the muddy bank waved small American flags.

On the pier, helmeted GIs in fatigues caught lines. The gangway was run across; several Army officers strode aboard and headed toward the bridge. And the rest of them waited for official word about their duties here, in the absence of which they theorized and speculated. They'd all become experts at that.

That evening, the Exec briefed them about their next passengers. "Most are Navy, some four hundred of them, plus a few merchant seamen. Surprisingly, the Nips actually picked up survivors once in a while. Other PWs were captured on Guam right after Pearl Harbor. But most came from ships they sank. A PT boat crew, a sub, a fleet tug, an oiler, a couple tin cans."

"A sub?" Adrenaline jolted Anna upright. "Which one?"

Up and down the table, friends glanced at her. "No idea," he said. "We'll find out when they board."

Throughout the briefing, her mind strayed to the mention of prisoners from a sub. Her mouth went dry, fingers turned cold and her heart raced, as if she'd been chased by a bear. Or a familiar ghost.

When they were dismissed, Mark pushed toward her. "Can you come to the office awhile, Anna?"

Surprised at the public request, she followed him up to C and down the passage. Luke was already at his desk; Mark gestured at the chair, and sat at his own. She shook her head and continued to stand. "What is it?" she asked, suspecting.

The two chaplains exchanged a covert glance. "Tell me, something, Anna," Mark said. "Why'd you ask which sub the survivors they'd found were from? Surely you don't think it's your husband's."

She shrugged, uncomfortable about admitting what he undoubtedly considered a pathetically foolish hope. "Well, it could be. See, when he was reported missing, I thought maybe if they sank the boat and took the crew prisoners, there might not be an official record. So I wouldn't have been notified if he was in one of these camps."

"Anna," Luke said soberly. "The International Red Cross has records of all PWs. If your husband was in this camp or any other, the Navy would know."

Waving off the suggestion, she noticed Mark's grave expression. "He's right," he said. "Nobody here is likely to be Dan."

"Look, Anna," Luke put in. "What are the odds that we'd meet out here, you and I, I mean, and you'd figure I was Lorraine's son? A million to one?"

"Of course. That's why I believe Dan could still be alive." She paced around, glancing out the porthole at thin rain dappling the harbor, veiling anchored ships and the bleak, colorless hills beyond. "See, when I joined the Nurse Corps, some people thought I was hoping to find him out here. I never did, though, I really never did. Until just now. My God, the crew of a submarine. That's more than coincidence."

"No, it's not," Luke said. "Dozens of subs have disappeared out here."

"I know that. And I'm not betting on it. Just saying it could be."

Both nodded. Mark said, "Well, we'll know soon enough."

More than willing to be dismissed, she hurried to her cabin and removed Dan's picture from a folder in the locker. Studying it again, she traced a series of possibilities that could have brought him here. Even as she cautioned herself against counting on any of them, she felt an uncommon exhilaration. An all-things-are-possible sort of exhilaration.

That evening at chow, Mark suggested a walk to the fantail. "But wear your foul-weather jacket. Damp and cold this evening."

They were the only ones there, likely because the earlier smell was more intense, a brown and black stink trapped under a gray cloud. "Can't we go somewhere that smells better, like your cabin?"

"You'll get used to it in a minute. Right now, I don't want to be distracted by the usual temptation."

She glared. "Well, okay. But I know what you're going to say...you think I'm crazy."

His eyes, the lines of his face were soft, his mouth tender. "Of course not, Anna. I understand completely."

"What is there to understand?"

"Oh, just that if one of the PWs is Dan, you'd still be his wife. So I'd be out of the picture. I guess Jim would too." He shrugged. "Your life would be much simpler, wouldn't it?"

The suggestion made her gasp. Mulling it over, she focused on a small, feeble-looking boat with virtually no freeboard chugging toward the far shore. Yellow smoke roiled from the stubby stack and drifted above the swirling wake. She shifted her gaze back to Mark. "Oh, maybe. But simplicity aside, finding Dan would be the best miracle ever."

His gaze didn't waver. "I can think of an even better one."

"What?"

"Well, suppose the hospital lied when you had your baby. Told you he was stillborn because they'd given him to another woman, say, because her husband outranked yours. Anyway, after Dan came home, you and he could claim the child. And live happily ever after. Now. Wouldn't that be the best miracle of all?"

She studied his expression: guileless and open. Nonetheless, disbelief rapidly escalated into anger. "What a heartless thing to say, Mark. How could you?"

He shrugged. "Because I love you. And I want to slap some sense into you."

She filled her lungs with the foul air. "Well, I feel

slapped all right. That was totally out of line. If you loved me, you'd never say something so hurtful."

"Sorry. But...well, it's just crazy to think you'll find Dan out here. Or anywhere. And you need to realize it. Not get your hopes up for nothing."

"That doesn't sound like you, Mark. Unless you've totally lost your faith."

"This isn't about faith, Anna. This is a fairy tale."

"Huh! I bet if you'd been there the first Easter, you wouldn't have believed Jesus rose from the dead either. Talk about fairy tales!"

He shrugged, touched the side of her face with gentle fingertips. "Sorry, Anna. Didn't mean to shoot you down. But...."

Unable to devise an exit line, she turned and fled to the sanctuary of her cabin. Tempted to fling herself on the bed like a hurt teenager, instead she wrote Jim a rambling, disjointed letter about the day's happenings. Editing out Mark's declaration of love, of course, but reporting other dialogues with him and Luke.

Funny, she mused later, Mark had blurted out "I love you," before, during moments of passion. Now, spoken in the putrid air of this war-ravaged port, the declaration had the ring of veracity. Wrapped in his blunt advice, however, it was easy to reject.

* * *

At chow the next morning, she passed Dan's picture around the table. "This is my husband. He was on a sub that went missing two years ago."

The explanation evoked surprised glances from other nurses. One gasped, "I didn't know you'd been married."

Anna's turn to be surprised. As prodigiously as all of them gossiped among themselves, she'd thought there were no untold tales left. You only needed to confide in one other girl to kick off a legend. Like the one that OH had been engaged to a World War One pilot shot down over Belgium by the Red Baron.

"But I think," she went on breathlessly, "I mean I'm hoping, he might be with the PWs we're evacuating."

No one replied except OH. She studied the photo, then passed it up the table to Anna. "When was this taken?"

"Uh, July, 1941. For his twenty-fifth birthday."

She shook her head. "Well, if he is here, you bet your life he won't look like this."

Anna stuck it back in the folder. "Oh, sure. I know that. I just thought, well, I'll be in Receiving, but I won't be able to see everyone who comes aboard. So I want the rest of you to know what he looks like. Or used to. I mean, if anybody looks even a little like him, let me know. Please? I'll recognize him. No matter how changed he is."

No one answered or met her gaze. Unable to swallow more toast and jam, she excused herself and crossed the wardroom to the table where Mark and Luke were gabbing with some surgeons. She passed the photo around there too, and repeated what she'd told the nurses. The only difference here was that nobody commented.

Finally Mark handed it back and said he'd walk with her to the ladder. When they were alone, he said, "Just want you to know, I'll keep my eye peeled today too."

"Oh? You don't think I'm crazy?"

The hint of a smile warmed his face. "Well, yes, I still do. But I understand. And if you want me to, I'll watch for him."

She leaned up and brushed her lips against his. "Oh, thank you. That means so much."

He nodded, his look warm and fond, yet patently troubled.

* * *

The first ex-PWs arrived later that morning in the back of open Army trucks. Assisted by corpsmen, they shuffled slowly up the gangway, skinny frames covered by GI fatigues, feet swallowed by oversize combat boots. Having recently been deloused, their hair was cut to the nub, their faces uniformly lined and gray.

"They say they look good now to what they did when we went into the camp last week," murmured the corpsman working with Anna. "And even then they were better off than before the B-29s started parachuting food to them. A wonder any of the poor devils made it out alive."

Studying the sad incoming procession, she felt her professional smile wilt.

As the former captives came aboard, before long they all began to resemble each other, wizened old men in whose sunken eyes she could see only a remote hope of rejuvenation. A few brightened as they stepped into the sanitized whiteness of Receiving, where medical personnel waited to examine them, then lead them to a bed with clean sheets and the promise of food as often as they wanted. Several actually got down on hands and knees and kissed the deck.

For hours they came, a few on crutches, some on litters, most upright and under their own power. Part of two groups checking them in, Anna focused on her line and tried to watch the other, but was soon caught up in making charts. Some had improvised records assembled by Army medics who'd reached the camp first, but for most she had to rely on dog tag information. Beside medical questions like, "Were you sick while you were in the camp?" the only other she asked was, "What ship were you on?"

So they arrived, one truckload after another packed with men in threadbare Jap uniforms or Navy-issue denims.

Anna's duty section was relieved for noon chow, then sent below again to escort new arrivals to the wards, push their wheelchairs, or walk beside their litters. See that they got chow, help them eat, treat them like human beings.

By the time they were processed and assigned beds, some had begun to recover from the shock of freedom. A few asked, "Am I dreaming, nurse? Am I really on an American ship bound Stateside?" But most were quiet and withdrawn, still watching unspeakable memories, like private horror movies in their heads

On previous deployments, commissioned patients occupied quiet rooms; on this one these cabins were assigned on the basis of condition. Some patients were gravely ill with diseases caused or exacerbated by malnourishment, including TB, and had to be isolated. Some had old fractures, healed only with the aid of improvised splints and bandages. A few were on the brink of starvation, despite what Anna had always believed were regular Red Cross food packages. But Floyd had learned the Japs had distributed very few, and then only after they realized the war was lost. No man had ever had mail from home. Several reported a Navy doctor with them had died a year before.

By the end of the day, *Compassion*'s medics had processed over two hundred patients. Among them, Anna had met Navy flyers who'd ditched at sea, seamen from torpedoed merchant ships, and corpsmen captured on Guam in December, 1941. One asked about the nurses who'd been taken prisoner with them. He was incredulous that even after they'd been transported to Japan, they were actually repatriated.

At no time, however, did she meet anyone from a sub. By nightfall, she was almost too weary to eat, but dragged herself to the wardroom and collapsed next to Mark. He'd learned nothing of any submariners either, except one man he'd talked to had confirmed there were some in the camp.

After chow, at the foot of the ladder again, he pulled her close for a surreptitious kiss, and the murmured invitation, "Want to come to my cabin a while?"

"Spirit's willing," she said, "but the flesh is too damned tired."

That grin, always disarming and appealing. "But suppose tomorrow you find your husband. They'll put him in a quiet room, and you'll spend every night with him all the way home. And if you do come to see me, it'll be adultery."

Astonished, she clapped one hand over her mouth. "My God, I hadn't thought of that. I mean, about the quiet room." Her consciousness returned to a baser reality. "But it's adultery now, isn't it?"

He shrugged. "Yeah, but only for me. Whereas if you find Dan..."

She stared, torn, but too weary to resist further. "Well, since you put it that way...."

* * *

The next day they received another two hundred thirty men, these more debilitated and worn down by longer captivity. And Anna finally met a radioman from a sub. He mumbled the name, but she didn't understand. "Did you say *Wolf Fish?*"

"No, ma'am, *Bullfish.*"

Disappointment rocked her. "Well, then. Ever heard of *Wolf Fish?*"

"Can't say I have. But that don't mean I ain't."

"So her crew might've been in your camp and you wouldn't have known."

"Well, no. See, we were there damned near three years. Every time we got new people, we all knew. It was the way we found out what was really going on, not the bullshit the Japs fed us. No, ma'am. When I said I might've heard of that sub, I'm talking about before. Like at Pearl, or when we tied up at the tender, there was plenty of boats coming and going."

During the rest of her shift she found others from the same sub. One, a jaygee, asked if *Wolf Fish* had ever been at Portsmouth, NH; he might have seen her there. This slim connection ignited a blaze of hope that compelled her to ask the circumstances of their capture.

"Funny about that. Only happened because the Old Man gave us a break. We'd just replenished, so we anchored off some little island they said was secure. Half the crew went ashore with beer for a picnic, while the rest of us stayed aboard to charge the batteries. When we spotted the Jap plane, he was on top of us before we could man the deck gun. Only dropped one bomb, but that was the end of the boat, and a dozen crewmen, and the Old Man. So the rest of us swam ashore and waited to be rescued. Finished off the beer, of course. We'd got off an SOS, so the next day, when we saw a ship on the horizon, we all hollered and waved. At least 'til we saw the rising sun on her flag." He shrugged, shoulder bones prominent under the denim shirt. "That's it. That's what happened."

The story was so similar to one of her early fantasies, her spirits soared higher. "Well then," she said, "what happened to your boat could've happened to *Wolf Fish* too. Only her crew was taken to another camp."

"Guess so, ma'am. But why're you asking? Know somebody on her?"

"My husband. He was Engineering Officer. Dan Donovan? Maybe you met him at Portsmouth?"

He shook his head wearily. "Sorry."

"That's okay. Now I've met your crew, I know he could still be alive."

His stare was blank, empty of any clues to his feelings. "Well, I wish you luck, ma'am. I sure do wish you luck."

At chow that evening, no one inquired about the search for Dan, not even Mark. Everyone was elated that after they'd embarked more ex-PWs in the morning, they'd get underway for Okinawa. There, they'd transfer some off, pick up others, then set course for San Francisco. Finally, finally, they'd be homeward bound.

Around her, Anna's friends were rejoicing, yet she was heavy with gloom. As if Dan were somewhere near, if not on Kyushu, then on another island; but once they sailed, she'd never find him. Even as she posited it, however, the logic began to drain from the theory. If he were anywhere in this conquered land, the Army of Occupation would find him and bring him back.

That night she wrote to Jim, but he'd once urged her to stop looking for signs about Dan, so she realized this latest notion would only elicit similar advice. Bad enough she'd had it from the chaplains. Even worse was Mark's supposition that if Dan were alive, she wouldn't be returning to Jim. Still, it was easier to imagine writing, "Sorry, Jim, but I have to stay with Dan. I'll always love you, but after two years in prison, he really needs me," than, "You were right, Jim. I have fallen for another man, just as you were afraid I would."

But under no circumstances would she ever tell him about Mark. Mark might proclaim his love in a thousand ways, but he'd never be Jim Millett, and she would never trust him as she did Jim. Passion was thrilling, but it was no substitute for steadfast, wordless trust.

CHAPTER TWENTY-FOUR

*T*he last of the ex-PWs came aboard the next morning, almost all on litters and in worse shape than the earlier groups. Again Anna searched their faces for Dan, only to realize he was not among these men either. Racked with disappointment, she nonetheless forced her focus from her own emotions to the medical needs of the new passengers. Which was what any nurse worth her salt did, wasn't it, no matter how her heart ached?

By noon, all had been charted, bathed, put to bed and fed egg custard, applesauce, and sweet tea. Too weary to climb ladders, she rode the elevator up to the main deck and headed for the smell of roast beef wafting from the wardroom. She'd just found a seat with Willi and Floyd when the Exec took the lectern and announced that all medical personnel with a rank of full lieutenant or above would be allowed to tour the bomb-flattened part of the city.

"Muster at the foot of the gangway at 1330," he added, "and be prepared to ride standing up in Army trucks. Now.

How many want to go?"

From the number of hands in the air and bursts of conversation all over the wardroom, Anna surmised everyone was wild to see the destruction. Then OH announced that anyone who wanted pictures should give her their cameras. A dozen junior nurses rushed out to get theirs. At another table, Mark found her with his eyes, then made his way across the room.

"Want me to take your camera?" he asked. "Or can you do without a souvenir of Japan?"

She gave him a wry smile. "Thanks, but I've seen enough. You can tell me about it later."

"Would you come too, if you had the rank?"

"Nope. Maybe if it were the ruins of Athens, and I were a real tourist..."

He smiled, squeezed her shoulder, and took off with unusual energy. Luke too was heading for the tour, along with Floyd, all the senior nurses and every medical officer except the MOD. The mood was so festive you'd have thought they were off to a garden party.

When the others had left, Anna and Willi stood at C Deck rail and watched the mob clamber into the same olive drab vehicles that had brought ex-PWs from the train. Another overcast day of cold, damp air full of the Stench.

Willi waved to Floyd. "Well, this'll be something to tell our kids, I guess."

Anna nodded, unable to connect thoughts of innocents with this nightmare place.

"Floyd wants to start having them--kids, I mean-- as soon as we're married. But I think we should wait a while. 'Til we're over the war."

"Oh, you mean, until his practice is established and he's bought the Packard?"

"Those are material things. I'm talking about what all this is doing to us." She shivered, pushed sunglasses higher on her nose. "Me at least. See, I don't want to hate the Japs the rest of my life, but everything I hear makes it worse."

Anna waggled her hand at Mark as the trucks chugged away from the pier in clouds of exhaust only slightly less offensive than the ambient odor. "A lot of people feel that way. Guess it's only natural, knowing what we do."

She nodded solemnly. "Remember the Aussies we picked up at Balikpapan last month? One told me the most horrifying story." She shuddered, wrapped her arms around her waist. "He said his best mate was killed in a battle, but they couldn't pick up the dead 'til the next morning. They didn't know the bloody Japs had booby-trapped the bodies in the night, so the first men in were blown up when they touched them. After that they had to machine-gun the corpses to make sure nobody else got killed." She paused, swallowed visibly. "He had to do that to his mate's body. Had to watch him explode. Then collect the pieces for burial."

"Dear God," Anna breathed. The scene played like a movie in her head, definitely one Hollywood would censor.

"He cried when he told me. Actually broke down. I didn't know what to say."

"What could you say?"

She shook her head. "Not a blessed thing. I heard some awful personal stories before, but that was the absolute worst."

"I bet our PWs could tell a few. Except you probably don't want to hear any others."

Willi's look was serious. "I do, though. See, Floyd and I feel we have a moral obligation to find out what they went through. So people back home can hear about it."

"Will that stop you from hating Japs?"

She shrugged. "Might make it worse. But I have to know."

Anna studied the other woman's profile, backlit by a sunlit rift in the clouds. "Well, if that's what you have to do...."

"What about you, Anna? You lost your husband. Don't you hate them for that?"

"No, not really. What I do hate is, the Navy never fixed the problems his boat had from the start. Sure, maybe the Japs sank it. But maybe it was an engineering snafu."

Even as she spoke, she was shocked to realize she was thinking of Dan in the past tense, as she had since she'd received the Killed in Action telegram in June, '44. As she did again now, with a sudden, inexplicable surety that he wasn't among the prisoners they'd liberated, not here or in any of the other Japanese islands.

Good Lord; she'd clutched at a straw too flimsy to support further hope. And everyone had known but her.

Willi's face brightened as sunlight touched it. "Floyd thinks we should write the PWs' stories. Thinks it'll help put the war behind us. And our new life, of course. Our new car. The kids we'll have. Then we'll forget what happened out here."

Anna inhaled deeply of the foul air. "Sometimes I have to make myself stop thinking about things. Like the men in the water after Indy sank. Then I sort of go numb inside. But it's better than pain."

"I can't do that yet. Wish I could."

"Maybe I've had more practice." Anna gazed away from Willi's wistful expression. "I started when my husband's boat first went missing in '43. So I'm good at it now."

"Floyd calls it dissociating. See, he wanted to be a psychiatrist before he went into dentistry."

They both smiled, but said no more, turning their gazes to a wash of lemony sunlight on the decrepit oriental buildings along the waterfront. Nothing anyone would ever use as a backdrop for an opera.

* * *

Those who'd toured Nagasaki's ruins returned just after three. No sooner had they arrived than a pilot came aboard, the gangway was retrieved and lines cast off. In midstream, one of the destroyers fired up too and weighed anchor. When *Compassion* had drifted away from the wharf and come about, the tin can fell in behind them in the serpentine waterway leading to the East China Sea. And a course that would bring them first to Okinawa, then California. Even imagining it gave Anna shivers of nostalgia.

While they were still in the harbor, she went to Mark's cabin and asked if he wanted to watch their departure from the usual fantail spot. "And tell me what you saw in the city."

He bit his lip, then tossed on his hat. "Okay. But there wasn't much to see. Just a valley full of rubble. And if you think it stinks here, you should smell it out there." He stood aside, let her precede him down the after ladder "I'm glad I saw it, but it was a nightmare place."

She shivered and took his hand as they came out on deck.

The fantail was packed with doctors and nurses silently staring at the receding panorama of gray hills and silver water behind their wake. As they plodded between hulks of sunken ships, the stench gradually dissipated in gusts of fresh sea air. By the time they'd dropped the pilot, Anna was able to inhale deeply for the first time in days.

As the pilot's launch chugged away, she turned to Mark. "Now. Tell me more about what you saw this afternoon. I mean details. So don't say nothing much."

He shrugged. "Okay. But it was just rubble. Acres and acres of it. And here and there, pieces of things people must've used. Like shards of pottery. Hunks of twisted metal. A burned shoe." He swallowed hard and compressed his lips before he continued: "And a doll's head. With blue eyes and blonde hair."

Anna winced at the image, horrifying enough even without imagining what had become of the child who'd loved it.

"And books. Totally charred, but you could tell what they were. Luke even found a prayer book under a chunk of concrete. They told us not to take anything because it might be radioactive, but he picked it up anyway. And took lots of pictures. To show his mother, he said. Thought she'd like to see the head of Jesus on the ground by the Cathedral."

Anna was sure the picture would horrify Lorraine, but if her son had taken it, she'd be proud he'd shared it. "You're right, those are nightmare images."

"Well, you asked."

By now there was nothing left to see of Japan except the mist-shrouded hills of Kyushu fading behind them, the trailing destroyer, and the long gray reaches of sea ahead. Suddenly chilled, she huddled closer. "You know, I just realized something. Pretty soon, this is going to end. With the war over, the Navy's not going to need us much longer, are they? So then what?"

He shrugged, as if the answer was obvious. "Why, then we'll all go home. You'll marry Jim and live happily ever after."

She blinked slowly and inhaled a couple of times before she knew how to respond. "That's not what I meant. I meant, nothing will ever be like this again, will it?"

He tucked her hand through the crook of his elbow. "I hope not. Oh, being with you, well, that's been wonderful. But the war, no, that can never happen again."

She sighed; others at the rail were straggling away. "It

just feels strange, knowing it's over."
"That mean you've stopped looking for Dan?"
She nodded, avoiding his concentrated gaze.
"Really? What changed your mind?"
"Don't know. Maybe the Lord spoke sense to me."
He chuckled, patted her hand. "Good. Then there's hope for me too."

CHAPTER TWENTY-FIVE

After chow that evening, they ran into heavy weather and slowed to half speed. By the time Anna came on duty at 2300, the ship was bucking and rearing like a raft in rapids. All the ex-PWs were awake, corpsmen handing out anti-emetics or scurrying with basins for those who couldn't make it to the head to throw up. She was shocked that men who had survived indignities and brutality beyond imagining were now terrified, clutching covers and bed rails with bony hands, eyes wide in their pallid faces. She knew that for this particular group, terror stemmed from having been in the water for two days after their destroyer was sunk, only to be picked up by another that also went down off Guadalcanal.

"Didn't you have rough weather on the tin can?" she asked a Negro to whom she'd brought a sleeping pill.

His jaundiced eyes were bright against a seamed, coffee-brown face. "Well, sure, Ma'am. But that was three years ago. Lost my sea legs since then."

"Well, by the time we reach Frisco, I promise you'll have them back."

"So long as we don't hit no more storms. Hate to think after what we went through, we'd end up shark-bait."

She used her confident nurse's voice. "No danger of that. This ship's lived through much worse." Then to distract him, said, "I see you were a mess cook on your ship. Did you do that in the camp too?"

His smile was studded with a few stubby teeth. "If you could call it cooking. Mostly they just gave us rice, and sometimes vegetables. Least I guess they was vegetables. Things I never seen before. But we cooked 'em up, and them boys, they ate every bite. Three times a day, though, it was rice. No ma'am, don't care if I never see another grain of that stuff, ever."

She glanced at his chart again. "It says here you helped the camp doctor, and after he died, the corpsman. Did you have medical training too?"

"Oh no, ma'am. But on the ship, see, they asked us cooks if we wanted to work with Marines on the beach. Even gave us rifles so we could help the medics bring out wounded. They was so short of men, they didn't care what color we was." He chuckled. "Helping them medics, it come natural once we got to the camp. Not that they was much we could do with what we had."

She tried to envision the horrific images in his memory, was about to ask more when the man in the next bed asked if she could please, please give him something to knock him out.

"I lived for this," he said. "Being on an American ship, getting the hell away from that shit-hole and them slant-eyes. Now, all I can think, it's a bad dream and we're all gonna die."

She gave him her best smile, patted his hand. "How long were you in the camp?"

"Three years, more or less."

"That's a long while to be in prison. I have no idea how bad it was, but there must've been times when you didn't think you'd make it. Yet you did. And here you are. This is just a storm. It'll soon blow over. I'll give you a sleeping pill, but you have to tell yourself, the worst is over. The war is over. The camp is behind you. Japan's behind you. You're going home."

She made her way to the nurse's station, grabbing bed frames for support as the deck lurched. God, she'd been as didactic and preachy as OH. What did she know about the myriad terrors that fed these men's fears, which presently made little sense to her neat American mind? She might just as well have slapped his face and commanded him, "Get over it, sailor!" She'd seen OH do that once with a hysterical battle fatigue patient. And yet she'd known the same terror during the squall off Guam; it had retreated only in the shelter of Mark's arms. Now here she was, glibly offering others the reassurance she hadn't been able to give herself.

She returned with the pill, watched him swallow it, then asked him to tell her about home. When he dozed off, she gave out a dozen more pills and reassured a dozen other former boys that they had nothing to fear. But all the while she was painfully aware that though they'd survived the worst war could do, their souls had no peace. If Mark were there, she knew he'd have comforting words for men who hadn't been comforted in so long they'd forgotten what it felt like. His faith may have waned, but she still trusted him to do that.

* * *

When she missed him at breakfast, she went to the chaplains' office. Luke said he'd gone below to hold a service. "After all, it is Sunday," he reminded her.

She shrugged. "Lately time doesn't have a day or a date on it."

"For me, saying Mass every day makes it even more confusing."

"Oh, that's right. I'd almost forgotten."

"Maybe you're still spending too much time with Whitmore. Thought you broke it off."

A red flame flared in her mind. She was tempted to challenge him, except she knew any discussion would invariably eventuate into a morality debate. Having been on duty all night, she was in no mood for polemics.

Without answering, she hurried to her cabin, showered and flopped onto the bunk. She slept so long she was late for noon chow and missed Mark again. She soon began to interpret this failure to connect as a sign from God they weren't meant to, at least that day.

She finally caught sight of him after *Compassion* docked at Naha, where they transferred a hundred more robust passengers to complete the trip home on a transport. He and Luke followed them down the gangway; neither showed up for chow later. By then her composure had yielded to a vague but familiar yearning. Trying to ignore it, she ate with the usual gang, then watched a Ronald Reagan movie that had just come aboard. When she kept falling asleep, she collected the latest mail and repaired to her cabin to read. The tone of all the letters was joyous: the war had ended, everyone was safe and she'd soon be home.

Lorraine Cropper was particularly ecstatic about meeting her son. She also reported Alex was engaged to an English girl whom she was sure Anna would get on with, because they were both nurses. As if nurseliness was what she prized most in friends. As if she didn't have Margie to remind her a shared profession meant nothing when friends had so few values in common. Or so it had seemed when she'd seen Margie the year before. Perhaps by now her own values had become just as tarnished.

* * *

The next morning, buses brought nearly three hundred liberated prisoners from other parts of Japan to the pier. Mark was with Luke at another table, but leaving the wardroom, he came over and sat on the edge of a chair beside Anna. He seemed jittery, as if en route to more urgent duties.

"Heard you were looking for me yesterday." His tone was so bland she couldn't tell if he was surprised, pleased, or merely wary.

"Yes. I wanted to talk about…well, the PWs. Because I don't know how to deal with them. Psychologically, I mean."

"You, Anna? All the time you've spent on the nut ward?"

"This is different. Look, can we talk more later?"

He grinned. "Want to come to my cabin? Or do you just want to talk?"

Her gaze sank into the dark depths of his eyes. "I can talk there too."

The rhythm of his breathing changed as he returned the look. For a moment, there was no one else within fifty miles. Then he compressed his lips, nodded, got to his feet. "You on duty again tonight?"

"I'll be in Receiving the rest of the day. Then I'm off until tomorrow afternoon."

"Good. See you at chow, then." He left without arranging a meeting.

She spent the morning checking in new arrivals, many in worse shape than patients from Nagasaki. Few could climb the gangway unassisted, even after six weeks of freedom.

Later, a corpsman told her this group had survived the Bataan Death March, only to be loaded onto a Japan-bound transport sunk by American planes. Then, picked up at sea by one of the infamous Hell Ships, they'd had neither water nor food on the voyage to Japan; those who'd survived became slave laborers in factories and mines. Now their emaciated frames were so stooped and bent she wondered how much nurture and rest it would take to restore them physically. If restoration was even possible.

That night the wardroom was packed with visiting dignitaries from the base. Naturally, the Uniform of the Day was dress blues with service ribbons and spit-shined shoes. Lined up in neat rows, Anna and other medical personnel sat feigning attention during endless speeches congratulating them for the ship's latest Silver Star, her third in as many years. They were also reminded they still had a big job yet ahead: getting ex-PWs home before Christmas.

As usual, she was at the junior nurses' table, Mark and Luke with the medical officers at another. Fighting boredom, she kept staring at Mark's profile, but he was in proper chaplain's mode; eyes straight ahead, smiling when appropriate, serious the rest of the time, applauding when everyone else did. After an hour, however, she caught him glancing at his watch, even stifling a yawn behind his hand.

It was after eight before they were turned loose. "Come on," he said as they mingled with the departing mob. "Let's get some air." He steered her toward the deck and the cool fog that had settled over the harbor. Not as pungent as Nagasaki, but still heavy with the stench of death from recent battlefields on this island.

They walked forward, leaned on the rail overlooking the pier where stevedores were hefting supplies aboard. Mist haloed lights, muffled the banter of others on deck and the crunch and thud of boxes.

"Now," he said, taking her hand. "What do you mean about dealing with the PWs psychologically?"

"I don't know how to comfort them." She related their fear during the storm. "So I wondered what you would do. You always knew how to deal with battle fatigue cases."

"That was different. Those guys needed to talk. It's too soon for these men. They're still… oh, scalded, you could say. Just barely alive after all that abuse and starvation. No one can comfort them yet. They need time."

"And the Lord. You didn't mention the Lord. Or don't you think he cares?"

"Still haven't decided."

"Well, tell me this. Do you pray with them?"

"If they ask. Most don't. See, they lost everything in those camps. Not just their health, but youth, and dignity…even hope. And faith, maybe faith most of all." He shook his head. "Damned hard to keep believing in a God that sends you to hell for no reason."

She shuddered. "Isn't there any way to reach them?"

"Nothing obvious. Eventually, even without psychological treatment, time'll heal them and they'll be easier to reach. In fact, I bet even before we get to Frisco, some'll be so much better they'll be lusting for you."

She laughed, but the comment seemed too banal to dignify. "I hope you're right. I mean, about time healing them. And all the rest of us. Especially you."

He looked away quickly, lips compressed, eyes cold. Then he turned again with the usual grin. "Hey, if lust's any barometer of healing, I'm already recovering."

Later, in the dim closeness of his bunk, she wondered if he'd felt a similar heat with his other women. She knew better than to ask. What would he say anyway? Probably a variation of, "Nothing was ever like this, Anna." She hated that about herself that she could totally shut out his egregious past, as if forgiving seventy times seven made her a fool. Her only hope was that eventually Jim's constant presence would expunge this unreasoning torment.

Even as her mind strayed to the notion of phoning Jim from California, Mark said, "Hey, sweetie, what do you say we get ourselves a room in Frisco? In a first-rate hotel. With a big double bed?"

She glanced down at their entwined bodies, arms and legs casually draped over each other's, like those of the piled corpses in Nazi death camps. How close they all were to the other side, she thought, picturing the hollow-eyed men in the wards who, unlike so many of their comrades, had narrowly escaped being sucked through the thin membrane dividing the living from the dead.

She shivered and forced herself back to the reality of their warm and lively flesh. "Can't wait. And I want a hot bath in a real tub."

He sighed. "It's going to seem like a dream after all this time. Being back in an American city, I mean."

"Will you try to call your wife?"

He tensed. "Why would I do that?"

"Maybe just to hear her voice."

"No," he muttered in such a way she knew not to ask more.

She did anyway. "Funny. You mentioned it once, but I can't remember her name."

He sighed, shook his head. "Look, Anna. We don't have much time left, so let's not waste it talking about my wife, okay?"

"Whatever you say."

"Anyway, scuttlebutt is we'll make one more run after this. Then the ship's scheduled for a major overhaul. And we'll go home, I guess. So all we have is nine or ten weeks more."

"What'll you do then? Resign from the ministry?"

"Don't know. First I'll go see my kids. And my parents.

And a bishop I used to work with. Maybe he can advise me about…you know, these doubts I've been having."

She was curious about whether he'd try to reconcile with his wife. But that subject was now officially off-limits. All they could do was pretend time would never run out. So she stroked his chest, inhaled the smell of his body, and tried to hear what two nurses outside the porthole were talking about, but their voices were too low, and they soon moved on down the deck. Then, from the passageway just beyond the hatch she heard a stifled female giggle and a male voice responding.

"Do you know," she said then, "how much desperate screwing there's going to be on this ship in the next nine or ten weeks?"

He laughed. "No. But I bet Luke could tell us. He and his cronies probably have a betting pool going."

* * *

In the morning, word went out that all patients who wanted a last view of the Orient should come topside before they sailed. "Because our next port of call is San Francisco, California, US of A," the Exec added. Unsurprising news, but goose bumps rose on Anna's forearms.

So they came, up the ladders or on the elevators, in wheelchairs, on crutches, with canes, or shuffling along on their own, their skeletal bodies clad in sailors' denims, makeshift khakis or Navy-issue pajamas and robes. By the time the last supplies had been loaded, the starboard rails on every deck were lined with these gaunt-eyed survivors of hell. On the pier below, a Navy band had been pumping out Sousa marches the past half-hour, and *California, Here I come.* But as the gangways were taken aboard and lines cast off, they broke into *Anchors Aweigh*.

Compassion drifted from the pier, the deck began to vibrate; the whistle blasted. Everyone on deck stood on attention, hands raised in salute or placed over their heart.

"Until we meet once more," Mark said quietly in time to the melody, "Here's wishing you a happy voyage home."

Anna couldn't speak. The familiar music wafted across the water, notes distorted by the wind. At her first sight of this ship thirteen months before, she'd been conscious of the spot-lit quality of the moment. Here was another, a perfect bookend for the past year.

They watched until a tug had pushed the prow around and the band music had been drowned by the blare of the squawk box announcing a briefing for all medical personnel in a half hour.

Mark's sigh was full of poignant irony. "Well, guess now it's back to work as usual."

* * *

If anyone had expected the next three weeks to be a pleasure cruise because they carried no critical patients, they soon learned otherwise. So few of the six hundred ex-PWs had been thoroughly examined, staff was tasked with doing complete work-ups on every man. Based on these findings, at the end of the voyage they'd be sent either to hospitals for further recuperation, or home for discharge and follow-up care.

"Besides those with unattended old wounds, some may be seriously ill. So we have to keep painstaking records for a basis of comparison," said the CMO between sips of coffee. "Therefore, I'm depending on all of you to maintain the same high professional standards you did throughout the war."

Once Anna might have groaned inwardly at this sententious speech; now she had a sand-through-the-hourglass sense of this deployment. The happy voyage home would be replete with dull routines after all. The band had stopped playing and the goose bumps had leveled out. Of course, they might run into squalls, and some patients would be terrified, but for the most part, they were beginning to heal, their craving for comfort attenuated by the evolving normality of their lives.

As Mark left the meeting, he gave her hand a surreptitious squeeze. The weary smile deepened the crows' feet around his eyes. "You on the graveyard shift tonight?"

"Uh-huh."

"Which ward?"

"Haven't checked the duty roster yet. Why?"

"Oh, I just thought…well, maybe I'll work wherever you are. Like we used to on H13." He pressed his lips together. "See, I want to be with you as often as I can, as long as I can."

The vulnerability in his admission sliced into her. Ridiculous, she told herself; he just knew how to play her. Lord knew, he'd had enough practice.

"That'd be nice," she said crisply, to conceal tenderness whelming like a sudden fever in her system.

CHAPTER TWENTY-SIX

They'd been at sea less than twenty-four hours when Anna realized she hadn't seen Floyd in the wardroom since they'd sailed. When he didn't show up the next day either, she asked Willi if he was sick.

"No, he's fine. Just busy." The smile crinkled her eyes. "You know, those PWs haven't brushed their teeth in years. So he's up to his eyeballs in cavities and pyorrhea. And he loves it."

Anna couldn't imagine loving anything about dentistry, but there was a lot about Floyd that was incomprehensible.

He finally turned up Sunday noon for the week's major meal. He seemed thinner, wirier, noticeably less garrulous. As if more attuned to his own thoughts than table chatter. Almost like someone incubating a grand plan, perhaps even a crusade, he ate hurriedly, cramming in food with seeming disregard for the fact the entree was baked ham. He even skipped desert, explaining he had to repair the Ops Officer's broken molar before he went back to his usual patients.

"Usual patients? On a Sunday?" By the time Nell got the

words out, he was already halfway across the wardroom.

Mark gazed toward the passageway where Floyd had retreated, lab coat flapping in his wake. "Never seen him so fired-up before. He's always been kind of blasé about dentistry."

Willi said, "Ordinarily he is. But these blokes have been through so much, he's doing everything he can while they're with us. Meantime, we're asking them about their experiences in captivity. See, he wants to know why some of them survived and others didn't."

Mark rolled his eyes. "Easy. Because they weren't shot. Or beaten. Or starved."

"I mean, besides obvious causes. Why, under the same conditions, are some alive while others died?" She swiped a glance at the clock, drained her coffee and got to her feet. "Anyway, we're looking for common denominators."

After she bustled out, the rest sat looking at each other. Then Polly yawned and Ed said he needed a nap before he went on duty. They left together without any pretense of retiring to separate cabins.

Mark smiled at Anna. "So preachers aren't the only ones who favor Sunday afternoon naps."

"Evidently not." She rose from the chair and excused herself. "Think I'll have one myself."

He followed her into the passageway. "Alone?"

She nodded. "It's that time of the month again."

"But sweetie, we can still sleep."

She gave him a dubious look, but followed him up the ladder.

It was a sullen day, clouds and ocean leaden, somber, wintry. Perfect for napping. And she might have, except that when they were lying together, Mark kept fidgeting, shifting positions in the narrow bunk, and sighing so loud and long she finally asked, "Can't you sleep without sex?"

"Don't be silly. I sleep without it all the time. Nope, I

was just thinking about that business Willi mentioned. You know…who survived the camps and who didn't. I'm wondering if faith plays a part in it too."

"Didn't you tell me these men have lost theirs?"

"Only an assumption. I need to know more, so I've been encouraging them to talk too. Not about religious beliefs, but maybe I should." His gaze shifted to hers. "Might even get Luke's take on it too."

She took his face between her hands and kissed his mouth. "That's a swell idea. Maybe it's something the two of you could actually agree on. And I could help. At least make notes of stories I hear. What do you think?"

His expression went serious, almost grim. "Might help me figure out what I believe too."

* * *

By now she knew what the Navy men from Nagasaki had endured. But among the new passengers, those in the quiet rooms were mostly Army men, survivors of the Bataan Death March in 1942. At the end of that enforced sixty-mile hike, they'd been interned in a camp in the northern Philippines where, for two years, their lives had settled into a pattern of deprivation relieved by the occasional Red Cross food package and the surreptitious offerings of natives. Not the best of all worlds, but at least survivable.

Then, as the invasion of the Philippines moved across Leyte and into Luzon, for no reason they could figure out, they'd been herded aboard a packed steamer where they slept in the hold on bits of straw and subsisted on a few tablespoons of raw rice and water each day. When this ship was sunk by American planes, they'd made it to a beach where rations were even tighter and potable water almost non-existent.

"They wanted us to die," said one skin-and-bones second lieutenant in Navy pajamas. "If they'd left us at Malaybalay, we'd've been liberated. But no, we'd surrendered and cowardice is the worst sin in the Japs' book. And they couldn't kill us outright unless we got out of line, so they pushed us to the edge, so we'd rebel. Or locked us in boxes where we couldn't stand or sit. And tried to starve us, like on that ship." He shuddered, face contorted. "Sometimes I envied the ones that didn't make it."

She recoiled. "Did you ever want to die too?"

His look was blank, as if she'd asked him to explain the theory of relativity.

"It'd been a lot easier," said his cabin mate, another shave-tail. "But see, we didn't want them to think they'd won."

"Besides," said the first, "other guys were hanging on, so I told myself I could too."

"See, it was just something we did. Staying alive, I mean. The only way we could rebel."

She nodded; his words made the sort of sense she could understand even vicariously. "What about God though? Did you ever pray?"

Lieutenant number one gave a rueful laugh. "Oh sure, at first. See, we had this padre who kept preaching the Lord'd give us strength. But then he got the shits and checked out, just like anybody else."

"I guess between us," said the other, "we said every prayer in the book. But nothing happened."

"Yeah, it did, Joe. Things got worse. You'd think it was as bad as it could get, then it got worse. Like when we heard the Japs were keeping Red Cross packages for themselves. Food and medicine too. So we figured, at least I did, what's the use of praying for anything?"

Anna nodded again, but with only superficial

understanding. "What about now? Now you're going home, do you think that God, I mean, can you look back and see He was with you all along?"

In their silence and sidelong glances at one another, she intuited they judged the question that of a do-gooding woman sheltered from war's harsh realities by gender and rank and naïveté. She resolved that henceforth she'd focus her queries only on their experiences, not the insubstantial fabric of their faith.

So night after night, she asked both those in quiet rooms and on the wards for their memories. Some closed up, preferring sleep to remembrance. Others would recall a few fragments, adding more from time to time as the ship plowed eastward. For once she was glad to work the graveyard shift where routines were fewer. Especially the third week, when many patients were finally more interested in talking than sleeping.

During this cruise, she saw almost nothing of Floyd and little of the chaplains. Intent on their respective projects, they often had chow with the patients instead of in the wardroom. When her path did cross Mark's and both were free, they scurried to his cabin, where they poured energy she didn't know they had into gratifying their bodies' need. At first, numbed by the PWs' tales of deprivation, she derived little pleasure from this activity. But after the first week, desire escalated into an unreasoning compulsion, a contact with sensation, a means of validating her own existence.

The phrase 'rutting barnyard animals' occasionally crossed her mind. Nonsense, she told herself, they were just two lonely souls trying to find their way home.

CHAPTER TWENTY-SEVEN

*C*n a Thursday in late October, *Compassion* approached the Golden Gate in rain, wind, and seas so rough no one manned the rails as they slipped under the rust-red bridge. Scuttlebutt was they'd tie up at Fort Mason, close to the heart of San Francisco where most of them planned to spend liberty. But instead, they steamed past piers packed with transports and capital ships, and headed under the Bay Bridge's suspension span. In the anchorage down the bay, mist blurred silhouettes of a carrier, a battlewagon, a cruiser and several smaller vessels.

Floyd had finally closed the dental surgery to join the group in the lounge. Scanning this flotilla with his well-worn binoculars, he muttered, "Looks like some kind of celebration." No one had asked, but he seemed frustrated he couldn't provide more specific information. Anna was far too caught up in recollections of her last view of this harbor to be curious.

"Remember flying out of here on the Clipper last year?" she asked Audrey as they watched their progress from the bank of windows in the lounge.

"Never forget it. God, thirteen months already. Can you believe it?"

Anna shook her head, surprised that instead of relief at returning to the Continental US, or the satisfaction of having completed a difficult mission, she felt only wistful. Faintly inexplicably blue, the color of illogical sadness.

Where was the exuberance she'd expected? Was it absent because this homecoming was merely symbolic: they could set foot on American soil for only a weekend before they sailed on one final deployment. Or did this nostalgic sense of ending, of no more, derive from the knowledge that the next would really be the last voyage?

Ah, that was it, she thought. The end of all this.

She glanced around at those nearby. And saw something similar mirrored in their eyes. But wouldn't ask. Who among them would dare admit he or she felt anything other than the triumphant sense of returning home as one of the victors?

The pier at the Oakland Naval Supply Depot was lined with gray Navy buses and ambulances waiting for patients. After the ship was tied up, Anna went down to Receiving to see them off, these former PWs she'd come to know like family during three weeks at sea. The Red Cross girls had staged farewell parties the night before, but this group was special, particularly the Negro cook from the sunken tin can. His war story was intriguing, so she'd asked about his earlier life too. And discovered such parallels between his youth in the segregated south and that in the prison camp, she'd taken down every word. Then, with a bottle of Chivas Regal she'd intended for her father, she bribed a Medical Records yeoman to type up two copies. Jesse was illiterate, but she gave him one to take home anyway.

By the time the gangway was in place, the rain had stopped, clouds shredding, opening to patches of brilliant cobalt and bursts of sunlight. As her patients debarked, she hugged them all, and watched until their busses had left. Then, dogged by a certain post-partum emptiness, she walked through the deserted, echoing wards to the dental surgery. Floyd was back at work, this time in a corpsman's gaping mouth.

"Did you get us rooms?" she asked. He and Willi were coming to a hotel with her and Mark, so he'd volunteered to make the reservations.

Still peering at the patient's teeth, he nodded. "Must be the last in the whole city. Saturday's Navy Day, so the fleet's in and the place is jammed."

"Which hotel?"

He consulted a notebook in his lab coat pocket. "Uh, the Fairmont."

"Oh, that's one of the best."

"Damned well ought to be for what they charge. I told them we'd just brought some PWs home, but they still didn't give us a break. Guess every gob in town wants a discount."

That evening at chow he outlined plans for their hotel stay. To offset the cost, he figured it was within walking distance of Chinatown and other free tourist attractions. Willi and Anna didn't care; their primary goal was to see a movie that wasn't six months old, in a real theater.

* * *

Liberty commenced after noon chow the next day. Floyd was all for riding the bridge train to the city and a cable car to the hotel. But the rain had returned, so they convinced him a taxi was a sensible option.

As soon as they piled in, the cabbie asked where they'd been. Floyd's eyes lit up as he launched into an answer. With his embellishments, the narrative of their most recent voyage lasted across both spans of the bridge, through the city and to the hotel entrance.

"So you been to Japan," the cabbie murmured with a shake of his head. "Boy, I seen what them devils did to Wainwright. Bet them PWs was skeletons too."

"Well, they were emaciated." Floyd glanced at the still-ticking meter. "Some had been tortured, and most had been slave laborers in factories or farms or mines. But as long as they did what they were told, they got by. Some even kept a sense of humor. In fact, one guy told us they didn't have toilets, just this long trough where they...well, you know. Then, when they cleaned it out, the guards sold the...uh, excrement to Jap civilians for fertilizer. And listen to this, they told them the officers'...uh, excrement ...was better than the enlisted, and charged more."

The cabbie guffawed and pounded the steering wheel. "Well, if that don't beat all, them sons of bitches screwing their own people." He finally raised the flag to stop the meter. "Listen, folks, been nice talking to you. And being tomorrow's Navy day, the ride's on me."

Mark pressed a wad of bills into his hand as the others hurried toward the hotel.

There was a long line at the desk, so while the men checked them in, Anna and Willi found seats in the lobby. On a nearby end table, Anna spotted a *Life* for October 15; the cover featured a languid model promoting new fall jewelry. Curious, she flipped through colorful ads for wondrous post-war products, but stopped dead when she came to the Picture of the Week: a full-page shot of the ruined Nagasaki cathedral with the head of Christ in the rubble.

She was still staring at it when Mark came over to ask if Willi objected to twin beds. She said she didn't, and he rejoined Floyd at the desk.

"I don't know why, "Anna said, "but he's been counting on a big bed."

Willi's smile was wise. "Maybe he really wants to sleep."

Blushing, she turned back to the magazine. Further on was a photo-essay for *The Lost Weekend*, a new Ray Milland – Jane Wyman film. She was wondering if it was playing somewhere in the city, when the men announced their rooms were ready.

"The clerk said the view from the one with the twin beds is much better than the one with the double," Floyd reported.

Mark said, "Don't worry; we won't be looking out the window anyway."

Then Anna showed them the Nagasaki picture. Before she realized what he was up to, Floyd hunched over the magazine and surreptitiously ripped out the page. Folding it in quarters, he handed it to her. "Here. Stick this in your pocketbook for Luke. This was what impressed him most about those ruins."

"You know, we could've bought him his own copy," Mark said as they headed to the elevators. "You didn't need to rip it out."

"Oh, that's right. I forgot. Christians are forbidden to deface other people's property."

"We're forbidden from all sorts of things. Fornication's another big one."

They all snickered as the elevator doors opened. Straightening their faces, they rode up in the company of a rear admiral, a two-star Marine Corps general, two Navy captains and a full commander WAVE. Worried that one of these august personages might sniff out either the purloined page in her purse or the fact that she wasn't married to the man on her arm, Anna kept her gaze on her shoes while Floyd's normally mournful face twitched with repressed laughter.

When they stepped off at the fourth floor, the door had

just closed when he erupted with, "God, can you imagine what their collective shit's worth?"

Mark began hefting their bags down the corridor. "Oh, go get laid, Einhorn," he called.

Their room might have been the smallest in the hotel; the only window looked into a courtyard. On the far side, a sliver of blue sky hung above another building. But the bed was wide and soft, with plump pillows, and a phone on the nightstand.

Mark dropped the bags and kicked off his shoes. "Look at this, Anna. Just look at this." Tossing his hat to a dresser, he flopped onto the brocade spread. "I swear I have died and gone to heaven."

"Good. Enjoy it while I call my parents."

While she talked to various operators, Mark shed jacket and trousers, draped them over a chair, then stretched out in skivvies. For ten minutes she heard only static on the line and occasional reminders to "Hold on, please." Finally, it began ringing on the other end. Her heart thudded when the thin, distant voice of the Reverend Thomas Cranmer Moss finally said, "St. Stephen's Rectory. Father Moss speaking."

She swallowed hard. "Hi, Daddy. It's me…Anna."

There was a small silence, then a gasp. "Oh sweetheart, is it really? Is it really you?"

She assured him it was, told him where she was. Her mother picked up the extension; both began talking at once. In answer to their big question, "When will you be home?" she said, "Not for a while. Another month or so. After we pick up another load of casualties."

"And then what?" her father asked.

"Then I'll come home. I hope before Christmas."

Her mother said, "Whenever you get here, dear, it'll be Christmas."

"What about Jim?" her father asked. "You call him

yet?"

"He'll be having office hours tonight. I'll try tomorrow."

"Maybe we should let him know. Oh my." Her mother began to blubber. "Are you all right, dear? You sound...oh, I don't know. Older. Yes, that's it. So much older."

She reassured them she was fine, and dutifully asked for their health before an operator said three minutes was up. They all sniffled and rang off. Mark seemed to be asleep, so she hung up her uniform and lay down beside him.

At first the silence was soothing, but gradually a sense of now what? began stewing in her chest. Here she was with Mark in a deluxe American hotel with nothing to do but unwind for the next forty-eight hours. Yet she couldn't shake the hunch that she needed to do something else. Something urgent. Something troubling.

Encircling his waist with her arm, she felt the steady rise and fall of his breathing, stretched her legs against the spread, and studied the wedge of sky, now purple with cloud. But when she stopped thinking about the weather and the city, she felt the PWs' stories hanging over her consciousness like a stone about to drop. Those men had left the ship, but so far, neither Mark nor Floyd nor Willi had mentioned the narratives they'd been collecting. If they'd set them aside, why couldn't she?

And then the phone rang. Floyd asked what time they wanted to go to dinner, and did Chinatown sound okay? She sighed with the relief of having some concrete, ordinary goal for the next few hours.

* * *

Knowing Jim would expect her call, in the morning Anna tried his number before they went down to breakfast. And again before they left for sightseeing; both times the circuits were busy, so she gave up. Then, based on knowledge of the city from her four months there with Dan, she led the others on a tour of the city, Golden Gate Park, Coit Tower, Fisherman's Wharf.

After lunch, she tried calling again, and again, and again. But by the time they left for dinner at the Treasure Island O Club, she still hadn't reached him.

It was after ten when they got back, full of good wine and good food, and worn out from dancing to what Floyd called, "Good old American music." Mark went into the bathroom, so she tried one last time. When she got the same all-circuits-busy message, she requested the operator to call whenever she got through. Never mind how late that night, or early the next morning.

Mark threw her a curious glance as he headed for the bed. "Why don't you wait 'til morning? Now I won't sleep for wondering if the phone's going to ring. And wake us up. Or worse."

"I'm sorry," she said primly. "Sorry if that inconveniences you."

He crawled under the covers, stretched, yawned. "Don't be silly. I just don't understand why you can't wait a few more hours."

"No, I guess you wouldn't, since there's no one you care about enough to call."

He blinked a couple times. "Well, I'll try my parents tomorrow. But tonight, hell, here we are in our big bed. And it might be the last night we'll ever have together. In a room of our own, I mean. I just wish you could give it all to me."

She got in beside him, switched off the light, but didn't answer. She might have reminded him they'd already had the previous night and most of the afternoon, complete with intercourse as often as he wanted. Therefore, she couldn't understand his reluctance to share her now with a phone call, just a damned phone call. She came close to saying as much, but better angels convinced her to remain silent. Tense, but silent.

* * *

It was still dark when the phone bell cut into her sleep. She turned on the light before she picked up: five-thirty. "Ready with your call to Maine," the operator said. "Go ahead, please."

She focused through the night's foggy residue. "Jim? Is that you?"

And he said, "Oh Anna. Finally. Your mother said you'd be calling, but then I began to think I was dreaming. So you're in San Francisco. If I knew what hotel, I'd have tried there."

She cleared her throat. "The Fairmont. Some of us are enjoying a little luxury before we go back to the Pacific again. There's still thousands of wounded out there, so we have to make one last trip. Then I'll be home as fast as possible. I hope before Christmas."

"Oh darling. And then what? Still want to marry me?"

Why had he asked? "Of course. More than ever."

"So you never found Dan?"

"No. That was just a pipe dream. Now, tell me how you are."

As she listened, Mark slipped out of bed, padded into the bathroom and silently closed the door. Without him beside her, she was able to picture Jim at eight-thirty on a Sunday morning, probably dressed for church. Smiling at the phone, at her voice, at the fact they were finally connected by something besides ink on paper.

Finally he asked, "Is Luke coming home with you? He hasn't told Lorraine yet."

"Not sure. But he's anxious to meet her."

"You think she'll like him?"

The question shocked her, until she remembered commenting in letters about Luke's judgmental streak. "She's his mother. Of course she will. Anyway, I ought to let you get to church. Does your nurse still go with you?"

He laughed. "Not since she met an old friend of her husband's. And started going to the Catholic church. Think there's a romance there."

"Then you're lucky I'm coming back. I can take over the job if she gets married."

"Even if you never set foot in the office, I'll still be the luckiest man alive."

Words retreated in a surge of longing. All she could do was blurt out, "Oh, I love you, Jim. I love you so much."

"And I, you, dearest."

When she'd hung up, Mark emerged from the bathroom and fell back into the bed. His breath was minty with toothpaste. But his words were crisp, even cold: "Tell me something, Anna. How could you do that?"

"Do what?"

"Lie like that. Here in this bed where we've loved each other, how could you make him think everything's still the same with you?"

Disbelief made her briefly speechless. Then, "That's really none of your business."

He reached for her left hand, and encircled the diamond with his thumb and forefinger. "If I weren't here, if I hadn't been with you all this time since Kailua, okay, it wouldn't be. But I love you. And I know what being of two minds is doing to you. That's why I left the room. I couldn't stand to see your face when you talked to him." He sighed, kissed the back of her hand. "Are you really serious about marrying that man?"

"Of course. Why would you even ask?"

"Because a woman who loves someone enough to marry him doesn't sleep with other men."

Something tightened in her chest, as if truth were a vise around her heart. "Look," she said. "When I'm with you, you're all I want. But just now with Jim, it was as if I'd never left Maine."

"So you're going to let geography decide it, are you? I mean, now that your first husband's not going to come along and rescue you."

"Maybe. I don't know." She knew she sounded pathetic and pleading, like a kid who's been reminded of some duty she's shirked.

"Well, you'd better figure it out soon."

It was just after six, still dark. She turned and draped her arm across his chest, but he didn't respond. Snuggling against his neck, she tried to visualize life without him. Unimaginable, at least in the Fairmont Hotel in San Francisco. But in St. Stephen's rectory in Portsmouth, New Hampshire, the person she wouldn't be able to imagine life without would be Jim. Now. Was that purely geography or an inherent flaw in her?

"Mark?" she whispered.

"Mmm...?"

"Did you ever wonder if I'm just fickle?"

He laughed without humor. "Fickle's too simple a word for you, Anna. Now, if you don't mind, I'm going to sleep another few hours. Then I'd like to go to church. Want to come along?"

"Oh, that's a fine idea. Grace Cathedral's right across the square."

"Uh-huh. Well, let's see how we feel after forty more winks."

He began to snore, and she continued to lie close, but it was a strange, superficial proximity that offered no comfort. Finally, distracting herself with notions of a movie that afternoon, she dozed too.

* * *

Two hours later, he woke her with the usual gestures that advertised his sexual intentions. Afterward, she used the bathroom and came back to the rumpled bed while he showered. When he emerged in clean skivvies, he sat on a chair by the window and leafed through the telephone book, then glanced at a city map from the lobby. She asked what he was looking for.

"A Methodist church somewhere close."

"Oh? Don't want to try the Cathedral?"

He shook his head. "Been so long since I've been anywhere but a Navy chapel, I'm homesick for a good old stateside Methodist service. Maybe it'll help me believe again."

"In that case, I'll stay here. Guess I'm homesick too…for Episcopal communion."

He nodded, replaced the directory in the nightstand, then withdrew his uniform hanging up in the closet. She watched him dress, knot the tie, square the hat in front of the mirror. In dress blues with service ribbons on the chest, he looked so fit, so masculine, so enticing that her heart clutched and she almost relented on the church choice. Until she realized to change it would be a metaphorical commitment, not just to Mark but to his vocation and the Methodist Church in general. That she'd turned away was based less on denominational bias than on the surety that nothing Mark Whitmore and she did, as shipmates, friends or lovers, could undermine her prior commitment to Jim Millett.

"Meanwhile," she went on, "I'm just going to lie here. Thanks to you, I haven't had much sleep the last two nights."

He grinned, lascivious in spite of the cross insignia above the two gold stripes on his sleeves. "See you later then, sweetie." Tossing her a quasi-salute, he left the room.

For a few minutes, his absence throbbed in her, so acute she intuited that his ghost would haunt her well into her brave new life. With her face in his pillow, she absorbed the familiar smell of his hair and felt the decision to let him go like a raw new surgical incision. She wanted to cry with the pain of it. But once again, tears failed her.

* * *

After they checked out, the four of them rode the cable car down the slope of California Street. As they passed Old St. Mary's Cathedral, Anna said, "On Christmas Eve, 1942, Dan and I went to Midnight Mass there with one of his shipmates. Afterward, he drove us back to our apartment and slept on our daybed."

The anecdote met with such polite lack of interest, she vowed not to speak of any other events they hadn't all shared. When they got off the trolley, they hiked over to the Ferry Building and boarded the side-wheeler *Eureka*. Watching the sun set behind the city, however, she felt her good intentions go dead in the water.

"This really brings back memories too," she said as they stood at the rail. "Dan and I rode this same ferry before his sub left for the Pacific."

Floyd and Willi nodded, while Mark moved almost imperceptibly further down the rail.

"I'd been out here for four months. I wanted to wait and watch the boat leave, but he insisted on taking me to the train. See, I was nine weeks pregnant, and he wanted to be sure I was safely on the way back to my parents."

"How ironic," Willi said, "considering neither of you was really safe, were you?"

Familiar pain tightened in Anna's chest. The sunlight was red now, flaring on windows on Yerba Buena Island, tinting the towers of the bridge. They passed underneath, traffic roaring above the splashing hiss-thump of the walking beam. As they rounded the island, the sun dipped behind Twin Peaks, throwing the stubby lighthouse in shadow except for its whirling beam. Ahead was the Oakland Mole and the great train shed where lines of coaches waited to carry returning servicemen home. And beyond that, the bulbous stern of the white ship being readied to carry them again to the Pacific's far reaches.

As they nosed into the slip, Mark stepped closer, slipped his arm around her. "Listen, sweetie. Next time you get on a train, I'll be there. Because we're probably never going to see each other again either."

She inhaled sharply, unable to answer his sardonic comment. She felt pricked by something pointed and vicious. Perhaps a thorn. Not of a rose, but one imbedded in the flesh. His subtle way of reminding her what they were to each other?

She was tempted to come back with, "Jim would never say something like that." But what was the use? Mark wasn't her future, and now it seemed he knew it as well as she did.

CHAPTER TWENTY-EIGHT

After they got underway the next morning, Anna stood on deck with the usual gang to stare at the passing city as *Compassion* headed for the Golden Gate. For the first time, she felt none of the exhilaration of slipping their moorings and edging into the stream toward new adventures. The only adventure this deployment promised was the fastest trip they'd ever had. With an eighteen-year-old ship that had been run hard for three years, the engineering philosophy had previously been slow and steady, conserving both fuel and the aging power plant. Now, with an overhaul in her future and oil no longer scarce, it was Full Speed Ahead. By the time they'd cleared the big red suspension span, the sense of speed was everywhere; in the oily smoke pouring from the stack, in the chattering dishes in the wardroom, the shriek of wind in the rigging and a vibration that hummed in everything Anna touched.

Floyd was quick to explain, though no one had asked the first question. "Do you know how much it costs to keep those troops out there? Especially the ones still hospitalized. Sooner we get them back, the sooner we can reduce the national debt. So yeah, running wide open increases the chances of malfunction, but it's one of those calculated risks BuShips loves to take."

"Calculated risk," Willi repeated. "Ah, something else for the sailors to bet on; exactly when will we go dead in the water?"

Floyd shrugged and laughed. Anna had never understood how he remained so cheerfully didactic in the face of everyone's polite but chronic disinterest. He seemed about to enlighten them further when the squawk box interrupted to announce a meeting in the lounge. Groaning with reluctance, they went through the wardroom to grab coffee on the way.

The CMO's topic was their primary goal for the next two weeks: basically, housecleaning all medical areas and inventorying supplies to account for every item on board.

"Don't anyone even think of trying to get out of it. No one's exempt," he added. "Stem to stern, keel to crow's nest. That is, if we had a crow's nest." He chuckled at his minor bon mot.

Mark caught up as Anna scanned the duty roster. "Damn!" she muttered. "Look at that. Willi and I are on H-13 again. They're still out to get us for the Kissing Mutiny."

"Maybe for last weekend too. Especially if somebody saw us together. Like Luke."

"Because we went to a hotel?"

"Well, I'm not going to worry about that today." They came out onto the covered main deck. The sea wind was chilly in spite of late morning sunlight. Behind them the California hills had receded to a green smudge where the wake met the horizon. "Anyway, I thought you and he were friends again. You talked to the PWs together, didn't you?"

"Not together. Yeah, we worked on the same project, but separately. He hasn't changed; he still makes little digs about us. You know. Our sinning ways."

"Oh, that worries me. Sooner or later, he's going to come to Maine, and I don't want him making nasty remarks to Jim."

Mark's shrug shouted indifference. "Then maybe you ought to tell him first."

She drew a deep breath of the crisp, briny air. "I will someday, when we're an old married couple. But God, not right off the bat."

"Then you're taking one of those calculated risks Floyd was talking about."

She watched the ocean rush past, deep ultramarine, foam-flecked and hissing as the screws pushed them westward. "Sounds like you think I deserve anything that happens."

He winced but clasped her hand on the railing. "Well, you can't have it both ways, Anna. Can't serve the Lord and the Devil at the same time."

"Is that what I'm doing?"

"Wish I knew. But even after all this time, I don't know what's in your heart."

"Well, that makes us even. Because I don't know yours either. Don't know if you really love me, or if I'm just another woman you love when it's convenient."

"Would knowing make a difference?"

She pondered the question as a trio of long, slow swells rolled under the hull, lifting them like the first low rises of a roller coaster. Then she had to admit, "No, not really."

"Ah," he sighed. "So that's how it is."

They stood awhile longer, silence congealing around them like a cold fog, until the PA system announced noon chow.

"You know," she said, "every time we talk, it gets more pointless. There's still four weeks before we go our separate ways, so let's stop analyzing and just enjoy whatever happens. Okay?" Frustrated with badinage that invariably failed to connect them, she stomped off toward the wardroom.

For the next hour, Nell, Audrey, Willi and Anna had a good gripe about their new assignments. Nell's and Audrey's were on H-Deck too, but forward, where the churning of the screws was less onerous, while Anna's and Willi's were toward the stern, always the hottest, noisiest place to stand duty. They figured that posting them to these areas was the CMO and OH's last attempt to remind them they'd strayed from their rightful places in the shipboard hierarchy.

"Lord, I'll be glad to get off this tub," Audrey exclaimed. "Go home and get married and forget there ever was a war."

The rest of them exchanged glances, as if they shared Anna's unspoken hunch that the past year had been the best of their lives. At least the most dramatic, the one beside which the rest of their days would seem pale, maybe even pointless. Sure, they all expected to marry, have kids or careers, and lives which would certainly not be without dramatic moments. But nothing would be like this again, when their senses were most alert and they were constantly challenged to rise above the trivial self-interests that had followed them out of adolescence into this odyssey. This long, often-brutal yet somehow beautiful odyssey that was finally winding down.

* * *

The next week Anna took an hour away from scut work so Floyd could replace a filling in an upper molar. Now that he no longer had the PWs' survival instincts to study or their teeth to fix, he was back on schedule for chow, but she still hadn't heard anything about his project. She made a point of asking as he approached with picks and mirrors, and just before he told her to open wide.

"Willi and I have a couple notebooks full." The intensity of his focus was magnified by the close range at which he was peering. "When did you lose the filling?"

"My tongue found it the other day. I felt this hole…"

His focus intensified as he began probing with a pointed steel instrument. After a few minutes of picking, he switched to a drill. Shortly he told her to rinse out, then gave instructions to a corpsman, who set to work with a mortar and pestle. Then Floyd said, "I understand you talked to the PWs on your ward too. What are you going to do with their stories?"

"Don't know. They're pretty gruesome. Especially those from the Bataan death march. At Nagasaki, I felt sorry for the Jap civilians, but now my attitude's not as charitable."

"Understandable," he said cheerily. "But let me tell you a story. It may give you a different slant on them." He stuffed cotton wads along her gums and squirted something warm and pleasant into the tooth.

"After the Germans took over Poland, Jews began to realize if they didn't leave Europe soon, they might never. The Nazis gave them problems, but a Japanese consul in Lithuania helped them get visas to Curacao in the Dutch West Indies. First they had to get to Japan, so they took the trans-Siberian railway to Vladivostok, and a steamer to Kobe. Once they got there, the Japanese gave them new visas to almost anywhere. A lot of them came to the States. Including a cousin of my mother's."

Anna wanted to comment, but he was still smoothing out the new filling; it squeaked under the instrument.

"Anyway," he went on, "that consul was one damned good man. And my family'll never forget him. Neither will the other two thousand Jews he saved from the ovens."

She could only widen her eyes to express amazement.

When he finished, she swished Lavoris around, spat out silver crumbs and removed the bib from her neck.

"That's a neat story. But I never thought all Japs were bad. In fact, some PWs said civilians often did kind things when the guards weren't looking." She slid out of the leather chair. "By the way, have you told Willi about him?"

He nodded with a faint frown. "She needs more than one good-works story. Oh well, we have the rest of our lives to deal with it."

"What about you, though? Don't you hate the Germans the same way?"

His eyes narrowed and he gazed into space a moment. "Just what they did to the Jews. But hell, Anna, you know as well as I do, hate's a killer. I can't afford it."

She wanted to ask more, but the corpsman was cleaning up, so she thanked him, then told Floyd, "Your dental practice is going to be so successful, you'll be able to afford two Packards. But remember their slogan: Ask the man who owns one. So ask my father. He's not awfully happy with the one he has."

He laughed, began washing his hands at the small sink. "Don't worry. A car'll be the last thing on my mind when I get back to Philly."

* * *

A week later as they neared Saipan, she and Mark sneaked to his cabin for the first carnal hiatus since San Francisco. By then, they'd done all their superiors had tasked them to do: the ship was ready, not just to go into the yard, but to carry home one last over-capacity load of convalescents. Suddenly she realized that beyond a few casual mentions, they hadn't discussed their project. Time was running out for this too.

Now, in the afterglow of passion, she asked if he was

still working on the PWs' stories.

He shot her a bewildered look from their shared pillow. "Oh that. No, not lately. Seemed like a fine idea at first. But then, well, I found out too much." He grinned. "Like collecting snow to build a snowman. After a while, hell, it was a damned avalanche."

The simile gave shape to her own feelings. "I have a notebook full, but I don't know what to do with it."

"Maybe the real virtue was getting them to talk, not looking for reasons why they survived."

"Did hearing them restore your faith?"

He grimaced. "Not really. Yeah, it's good to know what people can endure. But the other side of it—what other people let them endure without helping..." He shook his head, face troubled. "Makes me wonder even more where the Lord was in all of it."

Ah, there it was—the reason she'd immersed herself in the tedious business of housecleaning and inventorying as if it were a Holy Cause: it was the relief of dealing with things she could touch, see, feel, count, list, categorize, then walk away from with no overt emotion. After the mosaics of the PWs' horrific accounts, such ordinary routines had transformed her into a functioning, feeling nurse again.

"What about you?" he asked. "Is your faith still intact?"

"Don't know. Haven't analyzed it. Of course, I'm not clergy, so it doesn't matter if I have occasional doubts. But this year, I've discovered a side of myself that makes me wonder if I should go on calling myself a Christian."

He nodded. "You mean this? You and me?"

"Of course."

The smile was barely noticeable. "Listen, Anna. Half the people on this ship have secrets like ours. Or worse. See, I hear lots of confessions. So I know we're not the only ones sleeping together. Then there's Luke's attraction to men. A couple nurses are Lesbians too." As he talked, he stroked her hand, rubbed her fingers, intertwining them with his. "Ever heard about a still down in the engineering spaces?"

"No, never have."

"Well, top brass knows all about it, but they ignore it because they have their own rackets going." He shook his head. "And remember the powdered eggs rebellion? Actually, the CO does keep the fresh ones for his own mess. Plus plenty of other good stuff meant for the wardroom."

"I see. And what else is going on?"

He yawned. "For one thing, a black market on Guam; one of the CPOs sells them all the morphine and pain pills they want. And another chief's getting rich on a floating crap game ."

"Sounds like the ship's a big floating den of iniquity."

"Out of our complement of four hundred souls, how many do you think are saints?"

She gave him a wry smile. "Not you and I, for sure. So if everybody else is sinning, is it okay for us too?"

His shrug was so casual she took it for an affirmative answer. "No. Just that...well, how much do our private weaknesses matter in the larger scheme of things? After all, we did our jobs, didn't we? None of us went AWOL, or ended up in the nut ward, or shirked our duties, or hurt anybody. So we've done a little fornicating, sure. But regardless of our private moments, day in and day out, we were faithful to duty. That's what counts, Anna. Nobody expected us to walk on water too."

She couldn't dispute his logic, rich as it was with issues they might argue the rest of the night, perhaps even into perpetuity. To what end, though? Maybe one day her father might explain the essence of sin, but for the time being she had to conclude Mark was right: that they'd done everything the Navy had required of them was of far more consequence to the world than the sum of their personal and private falls from grace.

She kissed him lightly. "And we never did, did we?"

"What?"

"Walk on water."

He smiled, pulled her closer. She kissed him again, harder, in hopes he'd want to make love again and further distract her from the question of Sin. She had never bet on anything, but Mark's proclivities made this possibility a sure thing.

* * *

After embarking two hundred casualties at Saipan, they steamed to Guam for another five hundred, which filled the wards beyond capacity. Most patients were ambulatory but still in need of medical supervision. To accommodate this overload, hammocks were hung from the overheads in the wards, officers doubled up with others in private staterooms, and cots were set up in quiet rooms. Otherwise, the turnaround in Apra Harbor was to be merely routine, with yard oilers alongside to top off *Compassion*'s fuel tanks and supply trucks crowding the pier.

The night before they sailed, Anna joined the usual group at the O Club for one last taste of the overseas high life. She was scheduled for duty at 2300, so limited herself to a light rum and coke before dinner. Others, however, were so well-oiled that they broke into a round of lengthy, sentimental toasts and tearful choruses of *Auld Lang Syne*.

Awash in a sense of ending, she clung to Mark on the way back to the ship. The humid Guamanian night brought whiffs of the usual smells: dank water, garbage, oiled machinery, creosote, cigarette smoke, and urine. Not romantic scents, but a couple times between pier lights, he kissed her and said he wanted her.

"Don't even think about it," she said. "I have to get ready for another night on H-13."

"How about I help you shower?"

"Oh Mark. That sounds like the ultimate debauchery."

"Hey, sweetie, you'd better take debauchery while you can get it. Because once you marry that good doctor of yours, you'll have damned little of it."

And she said, "Oh Yeah? Well, the first time we ever did it, it was on the desk chair in his office. So there too."

He stopped walking and pulled her into a tight hold. "Oh, Anna, Anna," he murmured into her hair. "I can't stand thinking of you with anybody else."

"You should talk. All the women you've had. Probably dozens. And I've only ever slept with my husband and Jim."

"And me. Don't forget me. Bet you've had twice as much loving with me as you did with the other two combined."

She walked on, jaws clenched. He caught up and tried to kiss her again, but she broke away and told him not to touch her. When they'd boarded, he followed her up the ladder to C, and grabbed her again. This time, she yielded to the kiss and said, "Oh, what the hell? But be quiet. Last thing I need is to get caught sneaking you into my cabin."

"What'd they do then… make you stand duty on H-13 till we reach Frisco?"

* * *

In the morning, *Compassion* got underway before Anna's shift ended. She was disappointed, having wanted to mentally record the last of all the departures she'd experienced on this ship. Feeling mildly cheated, she left the patients with their breakfast trays and went into a quiet room to watch the green Guamanian hills recede as they stood out to sea. There hadn't been a band on the pier, so she hummed *Anchors Aweigh* under her breath until they'd cleared the breakwater. Then she shook herself back to the dull business of charting patients' food intakes.

For the next two weeks, her duties settled into a familiar pattern: Nights she worked on H-13. Mornings she read or went to meetings, and after noon chow, napped until supper. Several times Mark tried to talk her into coming to his room for what he euphemistically called "some quick loving". Now that he and Floyd were bunking together, they'd agreed that each would absent himself whenever the other wanted private time. But the arrangement seemed so déclassé, she turned up her nose. However, with Sunday night free, she invited Mark to her cabin again. This time the fact that it might be their last night ever so dampened their spirits they spent it merely holding each other in a state of low-grade misery. And in the morning, he was so concerned about escaping Nurses' Country undetected that he slipped away before she awoke.

In spite of an avowed aversion to debauchery, she felt robbed of some final momentous coupling. Like reading a great love story, only to find the last page missing.

CHAPTER TWENTY-NINE

Compassion's original ETA at San Francisco had been Sunday, 2 December. But four days before, her speed had slackened to the usual wartime crawl. Sure enough, Floyd reported, the engines had finally begun to break down, something about overheated bearings in the propeller shaft pedestals. Anna didn't understand the technicalities, just the end result: they'd be late arriving. This put the CO in a dither because the ship was due in the yard on the fourth.

Nobody else seemed to care except the patients. "Damn! Just when we're so close to California I can smell orange blossoms," said one young amputee who apparently had no idea orange trees weren't part of Northern California flora.

They finally cleared the Golden Gate on 6 December and put in to Fort Mason with Army men bound for Letterman General Hospital. Then, slowly and with a noticeable clunking from the engine room, beat their way over to Oakland and tied up at the Supply Depot. By the time personnel had waved the last of the Navy patients ashore, it was almost dark, corpsmen cleaning the empty wards with energy derived from the certainty this was their last such duty. The skipper summoned the rest of them to the lounge for a final briefing.

"Uh-oh," said Floyd as they filed in. "The Hail and Farewell speech. Thanks for a job well done. God, I hope the Old Man doesn't start sniffling."

The captain led off by announcing they'd have the next day to pack and pick up leave papers, but were to be off the ship no later than midnight. Then, "I know most of you want to go home immediately, but there are so many troops going back east, the railroads can't keep up with them. So first thing tomorrow, anyone taking the train needs to go over to the Mole and buy tickets ASAP. If you can't get out right away, you can bunk at the Treasure Island BOQ."

Then he got into an emotional speech about what good shipmates they'd been, and how they'd made him and the Navy proud, and how he'd be honored to serve with them again. After that the Exec paraphrased his remarks, then the CMO and even OH put in their two cents' worth. Anna stared at her hands, but other nurses were sniffling and wiping their cheeks. Finally, they stood at attention as their superiors dismissed them and proceeded to the CO's cabin for their own farewell dinner.

"Bet they're having filet mignon," Audrey griped as stewards set out their humble last supper: corned beef hash, stewed tomatoes, canned peas and all the Dixie ice cream cups they wanted. Only Floyd was his bright, cheerful self. Having been charged with getting everyone's tickets, he went around taking copious notes to make sure he got them right. Of the usual group, only Nell and Nick weren't leaving: he had orders to Treasure Island; she'd been assigned to the dispensary there FFT. Floyd was taking Willi to meet his parents in Philadelphia; Audrey wanted to go to Harrisburg, Pennsylvania. Mark needed to get to Charleston, which meant the southern route out of LA.

Luke was going to Baltimore, while Anna headed for Boston.

"Baltimore," Anna said. "Don't you want to meet Lorraine right away?"

"No. Want to see some old friends at home first."

"When will you come to Maine?"

His eyes darkened. "Maybe the week after. Depends."

She wanted to ask Depends on what? but something in his manner warned her off.

As they planned their trips, she remembered that 6 December was the anniversary of her marriage to Dan. It had been only four years, but the memory was so thin and pale it no longer stirred more than a faint wash of sorrow. Subsumed in it, she only gradually became aware of Mark's scrutiny at the now-empty table.

"What?" she asked.

"Tonight really is our last," he said quietly. "We should celebrate."

"Celebrate?"

"Okay, then. Make it memorable."

"How? The usual way?"

He smiled, flipped a stray lock of hair back from her forehead. "It won't seem usual tonight."

She got to her feet. "We still have tomorrow 'til midnight, you know."

"Look. You can stay aboard as long as you want, but I'm getting off soon as I pick up my leave papers. Hanging around until the last trumpet blows only makes it sadder."

"And then what'll you do? Get on a train? "

"Not right away. I'm not leaving till you do. Remember, I promised to see you off? It'll break my heart, but that's how it has to be."

Waves of cynicism crashed on the sands of her tenderness as she reminded herself his aim was probably not to win her as a wife but to tempt her away from Jim. Oh well, what did it matter? Time was bearing them away from each other just as surely as the tide would bear *Compassion* into the channel tomorrow without them.

"Then I guess we'd better take advantage of tonight," she said.

By now, though the routine was as familiar as breathing, he'd been right. Nothing felt usual. With so many personnel already gone, the ship was too quiet, no muffled conversations on deck outside or in the passageway, no slamming hatches or loud radios in other cabins. Even the squawk box was silent. And since they weren't underway, nothing vibrated or trembled.

Neither of them mentioned again that they'd come to the final night together, but that sense pulsed in her bloodstream, as it must have his: for the first time, he was impotent.

She said, "Just as well. I'm too sad to be sexy." Because there it was, the end of all the voyages, the end of the mission, the common purpose, the coupledness. The time chasm ahead would quickly widen from a trickle to a stream, then a river and finally an ocean on which one day she'd look back on this ship as an island in time. Hope Island was a fixed, enduring reality; this was ephemeral, bridged only by the flimsy strands of memory.

They slept entwined, inhaling each other's breath. Whatever he was now or had once been no longer burned in her consciousness. In the morning, refreshed by sleep, he loved her the last time. Neither commemorated the finality of the act with sentimental phrases, but she felt it in her bones, in every cell of her body. Afterward, he went in to the head, while she got into uniform, then made the familiar trip up the passageway to the ladder, then down to C Deck and forward to Cabin C-14. There, she reluctantly showered away traces of their last act of love.

* * *

Although she'd hope to pack quickly, she'd accumulated so much stuff she had to buy a suitcase at the Exchange. At noon chow, Floyd handed out tickets. Audrey would be the first out, at three the next afternoon on a Pullman. Since he, Willi, Luke and Anna wanted to stay together to Chicago, they couldn't get a train till four days later, and then they'd be in coach seats all the way. "Guess we'll have to play a lot of cards," he grinned. Mark would go last; his train left an hour after theirs.

Luke scanned his tickets. "Oh, look. I'm on 'The Cardinal' from Chicago to Washington. Maybe that's a good omen for my future in the church."

"It's the bird, not a Roman Catholic primate," Floyd told him, as if he had no idea.

Although Anna had finished packing by four, her usual group stayed aboard for one last meal. By then most of the medical staff had left too, with little overt sentiment except handshakes, pats on the back, a few hugs between nurses, and the exchange of addresses. Those staying on in the Bay Area promised to get together for dinner soon. OH even suggested a reunion in a few years; she'd organize it and notify the rest of them.

"Don't worry, ladies; wherever you are, I'll find you. I was always good at that."

"We noticed," said Willi. The ensuing laughs were feeble. Then they saluted and watched OH stride, purposeful and stoical as always, toward the gangway.

Even the stewards were apologetic for that final meal: grilled cheese, mystery meat sandwiches, canned bean soup, a few sawdust-dry cookies, more Dixie Cups. Afterward, Anna checked her cabin one last time, dragged her sea bag down the ladder to the main deck, then gave a steward ten dollars to carry it down the gangway.

A misty, winter darkness enclosed the waterfront, shrouding lights, muffling the blast of foghorns, intensifying the smell of brine and oil. As she waited for the others at the head of the gangway, she studied the superstructure, memorizing details to return to in memory when the real thing was gone from her life. Brilliantly lit as usual, bridge and wings of the bridge, pilothouse and covered decks, masts and stack shining white in the spotlights that illumined the red crosses on stack, decks and hull, marking *Compassion* as a non-combatant throughout the war. The hushed whir of ventilating blowers still wafted the smell of cigarettes and coffee and inevitably, oily machinery. Everything seemed routine, just as if tomorrow everyone would line the rails and set off on another deployment. Instead, manned by a civilian skeleton crew, the ship would creep up the bay toward a Vallejo shipyard from which she might never sail again. At least not in her present identity.

Regarding *Compassion's* familiar lines, Anna remembered the first sight of her on approach to Brisbane fourteen months before. The sentimentality that had shivered through her then, she knew now, had stemmed from a starry-eyed view of her mission, a sanitized Hollywood permutation of her reality. Maybe everyone, including Bobby McWherter, boarded a new vessel with the same romantic wonder, uplifted spirits and noble sense of purpose. Armored with chauvinism, they set foot on the gangway and became part of the living organism that was their ship, their new mother.

No wonder vessels were referred to as "she". No wonder Anna was leaving this one with the sense of being wrenched from a secure womb.

Talking loudly, the others came up behind her, showed leave papers to the OOD, saluted both him and the flag, and stepped onto the gangway for the last time. At the foot, a taxi waited to take them to Treasure Island. No one spoke of anything but trivia while they folded themselves and their luggage into its cramped interior.

When they pulled away, Anna turned to keep the ship in sight as long as possible through the rear window. Until they rounded a corner, and *Compassion* disappeared behind warehouses, only the stack and masts, one still flying the Geneva pennant, visible above them.

Willi sighed. "Funny, isn't it? Seemed like it'd never end, and now, it's already starting to seem just a dream."

"High time," Audrey said in her usual acerbic tone. "I've had enough of the damned Navy."

Anna said, "Right now, I can't think of a thing to gripe about."

"What about all that powdered stuff?" Willi asked. "Eggs, even milk."

"They were nothing."

Mark grunted. Floyd, for once, was silent.

* * *

The next afternoon at the BOQ, Willi and Anna helped Audrey carry her bags down to the shuttle bus that would take her to the train. The gesture had been Willi's idea because they'd flown out with her from this very base to join the ship. Anna was lukewarm; Audrey had been part of the experience, true, but she couldn't imagine missing her.

"Come on, now, Anna," Willi'd cajoled. "It'd be a shame to let her leave without at least waving her off."

Floyd was at the bus stop too. He carried the luggage aboard, then returned for a hug. When Audrey cringed, Anna wanted to slap sense into her, but knew better than to attempt one now. So she extended her hand for a shake, and told her she'd enjoyed serving with her.

"Same here, Donovan. Keep in touch, okay? Let me

know when you marry that doctor of yours so's I can send a card. And give me your address in Maine. So's my fiancé and I can come visit. Of course, he'll be my husband by then." Her gaze landed on Willi. "You too, Wilhelmina. Especially if you end up in Philly. Only a few hours from Harrisburg on the turnpike." They shook hands too; Audrey hefted the purse strap to her shoulder. "Everybody be good now, you hear?" She gave Floyd a weak smile. "If you can't be good, be careful. And if you can't be careful, name it for me."

Everyone laughed, a little too enthusiastically. With a last casual wave, she boarded the bus, leaving the rest of them to watch it pull away, cross the causeway to Yerba Buena Island and enter the bridge to Oakland. Anna wanted to make some remark that would close out the time she'd spent in Audrey's company, but all she could think of was, "She was a good shipmate, but I'm glad we weren't cabin mates."

Willi said, "Amen to that."

And Floyd looked at his watch. "Think it's too early for a drink?"

Anna said, "Well, the sun's over the yardarm."

"Good. Then I'll find Mark, and meet you at the O Club."

* * *

Wednesday morning, the same foursome plus Luke rode the same shuttle to the Mole. Their Chicago-bound train left at 11, Mark's to LA at noon. In the long shed, theirs stretched into the distance to a pair of locomotives puffing steam like horses on a cold morning. The air was heavy with coal smoke and the metallic and greasy smell of the cars, and always and inevitably, whiffs of urine and cigarette smoke.

As they merged with a crowd moving along the string of cars, Anna caught sight of a dark red Boston and Maine day coach. "Oh, look. One from New England," she said, aware that no one else understood her enthusiasm. "Wonder what it's doing way out here?"

"Every railroad in the country's deadheading coaches to California to handle the troops heading east. Millions of them." Floyd pointed to others; a New York, New Haven & Hartford, a Pennsy, a Chicago & Northwestern, a veritable rainbow of mismatched cars. Except for the train across the platform-- a handsome stainless steel Southern Pacific with a Diesel engine. The one Mark would take to Los Angeles.

"I change there for New Orleans," he explained. "Then Jacksonville, Florida. And finally, the Seaboard Air Line to Charleston."

Pausing at the rapidly-filling Boston and Maine car, they all stood looking at each another, as if no one wanted to be first to break away.

Until Luke said, "Well, hate to rush things, but we ought to make sure we find seats together." He extended his hand to Mark and murmured something about having been glad he'd worked with him. "In spite of our differences."

Anna frowned at his back as he climbed the steps into the coach. Floyd seemed about to shake Mark's hand too, but pulled him in for a quick, abashed hug. Willi leaned a kiss on his cheek, promised to take care of Anna on the trip, then followed the men aboard.

Anna watched their progress up the aisle to a pair of facing seats halfway up the car. Then, with a quivery sensation in her chest, turned back to Mark and the scene she'd previously only imagined. And dreaded.

She forced her trembling lips to smile. "Well, I guess this is it. You know. Now is the hour?"

He grimaced. "Damn. I knew this'd be bad that night at Pearl Harbor. I mean, when we just danced. Even before we loved each other."

She nodded; the smile had begun to feel like a death mask.

"But this is worse," he said. "Worse than I imagined."

Another tight nod.

"Not for you though, is it? You have someone to go home to. Something to look forward to. I don't know what I'm going to find."

She reached for his hand. "That doesn't mean this is easy, Mark." No matter how often she blinked, his image was distorted by tears. "Because of my feelings for you. I'm not going to be able to turn them off. No matter what happens with Jim."

He took a deep breath, raised her fingers to his lips. "Oh, Anna."

"What?"

"At least promise to stay in touch."

"Of course."

"Even after you marry Jim."

She nodded mutely; tears pushed out of her eyes. Leaving Mark was harder, so much harder, she realized with a shock, then it had been to leave Jim fourteen months before. Because now there was no promise of anything except the paper-thin connection of the occasional letter, fewer and fewer as time leached the intensity from their memories.

She inhaled to regain self-control. "You know what this is, don't you?" she asked, and before he could answer, "The wages of sin, that's what. Oh, not death, except the way it feels."

"Yeah. That's what it is, all right." He glanced toward the window up the car where Luke was now in a seat facing Willi and Floyd but watching Anna and Mark.

"Look at Luke," he said. "Bet he's gloating right now."

"Screw him," Anna said miserably.

A conductor strode by, frowning at the pocket watch in his hand, then waving at another conductor farther up the train. A group of sailors in pea coats came hurrying down the platform and swung up the steps into the coach as the conductor called the All Aboard.

Mark grabbed her, so close she inhaled the faintly bitter smell of the woolen uniform, the medicinal tinge of Lifebuoy from his last shower, the licorice of the Black Jack he'd chewed on the bus.

"Damn, I hate this," he whispered. Up forward, the locomotives' bells were clanging, two different notes, like the start of some musical number. "Remember me, Anna, okay? Remember I love you?"

She leaned toward him again for a desperate kiss, teeth touching, bill of his cap knocking hers askew. Then she looked up, memorizing the wide set of his eyes, the crow's feet around them, the firm lines of his mouth, the fading tan, even the faint shadow of beard. "I'll remember," was all she could say before she broke away and pulled herself up the steps, groping her way into the car and up the aisle through a curtain of tears.

As she approached, Luke greeted her with a grave smile. "Hope you don't mind being so far from the lavatory, but Floyd says the ride's better when you're not over the trucks."

He'd saved the window seat for her, facing backward. Mark was right outside.

The conductor stepped aboard, yanked the signal cord. She held Mark's face in her gaze as the train jerked a couple of times, then began to creep forward. For a while, he walked alongside; his cheeks glistened with tears; he looked old and haggard. She blew him a last kiss as, gaining speed, they moved into the sunlight beyond the shed, beyond the platform, where he stood, still waving.

Beside her, Luke grabbed her hand and held it tight. She

appreciated that he said nothing. Nor did anyone else. But for the next two days and nights to Chicago, the four of them would be sitting there, staring at each other. Even if they played cards the whole time, she found it hard to imagine that any of these close friends would fail to comment on the parting they'd just witnessed. She could only pray that when they did, she'd have regained the ability to speak of it, calmly and without tears, just as if her heart wasn't breaking.

CHAPTER THIRTY

When the Boston Limited rattled out of Albany the following Saturday, Anna was in a coach that looked clean and new, but reeked of the eye-smarting fumes of hot metal. After sitting upright for three days and nights, however, she was too uncomfortable to worry about being derailed by bad brakes or overheated wheel bearings: her fingers were so swollen she couldn't have removed the engagement ring if her life depended on it; the bags under her eyes felt as big as her boobs, and a gnawing in her belly reminded her she hadn't eaten since halfway across New York State. But these thorns in the flesh had taken her mind off the other, more pervasive thorn she'd left on the platform at Oakland four days before.

Wiggling circulation back into her feet, she stretched cramping legs across the empty seat beside her. Outside, the landscape was bleak and lunar under a clabbered milk sky. She'd almost forgotten what winter looked like. Or how it felt; in the taxi between Chicago stations, cold had set her teeth chattering. Now, even huddled into the heavy topcoat, she was conscious of icy drafts from the window.

Wrapping the scarf tighter, she pulled on gloves and closed her stinging eyes against the jolting of the car. It was only when she dreamed of a succulent pork roast that she realized she'd dozed off. She popped a stick of Juicy Fruit, all she had in her purse to placate a growling stomach.

The train rocketed across Massachusetts without a stop till Springfield, The city looked worn out and down-at-the-heels, like the crowd that poured into the coach. All except a young sailor who paused in the aisle and eyed the seat beside her. "Excuse me, ma'am. Mind if I sit here?"

Was he being polite, or worried about the Navy's segregation of officers and enlisted? She was used to it, but at this time and in this setting, the rules of that petty bureaucracy seemed more offensive than they had even when they'd worked in her favor.

She smiled. "Please do." The band of his flat hat was embroidered with *USS Callaghan*. She waited till he'd stuffed his peacoat into the overhead rack before she said, "Judging by the name, your ship must be a tin can."

"Yes, ma'am. Least she was. Kamikaze got her off Okinawa. Last ship they ever sunk with one of them planes."

"Really? I was on *Compassion*. The hospital ship? We picked up plenty of casualties from those attacks."

His stare was blank. "It was a LCT picked us up."

"Oh? Well, anyway…thank God it's all over now. You on your way home too?"

"No, ma'am. Been Stateside since September. Just home for the weekend. See, I'm a fireman striker, but there ain't no future in that, so I'm going to A School at Chelsea. Studying for Pharmacist's Mate."

"Good for you. Our ship couldn't have operated without corpsmen." Bobby McWherter's eager face smiled in her mind. One day she'd find his family in Boston and tell them how much she'd esteemed him--and regretted his death. Perhaps even more than she did that of the Marine captain; true, Bobby's choices had sealed his fate, but you could hardly accuse him of voluntary suicide.

When the sailor lit a cigarette, she turned her face to the window. At first she assumed the whirling white speckles were spots before her weary eyes. Then she realized what they really were. She pointed. "Look. Snow. Haven't seen any for two years. Haven't even been cold."

He drew on the smoke, exhaled, nodded. "Takes some getting used to."

"Indeed." She waited till the tobacco haze dissipated. "Now. Would you mind if I asked something personal?"

Faint wariness touched his features. "Okay, I guess."

"Well, I was just wondering. Does your family, I mean, the people at home, do they want to hear about the war?"

His gaze shifted to a conductor swaying down the aisle, ticket punch in hand. "Hard to say. Then again, I'd just as soon not talk about it myself."

"Oh. You want to forget?"

"Well, some. Like, when we abandoned ship. But other things... I won't say it was good, but we was part of something. You know? Hard to explain to folks who wasn't there."

She nodded at the sense in his words. "I've been gone so long, I have no idea what to expect."

"Well, they ask. Like maybe they do want to know. But I don't think, I mean, you had to've been there. Like we was." He drew on the smoke. "Say, that wasn't your ship got hit, was it?"

"No, that was *Comfort*. A Kamikaze buzzed us once though. Bad enough."

He nodded, averting his gaze. She glanced at her watch. One o'clock. Hard to believe, in less than an hour, this coast-to-coast torture would end. "Well, I'm sure being home will be wonderful. I can't wait."

Another nod, deferential but brusque, before he unfolded a *Time* from his ditty bag and began scanning it. "Well, nice talking to you, ma'am. Wish you lots of luck."

"The same to you." Feeling faintly dismissed, she pressed her face against the frigid glass to watch for the Boston skyline in the milky distance.

* * *

Finally, finally, she was walking the long platform at South Station, past emptying coaches and the sighing locomotive that had pulled them from Albany. Trailing, a red cap pushed a baggage cart with her luggage. In the stream of passengers, she was one small ripple in a flood tide of returning service personnel huddled into winter gear, hurrying along with intense, tired faces and fading South Pacific tans. All of them no longer driven by the exigencies of war but by a homing instinct, that long-neglected pulse waiting to burst forth. As hers had when the band at Okinawa had played *Anchors Aweigh*. And in San Francisco, when she'd heard the phone-thinned voices of Jim and her parents. And now, counting off these last few minutes before she saw them again, no longer only grayed images on paper but flesh-and-blood real.

Even bursting with anticipation, she had to wonder: after homecoming, what? New challenges, accomplishments, new purposes? Or ordinary times, when the view from the windows didn't change nor did the floor tremble and rock; when there were no shattered bodies or bent minds to deal with, no wardroom camaraderie, rumors, gossip, or speculation. Most of all, no Mark. Would existence on such a stationary, stable plane content her, as it once had? Or had she gone too far, for too long?

Pushing through the smoky air of the thronged waiting room, she headed for the main entrance. Not an empty seat in sight, so she gave the porter a dollar and said she'd wait there.

He tipped his cap, set the bags on the filthy wet marble floor and rejoined the massed humanity moving toward the trains. Outside, traffic crawled by, the gentle snow whitening a line of taxis and the familiar cityscape beyond. The perfect Christmas card to greet someone just back from the tropics, especially when viewed from inside, with the crowd flowing around her like river water around a rock.

Focusing on each pink-cheeked incoming face, she almost missed the civilian who leaned on a cane as he walked haltingly toward her. He paused; their gazes connected. Her heart banged as she stepped closer to his tentative smile. And the multi-colored scarf she'd knit for him two years before.

They stared a moment longer. Then his arms opened; his eyes held recognition and relief. Walking into his wet woolen embrace, she tried to say his name, but her throat closed. Finally she was able to croak, "Jim...I was expecting my parents."

He shook his head, flinging snowmelt from the hat brim. "Tried to talk them into coming too, but they said we needed time to ourselves."

"Oh," she sighed. "Oh my goodness," and kissed him at last. Then again, until she believed it was really he, close enough to taste his mouth, inhale his breath, and hold his warm reality. And kiss him again and again, because it had been such a long time and she'd been gone so far.

Still smiling he asked, "Where's your luggage?"

She pointed to the crumpled sea bag like a shrouded corpse behind her. "If you bring your car, I'll drag it outside."

"Just down the street." He stooped to lift her smaller bag. "Be right back."

Hoisting the purse strap to her shoulder, she grabbed the

other case, and began pulling the sea bag by its cords. A soldier stepped up, saluted minimally and said, "Here, let me help, ma'am."

She smiled, thanked him. By the time they reached the sidewalk, Jim was double-parked beyond the taxis, the Buick's trunk gaping open. Effortlessly, the Army private hoisted the elephantine bag inside, saluted again and disappeared into the crowd before she could press a dollar bill into his hand.

Jim slammed the lid as she got in the front seat. The sedan smelled musty and greasy, which it hadn't before. Like all the country's hard-run trains, it was probably wearing out too.

Shifting into low, he scanned the rearview mirror and edged into traffic. His face seemed more creased than when she'd left, pinched and lined, as if he was wearing out too. Of course, it was winter; most New Englanders' faces were pinched and lined. Besides, he'd been the only doctor in Penobscot County since the war started. At forty-one, how long could he sustain such non-stop responsibility?

Well, she was back now; that would change. She'd see that it did.

Around them, feathery flakes veiled the city like dotted Swiss curtains, lending another layer of unreality to her disoriented consciousness. While he navigated the turns toward Route One, she sat straighter, stared through the swiping wipers at the passing city. And tried to think of some celebratory line to mark the moment. The only thing that came to mind was, "Well, I see you're still wearing the scarf I made."

He grinned. "Got it out of mothballs last week. So you'd find me in a crowd, in case you forgot what I looked like."

She patted the heavy wool of his sleeve with her gloved fingers. "Even if I hadn't seen your picture every day, I'd still remember you."

"Well, I hoped you would. But it's been a hell of a long time." He pumped the brake as a light ahead went red.

She ignored a small ping of alarm in her head. "You didn't drive all the way from Maine today, did you?"

"Sure. Why? When did you leave California?"

"What?" She had to think. "Umm... Wednesday morning. Why?"

"Three nights. And how much did you sleep?"

She grimaced. "Oh, some. But...you know how it is sitting up in a day coach."

"Well, while you've been awake on a train, I've slept real well. So driving from Rockhampton to Boston is no sacrifice." He let go the gearshift knob and squeezed her hand.

Relaxed by the rumble of his calm, steady voice, she felt the self-constructed ice dam in her chest yield to pressure of unshed tears, months and months of them. Here on this silver afternoon in this old city, it began to shift, buckle and crack.

No, not yet, she warned herself; she had to hold together long enough to convince Jim and her parents she hadn't been undone by the war. That ground down though she was, her identity was unchanged by the experiences of the past fourteen months. Or the other souls with whom she'd shared them.

Somewhere outside her consciousness, Jim asked if she was hungry. "Diner up the road makes the best clam chowder in the state. How's that sound?"

Snapping back to the present, she focused on the emptiness of her belly. "Swell. All we had on the ship was the canned stuff." Just mentioning it brought the faintly metallic aftertaste of Sunday night suppers to her mouth, along with a full-body sense of Mark's presence beside her in the wardroom. She took a sharp breath and clenched her hands.

Jim's face was rejuvenated by a boyish grin. "Say. Didn't we have clam chowder at the Rockhampton coffee shop the night we... I mean, after you found all those condoms in my car?"

"Oh, Jim. I don't remember what we ate. Only how shocked you were when I...you know." Still couldn't bring herself to say *seduced you.*

He chuckled. "That memory kept me warm every night you were gone."

Like flaming arrows out of nowhere, new Mark images pierced her, contrasting with the roadside landscape of modest houses with whitened roofs and yards where bundled kids rolled snowmen and pelted each other with frozen handfuls. And in the misty distance, the flashing neon of the State Line Diner's big sign. She squeezed her eyes closed, and prayed the silent Jesus, Jesus, prayer.

The air in the diner was equatorial, engulfing them in the smell of cigarettes, hot grease, stale coffee. And the noise of the juke box blasting *Hubba, Hubba, Hubba.* Like one at the Guam O Club after *Indy* had gone down. She slid into a booth just as Perry Como sang: "It was mighty smoky over Tokyo..."

"I wonder why they don't mention Hiroshima or Nagasaki," she said. "Maybe because they had mushroom clouds, not just smoke."

Jim eyed her curiously. "What's that?"

"That song. I never noticed before."

His eyes changed, as if veiled. "That's right, you were at Nagasaki, weren't you?"

She nodded, loosened her scarf and unbuttoned her coat; Jim hung his on a hook with his hat. In a dark blue suit, white shirt and gray tie, he seemed thinner, hair more silver than beige, cut almost to the scalp over the ears. When a waitress brought menus, he ordered clam chowder for both of them, coffee for himself and milk for Anna.

As the girl slouched away, Anna said, "How did you know I wanted milk?"

"Have any idea how often you wrote about the lumpy powdered stuff on the ship?"

"I did? Don't remember. Anyway, I had the real thing in San Francisco. Just not enough."

He extended both hands across the red plastic tabletop. "Well, your mother'll see you get plenty now." His gaze dropped to her diamond. "Oh, you're wearing my ring. Thought you weren't allowed to in uniform."

She clasped his warm, competent hands. "I put it on when we left the ship. By then nobody cared about silly little rules like that."

He toyed with it a moment longer. "Now. Let me get a good look at you."

"Don't tell me. I look like hell."

"No. Just tired. But beautiful as ever."

Tears welled. Not now, not now, she thought again, biting her lip and blinking them away. "Sorry. This is all so…so overwhelming. Being here, I mean. Finally being back. Like a dream."

"A good one, I hope."

"Oh, of course! But now I know how the PWs felt. After they came aboard, they kept saying, 'This must be a dream.' Now I understand. You wait so long for something, but then…"

"What?"

She shrugged. "Don't know. My body's here, but my mind's still out there." A few more tears, easily wiped away with her fingertips. "As if it's not really over. Yet I know it is; the ship's in a yard for a long overhaul. When she comes out, all the casualties will be home. We won't need hospital ships any more. Still…"

"Go on."

"I can't stop feeling I should still be back there. On the

first train, I had Willi and Floyd and Luke to talk to. But we went our separate ways in Chicago. The rest of the trip, I'd doze off, then couldn't remember where I was. And when I did, I'd feel.... oh, just sad. And that doesn't make sense, does it? I mean, this is what I lived for the whole time. Yet now, it's as if I'm... uh, grieving because it's over."

His gaze was kindly and concerned, the doctor assessing a patient with all the objectivity he could bring to bear on one who was also his fiancée. "Well, maybe you are. Oh, not for the war, but your friends on the ship. And your work. Must've been intense."

She nodded, concurring with the adjective. "That's what it was. Intense. I mean, when we had patients. The rest of the time..." She paused, wondering if the sailor on the train had been right: did civilians, even Jim, really want to hear about it? And even if they did, what could she say that would convey the total reality of the experience? "Listen, I'll talk about it another time. Just not yet, all right?"

"Of course. No hurry." When he cleared his throat, something in the innocuous gesture made her tense. "Uh, you mentioned your friends from the ship just now. But what about the other chaplain? Wasn't he with you on the train too?"

Her heart paused. "Oh, you mean Mark?"

"He was going back east too, wasn't he?"

She swallowed tightness in her voice. "Charleston, South Carolina. But he went the southern route, through Los Angeles." She turned on the practiced, impersonal smile she'd used with patients. "Good he did, or we couldn't all have sat together. Not that we didn't get bored playing cards and talking about...oh, everything. But at least we had each other for company."

Jim's gaze stayed on her a fraction too long to reassure her that he was free of suspicions. "Well, whenever you feel like telling me the whole story, I want to hear."

The whole story? Of the war, or of sharing it with Mark? She said, "Okay," then drew a heart in the steam on the window by the booth. And inside, J.E.M. and A.M.D. "Look, Jim. You wondered if I'd remember you. Of course I do. Even your middle initial. E for Edward."

He chuckled. The soup came then, so thick the spoon almost stood in it. Her milk was in a tall, cold-beaded glass, and there were oyster crackers in a basket. Letting go of his hands, she dug in as someone fed the juke box and *Now is the Hour* began. She tried not to listen, but a replay of the dance with Mark instantly flooded her mind, pricked her heart and filled her eyes.

She sniffled, blew her nose and resumed eating. "Sorry, Jim. But I was just thinking, this time last week we were still on the ship. Then, after supper, we went to the BOQ on Treasure Island. Where they had the World's Fair."

"Where you left on the Clipper last year, right?"

"That's right. I forgot you knew." She took another spoonful. "But listen, why don't you talk now? Tell me everything. I mean, about the island, Lorraine and Cleve and Johann. And Alex. Did he come back yet?"

As he filled the blanks, she felt herself drifting again, sucked back into a world that no longer had form or substance, the inhabitants of which had migrated to other worlds. God, why was she so drawn to a life that was over? Common sense dictated that what she wanted was here, had always been here, with this man. Still she felt split in two, unable to reconnect the disparate halves of her private self.

When the soup was gone, she drained the creamy milk, only dimly aware he'd stopped talking. "I'm sorry, dear. What did you say?"

"Oh, just wondering when Luke's coming to meet Lorraine. You can tell me later, though. When you're feeling better."

"God, I hope it's soon."

"It will be. Today's probably the worst, because you're behind in your rest. But another month or two, why, maybe we can even talk about marriage."

She gasped. "A month or two? No, not that long. We've already lost too much time."

The waitress brought the check. Frowning, he pulled a worn brown wallet from his coat pocket, extracted a crumpled five. "We'll talk more in the car. Right now we need to get you home before the roads turn slick."

Outside, the silver day had dulled to premature evening; the damp air was scented with wood smoke and the salt tang of the nearby sea. With the snow falling more heavily, she stayed silent to let Jim concentrate on navigating the slippery highway. And give her own jumbled thoughts a chance to settle.

But after they'd crossed into New Hampshire, he reached for her hand again. "Now, darling. What were you saying about marriage?"

From a slow start, she talked a long while, rambling, repetitively trying to present cogent reasons why sooner made more sense than later. But the most compelling argument was unspeakable, that making their commitment legal would chase Mark from her thoughts.

She settled for, "Look, Jim. We love each other. And we've waited long enough. So let's get on with life, as soon as possible. Next Saturday, if we can talk my parents into it."

His hand tightened around hers. "I'd rather you took longer to get over the war, Anna. Be sure you really want to be married. To me, I mean. Besides, aren't you still in the Navy?"

"Oh that. Well, yes. I'm on thirty days leave, but I can get out any time. Anyway, I'm sure right now. Hell, I was sure last year before you even knew I loved you."

" Okay." He shrugged, smiled. "No sense arguing about

it then."

* * *

By the time they rolled into Portsmouth, slush glazed the streets and the darkness glittered with snow-wreathed Christmas lights. When they pulled up at the rectory, he tooted the horn until her parents burst from the front door, her mother wielding a big black umbrella. After a corset-stiff hug, she held it over Anna as she stepped into her father's tobacco and mothball-tinged hug. Then all of them scurried up the walk toward lights in every window and beside the door, where two service stars still hung, gold for Dan, blue for Anna.

In the entry, the first thing she smelled was pork and sauerkraut. Or was that just an olfactory manifestation of wishful thinking?

"No, that's what it is, all right," said her mother in answer to her question. "Remember, that's what you wanted for your homecoming dinner?" Mrs. Moss led her to the kitchen and pointed to a V-mail taped to the fridge. Sure enough, there it was in Anna's own handwriting.

As she read it, her mother scrutinized her with narrowed eyes. "Oh my. You look so peaked, dear. So thin. It must've been much worse than you let on."

"No, it wasn't that bad." Shrugging off further inquiries, Anna carried her coat to the front hall where Jim and her father were pushing and pulling the sea bag up the steps like a balky donkey.

* * *

Dinner was a feast served on the best china, with the good silverware, tiny crystal glasses of sherry, and joyous confusion. Her parents barely ate for pestering her with non-stop questions. Until Jim announced they'd decided to be married the following Saturday. Then the old folks settled down, attention shifting to the nuts and bolts of planning a wedding on short notice. Especially her mother, who'd been cheated of this joy when Anna had married Dan in a perfunctory service in the Catholic chaplain's office on the Navy base the day before Pearl Harbor.

"It was one of those awful little ceremonies they insist on when a Catholic marries an unconverted Protestant," she said to Jim, her voice still bitter. "My husband couldn't even be part of it, except to give her away. Oh, she bought a nice new suit, but that's not the sort of wedding a girl dreams of. We didn't even have a reception, just took them out to dinner afterward." Her eyes blazed in the dazzle of the crystal chandelier. "Now this one, this is going to be a proper wedding."

Jim's look on her was so patently tender, Anna felt the sting of tears again.

Leaving half her outsize portion of apple pie a la mode, she could hardly wait to excuse herself on the grounds of terminal fatigue. Just after seven, she dragged up to her old room, her mother right behind to get out flannel pajamas and fold back the chenille spread. Turning her back to undress, Anna asked if Jim was spending the night.

"Well, of course. We couldn't expect him to drive all the way back to Maine tonight, could we?" Anna crawled under the covers; her mother switched off the bedside lamp, opened the curtains. "Oh my, it's still coming down. He might have to stay over tomorrow too."

The night before Anna had left for the Pacific, Jim's presence in the nearby guest room had been a source of irresistible temptation. Now she felt no urge as strong as the one for sleep. She dropped off so quickly; she had time for only two prayers: one of gratitude for a safe homecoming, the other a plea that the Lord of the Universe, now that he no longer had to help the Allies win the war, would use his infinite power to purge Mark Whitmore from her mind and heart.

"Help me stop remembering," she whispered into her folded hands. "Help me stop missing him." And most important: "Help me stop feeling like hell about what happened with him."

Even with the Lord, or maybe especially with the Lord, she couldn't bring herself to call what had happened with him what it really was. Or at least the words her conscience kept spitting at her.

CHAPTER THIRTY-ONE

*T*he next morning she was awake long before her parents stirred, before the smell of coffee and bacon drifted up the stairs, before the first sunlight touched the white landscape outside and glinted on the copper cross the church steeple lifted against the bluest sky she'd seen since Hawaii. When she was sure the others were up and about, she put on a clean shirt and got into dress blues, because her mother would undoubtedly insist she wear the uniform to church so even total strangers could recognize her as the angel of mercy, finally home from the wars.

Jim's door was still shut, but downstairs her father was in the study making last-minute changes to his sermon, her mother in the kitchen dithering over lunch so Jim could get an early start back to Maine after the service.

She scanned a red and white line of Campbell's soups in the cupboards. "Maybe a nice Welsh rarebit," she said, then took out a can of Tomato and one of Mushroom. "Maybe with chopped olives for extra flavor. And lots of nice sharp cheese. Think he'd like that, Anna?"

"Can't think of anything he'd like more," she said, tempted to add, "Except taking me to bed," but knew it might cause her mother a fatal stroke.

By then Jim was in the parlor, in the wing chair beside a stack of magazines. "Anna, look at this," he said, gesturing toward the *Life* he was holding, the one with the Picture of the Week of the devastated Nagasaki cathedral. "You didn't go out to see it, did you?"

"No. But a lot of officers did. Including Luke, He took pictures. To show Lorraine, he said." She considered sharing the rest of the story about Floyd ripping out the magazine page in the Fairmont lobby, but even without Mark's tacit, peripheral inclusion, the innocence in Jim's eyes exacerbated the sting of her betrayal.

"Can't wait to meet him," he said. "And that Floyd you wrote so much about. Maybe next summer we can invite some of your friends for a visit. Hotel on the island ought to be open by then."

"Oh yes, yes," she said with feigned enthusiasm. "That's a swell idea."

* * *

By the time they got to the church, the sanctuary was packed with enthusiastic singers, minor key Advent carols notwithstanding. And when Rev. Moss invited everyone to the wedding the next Saturday, the congregation applauded, actually applauded. Mrs. Moss looked askance at this breach of decorum, but after the service, introduced Anna and Jim to everyone within range.

"Would you believe she just got back from the war yesterday?" she said over and over. "She's been on a hospital ship this whole past year!"

Escaping a multitude of well-wishers took so long, Jim began consulting his watch, a sure sign he was anxious to start for Maine. Nonetheless, Anna asked him to walk with her to the baby's grave. The sexton had shoveled the brick paths to the big tree with the bench, but they had to step in snow the rest of the way to the little stone. Without speaking, she bent to brush a layer of soggy flakes from it.

Jim squeezed her hand. "Sweetheart, I know you want another baby as soon as possible, so don't worry. I'll do my best."

"Last year you did your best even though we didn't want one."

He laughed and pulled her to him. "Good thing you didn't sneak into my room last night. See, I didn't bring any protection."

"It wouldn't matter now, would it?"

He laughed again, but so nervously she sensed his reluctance to discuss it further. So, reminding him her mother hated to be kept waiting at mealtimes, she linked her arm with his and began walking toward the rectory.

After a lunch of Welsh Rarebit, fried Spam, the finest Waldorf Salad ever and another round of wedding plans, Jim declined dessert so he could get on the road. His rationale was that he wanted to be home before dark, but Anna concluded he needed nothing so much as to escape this non-stop domesticity. He would marry her and be the best husband ever, but weaving together tedious wedding details was foreign to his nature.

"Just leave everything to me," she said as they walked to his car, "All you have to do is show up for the wedding."

"Easiest thing I'll ever do." He leaned toward her for a kiss, then got in and started the engine. She watched him drive away and turn the corner toward Route One. Then, feeling deflated, came back into the house in hopes of sneaking upstairs for a nap. Before she reached the steps, however, her father called from the kitchen. She straggled in; he was drying dishes as her mother washed. And chattered and chattered and chattered. About the wedding, of course.

Anna yawned. "Let's talk about this later, Mother. I need a nap."

"Of course, dear. You still look so peaked. We need to get the roses back in your cheeks before the wedding."

"Jim says I have a lot of rest to catch up on."

"Well, then, listen to him. Doctors know best."

One arm over her shoulder, her father walked her to the foot of the stairs, then stood regarding her from under craggy brows. Her mother was plumper than ever despite years of food rationing, but he seemed diminished and frail, far older than his sixty-seven years. Feeling the pressure of tears, Anna hugged him. Even through the thick tweed jacket, he felt bony.

He touched her cheek lightly with one finger. "Oh, sweetheart. You seem so sad. What is it? What's the matter?"

She gave him one of her practiced smiles. "Nothing, Dad. Just not used to being home yet, I guess. Like part of me's still on the ship."

"Well, of course. It must've been a great adventure. Today at church, if it wasn't Advent, I'd have had us sing *Amazing Grace.* In honor of everything you've been through."

She took a deep breath. "Appropriate. Especially the part about grace leading me home."

"Thanks be to God for that." His voice trembled.

Then, as he'd done for as long as she could remember, he closed her against the clerical shirt with the silver pectoral cross and the jacket with his pipe in the chest pocket. Patted her head and said he loved her better than anyone in the world, and was so happy she was back he'd almost danced the processional that morning. "And anytime you want to talk… I mean, about what it was like out there,

I'll be all ears. And I won't tell your mother anything you don't want me to."

She promised she would, brushed her lips against his whiskery cheek, then turned and plodded up the stairs. By the time she closed her door, tears had retreated, so she hung the uniform away, wrapped up in her old chenille robe and stretched out on the bed.

Comforted by her father's gentle thoughts, she drifted off right away, only to awake with a start a few minutes later. As if someone had called her name, or a PA system had blasted out Now hear this! Now hear this!

But it hadn't, and wouldn't again. Perhaps what had woken her, then, was this very absence of sound: the stillness of her childhood room and downstairs, the muffled hush of her parents quietly congratulating themselves on having a daughter who'd come home safe and made them proud in front of the whole congregation. A fine girl, who'd survived losing a husband and a baby without ever a murmur, then gone off to serve her country in a strange and dangerous part of the world. And was now about to marry a dedicated doctor with whom she'd soon be working to alleviate still more suffering.

What more could any parents want?

Subsumed in irony, she lay a few minutes longer before an unaccountable restlessness urged her from the bed. Opening the small bag still unpacked on the floor, she found her writing kit with the fountain pen she'd last filled at the Treasure Island BOQ, and a well-thumbed address book in which she'd listed Audrey's, Willie and Floyd's, Nell's and Luke's. And of course, Mark's at his parents' home in Charleston.

With no idea what to write, but compelled by an urge to communicate something, she sat at her old desk and began with the date. Then,

Dear Mark,

Still trying to believe I'm home even after 24 hours. Jim met me in Boston, in the snow. Like homecoming in a movie. Just want you to know we're going to be married next Saturday. Don't know why it seems important to tell you, though, maybe because I'm wondering if Luke will be here, and if he is, will he tell him about you and me?

Either way, all I can do is trust Jim loves me enough to understand something I don't quite understand myself. Unless the war brought out weaknesses I didn't know I had, like needing comfort so much I ignored my commitment to Jim, and my innate belief in morality. Now I'm haunted by what we jokingly called our "debauchery". Of course, as you said, we can take pride in having done our duty and been faithful to our mission But that other part...well, someday I'll tell Jim, because married people shouldn't have ugly secrets from each other. But not just yet. Not till I make my own peace with it.

Anyway, I wish I could talk to you again, but maybe we can write now and then.

You were such an important part of my life on the ship, I hope we can stay in touch. Meanwhile, I'm trying to picture you back home, and wondering if you feel as disconnected from your old life as I do. I never expected it to be like this. Jim says I just need to catch up on rest and I'll be good as new. I hope that's what it is.

Guess that's all for now. I hope you're well, safe and happy with your family. I look forward to hearing from you, and wish you my very best always.

With love, Anna.

Satisfied she'd expressed herself as well as mere words could, she folded the sheet into an envelope. For the return address, she almost wrote Ensign A.M. Donovan, USS *Compassion* AH-4, c/o FPO, San Francisco, Calif. And FREE where the stamp would go. One more aspect of the life she'd lived to completion. Like a thousand other small details that had no bearing on the present, this was still imbedded in her consciousness. Another souvenir of the war. Not quite as noticeable as shrapnel in flesh, but enough to remind her she'd been part of it.

She set the envelope on the nightstand so she'd remember to mail it if she walked later. When she replaced the pen in the writing kit, she noticed the menu from *Compassion's* Christmas dinner, 1944. Almost a year since she'd stuck it there. Now, in the lowering light of a winter afternoon with shadows purpling the snow outside, she studied the cover picture of the ship and the group shot of officers on the back. Touching each face with her fingertips, she named them all, even those she hadn't known except anecdotally and distantly, as well as those whose lives had intersected closely with hers, in the wardroom and Nurses' Country and Receiving, on the wards and on liberty, and at funerals, meetings and movies.

Like hers, their memories would be newsreels of the Kamikaze attacks, the kissing mutiny and the Marine's suicide, of Roosevelt's death, the loss of Indy, the VJ-day celebration, shore leave in Brisbane, the foul air at Nagasaki, and the hesitant joy of returning PWs. And in the final frame, the last glimpse of the ship at Oakland after they'd finished what they'd needed to do and turned their faces homeward.

So it wasn't only Mark's absence she grieved now, she realized, but that of a whole family of others, all of them part of the same big Something the past fourteen months. A multitude of brothers and sisters, and those to whom she felt an even deeper bond, like Willi and Floyd. And one closer yet than the any other.

For a while longer, she sat on the edge of the bed holding the menu with all those faces smiling back from the small picture. Then, with these black and white images adrift in her memory, she returned the menu to the folder, put it into the nightstand drawer and lay back on the bed.

Closing her eyes, she felt the remnants of sorrow begin to swell. Before long they built into a sense of loss that filled her so totally she was capable of feeling nothing else, not love for Jim or her parents, not gratitude for having safely returned, not even the absence of Mark. It burned like acid in her system, stirring up tears she knew better than to resist. To muffle the sobs they generated, she buried her face in the pillow and prayed her parents didn't hear..

She had no idea how long the anguish gripped her, but the light filling the window was ruddy with sunset when she finally wiped her eyes and blew her nose. Empty at last, she was limp and drowsy. Yet as she drifted into sleep another absence, insignificant in the larger scheme of things, began to gnaw at her. Until she left the bed again, this time to dump her sea bag on the floor. Shoes and hose and underwear, khaki shirts and slacks and nurses' whites tumbled out in rumpled disorder. Like mental images of the times she'd worn them.

Finally the old Westclox alarm clattered to the floor. It had stopped at seven; she wound it till it started ticking again, set the hands to 3:35, then placed it on the nightstand where it had lived before she took it to Hope Island in 1943, and the next year, to the South Pacific where it had lulled her to sleep for all the months on the ship. Several times it had crashed to the deck in rough weather, but undaunted, kept ticking.

She no longer trusted the time it kept. But time was not what she wanted it for now, rather the full-circle sense that the hours it measured had returned her to her starting point. And would continue to do so, on her honeymoon, then in Jim's old Victorian house in East Point, Maine. And wherever else the future led her.

Back in bed, eyes closed against the dimming day, she saw Mark's face again, and was hit by another small jolt of pain. It soon faded, replaced by the more immediate memory of Jim at South Station, snow melting on his hat, smiling, holding out his hands as they closed the last space between them.

Welcoming her back into his life, just as she was. And even with no idea of the changes he would eventually discover in her, ready to love her forever.

Or at least as long as she let him.

-The End-

SHORT GLOSSARY OF NAVY TERMS

AH - Hull designator for Hospital Ship, followed by a number: *USS Compassion* is AH-4. The A in any designator indicates that vessel is an Auxiliary, part of the Service Force. Others are AO-Fleet oiler; AE-Ammunition ship; AR-Repair ship; AF-Refrigerator cargo ship, etc.

CO - Ship's Commanding officer, aka Old Man, Skipper or Captain.

XO - Executive officer, or Exec; ship's second in command.

MO - Medical officer [doctor or surgeon] MOD -- Medical Officer of the Day: the doctor assigned to duty when others are not on call. CMO-Chief Medical Officer, a senior doctor in charge of a unit of medical personnel.

CMAA - Chief Master-at-Arms, a senior non-commissioned officer in charge of maintaining shipboard order and generally functioning in a police capacity.

OOD - Officer of the Deck: commissioned officer assigned to stand duty at the gangway to check papers and IDs of those departing and boarding.

OinC - Officer in Charge of a unit of personnel, as with the Marines transported on *Compassion*

Corpsman - Common term for World War II Pharmacists Mates trained to work with doctors and nurses or as battlefield medics; now officially Hospital Corpsman.

Swabbie - vernacular for a low-rated enlisted man, aka swab jockey [from swabbing the decks], also bluejacket, white hat or sailor

CPO - Chief Petty Officer; an enlisted man who has advanced from Apprentice Seaman through Third, Second and First Class ratings to a position of responsibility in a particular division.

Plan of the Day – official shipboard daily publication providing general information such as uniform of the day, times and titles of movies to be shown, times of sunrise and sunset, of sick call, church call, funerals, liberty, and any special events, as well as open hours of the Gedunk (Snack Bar), ship's store, library, post office, etc.

AUTHOR'S NOTE

When I began writing my first novel about Anna Moss Donovan, the ending seemed a fait accompli. All signs indicated she'd marry her fiancé and live happily ever after. But as I took her down that path, I began to realize that yes, she loved Jim, but before she put on his ring, she had another dream to fulfill. Since her first husband, a submariner, had been lost in the Pacific, logic suggested she join the Navy Nurse Corps and request duty in the same theater of operations…on a hospital ship. And thereon hangs the plot of *Odyssey of Angels*, the sequel to *Ministry of Angels* and prequel to the last in the trilogy, *Ordinary Angels*.

At that time, I knew almost nothing of these non-combatant vessels. If they were mentioned in the news during World War II, I never noticed; as a teenager, my view of life was more romantic than realistic. Later, during the Vietnam conflict, it was only when I met a surgeon serving on one that I realized their vital role in the care of battle casualties. I might have figured it out earlier if Hollywood had realized the romantic potential of the only vessels on which personnel of both sexes served together in close quarters and dramatic circumstances. Such conditions usually enhance the natural magnetism between men and women, but I don't remember any film that developed that theme in depth.

As I got deeper into research, I concluded that the service of these auxiliaries—just in the Pacific-- comprised a saga far larger than I had realized. (Some served in the African and Italian campaigns, but the Army Transport Service did the bulk of the work in the European conflict.)

To illustrate the point, consider the story of *USS Solace* [AH-5]. Built in 1920 as *SS Iroquois*, she was converted to a hospital ship in early 1941. After commissioning, she was sent to Pearl Harbor, where she became the only such vessel in the Pacific Fleet. Another, *Relief* [AH-1], was the Atlantic Fleet's single hospital ship; she operated primarily off Maine, where convoys for England formed up before setting out into the U-boat-infested North Atlantic.

On the morning of December 7, 1941, *Solace* was tied up at the destroyer piers at Pearl Harbor. Shortly after the attack began, she shifted berths to one less likely to be targeted, then launched a series of small boats to rescue men from the fiery waters off Battleship Row. This story is told in spare but stunning detail in the official battle report from her commanding officer, Benjamin Perlman.

In the months following, *Solace* saw intensive duty caring for and transporting wounded from battles and invasions to hospitals in Brisbane, Australia and Auckland, New Zealand. These had been built by SeaBees after the huge number of early casualties caught the Allies unprepared. Eventually Allied forces recaptured enough territory to construct fleet hospitals closer to the fighting. But in early 1942, *Solace* was the only lifeline between bloody South Pacific beachheads and these distant hospitals. Some casualties had had no prior treatment; one sailor from *USS Vincennes*, a cruiser sunk off Guadalcanal, told of spending hours in the water with shrapnel wounds, then climbing the cargo net of a transport, where he lay on deck overnight before he was taken aboard *Solace*. Following surgery there, he spent the rest of the war in the Navy hospital in Auckland.

By the final year of the war, the U.S. Navy was operating nine hospital ships in the Pacific, three staffed by Army medical personnel. Like *Solace,* most were converted liners, transports or freighters. As the conflict moved closer to Japan, however, six new constructions joined the fleet. Originally intended as tankers, they were transformed instead into vessels large enough to provide for the million casualties expected from the planned invasion of the enemy's home islands.

While their main mission was standing offshore to evacuate wounded soldiers and Marines from invasion sites, these white ships also treated victims of accidents, naval battles and Kamikaze attacks, and served as dockside dispensaries. Even in war zones, they traveled unescorted, fully lit and unarmed, their only defense a green stripe along the hull, red crosses on stacks, decks and hull, and the Geneva Convention pennant. Officers were permitted sidearms for personal protection, but the ship carried neither radar nor sonar, even for navigational purposes.

Besides ship's company, the original ships were staffed by an average of fifteen medical officers, thirty nurses, several Red Cross workers, one or two chaplains and about ninety Pharmacist's Mates (now known as Hospital Corpsman). They had berths for between four and six hundred patients, though more could be accommodated in dire circumstances. By comparison, the newer ships had a capacity of eight hundred and were air-conditioned. Still relatively fresh, some later served in Korea and Vietnam; one—*Benevolence*, [AH-13]--was sunk when rammed by a freighter off San Francisco in 1950. In World War II, none was ever lost to enemy action, though *Comfort* [AH-6] with Army medical personnel, was seriously damaged by a Kamikaze off Okinawa with a loss of twenty-eight lives. Other were bombed, strafed or targeted by torpedoes, fortunately with little effect except to morale.

Although personal narratives of some hospital ship nurses are available, no comprehensive memoir is in print, to my knowledge. *Odyssey of Angels* is an attempt to fill that void with a representational, albeit fictional, memoir of one junior nurse serving aboard one such ship in the last year of the war. *USS Compassion* and her hull number [AH-4] are fictional, but her itinerary is based on those of actual ships of that type. As a backdrop, the progress of the war is threaded through the story. The incident referred to as "The Kissing Mutiny" is a product of my imagination, but other events referred to actually took place, including the large-scale transport of former POWs home from Japanese camps.

Despite the title, my intention in writing this novel was not to portray Anna Donovan or her sister nurses as angels. Instead, I've tried to recreate their probable emotions as they carried on the tough, monotonous and emotionally draining work of caring for wave after wave of wounded men, most no more than boys. Besides dealing with physical trauma, they also cared for those with "Battle Fatigue"; in the Okinawa campaign alone, these accounted for a shocking one-quarter of the total casualties.

I've also explored medical personnel's all-too-human attempts to deal with personal loss as well as the chilling expectation of a proposed invasion of Japan. The term "Post-traumatic stress disorder" had not yet been coined, but its early counterpart offers a window on the devastating emotional effects of long-term exposure to war's brutal consequences.

Finally, I hope this novel adds another small layer to the still-growing mountain of knowledge about the grinding war that enveloped the world seventy years ago. By now the big stories are familiar enough to be clichés. Yet within each are personal accounts of individual heroism, mindless drudgery, endless confusion, numbing boredom, sudden terror, stoical endurance, and even occasional flashes of blessedly comic relief. Such small pieces form the mosaic of a conflict so enormous and horrific that even now it defies comprehension. At the same time, they illuminate the resilience of the human spirit even under unrelenting duress.

It is my hope, then, that this, the fictional story of Nurse Anna Donovan, provides the reader with a realistic glimpse of the demanding but heroic mission of the equally fictional *USS Compassion* and her fifteen real-life sister ships.

ACKNOWLEDGMENTS

While I'm tempted to thank the many friends and family members who encouraged me to write, the possibility I might inadvertently omit some names suggests I express strictly generic appreciation. However, a few must be recognized for specific above-and-beyond-the-call-of-duty help: my sons, David and Richard Iobst; my daughter, Barbara Gonda; old friend Ed Beyersdorfer, whose dream first turned me on to Anna's story; and my brother, Bob Hartzel, a maritime genius who supplied more engineering detail than I could possibly use. I'm also grateful to Bob Gelhard, a church friend who shared his experiences on *USS Solace* after his ship was torpedoed; and to Bill Rouse, who served in the engine room of *USS Rescue* as a young sailor. His observations of shipboard life added richly to my understanding of everyday happenings on a hospital ship in 1945.

Finally, for their generous encouragement, I must cite Lenore Hart and David Poyer. Without their guidance and inspiration, I'd probably have continued writing solely for my own amusement for another seventy years. It might have been an easier way to spend my old age, but it wouldn't have been half as interesting. My gratitude is boundless.

ABOUT THE AUTHOR

Chronically discontented with ordinary life, Joan Hartzel La Blanc began writing fiction during her childhood in Philadelphia. While she set this addiction aside to raise four children, it later enabled her to survive marriages to two career Navy men and one with Alzheimer's Disease. Now in her "golden years", it continues to offer romance, travel, and the adventures of an international spy without the associated dangers. After retiring from a real career as a PR and non-fiction writer, she specializes in circumspect prose for church publications, at least between visits to the various parallel universes that provide her greatest inspiration and creative fulfillment.

Northampton House Press

Northampton House LLC publishes carefully selected fiction, as well as lifestyle nonfiction, memoir, and poetry. Our logo represents the muse Polyhymnia. Our mission is to discover great new writers and give them a chance to springboard into fame. Our watchword is quality, not quantity. Watch the Northampton House list at www.northampton-house.com, or Like us on Facebook – "Northampton House Press" – to discover more innovative works from brilliant new writers.

www.ingramcontent.com/pod-product-compliance
Lightning Source LLC
LaVergne TN
LVHW012153200225
804227LV00029B/641